PENGUIN BOOKS

THE ANGEL MAKER

Stefan Brijs is the author of four novels. He lives in Antwerp, Belgium.

To access Penguin Readers Guides online, visit our Web sites at www.penguin.com or www.vpbookclub.com.

The Angel Maker

A NOVEL

STEFAN BRIJS

Translated from the Dutch
by Hester Velmans

PENGUIN BOOKS

PENGUIN BOOKS
Published by the Penguin Group
Penguin Group (USA) Inc., 375 Hudson Street, New York, New York 10014, U.S.A.
Penguin Group (Canada), 90 Eglinton Avenue East, Suite 700, Toronto,
Ontario, Canada M4P 2Y3 (a division of Pearson Penguin Canada Inc.)
Penguin Books Ltd, 80 Strand, London WC2R 0RL, England
Penguin Ireland, 25 St Stephen's Green, Dublin 2, Ireland (a division of Penguin Books Ltd)
Penguin Group (Australia), 250 Camberwell Road, Camberwell,
Victoria 3124, Australia (a division of Pearson Australia Group Pty Ltd)
Penguin Books India Pvt Ltd, 11 Community Centre,
Panchsheel Park, New Delhi – 110 017, India
Penguin Group (NZ), 67 Apollo Drive, Rosedale, North Shore 0632,
New Zealand (a division of Pearson New Zealand Ltd)
Penguin Books (South Africa) (Pty) Ltd, 24 Sturdee Avenue,
Rosebank, Johannesburg 2196, South Africa

Penguin Books Ltd, Registered Offices:
80 Strand, London WC2R 0RL, England

First published in Great Britain by Weidenfeld & Nicolson 2008
First published in the United States of America by Penguin Books 2008

1 3 5 7 9 10 8 6 4 2

Originally published in Dutch as *De engelenmaker* by Atlas, Amsterdam

PUBLISHER'S NOTE
This is a work of fiction. Names, characters, places, and incidents are either the product of the author's imagination or are used fictitiously, and any resemblance to actual persons, living or dead, business establishments, events, or locales is entirely coincidental.

LIBRARY OF CONGRESS CATALOGING IN PUBLICATION DATA
Brijs, Stefan, 1969–
[Engelenmaker. English]
The angel maker : a novel / by Stefan Brijs.
p. cm.
ISBN 978-0-14-311309-6
I. Title.
PT6466.12.R53E6513 2008
839.31'364—dc22 2008040397

Printed in the United States of America

The Angel Maker

I

1

Some of Wolfheim's inhabitants maintain to this day that they heard the crying of the three babies in the back seat first, even before they heard the taxi's engine as it drove into the village. When the taxi halted in front of the old doctor's house at number 1 Napoleonstrasse, the women of the village promptly stopped sweeping their front porches, the men came out of the Café Terminus still clutching their beers, the girls halted their game of hopscotch, and in the town square Lanky Meekers fumbled and lost the ball to Gunther Weber, deaf from birth, who drove it home right past the baker's boy Seppe, who was looking the other way. That was on 13 October 1984. A Saturday afternoon. The clock in the bell tower struck three.

The passenger got out of the taxi and what everyone immediately noticed was the fiery hue of his hair and beard.

The deeply devout Bernadette Liebknecht hurriedly crossed herself, and a few houses down the street old Juliette Blérot clapped her hand to her mouth and muttered, 'My God, the spitting image of his father.'

Three months earlier, the inhabitants of the Belgian hamlet that was adjacent to the place where three borders met, which for its entire history had lain pinned between the sturdy thighs of Vaals in the Netherlands on one side and the German town of Aachen on the other, had been advised of Victor Hoppe's impending return. The skinny clerk from Notary Renard's office in Eupen had come to remove the yellowing 'FOR RENT' sign from the front gate of the deserted house and had told Irma Nüssbaum, who lived across the street, that *Herr Doktor* was planning to return to Wolfheim. The clerk didn't have any further details; he couldn't even give her a date.

It was a mystery to the villagers why Victor Hoppe should be returning to Wolfheim after an absence of nearly twenty years. The last anyone had heard was that he had been practising medicine in Bonn, but that information dated from quite a few years back, so people came up with all sorts of hypotheses for his homecoming. This one thought he was out of work, that one blamed his return on heavy debts; Florent Keuning from Albertstrasse thought he was only coming back in order to do up his house and sell it, while Irma Nüssbaum suggested that the doctor might now have a family and want to escape the hustle and bustle of the city. It turned out that Irma was closest to the truth, even though she would have been the first to admit that it had come as just as much of a shock to her as to everyone else to find out that Dr Hoppe was now the father of a set of disfigured triplets who were just a few weeks old.

It was Lanky Meekers who made the disconcerting discovery that very afternoon. As the driver of the taxi stepped away from his car to help Victor Hoppe open the rusty gate, Lanky Meekers, drawn by the incessant screeching, crept over to peek in at the side window. What he saw on the back seat gave the skinny lad such a fright that he fainted clean away, thereby becoming the doctor's first patient. The doctor brought him round with a few smart slaps to the cheek, upon which Lanky Meekers opened his eyes, blinked, glanced from the doctor to the car, scrambled to his feet and scurried back to his friends without a backward glance. Still a bit unsteady on his feet, he threw one arm over the burly shoulders of his classmate Robert Chevalier – they were both in the fourth form – and draped the other over the left shoulder of Julius Rosenboom, who was three years younger and two heads shorter.

'What did you see, Lanky?' asked Seppe the baker's boy, who was standing across from his friends, the leather football tucked under his arm, his face turned towards deaf Gunther Weber so that the latter could follow what was being said.

'They . . .' Lanky Meekers began, but he paled once more and didn't go on.

'Oh, stop being such a wuss!' Robert Chevalier prodded Meekers with his shoulder. 'And what do you mean by *they*, anyhow? Is there more than one in there, then?'

'Three. There's three of them,' Lanky Meekers answered, holding up the same number of spindly fingers.

'Thwee giwls?' asked Gunther, grinning broadly.

'I couldn't tell,' said Lanky Meekers. 'But what I did see . . .' He crouched down, glanced over to where Dr Hoppe and the taxi driver were in the process of opening both sections of the gate, and motioned his four pals to come closer.

'Their heads,' he said slowly . . . 'their heads are split apart.' And extending his right hand, he made a swift slicing gesture down his forehead, over his nose and right down to the underside of his chin. 'Whack!' he said.

Startled, Gunther and Seppe took a step backward, whereas Robert and Julius couldn't stop staring at Lanky Meekers' disproportionately small head, as if that too was likely to be split asunder at any moment.

'I swear. You could see all the way back, right to their throats. And that's not all, honest to God – you could even see their *brains*.'

'Their *whaa*?' demanded Gunther.

'Brai-hains!' Lanky Meekers repeated, tapping his index finger against the deaf boy's forehead.

'Gross!' Gunther exclaimed.

'What did their brains look like?' asked Robert.

'Like a walnut. Only much bigger. Slimier.'

'Jesus,' said Julius, shuddering.

'If the window had been open,' bragged Lanky Meekers, 'I could have just snatched them – like this.'

Open-mouthed, the other boys followed the movement of his hand, cupped like a claw. But then suddenly the hand shot forward again, pointing, thereby directing everyone's eyes back to the taxi, some thirty metres from where they were standing. Victor Hoppe opened the rear door, ducked into the car and re-emerged a few seconds later with a large navy-blue carrycot, from which there arose a terrible wailing. Lifting the cot by its two handles, he carried it along the path into the house, with the taxi driver, who was lugging two large suitcases, following close behind. The village square was all abuzz; two or three minutes later the driver came out again, pulled the front door shut, hurried back to his car, and drove off with visible relief.

At the Café Terminus that afternoon, Jacques Meekers had the floor. He gave a detailed account of what his son had seen, not refraining from hyperbole when called for. The older villagers especially were all ears, and were able to tell the others that Victor Hoppe had been born with a facial disfigurement himself.

'A harelip,' Otto Lelieux explained.

'Just like his father,' Ernst Liebknecht remembered. 'His spitting image, too.'

'Spit from a rusty tap,' laughed Wilfred Nüssbaum. 'Did you see his hair? And that beard? As red as . . . as . . .'

'As the hair of the devil!' cried one-eyed Josef Zimmermann suddenly, whereupon the café suddenly fell silent. All eyes were on the slightly inebriated old man, who was pointing an admonitory finger in the air. 'And he has brought with him his avenging angels! Keep your eyes peeled, because they will strike as soon as they get the chance.'

It was as if his words had opened the floodgates, because all of a sudden others also found themselves recalling stories that showed the doctor in rather a poor light. They all knew something or other about him or his parents, and the later the hour, the more yarns were exchanged. Most of the tales were only hearsay, but no one seemed to question their veracity.

'He grew up in an asylum.'

'He got that from his mother. She died of insanity.'

'He was christened by Father Kaisergruber. The child screamed bloody murder.'

'They say that his father . . . you know . . . from the tree next to his house.'

'The son didn't even come to the funeral.'

'He was never seen again after that.'

'The house was only rented once. The tenants left after just three weeks.'

'Poltergeists. That's what they said. There was this constant knocking.'

Over the next few weeks Dr Hoppe would make forays into the village as regular as clockwork. Every Monday, Wednesday and Friday morning, at half past ten on the dot, he would follow the exact same trajectory, from the bank on Galmeistrasse, on to the post office on Aachenerstrasse and then Martha Bollen's grocery shop across from the village square. He rushed from one stop to the next at a brisk pace, head bowed, as if he knew he was being observed and was intent on getting home again as quickly as possible. However, his hurry only served to draw even more attention to him. The villagers would cross the street and watch him from the opposite pavement until he disappeared from view.

Martha Bollen, as well as Louis Denis the bank teller and Arthur Boulanger the postmaster, all reported that Dr Hoppe was a man of few words. It seemed that he was rather bashful, yet amicable in his own way. He always had a '*Guten Tag*', '*Danke schön*' and '*Auf Wiedersehen*' for them – pleasantries that betrayed his speech impediment.

'He tends to swallow some of the sounds,' said Louis Denis.

'His voice is very nasal,' said Martha, 'always droning on in the same tone of voice. And he never looks at me when he's speaking.'

To the frequent question as to what the doctor had purchased, she always gave the same answer: 'Oh, the usual. Nappies, formula, milk, cereal, detergent, toothpaste – stuff like that.'

But then she would lean over the counter, shield her mouth with the back of her hand and continue in a whisper, 'He also buys two packs of Polaroid film every time he comes in. Why would anyone want to take that many pictures of children who look the way they do?'

Her customers would profess surprise, encouraging Martha to beckon them even closer. In a tone implying some criminal wrongdoing, she'd end with, '. . . And he always pays with thousand-mark notes!'

Louis Denis was able to explain the derivation of those banknotes: he reported that the doctor sometimes came in to exchange German marks for Belgian currency. He had not yet opened an account, however, so he must be keeping all that cash somewhere in the house.

Since Dr Hoppe was not making any effort to attract patients and had not hung a sign on his gate listing surgery hours, some burghers decided that he must be living off past earnings of some sort or another. Still, it did look as though he was intending to practise his calling in the village eventually, because in those first few weeks a lorry from Germany had stopped in front of his house at least three times to deliver medical equipment. From behind the curtain of her kitchen window, Irma Nüssbaum would jot down the registration number and time of delivery, and what the delivery consisted of. Some of the goods she had been able to recognise straight away, such as the examination table, a large set of scales and some IV-drip stands, but most of the wooden crates kept their contents hidden, so she had to use her imagination to flesh out the rest – monitors, microscopes, mirrors, flasks, flagons, test tubes. After each delivery she would give the other women of the village a full report, and when, one bitterly cold morning some time at the beginning of January, she saw her neighbour emptying his postbox in a white lab coat with a stethoscope around his neck, she announced to all and sundry that Dr Hoppe's surgery was officially open for business.

A few brave villagers had admitted they were planning to have themselves looked at by the doctor – if only because they wanted to catch a glimpse of the children, for the latter had been kept out of sight all these weeks, so that little by little their existence had grown into a mystery greater than the Holy Trinity itself. But at the next Sunday Mass a sermon given by Father Kaisergruber, who had been ministering to the parish for almost forty years, had alarmed even the most confirmed sceptics.

'Believers, beware!' he had cried from the pulpit, his index finger in the air. 'Beware, for the great dragon is at hand, the old serpent, whose name is Devil and Satan, and who leadeth the whole world astray! I tell you, he is cast down here upon the earth, and his angels are cast down with him!'

After that the village shepherd had paused briefly, letting his eyes roam over his two hundred or so parishioners. Then, pointing his finger at the front row, where the village boys sat side by side in their Sunday best, their hair neatly slicked down, he had warned in a thundering voice: 'Take care, and be vigilant! The devil, thine enemy, prowls about like a roaring lion, seeking those he means to devour!'

And all the parishioners had seen how, as he spoke those last words, his trembling finger had pointed straight at Lanky Meekers, who had turned white as a sheet and did not dare show his face in the village square for the next few days.

2

The catastrophe that had been predicted for Wolfheim did not come to pass. In the months following Dr Hoppe's arrival, the villagers were spared death, accident, neighbourly strife, thievery and other such troubles. Not only that, the winter was mild for the first time in years and the spring, too, was warmer than usual, so that by the last week of April the lilacs next to the Maria Chapel were already in full bloom; many citizens took this as a good omen.

During all this time Dr Hoppe had stuck to his routine, making his rounds three times a week. He never had the babies with him. No one had seen or heard them, neither at the window, nor in the garden – this despite the fact that several villagers made a point of peering through the hawthorn hedge on a regular basis. There were some, therefore, who began to ask themselves if Lanky Meekers could have made the whole thing up, and in more and more living rooms the cautious consensus was reached that perhaps the doctor ought to be given a chance. Still, nobody had the nerve to take the first step, and it wasn't until one Sunday in May 1985, seven months after the doctor's return, that the first villager turned to him for help, albeit not really by choice.

That Sunday, around noon, George Bayer, an asthmatic toddler residing at 16 Galmeistrasse, took an orange-flame marble out of his pocket, which he had found some days earlier in the playground. The little fellow first licked it, and then, as his father, on the sofa, was turning the page of the Sunday paper and his mother, in the kitchen, was putting on the potatoes, he stuck it into his mouth. George let the marble roll around his tongue like a gobstopper, from left to right and from front to . . . The marble rolled into his throat, got stuck in his windpipe and no matter how hard little George coughed, he couldn't manage to dislodge it. His father also tried to get the marble out – first he slapped the kid on the back a few times and then stuck two fingers down his throat to fish the marble out – but it was no use. Suddenly he hit upon the notion of calling on Dr Hoppe, even if it meant having to sell him his soul.

Not even two minutes later, Werner and Rosette Bayer's car came squealing to a halt in front of the doctor's house. Werner snatched his son out of his wife's arms and rushed to the gate, yelling at the top of his lungs, 'Doctor! Help! Doctor! Please help!'

On all sides curtains promptly began twitching and the first neighbours came rushing outside. Only in Dr Hoppe's house was there no sign of life, so that Werner began to holler even louder, lifting his son's semi-limp body high up in the air, as if he were bringing an offering. That was when Dr Hoppe finally appeared in the doorway, immediately took in the gravity of the situation and ran to the gate with a bunch of keys in his hand.

'There's something stuck in his throat,' said Werner; 'he's swallowed something.'

With four or five bystanders watching, Dr Hoppe took little George from his father's arms. The neighbours' curious eyes were more intent on the red-haired pate bent over the child than on the child's face itself, which was beginning to turn blue. Without saying a word, the doctor tucked his arms around the torso of the unconscious boy from behind, locked his hands together and, with a vigorous thrust to the skinny little chest, expelled the obstruction from the victim's throat. The marble bounced onto the pavement and then rolled to a stop at the feet of Lanky Meekers, who had come to join the group of bystanders.

Next Dr Hoppe laid the toddler down on his back, knelt beside him and pressed his mouth against the child's. You could hear a loud gulp or two from the spectators. George's mother was sobbing, while Irma Nüssbaum made the sign of the cross and began to pray out loud. Some of the other bystanders couldn't bear to look, and only heard the doctor over and over again taking in a mouthful of air and then blowing it into the boy's lungs. Irma had just called out to Saint Rita when suddenly a shudder went through George's body and he began to gasp for air.

A sigh of relief went through the crowd and Rosette Bayer, rushing to her son's side, gathered him up in her arms. 'My boy, oh my little boy,' she wept, dabbing at the saliva that was dribbling down his chin. She picked the toddler up, tucked his head against her shoulder and gazed with tears in her eyes at Dr Hoppe, who had taken a few steps back, as if eager to return inside.

'Thank you, Doctor, you saved his life.'

'You are welcome,' said the doctor, and even though he had only spoken three words, the effect of his voice on the onlookers was like being stabbed with a knife. No one knew where to look, or how to react.

'Doctor, please tell me what I owe you.' George's father broke the awkward silence.

'Nothing, Herr . . .'

'Bayer. Werner Bayer.' He stuck out his hand, then let it fall again, but extended it once more upon receiving a discreet poke in the back from his wife.

'Nothing, Herr Bayer, you owe me nothing,' said Dr Hoppe. He gave the extended hand a quick shake, looking the other way, embarrassed.

'But I do want to thank you – some way or other. At least let me buy you a drink at the Terminus.'

Werner, glancing over his shoulder, indicated the café opposite the church. Dr Hoppe shook his head and nervously stroked his beard, which was a jumble of stringy tufts of red hair.

'Oh, come on, Doctor, just one little drink,' Werner insisted. 'It's on me. I'll buy everyone a round. *Tournée générale!*'

Voices were raised in approbation and now the other villagers also did their best to convince the doctor. Lanky Meekers made use of the commotion to bend down surreptitiously, pick up the marble, and furtively slip it into his jacket pocket.

'Yes, Doctor, let's drink to it!' he cried. 'To the miracle! Long live Dr Hoppe!'

There was a moment of hesitation from the bystanders, but then little George lifted his head from his mother's shoulder and gazed around, teary-eyed. Irma Nüssbaum was ecstatic. 'Yes, it's wonderful! It's a miracle! Long live Dr Hoppe!' Her cheer dispelled any remaining tension, and there was a sudden din of shouting and laughter.

'I can't, I'm afraid,' said the doctor, shaking his head. His voice carried easily over the brouhaha. 'My children, they . . .'

'But then bring your children with you!' cried Werner. 'A sip of gin will make them grow big and strong! Besides, we'd love to have a look at them, finally.'

Some of the bystanders nodded their agreement; others held their breath, waiting for the doctor's reaction.

'I . . . just give me five minutes, Herr Bayer. I have to take care of some things first. You go on ahead and I'll be along shortly.'

Then the doctor turned on his heels and strode down the garden path. Some of the villagers returned to their homes, but most headed straight for the Terminus, so that the little café was bursting at the seams in no time at all and Maria, the daughter of café owner René Moresnet, had to come over to give him a hand.

Josef Zimmermann had watched the entire incident from his usual table by the window, and when Werner Bayer arrived and began to sing the doctor's praises, the old man shook his head, drained his glass of gin in one gulp, then exclaimed, 'Only God can perform miracles!'

Werner waved his pronouncement away, and a glass of gin, compliments of Werner, did much to soften old Zimmermann's objections, so that after a little muttering he finally fell silent. Every time the door of the café swung open, everyone would stop talking and look up. But it always turned out to be yet another villager who had just heard the news.

'René, pour the man a drink,' Werner would call each time from his bar stool.

The tension grew by the minute, and when Jacob Weinstein, the village sexton, arrived and shouted that he had seen the doctor leave his house with a carrycot, wagers were hurriedly made: bets on the babies' sex and hair colour, but especially on the dimensions of their facial cleft.

'Here, write it down: eighteen centimetres,' Lanky Meekers said to his father, whose pen was poised over a beer coaster. 'I'm sure of it, Pa! I'd bet at least twenty francs on it if I were you!'

'If I lose, it's coming off your allowance,' said his father before scribbling down the bet and handing the coaster, with a twenty-franc coin, to the bartender.

Dr Hoppe, who had swapped his lab coat for a long grey overcoat, came into the Café Terminus backwards, so that the first thing the villagers saw was his hunched back and only afterwards did they catch a glimpse of the navy-blue carrycot he was toting. Even though everyone saw the difficulty he was having manoeuvring the cot through the doorway, nobody jumped up to give him a hand. It wasn't until he was finally inside and uncomfortably looking around for a place to put down his heavy load that Werner Bayer stepped forward, swiftly cleared some glasses off one of the tables and pointed magnanimously at the empty table top. Florent Keuning, who had been sitting there, hastily moved over to another table.

'Here, put it down here,' said Werner.

'Thank you,' said the doctor.

Again his voice startled the onlookers. Lanky Meekers' dad brought his mouth up to the ear of Jacob Weinstein and whispered, 'It's on account of the harelip. Makes him take in too much air.'

The sexton nodded, even though, being hard of hearing, he had hardly understood a word. Open-mouthed, he followed the doctor's every movement as he leaned over the cot and began to remove the plastic rain shield.

'What would you like to drink, *Herr Doktor*?' asked Werner.

'Water.'

'Really? Water?'

The doctor nodded.

'René, a glass of water for the doctor. And for, uh . . .' He waved his hand at the cot doubtfully.

'They don't need anything,' said the doctor, and as if he felt the need to justify himself, he added, 'I take good care of them.'

'Oh, I have no worries about that,' said Werner, though everyone heard how forced his answer sounded. Everyone, that is, except for the doctor, because he showed no reaction. Bending over the cot, he pushed the hood down, unhooked the cover and pulled it off. The onlookers standing closest took a few steps back. Only the villagers standing at the back weren't afraid to stare directly at the cot, even craning on tiptoe; but still no one could see what was inside.

The doctor, swaying a little on his feet, stood silently beside the cot. Except for the hum of the old ceiling fan, there was an awkward pause, and Werner felt all eyes on him.

'Hey, Werner, give the doctor his drink,' cried René Moresnet. The bartender held out a glass of water. Everyone watched as Werner handed the glass over to the doctor, who accepted it with a polite nod.

'Thank you very much,' he said, stepping aside to free up a space right next to the cot. 'Please, be my guest, Herr Bayer.'

Werner took a hesitant step forward. 'They're so quiet,' he remarked. 'Are they asleep?'

'Oh, no, they're awake,' replied the doctor with a cursory glance into the cot.

'Ohhh.' Cautiously Werner leaned forward; he thought he could make out the tops of the babies' heads. 'Girls?' he asked.

'No, three boys.'

'Three boys,' Werner echoed, swallowing audibly. He inched past the doctor to the side of the cot. 'What are their names?'

'Michael, Gabriel and Raphael.'

A buzz went round the café and Freddy Machon exclaimed in alarm, much louder than he'd intended, 'The angels of vengeance!'

It was clear that Dr Hoppe didn't know where to look. In order to cover his embarrassment, he took a sip of water.

Jacob Weinstein, who had not caught Machon's exclamation, chimed in: 'Just like the archangels, right, Doctor? God's messengers,' stated the sexton emphatically, as if to show off his biblical knowledge.

The doctor nodded, but remained mute.

Werner was still dithering next to the cot. 'How old are they now, Doctor?'

'Nearly nine months.'

Werner tried to recall what his own son had looked like at that age – how big had the boy been; and had he had any teeth?

His hands behind his back, his eyes squeezed shut, Werner leaned in slowly, screwing up his face as if he were biting into something sour. René Moresnet watched from behind the bar as Werner opened first one eye, then the other. Twice his eyes scanned the cot, from side to side and back again.

Then his face lit up. 'It's incredible! They look so much alike, all three of them!' he exclaimed, with a sigh of relief.

Dr Hoppe nodded. 'Quite. And nobody thought I could do it.'

Some of the patrons laughed, but the doctor's face remained serious, so that several people began to wonder whether it really was meant as a joke.

Werner took no notice; he was waving the bystanders over. 'Come on, you've got to see this!'

René Moresnet emerged from behind his bar, pushing Wilfred Nüssbaum ahead of him. It wasn't until the two men had leaned over the cot and reacted with an enthusiasm equal to Werner's that the other villagers felt it safe to approach. There was some pushing and jostling, and as the cries of *Oooh!* and *Aaaah!* proliferated, everyone tried to catch a glimpse of the three infants.

The first thing that everyone noticed was the way in which the doctor had had to arrange the babies in the cot, because they no longer quite fitted. Two of them were lying head-up: one had his left ear pressed against the side of the cot, the other his right. The third boy lay with his head at the foot of the cot, his feet sandwiched between his brothers' heads.

'Like sardines in a tin,' whispered Freddy Machon.

There was no blanket, but to ward off the cold their father had dressed the babies in mouse-grey woollen jumpsuits that covered them from neck to toe. All three jumpsuits had a sailboat on the left breast pocket, but most of the villagers did not notice this until they had closely examined the three little faces, none of which betrayed any sign of the wide-open gash Lanky Meekers had described. As it turned out, each infant did have a stitched upper lip, leaving a diagonal scar that extended, as in the doctor's own case, halfway up the wide, flattened nose. Their bulging heads – 'I thought for a moment they were wearing helmets,' René Moresnet remarked later – sprouted stringy ginger hair that was still too sparse to mask the entire skull. They had also inherited their father's grey-blue eyes, and his pale complexion. The skin on their high foreheads and cheeks was flaky, as it was on the backs of their hands.

'Their skin is too dry. He ought to use Zwitsal soap on them,' whispered Maria Moresnet, mother of a pair of illegitimate eighteen-month-old twins.

In any case, everyone agreed that the three brothers looked uncannily alike, and were nothing like the monsters most people had been imagining. The boys certainly weren't cute, and if you had said that they were ugly, nobody would have been likely to contradict you. However, for most people, especially the young mothers, the sight of the boys didn't evoke disgust, only pity – although no one was actually tempted to touch them, pat their ginger hair or say their names out loud, as if the people were all afraid that doing so would summon the children's celestial namesakes. The villagers shuffled round and round the cot, their heads bobbing above the three little boys like so many balloons. Anyone expecting the babies to react with alarm, now that they suddenly found themselves the centre of attention after so many months of confinement, would have been sadly mistaken. They simply didn't react at all. The spectators decided the babies must be overwhelmed by all the new things to see, because even pulling a funny face at them, or crooning *ga-ga-ga* or *boolle-boolle-boolle* did not make them as much as blink.

'They seem drugged,' whispered René Moresnet.

When just about everyone had had their turn at the cot, Lanky Meekers and his father came to have a gander.

Meekers promptly gave Lanky a poke in the ribs. 'Eighteen centimetres? Idiot!' his father hissed at Lanky, causing quite a bit of hilarity among the bystanders. Quickly, to change the subject, he turned to the doctor. 'Can they talk yet?'

From behind the bar Maria Moresnet said scornfully, 'At nine months? Surely not!'

But Dr Hoppe nodded and said dryly, 'Indeed they can, ever since they were six months old.'

Meekers looked up triumphantly. 'See? I was right!'

'Really? That soon, Doctor?' asked Maria incredulously.

The doctor nodded again. 'In French *and* German,' he added.

Now Maria began to laugh, 'Oh, you're joking.'

But the doctor wasn't joking. He even seemed to be slightly

offended. 'I have to go,' he said abruptly, walking over to the cot and yanking up the hood.

'Wouldn't you like another drink, Doctor?' René Moresnet suggested. The doctor shook his head, stretching the cover over the cot.

'Doctor?' The question came from somewhere at the front of the bar – a voice that had not been heard from before. Whoever it was cleared his throat and cried again, louder this time, 'Doctor, would you mind if I had a look at your sons too?'

The doctor was startled. He turned his head to see where the voice was coming from. A man with a wrinkled face, squinting out of one eye, stuck his gnarled hand up from his seat at a table by the window.

'My name is Josef Zimmermann, Doctor.'

There was some tittering. With his good eye Zimmerman glared around the café. 'Could you bring them over here for a minute?' he said, turning to the doctor. 'I'm not too steady on my feet, you see.' With a nod of the head he indicated the walking stick that was hooked over the arm of his chair.

'If you like, Herr Zimmermann,' said the doctor.

The café had gone quiet again, and the patrons held their breath as they watched Dr Hoppe pick up the cot and swing it down off the table. He crossed over to where Zimmermann was sitting and, crouching down, placed the cot on the floor right next to the old codger's scrawny legs.

'Thank you,' said Zimmermann, staring at the bowed back in front of him.

The doctor let the cot's hood down once more, then stood up. The old man was scrutinising him intently with his one functioning eye, the inky pupil of which filled almost the entire cornea. The other eye was just a horizontal split ringed with yellowish crusts.

'I knew your father and mother,' said Zimmermann.

The doctor cringed as if he'd been stung, but rose to his full height, trying to look nonchalant.

'Your father, now *there* was a good doctor,' the old man went on. 'They don't make them like that any more.'

It was a mean thing to say, but Dr Hoppe did not react. He simply stared at the cot and didn't say another word. Josef Zimmermann gave an audible sigh and slowly bent forward over the head of the cot.

'Well, well, so there they are. They look just like you.' He paused for a second, then said, 'Where is their mother, if I may ask?'

Behind him, some of the villagers exchanged looks of surprise. Everyone had been wondering the same thing for months, but nobody had had the guts to come right out with it and ask the doctor.

Dr Hoppe did not seem fazed, as if he had been expecting the question. He took a deep breath and then replied, 'They don't have a mother. Never had one.'

Josef Zimmermann looked baffled, but then he shook himself and said, 'I'm sorry, Doctor, I didn't know . . .'

All of a sudden the babies made their presence known. All three simultaneously opened their mouths and began to cry, and their voices were so exactly alike that it almost seemed as if the wailing were emerging from a single throat. Their shrieks set the bystanders' eardrums ringing. Even hard-of-hearing Weinstein covered his ears. The doctor reacted nervously to the screams, but did not make any attempt to hush his offspring. He pulled the hood of the cot back up and snapped the plastic rain shield into place. Then he picked up the cot and manoeuvred it between the tables and chairs towards the door, which he struggled in vain to open. Werner Bayer rushed forward and flung the door open wide, nodding his head nervously. He stared after the doctor as he crossed the street, then shut the door, turned round and glared angrily at Josef Zimmerman.

'Was that really necessary?' he cried. 'Was it? He saved my son's life, for God's sake!'

3

Any villagers who had still been hesitant about going to Dr Hoppe's surgery in the days following the incident with George Bayer changed their minds after Father Kaisergruber went to see him about his gastritis. In fact, the pastor's chronic complaint wasn't the real reason for his visit; it was curiosity. His conscience, too, played a part in his decision. Certain things had happened in the past, and he wondered what, if anything, the doctor still remembered.

'You look very much like your father.'

That was how he began the conversation, upon being received by the doctor in a rather cool and businesslike manner in the former consultation room. It was still stacked with boxes, and otherwise furnished with an old desk and two chairs.

Victor Hoppe responded to his remark with a curt nod, then asked him to describe his symptoms precisely.

The priest tried again a little later: 'Your mother was a good and devout Christian.' *She* was, at any rate, he would have liked to add.

Again, just a nod of the head. But this time the priest noticed a slight hesitancy. At least that was something.

The doctor asked him to take off his cassock. He complied, although it felt as if he were taking off a piece of armour that protected him from evil. As he was being examined, therefore, he kept conspicuously fingering the little silver cross that hung from a chain around his neck, in the hope that that would make the doctor think twice.

Then he mentioned casually, 'The holiday of St Rita is coming up next week. The entire village always goes on pilgrimage, to Calvary Hill at La Chapelle. The convent of the Clare Sisters.'

The doctor palpated his stomach, prodding hard where it hurt the most. The priest cried out in pain and only just managed to swallow an oath.

'That's the spot,' Dr Hoppe said, nodding, 'right where the oesophagus joins the stomach.' The doctor had managed to dodge the subject, but Father Kaisergruber knew that his own remark had touched a sore spot as tender as the one the doctor's probing thumb had just found.

The doctor gave him a home-made elixir for his ailment, and when the priest asked what he owed him, Victor Hoppe just shook his head and said, 'It is my duty to do good. It would not be right to take money for it.'

The priest was astonished. He wondered if the doctor was being ironic. He responded perfunctorily that that was very noble of him, and departed somewhat befuddled, the acid burning in his stomach.

At home he took a spoonful of the elixir, though less than the prescribed amount – what if it was poison? he asked himself fearfully – and very soon the burning sensation in his stomach began to abate. Two days later it was almost entirely gone and after another two days he felt great, as if his stomach upset had never existed. That in itself was such a relief that at the next Mass he read from chapter 6 of the Gospel according to St Luke, even though a different text was specified by the liturgical calendar. '*Judge not*,' he preached that Sunday, '*and ye shall not be judged. Condemn not, and ye shall not be condemned. Forgive, and ye shall be forgiven*.' And the entire congregation had witnessed how, for the first time in many weeks, the priest did not grimace in pain on swallowing the cheap sacramental wine.

A bunion, a dry cough, chilblains, a boil, a grazed knee: ever since Father Kaisergruber's recovery, even the most negligible complaint was excuse enough for the burghers of Wolfheim to ring the surgery bell. But villagers with incurable ailments – a chronic hernia or, in the case of Gunther Weber, congenital deafness – also went to Dr Hoppe, hoping, of course, that he would bring about another miracle.

Although Irma Nüssbaum had claimed the contrary, it turned out that the doctor was not quite ready for so many patients to come knocking at his door. As the priest had already discovered, he did not yet have a proper examination room, and the former waiting room had not been refurbished either, so that patients occasionally had to wait in the little hallway by the draughty front door.

The doctor begged his patients to excuse the inconvenience and said he had not had the opportunity to unpack everything, so that he was frequently obliged to leave the room during the consultation to fetch something he needed, such as the blood-pressure gauge or some disinfectant.

Dr Hoppe was invariably attentive and amiable, and never asked for payment, which made him – inadvertently perhaps – even more popular with the villagers. They certainly flocked to the surgery at all hours of the day, from as early as half past six in the morning until late in the evening. Sometimes they even rang in the middle of the night, like the time when Eduard Mantels of 20 Napoleonstrasse just couldn't get to sleep, even after two cups of linden tea laced with rum, and had roused the doctor from his bed for a sleeping pill.

4

One fine Saturday in July, some weeks after George Bayer's resuscitation, a sign went up on the gate of the doctor's house posting surgery hours: from 9 to 11 a.m. and 6.30 to 8 p.m., weekdays only. And if anyone needed to see the doctor outside those times, an appointment would have to be made by telephone. This caused a fair amount of indignation, for some of the villagers thought a doctor ought to be always at his patients' beck and call, but on the whole most condoned the doctor's decision, especially since he was having the waiting and consultation rooms refurbished. The doctor delegated this job to Florent Keuning, who often moonlighted as a handyman. Florent gave the walls a fresh coat of paint, the doors and windows too, and sanded and varnished the wooden floors. The rest of the house was also in need of all sorts of repairs. Hinges and latches had to be oiled, windows and doors that were sticking needed adjustment, there were damp spots on walls and ceilings to be patched, and plumbing leaks to be soldered, so that altogether Florent had at least four weeks of work ahead of him.

During the month he worked at the house, he'd catch a glimpse of the triplets from time to time. Ever since the doctor had shown his children to the patrons of the Café Terminus, they had not been seen again. Nor did anyone hear them crying, even though the villagers who attended the surgery were particularly alert to that possibility.

'Are the children always so quiet?' they asked the doctor on several occasions.

'They're very calm babies,' was his usual reply. 'They're hardly any trouble.'

Florent was asked the same question when he told the patrons of the Café Terminus that he had seen the little boys.

'It's true, they were ever so quiet,' he confirmed. 'They were sitting in those little rocking chairs – you know the kind – just staring off into space, as if they were trying to work out some complicated problem. They didn't even look up when I hammered a nail into the wall right next to them. I don't think they even noticed me.'

'Valium, I expect,' said René Moresnet.

'Oh, come off it,' his daughter broke in; 'maybe they were just a bit under the weather, or exhausted or something. You always assume the worst.'

Maria wanted to know if the boys still looked so *weird*. What she really meant was ugly, but she didn't say so out loud.

'Their hair is an even brassier colour than the first time we saw them,' the handyman replied. 'Not the doctor's kind of garish red – it's more of a rusty colour, as if they'd had their heads dunked into a jar of red lead.'

'And what about their . . .' said Jacques Meekers, pointing to his upper lip.

'The work of a clumsy joiner. You know, the kind that tries to fill a crack in the wood with some putty and sawdust. A half-arsed job, if you ask me.'

'And do they really know how to talk?' Maria wanted to know.

Florent shrugged. 'Not that *I've* heard, anyway.'

'Just as I thought,' said Maria.

Over the next few days Florent Keuning was often stopped on the street. Some of the ladies were curious to know if the doctor could manage the housework all by himself.

'I think so. It's always neat as a pin. And he's always asking me to keep the dust down.'

'But does he change the babies' nappies often enough?' asked Irma Nüssbaum, the mother of two adult sons.

'And are their clothes clean?' asked Helga Barnard, who had raised three daughters.

'Does he test the milk first, to check if it isn't too hot?' asked Odette Surmont, grandmother of six.

'Oh, I couldn't tell you,' said Florent; 'that isn't a man's business, is it?'

'See what we mean? It can't be easy for him without having a woman around. The doctor really needs someone to help him,' they decided.

One after another, the ladies swiftly made good on their words. Feigned spells of the migraine led to inquiries about whether the doctor needed a housekeeper or a babysitter; he thanked each and every one of them for their kind offer, maintaining that he could manage by himself. He did, however, accept any tips they offered with evident interest – what to do about teething pains, for example.

'Have them chew on a crust of frozen bread, Doctor,' Odette Surmont advised him, while Helga Barnard swore that in the case of her two daughters raw onion rings had done the trick.

So it was with some consternation that Irma Nüssbaum, Helga Barnard and Odette Surmont found out from Florent Keuning a few days later that Charlotte Maenhout was going to be looking after the doctor's brood. The three women, on porch-sweeping patrol late that afternoon, had gathered at the corner of Napoleonstrasse and Kirchstrasse, and there they ambushed the handyman, who had just finished his last day of work at the doctor's and was on his way to spend his nice big tip at the Café Terminus. The news was dire enough to stop their brooms in mid-air, whereas the ladies themselves exploded in indignation. It was true that, as a former schoolteacher, Frau Maenhout had some experience educating children – she had taught the reception class at the Gemmerich schoolhouse for many years – but she had never had any children of her own, to say nothing of a husband. So how could she be expected to know how to look after a bunch of little tykes?

Helga asked the handyman if he was absolutely sure, whereupon he told the ladies how that morning, as he had been giving one of the doors a final coat of paint, he had peeked through the crack and seen Dr Hoppe showing Frau Maenhout into the kitchen, where the little boys were seated as usual like rag dolls in their rocking chairs.

'Was it really Charlotte Maenhout?' Irma promptly broke in. 'From Aachenerstrasse?'

Florent nodded confidently, and said he'd recognise Charlotte

Maenhout from a kilometre away, which nobody could refute, since there was no other woman in the village with as hefty a build as the sixty-eight-year-old retired schoolteacher who had come to live in Wolfheim three years ago. She was tall – one metre eighty-four – and her broad back was hunched from years of hovering over her young pupils, guiding their inexperienced hands in the art of writing. Her bowed back caused her neck to sink down between her knobbly shoulders, and in order to lengthen it, she always wore her long silver hair in a bun at the nape, or twisted it up with a wooden hairpin. Another conspicuous thing about her was her generous bosom, or, as Florent described it, her 'stack of wood at the front door'.

'What did she say? What did the doctor say?' Helga wanted to know.

'First the doctor introduced his children to her,' the handyman answered, pinching his nose to mimic Dr Hoppe's voice: 'This is Raphael. He has the green bracelet. That is Gabriel, with the yellow bracelet. And the one with the blue bracelet is Michael.'

Florent went on in a normal voice: 'They have these little plastic bracelets around their wrists. Like newborns in hospital, you know? And then the doctor turned to his sons and told them that Frau Maenhout would be coming to look after them.'

The three ladies shook their heads and Irma Nüssbaum said aloud what the other two were thinking: 'Why *her*, in God's name? She isn't even from around here.'

'Wait,' the handyman broke in, 'because that wasn't all. The doctor had just finished telling the children that she'd be looking after them when all three boys raised their heads at the same time – and they *winked* at her.'

The ladies looked at him open-mouthed.

'That's what it seemed like to me anyway,' he added, watering down his testimony somewhat.

'And then? What did Frau Maenhout do then?' asked Odette.

'Nothing. She asked the doctor what time he wanted her to be there and the doctor said 8.30. Then she left. And now I must be going myself, ladies. I have urgent business spending a nice big tip!'

He forged his way out of the circle of muttering women and started walking off, but turned back one last time. 'The doctor pays well. I don't think Frau Maenhout will regret her decision.'

Then he turned on his heels and made straight for the Terminus. Behind him there was a brief silence, and then the tongues started wagging again.

Half past eight the next morning found Charlotte Maenhout striding resolutely along Napoleonstrasse. Passing the churchyard, she nodded at Jacob Weinstein, who was weeding the paths; he stuck his chin in the air by way of greeting. From across the street, Irma Nüssbaum, who had been at her post behind the kitchen curtain for a good half-hour, watched her approach. The former schoolteacher had flung a white crocheted shawl around her broad shoulders and every now and then the thick lenses of her horn-rimmed glasses would catch the rising sun. She was wearing her hair pinned up, and Irma guessed that the red fabric sticking out of the wicker basket on her left arm must be an apron. When Frau Maenhout rang the bell at the doctor's gate, she glanced over her shoulder, showing her face, its roundness in marked contrast to the angular build of her heavy-set body. Her gleaming eyes wore their usual amiable expression, which had always put the little children she taught at ease from their very first day at school.

When she heard the doctor's front door being unlocked, Frau Maenhout turned forward again. Irma saw Dr Hoppe in the doorway, awkwardly raising his hand in greeting. He was already wearing his lab coat, but had not buttoned it. With long strides he walked to the gate and opened it, inviting Frau Maenhout to come inside and leaving the gate unlatched for the patients who would be streaming in over the course of the next two hours.

Following the doctor inside, Charlotte Maenhout couldn't help recalling the conversation of the day before. She had gone to see the doctor about her raised blood pressure, and Dr Hoppe had made use of the occasion to give her a thorough check-up and ask all sorts of questions for the medical file that he began for every new patient. He'd asked about previous complaints, about any surgery or illnesses or abnormalities in the family. He had also wanted to know about her lifestyle, her eating habits and whether she drank or smoked. Her answers had met with his approval, but she had not admitted to him that she had a sweet tooth. Then he had asked if she was married or had any children – 'The doctor is looking for a new wife,' Odette Surmont told her friends after he had asked her the same question on her first visit – whereupon she had said, smiling, that forty years ago, a teacher at a convent school was expected to remain single and live in, and that now she was too old and too wise to take a husband. The doctor hadn't seemed to get the joke. But at least he now knew not to try anything with her, she had thought at the time. She didn't find him at all attractive; on the contrary, she was even slightly repelled by him. Never having seen him before, the moment she laid eyes on him she had decided that Martha Bollen was not exaggerating when she'd said that the doctor had been last in line on the day that God was doling out good looks. The hair on his head, on his arms and on the back of his hands was the colour of baby carrots. His beard was darker, sprouting from his chin and jaw like a rusty tangle of barbed wire, with sparser tufts of hair growing on his cheeks and the region just below his mouth. Since the scar of his cleft lip was hairless, it looked as if someone had taken a razor and roughly carved a strip out of his moustache. And then there was his nasal, monotone voice; the consonants normally produced by touching the tongue to the roof of the mouth, such as the 't' and 'l', almost vanishing into the mouth cavity, so that they were barely audible. Only his sober clothes – brown corduroy trousers and a beige shirt – were unremarkable.

As the doctor had examined Charlotte he had been punctilious about telling her what he was about to do, asking her direct questions all the while. So it had turned out that he was most interested to hear that she could speak French, German and Dutch.

'*Niederlandisch*,' he had said, and then he'd asked if she knew a song in that language called 'The little flowers nodded off. The lovely smells had worn them out.' He'd said the words with a strong accent, but she'd known which song he meant.

'It's called "The Sandman".'

'What?'

' "The Sandman". *Das Sandmännchen*,' she'd clarified.

As long as he doesn't ask me to sing it, she'd prayed, but he hadn't. He had asked some more questions, including about her former profession. Again he'd showed great interest when she told him that she had spent almost her entire career teaching first years at Gemmenich and had initially been in charge of the nursery school. It had not immediately dawned on her what the doctor was getting at, so when he had suddenly asked her point-blank if she would babysit for his three little boys during surgery hours, she had been so bowled over that she hadn't been able to think of what to say. Nor had he waited for her answer before showing her his children. The doctor had led her into the kitchen, where the three little ones had been sitting in their rocking chairs.

She had been taken aback, despite having heard the many stories circulating about the children. They looked the way a child might have drawn them: the proportions weren't right. Their heads were too big in relation to their bodies and the eyes were much too big for their heads. That was what she had noticed first.

Then the doctor had told her the boys' names, showing her the little coloured band each wore around the wrist. Indeed, it was quite impossible to distinguish one from another with the naked eye. At the same time, she had seen how much they resembled their father: hair, skin, eyes and, alas, cleft palate, on the same side, too – the right.

In the short time that she was with them, she had noticed something else: they would not look at her. In that way too they resembled their father. It had struck her during her physical examination that he tried to avoid any and all eye contact. The way he accomplished this was by looking down at the floor a lot, whereas his three sons had been chiefly absorbed by their own hands, which were in constant motion, as if palpating some invisible object.

'Frau Maenhout is going to look after you, starting tomorrow,' she'd heard the doctor say, to her considerable surprise.

She had wanted to object, but then all three boys had lifted their heads and looked up at her for an instant with their disproportionately large eyes. She had made her decision right then and there. 'What time do you want me tomorrow?' she had asked.

'Eight thirty,' he'd answered.

Then she had left, and it wasn't until she was outside that she'd realised she hadn't even said goodbye to the boys.

'Are you ready?' asked the doctor as he opened the door to the kitchen.

She wasn't sure, for she had no idea what the doctor expected of her. They had not yet discussed it. They hadn't talked about the children at all, and even the subject of money had not come up. Rarely had Frau Maenhout been so impulsive.

'I think so,' she said, and again she was surprised at her own reply.

The little boys were in their rocking chairs, just as they had been the day before. Again they were concentrating on their hands, which they couldn't seem to keep still. There was even a kind of rhythm to their movements, which gave them a rather robot-like air.

Maybe they're bored, Frau Maenhout thought, because she had noticed that there were no toys or stuffed animals around. 'Hello, boys,' she said.

There was no reaction.

'They're a bit shy,' said the doctor.

She walked over to them and scrutinised them carefully. They were too thin, she decided, and with such delicate, almost transparent skin, they seemed rather fragile – as if they were made of glass.

'Please feel free to pick one of them up, if you want.'

She nodded and pussyfooted towards them. She didn't know which one to choose. None of them seemed eager to be picked up: they didn't raise their arms in the air or anything like that. Kneeling down in front of the middle chair, she unbuckled the strap. For a moment she held her breath, having to conquer her trepidation. It was the same kind of fear she had felt in class about ten years earlier, the first time she'd had to take Julie Carpentier's badly charred hand in hers in order to show her how to move it across the page. Just as she had then, she now counted to three under her breath, then swooped down and lifted the boy up from his chair. He weighed very little and showed barely any reaction upon finding himself in her arms.

'That's Raphael,' said the doctor, pointing at the blue bracelet.

'Raphael,' she repeated.

She thought it was a lovely name, but in combination with the other two names, it was a rather odd choice, to name the three kids after the three archangels, and Frau Maenhout wondered who had decided on this. The father or the mother? Or someone else?

'They are so quiet, such good boys,' she remarked. But as soon as she said it, she was struck with the alarming thought that there might be something wrong with the children. They might be retarded or something.

'They still have to get used to you,' said Dr Hoppe. 'They have a hard time adapting to new situations, I've noticed.'

His reply did nothing to ease her fears. As if he had read her mind, the doctor added, 'But they can talk. Sometimes they'll suddenly say a word they've overheard. Either from me, or from the radio. And it might be in French, or in German. They are extremely intelligent.'

'That is quite remarkable, yes.'

She didn't know whether to believe him or not. In her profession she had had occasion to speak to parents who perceived abilities in their children that did not actually exist. Every woman thinks her child is special, she used to remind herself every time it happened.

'I wish to stimulate their language skills,' the doctor continued. 'I've been alternating between German and French with them, but if you speak only French to them from now on, and I restrict myself to German, it should help them to distinguish the two languages from each other more quickly, don't you think?'

She had to agree, nor did she find it an unusual request. In this region, at the crossroads of three cultures and three languages, most of the children were raised multilingual. Nearly everybody spoke German, and usually also knew some French or Dutch. Some children learned all three languages at once, depending on which school they attended or who their playmates were.

It had been the same for her. She had been born in Gemmenich and her parents had raised her to speak German. She had picked up French in the street, and later, in secondary school, she had been taught Dutch. Suddenly she understood the reason for the doctor's interest in her language abilities the day before, especially when he mentioned the Dutch lullaby again.

'The one about the flowers,' he said, 'could you sing it to them from time to time?'

'As you wish,' she said, even though she thought it rather a strange request.

The doctor looked at his watch. 'Come, I'll give you a quick tour of the house. The first patients will be arriving any minute now.' He turned on his heels and disappeared through the door leading to the corridor, leaving her standing there somewhat befuddled.

Shaking her head, she carefully put Raphael back down in his little chair. 'I'll be right back,' she said to the boys in French, wondering what on earth she had let herself in for.

In the hall the doctor was waiting by a door opposite the examination room. 'The children and I have been sleeping downstairs for the time being,' he said, and stepped into the room.

She hesitated, hanging back in the doorway. The room was immaculate. At the far end, centred on the wall, was a single bed, its bedspread stretched taut, without a single crease. There weren't any books or clothes on the two chairs stationed on either side of the bed, nor were there any children's toys or paraphernalia on the floor. Three metal cots on wheels were lined up side by side against another wall. These too were neatly made; there wasn't a crease in the spotless white sheets or pillowcases. At the foot of each bed hung a little nameplate. Michael slept in the bed on the right, to his left was Raphael and next to that, Gabriel. The walls appeared to have been freshly wallpapered, but aside from that they were quite bare. There were none of the pictures one would have expected to see: a portrait of the doctor's wife, perhaps, a wedding picture of his parents, or at the very least a photo of the children. The entire room radiated anonymity. It was an impersonal space; the spotless white of the bedspread and the sheets made it feel like a hospital ward more than anything else.

'The bathroom is upstairs,' said the doctor, 'but since it's difficult to carry the children up the stairs every time, I've been washing them in a tub in the kitchen.'

'Just as in our own day.' Frau Maenhout smiled.

The doctor remained impervious. No sense of humour, she thought.

'Frau Maenhout . . .' There was a pregnant pause, which made her look up. 'There is something else. There's something wrong with their health,' he stated flatly.

Although she had been wondering about the children's health, the news still came as a shock. She wondered why the doctor had waited so long to tell her.

'It's nothing too serious,' he said, 'and I'm dealing with it, but I thought you ought to know. It means they do have to be kept indoors for the time being.'

'You might have told me before . . .' she began, but was interrupted by the sound of the doorbell.

'Ah, there's my first patient,' said the doctor in a rush. 'I must get started. And so must you.' He turned and, brushing past her, hurried out of the room. It was almost as if he were running away, and she stood there perplexed. 'Are you coming, Frau Maenhout?' she heard him say.

I'm not doing this, she thought, I mustn't. Flustered, she stepped out of the room. 'Doctor,' she said, 'I—'

'Hello, Frau Maenhout.'

It was Irma Nüssbaum at the end of the hall, nodding at her. Charlotte Maenhout had seen her watching from the house across the street just a short while ago.

'Will you be looking after the doctor's children then, Frau Maenhout?' asked Irma.

There was a note of spitefulness in the way she had pronounced her name. The doctor had stopped and posted himself in between the two ladies, like the referee in a duel.

'Yes, Frau Nüssbaum,' Charlotte Maenhout replied without moving a muscle. 'I was asked to, and said I would.' Turning on her heel, she walked towards the kitchen.

In those first few weeks the children did not strike Charlotte Maenhout as being particularly intelligent; on the contrary, they continued to be quite unresponsive and had not spoken a word. She was growing increasingly convinced that all three were mentally disabled and surmised that that was what the doctor had meant when he'd said there was something wrong with them.

Slowly but surely, however, Michael, Gabriel and Raphael began to warm to her. Indeed, it was as if she'd had to earn their trust. She had done nothing special to earn that trust, other than being consistently kind and patient with them, which was the hardest part, really. There were times when she had felt like shaking them one by one, hoping to wring even a smidgen of emotion from them. Luckily she'd been able to control herself, however, for one fine day, when Napoleonstrasse was, as so often, chock-a-block with cars and coaches on their way to the three-border junction, there was a sudden breakthrough. She had picked up Michael in her arms so that he could look out the window, when suddenly the boy cried, 'Au-o!' and a second later one of the other two behind her cried, 'A-ee!' Later the doctor said his son had probably meant 'taxi', because it was in a taxi that they had travelled from Bonn to Wolfheim all those months ago. Charlotte Maenhout was flabbergasted.

After that, things progressed rapidly. Either their vocabulary was already extensive to start with, or it was growing by leaps and bounds, because over the next few days the three boys kept uttering new words, repeating what one of the others had said or adding to it. Sometimes it almost seemed as if the children were making a game of it. She'd be preparing some fruit for them to eat and the boys would start naming fruits one by one, in French, because they had cottoned on to the fact that this was the language she spoke. All three were quite hard to understand, of course, not only because they were so young but also because, like their father, they had trouble with certain sounds on account of their cleft palates. But *she* understood what the boys were saying, and that was all that mattered – at first, anyway.

Shortly after this the children gave her another demonstration of their talents. As the doctor had requested, she sang them the Dutch lullaby about the little sandman every night before they went to sleep, and one evening, about fifteen minutes before their usual bedtime, Gabriel suddenly said, in Dutch, 'Tired.' She didn't understand at first what he meant, but when Raphael promptly chimed in with, 'Sleep,' in Dutch as well, and then Michael piped up and said, 'Night-night,' she knew that the triplets had spontaneously applied the Dutch words they had learned from the lullaby to their bedtime ritual.

When a few days later she told her friend and former colleague Hannah Kuijk about it, Hannah said, 'That's because they don't have a mother. It means they're not bound to any mother tongue.'

Charlotte Maenhout thought it a rather far-fetched explanation. Next her friend suggested that the boys' brains might be linked via some invisible neurological network into a single overarching superbrain. Frau Maenhout had heard of a similar idea before, and also that multiple siblings were sometimes able to read each others' minds or feel one another's emotions, even when miles apart. Still, she preferred to stick to the simple explanation that they had inherited their father's intelligence, as well as his passivity – unfortunately, because notwithstanding their verbal abilities the triplets were still frustratingly taciturn when it came to expressing or showing emotion.

For the four hours that Frau Maenhout watched the children – from half past eight in the morning until half past ten, and from six until eight in the evening – she kept them busy with an energy and enthusiasm that she had not thought herself still capable of. She made silly faces and rolled her eyes, erected precarious towers with building blocks and cardboard boxes, set the boys on her lap one behind the other and bounced them up and down, drove toy cars down imaginary lanes and little wooden trains through dark tunnels, and told them fables and fairy tales, taking on the role of the witch, the fairy or the queen. Yet notwithstanding all her exertions she never managed to get any of the three boys to chortle or laugh, except once; but then they hardly ever cried either.

'Oh, it will come, Charlotte,' was Hannah Kuijk's opinion. 'Those children are probably dealing with some kind of trauma. They didn't receive any love for the first months of their lives. They didn't get it from their mother, since she was dead, nor from their dad, because he's such a cold man. The very fact that he wants them to call him "Father" and not "Dad" or "Dada" proves that he wants to keep them at arm's length. I wouldn't put it past him to insist, later on, that his children address him as "Sir".'

'But he's constantly taking pictures of them,' Frau Maenhout objected. 'Surely that must mean he's fond of them?'

'I'm not saying he isn't. But if you ask me, it's a matter of sublimation. He's just trying to cover up his own inability to express love. He thinks taking pictures of them is a way to bond with them. No, Charlotte, keep on doing what you're doing; it's good for those poor kids that you're there. That way at least *someone* can teach them about feelings.'

'Right, Hannah. I'll bear that in mind.'

5

'A pound of those delicious ginger snaps, please.'

'Are they for the doctor's sons?'

Frau Maenhout shook her head, smiling. 'No, they're for me, actually.'

Martha Bollen began rummaging in the glass jar of home-baked ginger snaps that sat on the counter. She slipped the biscuits into a paper bag and plumped it down on one of the scales' copper pans, placing a weight on the other.

'I'm giving you three extra,' said the shopkeeper, squinting at the needle on the scales. 'For the boys. With love from Martha, tell them, from the shop.'

Frau Maenhout wanted to refuse the offer – the doctor's children weren't allowed any sweets – but being afraid that Martha would pepper her with all sorts of unpleasant questions again, she just nodded her head and said, 'That's very nice of you. Thank you.'

She took the bag and stuffed it into the shopping trolley that held the fresh goods she came here to buy for Dr Hoppe's household nearly every day. Her wicker basket was full as well, brimming with, amongst other things, tissues, talcum powder and a packet of nappies.

Frau Maenhout had started taking on more and more of the doctor's housekeeping. While she was looking after the children, she'd do some polishing, as well as cooking and doing the laundry. She always took the ironing home as a matter of course. The doctor hadn't asked her to do any of this, but she had taken it upon herself voluntarily, largely for the sake of the little ones, for she had too often seen them dressed in grubby clothes. In her eyes, they weren't being fed a sufficiently varied diet, either. The doctor mostly bought tinned goods, or ready-made food in jars.

Martha began punching the keys on the cash register. 'Aren't you ever going to bring the boys with you? We never see them out,' she said.

'They're still too young, Martha.'

'Too young? They must have turned one by now – haven't they?'

'Yes, last Saturday.'

'Last Saturday? September the twenty-ninth?'

'That's right.'

'But that means their birthday is on their saints' day.'

Frau Maenhout stared at the shopkeeper in surprise.

'September the twenty-ninth', said Martha, 'is the feast of St Michael, St Gabriel and St Raphael.'

'Is that so? I didn't realise.'

'My husband's name was Michel. That's how I know it. Maybe the doctor named his children the way he did because they were all born on that day.'

'It would be an uncanny coincidence otherwise.'

'Nothing is coincidence,' said the shopkeeper, wagging her finger in the air. 'But tell me, did the children have a nice birthday party?'

Frau Maenhout nodded, averting her face, because she felt herself turning red. She should have told the truth, but it still upset her to think of it – the doctor had sent her home when she arrived that Saturday morning with a bag full of presents, including some picture books. His sons were very ill, Dr Hoppe had told her, and he'd decided that they would have to spend the rest of the weekend in isolation, in a sterile room – he'd used the word 'quarantine', which had an unpleasant ring to it. When she'd asked the doctor what ailed them – they had not shown any sign of illness the night before – he'd answered that they had taken ill in the middle of the night and that he was still in the process of working out what was the matter.

It was the first time that all three had been ill at the same time. There had been one or two previous occasions when the doctor had sequestered one of them in a separate room next to his office for a few days largely as a preventive measure, having noticed symptoms that might indicate an illness brewing: a red throat, a slight cough, loss of weight or a suspicious rash.

Frau Maenhout had thought it all a bit odd, but who was she to question the doctor's professional opinion? Besides, Michael, Raphael and Gabriel had always returned from these separations hale and hearty.

Actually, hale and hearty wasn't exactly the right expression, because there did seem to be something seriously wrong with them. However, Frau Maenhout had not quite deduced what it was. The doctor was always a bit vague about it, as if he didn't want to come out and admit that he wasn't sure either. In referring to their illness he used words she did not understand, and kept telling her he was still running tests. She had once made the suggestion that he call in a specialist, but the doctor had seemed so offended that she had not raised the subject again.

'Any other doctor wouldn't know the first thing about it,' he had said, before stalking off.

The worst thing for Charlotte was that she had no idea what the children's ailment looked like, nor how it might manifest itself. Other than the fact that the children tired easily and couldn't really tolerate being touched, she hadn't noticed anything that might indicate a serious condition.

'What should I be looking out for?' she had asked Dr Hoppe early on.

'Oh, it will be plain enough,' he'd replied.

Martha Bollen's voice roused Frau Maenhout from her musings. 'And how well are they talking now?' asked the shopkeeper. 'Rosette Bayer said that they can speak Dutch as well. She heard them singing a Dutch song.'

'Singing isn't speaking, Martha. You mustn't believe everything people tell you. The boys just like to copy what I say.' She'd deliberately twisted the truth a little, for she had noticed on other occasions that mentioning the triplets' unusual ability with languages tended to provoke envy or disbelief. Some people thought Charlotte was just showing off what a good teacher she was.

'But they're smart little fellows, aren't they?'

'They get that from their father.'

'And a good thing too,' said Martha sotto voce. 'It doesn't bear thinking about, does it – if the only thing they've inherited from him is his looks. And how *is* our doctor, anyway?'

'Busy, very busy. People think he can work miracles.'

'And so he can! Last week he cured Freddy Machon of his chronic gout. Gave him five shots and then it was all better. The doctor told him they've been using the stuff in Germany for years. You know what it is, Frau Maenhout? We're very behind, here in Belgium, as far as medicine is concerned. It's too bad the doctor didn't get here sooner. Maybe he'd have been able to cure our Michel.'

'You shouldn't be thinking that way, Martha. What's done is done. How much do I owe you?'

Martha, peering at the bill to check that she had not forgotten anything, then said, 'Nine hundred and twenty francs, please.'

Frau Maenhout took out her purse, removed a thousand-franc note and placed it in the shopkeeper's stubby hand. After putting away the change, she left, wheeling the shopping trolley behind her.

'Will you please give the doctor my regards?' Martha called after her as she reached the door.

As Charlotte crossed the street, the plastic wheels of the shopping trolley clattered loudly over the cobblestones, attracting the attention of the three youths in the square, who began waving at her. She recognised Fritz Meekers, Robert Chevalier and deaf Gunther Weber, who used to come to her for weekly speech lessons because his parents couldn't afford a trained speech therapist. She hadn't really been all that happy with the result, but at least he could now make himself understood and appeared to be taking great strides since he'd started attending a special school for the deaf in Liège last year.

Waving back at them, she hurried on, urged by the church bell, which had started to strike six o'clock. It had been over two days since she'd seen the triplets. She'd sat by the phone all weekend, as usual, in case Dr Hoppe rang to ask her to mind the children while he went out on an emergency call. But nothing of a serious nature had happened to any of the villagers – she was ashamed to admit that she almost wished it had – so she had waited in vain, working herself up into a state about the boys' condition.

This morning she hadn't been allowed to see them either. The doctor had told her they were quite a bit better, but they were still asleep. He wanted to let them sleep on, so she had just tidied the place up and done a little cleaning, keeping an ear open for any sound from the boys. When it was time to go home, Michael, Gabriel and Raphael were still asleep. When she rang the doctor some time around three in the afternoon, he told her they'd finally woken up at 1.30, which came as a great relief.

As she rang the bell at the gate, the sixth and last peal of the church bells was dying away over the roofs of Wolfheim. She peered wistfully through the railings, hoping to see Dr Hoppe with one of the boys in his arms on the lookout for her through one of the street-facing windows. Alas, he wasn't there.

She had become attached to the children, and they had become attached to her. Even though it did still feel as if the three boys had put up a wall around themselves, she had the impression that they were beginning to lower their guard every once in a while. There was definitely a change in their facial expressions when she arrived, and also when she left. If you hadn't known them before, you wouldn't have seen the difference, but she had learned to notice the most trivial things: a slight tug at the corner of the mouth, a glance, a twitch of the hand.

'Frau Maenhout stay,' Michael had even said the last time she left, as if he'd had a premonition that she would be forced to stay away longer than usual. 'Vow aynot yay.' That's the way it had sounded.

Meanwhile, the boys were learning fast. Frau Maenhout estimated that they were at least six months ahead of other children their age. They understood almost everything she said to them, and came out with simple sentences in German and French. They could put together wooden puzzles aimed at eighteen-month-olds, and identify objects in picture books or comics.

Physically they were a little slower. They were not yet walking, and also had some trouble with their motor skills. This was made plain, for instance, when they tried to feed themselves or to pick something up. But that, Frau Maenhout thought, was only because she had limited time to devote to each of the three boys. There wasn't enough opportunity to give them individual attention. 'I only have two hands!' she'd often exclaim.

Besides, she suspected that the doctor didn't spend very much time with the children after she went home. He would plop them down in their little chairs or in their playpen, and then barely pay them any attention, except to put them through more medical tests.

'Isn't the doctor home?' she suddenly heard a boy's voice calling.

Frau Maenhout was startled. The doctor hadn't yet appeared, and the boys who had been playing in the village square were now ambling towards her.

'Oh, he is,' she said; 'he'll be coming out in just a minute.'

'How are they doing, then, the Hoppe brothers?' asked Lanky Meekers.

'Very well. How about you? I see you're still growing. You'll soon be a head taller than me.'

The doctor says I'm going to be at least two metres,' the boy responded, not without some pride. 'He examined me the other day.'

'His dad kick im in pants all de time!' Gunther Weber remarked. 'Thas why he's so tall!'

'And yours doesn't kick you often enough!'

'OK, no bickering, boys.'

Frau Maenhout glanced at the front door, but there was still no sign of life.

'My dad says the doctor's sons are geniuses,' said Robert Chevalier.

'Gee-whah?' cried Gunther, pointing at his ears.

'Gee-nee-uses,' said Robert, enunciating carefully. 'Exceptional.'

'Well, aren't all of you?' said Frau Maenhout with a wink, and saw all three puff up with pride. 'Here, I've got something for you.' She put down her basket, rummaged in her shopping trolley and drew out the bag of gingersnaps.

'From Martha the shopkeeper,' she said, glad that she could at least make someone else happy with the biscuits.

'Mmmmm!' said Gunther.

'Thank you, Frau Maenhout,' said Lanky Meekers and Robert Chevalier in unison, eagerly taking one biscuit each.

'Dwhere is de doctor.'

Gunther was pointing at the house. Dr Hoppe had opened the door and was coming down the front steps.

'When can we come and play with the doctor's boys?' Lanky Meekers asked quickly.

'Later on, when they're bigger.'

'Hello, Heaw Doktow,' Robert said with his mouth full.

The doctor nodded and clicked open the gate. 'Please come in, Frau Maenhout.'

'Can we help you?' asked Lanky Meekers.

The doctor acted as if he hadn't heard him. He bent down, picked up the basket and said again, 'Please come in, Frau Maenhout; we don't want to leave the children unattended for too long.'

Lanky Meekers scowled at his friends. Frau Maenhout, grabbing the handle of the shopping trolley, nodded goodbye to the boys. They stared after her as she walked up the path. At the door the doctor took the shopping trolley from her.

'How are the children, Doctor? Are they all better?' asked Frau Maenhout before going inside.

No response. He stopped to let her pass. 'I'll take this into the kitchen,' he said. 'You go on ahead.'

She didn't have to be told twice and hurried down the corridor.

Behind her she heard, 'Frau Maenhout?' There was some urgency in the doctor's voice.

She looked back at him quizzically, and thought she could see his left eyelid twitching. The same thing happened to his sons sometimes, when they were under stress.

'Something has happened, Frau Maenhout.' And his eyelid twitched again.

6

By the time Dr Hoppe had been back in the village a year, Wolfheim had settled down again; the gossips' brooms could therefore be put to their time-honoured use once more. In winter the brooms brushed the snow from the front porches; the following summer, a dry one, they whisked away the dusty sand blown down into the valley from Mount Vaalserberg, and when autumn came, they swept up the dead leaves that the old lime tree in the town square had shaken from its branches. Dr Hoppe continued to carry out his profession in an exemplary manner, relieving the villagers of their coughs, sunburns, influenzas, kidney stones and other ailments with his home-made tonics, poultices and pills. He hadn't performed any more miracles, it was true; but these things take time, Father Kaisergruber proclaimed in one of his Sunday sermons. In any case, everyone always talked about the doctor with the greatest respect, and his sons were rarely discussed, even though more and more people were starting to wonder why no one ever saw the three little boys, either indoors or out. In winter their absence hadn't been all that surprising – there had been a bitterly cold spell that lasted several weeks – but when both a lovely spring and a hot summer went by without even a glimpse of the children, people began to raise their eyebrows. No one was overly concerned, however, because from their little voices, which were sometimes heard out in the waiting room, the patients could tell that the threesome was doing fine. This was confirmed more than once by the doctor himself, as well as by Frau Maenhout, who still spent several hours a day with them.

After a while, however, two possible explanations for the three little boys' hidden existence began to make the rounds. Léon Huysmans, who had long ago studied medicine at the University of Liège for a year before dropping out, thought that they might have elephantiasis – an affliction that could make your head swell up to the size of an elephant's. He drew this conclusion from the fact that for months now the doctor' s desk had displayed the same picture – a Polaroid of the children just prior to their first birthday. Their heads had already been quite large at that stage, and Léon suspected that the transformation had been so quick that the doctor didn't have the heart to display a more recent photo, even though, according to Martha Bollen, he was still buying film.

Helga Barnard, on the other hand, had been passing around an article from *Reader's Digest* about people who were allergic to sunlight, and had to live their entire lives in the dark. 'When they're exposed to daylight, their skin immediately starts to burn. It must be something like that.'

It wasn't until September of 1986 that the truth came out – or at least in part. It happened one evening during Irma Nüssbaum's umpteenth visit to Dr Hoppe, this time to have her blood pressure checked. Other visits had been occasioned by backaches, ringing in the ears or memory loss; sometimes it was her stomach or her guts, although, if you asked her husband, it was all in her head.

Young Julius Rosenboom, a diabetic who came every day for his insulin shot, was already in the waiting room when Irma Nüssbaum entered. She sat down across from him so that she could keep an eye on the door of the consultation room, and chose a women's magazine from the pile on the table.

'Hasn't the doctor started seeing people yet?' she asked.

Julius shrugged his shoulders without raising his eyes from the comic book on his lap.

'Have you heard them yet?' she asked.

'Who?' asked Julius.

'The doctor's sons.'

Again Julius shrugged. Just then a door slammed somewhere in the house, and then a child's voice cried out, 'No, I'm not gonna!'

'That must be them,' Irma said, delighted. She cocked her head in order to listen. The noises seemed to be coming from upstairs.

'Michael, don't be naughty. Come here!'

'Frau Maenhout obviously can't handle them,' Irma said. She looked at Julius, who was turning a page. 'Does this happen often?'

'Not as far as I know,' said Julius, jerking his head towards the office door. 'I think the doctor's coming. You go in first, I haven't finished reading this yet.'

Irma was only too happy to take the boy up on his offer and she got to her feet as soon as Dr Hoppe opened the door.

She always needed a moment to get used to his appearance again. Her eyes were continually drawn to his hair and beard, and she often caught herself staring at his scar, which he tried to camouflage with his moustache.

'Come on through, Frau Nüssbaum,' the doctor said.

In the consultation room he took a seat at his desk and bent down to find her file in one of the drawers.

Irma Nüssbaum took the opportunity to turn the framed picture sitting on a corner of the desk towards her. 'It amazes me every time, Doctor, how much they look alike,' she said.

The doctor glanced up briefly and nodded.

'They must have changed quite a bit since this picture was taken – am I right?' Irma went on.

Placing the patient file on the desk, the doctor nodded again.

'Do they still look alike?' she insisted.

'They do.'

'And how are they, Doctor? I thought I heard one of them yelling just now.'

'Frau Maenhout is trying to give them a bath, I think. They aren't very fond of baths so, naturally, they resist. Wouldn't you?'

'Tell me about it! Just wait until they're a little older. I'm glad my two have finally left home. How old are the boys now?'

'Almost two. But please tell me—'

'You should soak it in cold water,' Irma interrupted the doctor.

'Excuse me?'

'That spot,' she said, pointing at the doctor's lab coat, the left sleeve of which had a stain on it the size of a coin. 'That's blood, isn't it? You can get rid of the blood by soaking your coat in cold water for an hour or so, and then washing it at sixty degrees. Doesn't Frau Maenhout know that?'

He seemed bewildered for a moment, and rubbed at the dried stain.

'Or is it ink?' She was pointing at a fountain pen lying on the desk. 'If that's what it is, you ought to use vinegar, or lemon juice.'

'I'll tell Frau Maenhout,' said the doctor, scratching at the spot with his fingernail.

'Don't do that, it'll only make it worse,' said Irma sternly.

The doctor drew back his hand involuntarily. He sat up straight and began leafing through her file. 'So. What were you here for, again?'

Before Irma Nüssbaum was able to answer him, or even remember what she had come for, there was another noise from upstairs, this time a loud thudding. It sounded as if someone was storming down the stairs, and both Irma and the doctor turned to gaze at the door leading to the corridor, which was flung open wide the next instant. Frau Maenhout stood in the doorway. Her face was red and she was panting for air, her hand clenched on the doorknob. Her mouth was twisted into a grimace and behind her glasses her eyes were gleaming with anger.

Irma, in her chair, cringed at the sight of the tall figure stomping towards her. She raised her arms to defend herself, but she wasn't the one Frau Maenhout was after. Skirting the desk she marched right up to the doctor, who was gripping the arms of his chair, raised her hand, leaned forward and wagged a threatening forefinger right in the doctor's face.

'If you ever again so much as raise a finger,' she cried out, 'against your children, I'll report you to the authorities! Just remember that, Doctor!' Then she turned on her heels.

Irma Nüssbaum slapped her hands to her mouth. But Dr Hoppe didn't seem the least bit cowed, for he had risen to his feet before Charlotte Maenhout had gone three steps.

'Frau Maenhout, what on earth do you mean? I don't understand . . .'

She halted and turned around. 'How dare you?' she cried. 'How *dare* you act as if nothing has happened?'

'Truly, Frau Maenhout, I . . .'

Irma glanced from Frau Maenhout to Dr Hoppe and back again. She was asking herself whether she should try to intervene, or just stay out of it, when suddenly the doctor's three little boys appeared at the doorway, each wrapped in a towel.

Bald. That was the first thing she noticed. The boys' heads were completely bald. There wasn't a single red hair to be seen, so that their skulls, already large to begin with, appeared even larger. Just under their thin skin was an intricate network of blue veins.

'Like looking at three huge light bulbs,' Irma later told her husband, who was pressing her for more details, but in vain, because before she'd had the chance to have a good look at their faces, Charlotte Maenhout had rushed over and gently herded the boys back into the corridor.

'Come, you still have to have your baths,' she said, leaving the room without looking back. Irma could hear her telling the boys that everything would be all right, and then it was quiet.

Opposite her Dr Hoppe leaned forward, rubbing his hands together as if nothing had happened. 'Now, what can I do for you, Frau Nüssbaum?'

'No I'm not gonna!' Michael slammed the bathroom door shut and planted himself out in the hall, his arms crossed.

Frau Maenhout called out to him from the other side of the door, 'Michael, don't be silly. Come back here!'

She opened the door and stepped into the corridor. Michael was standing by the staircase, ready to hurtle downstairs if she came any nearer. It wasn't the first time there had been a battle to get the boys into the bath, but they had never put up this much of a fight before.

'Do it ourselves,' said Raphael, who was now standing in the bathroom doorway with Gabriel, his hands tucked under his armpits to show that he wasn't going to cooperate today either. Gabriel nodded and added, 'Undress, wash, dry. Can do it all by ourselves.'

Michael nodded his agreement. 'All by ourselves.'

'Fine,' said Frau Maenhout. 'Have it your own way. Just this once. Come on, Michael, get inside.'

Michael followed his two brothers into the bathroom. Frau Maenhout shook her head. The boys had been going through a phase in which they wanted to know everything that was going on. *Why this?*

Why that? How come? Every answer led to another question. They wanted to try to do everything by themselves, even though they weren't really capable of it yet. She should be stricter with them, she knew, but she just wasn't able to. She felt sorry for them.

She stepped back into the bathroom and saw that none of the three had begun to undress. 'Well, what are you waiting for?' she asked.

'First brush teeth!' cried Raphael all of a sudden. He rushed to the sink, followed closely by the other two. They climbed up on a little bench so that they could reach the tap. Raphael doled out the toothbrushes that were the same colour as their bracelets.

Frau Maenhout could see their bald heads in the mirror. She remembered how she had wrongly berated their father when confronted for the first time with their baldness a couple of days after their first birthday. She had assumed that Dr Hoppe had shaved their heads, either because he was conducting some kind of test, or simply on a whim. But it turned out that their hair had fallen out by itself, all in a single night. As proof, Dr Hoppe had shown her three plastic bags full of hair, which he had gathered from the boys' pillows. The boys had confirmed his story themselves.

'It will come out all right in the end,' the doctor had said, adding that the baldness was only of a temporary nature. Yet almost a year had gone by and still their hair had not grown back. The doctor was also constantly subjecting his sons to all kinds of tests that he hoped might throw some light on the problem. These included routine check-ups, such as listening to their hearts and lungs, taking their blood pressure and testing their reflexes, but also other kinds of procedure: for example, he would take skin samples, using a metal implement to scrape off a layer, or draw blood from their scrawny little arms with a big hollow needle – unpleasant ordeals the children told her about matter-of-factly, as if they had simply witnessed the treatment instead of undergoing it themselves. Indeed, on that score she had sadly seen little change in the past few months. They still didn't seem to know how to react to things, or else – and Frau Maenhout wasn't completely sure which was the case – perhaps they did, but were simply incapable of showing their feelings. The upshot was that they were still extremely unresponsive, except when disinclined to do something, which was happening more and more frequently. Then all three would show themselves to be extraordinarily stubborn and Frau Maenhout suspected that this was their way of showing they were afraid.

Looking at the three boys in the mirror again, she wondered if they could tell that their scars seemed to stand out more sharply in the mirror than they did in reality, making their deformity even more noticeable. They must be able to tell just by looking at each other, Charlotte thought. That was one big advantage of looking so much alike: if they wanted to see what they looked like in other people's eyes, they had only to gaze at each other. But this was a *dis*advantage as well, since looking at his brothers would immediately confront each boy with his own disfigurement. There was no escaping it. Frau Maenhout wasn't really sure if they were conscious of the fact that they looked odd, because they hardly saw any other children or adults. She had never discussed it with them, and their father would certainly never mention it.

Even though they had changed quite a bit in the past year, the brothers' resemblance to each other was still uncanny. They were all three equally short and skinny, whereas their heads were still abnormally large. They also had the same number of crooked teeth growing in a similar pattern in their mouths, and the scar, too, had grown identically. Whether from close up or far away, not even a kink or squiggle in the veins on their skulls showed the slightest variation; they all had the exact same sickle-shaped vein starting behind the right ear and running right round the back of the skull.

When Frau Maenhout had first started working for the doctor, she had been confident that she would soon be able to tell them apart with the naked eye. That had been her experience with all the twins she'd encountered in her classroom. But she'd had to admit that the doctor had been right when he'd told her right at the outset that she would never succeed, and even to this day she was unable to tell them apart.

'All done!'

One of the boys put down his toothbrush and jumped off the stool. He turned and showed her his teeth by tugging at his upper lip and sticking out his lower jaw. Frau Maenhout automatically glanced at the child's wristband, to see its colour. She was on her guard about this because that morning the boys had tried to switch places. They had tried it before, but she had always been able to tell which she was dealing with by the coloured wristbands. This morning they'd finally succeeded in getting the little catch open. Raphael had snapped his around Gabriel's wrist, who had given his to Michael, and Raphael had in turn taken Michael's. Their identity swap had not lasted long, however. Frau Maenhout hadn't noticed it herself, but when she had asked Raphael a question, glancing at his wrist and addressing him as Michael, the real Michael had blurted out, 'He's Raphael. *I'm* Michael.'

Any other child would have yelled, 'Ha, ha, gotcha!' and screeched with laughter, but the boys had just nodded, as if to say, 'Didn't I tell you so?' Frau Maenhout understood that they were hoping she would mix up their names again, and so she had proceeded to do just that, several times, on purpose. When, at 10.30, she was getting ready to go home, the toddlers, putting their fingers to their lips, had whispered that she shouldn't tell their father. She realised that they had not yet tried their trick on him.

'Iz goo nuff?' asked Michael now, not moving his lips.

She gave his teeth a cursory glance.

'Well done, Michael. But there's still a little toothpaste in the corner of your mouth.'

Raphael and Gabriel stepped down and, without needing to be asked, also showed her their teeth. Frau Maenhout nodded, satisfied.

'You see, we can do it ourself,' said Gabriel.

'Soon you won't be needing me any more,' she said, winking at them. 'OK, now get undressed. I'll run the water for the bath.' It took her a little while to get the temperature of the water right, and when she turned round again, she saw that Gabriel was the only one who'd managed to take off his jumper. Michael had got no further than taking one arm out of its sleeve and Raphael, struggling to pull his sweater over his head, was still fumbling with the back of it, his elbows sticking out in front of him. It was then that Frau Maenhout noticed something in the mirror she had not seen before.

'What's that?' she asked, pointing at Raphael's bare back in the mirror.

'Father did it,' he said quickly.

She walked up to him and pulled off his jumper. There was a postage-stamp-sized piece of white gauze stuck to the skin with tape.

'We weren't allowed to,' Raphael added.

'What wasn't allowed?' she asked. Fear gripped her heart.

'Our wriss-banns . . .'

She began to peel off the tape. Her hands were shaking. She felt a great rage taking hold of her, even though she still wasn't exactly sure what was going on. Carefully she removed the piece of gauze. The skin beneath it was red and swollen, but she could clearly see three small black spots.

'What in heaven's name . . . ?' she said. A terrible thought occurred to her. She rubbed at the spots, but they did not disappear, not even when she wet the tip of her finger with saliva. She looked at Gabriel and Michael, who were staring into space. Hoping that she was wrong, she went over to Gabriel, who was standing with his back to the wall. Taking him by the shoulders, she turned him around. On his back was a similar square of gauze. Carefully she peeled it off and what she had suspected proved to be all too true: his back had the same little black dots, but this time there were only two. For a moment she stood there perplexed. Oh, it can't be, she thought to herself, yet at the same time she just knew that Dr Hoppe would indeed be capable of such a thing. She turned to Michael and although there was no need to examine him, she did it anyway, if only to fuel her indignation. She pulled off Michael's patch and discovered a single spot, the black ink a permanent blot on the boy's skin.

'Stay here,' she ordered the boys and ran out of the bathroom.

After Frau Maenhout's outburst Wolfheim was gripped by an outbreak of gossip fever. Irma Nüssbaum was the first carrier, and she was responsible for spreading the virus, which found an easy target in the womenfolk, spreading from mouth to mouth like wildfire. For weeks Dr Hoppe's waiting room was even more congested than usual, and even though the patients swore they were suffering from ringing in the ears, headaches, a stitch in the side or dizziness, it was clear that they were in truth suffering from one and the same stubborn ailment. Each one had her own explanation for Charlotte Maenhout's tantrum, and would air her opinion, preferably while in the waiting room for all to hear, in the hope that her words would reach as far as the examination room or kitchen. Remarkably enough, it was never the doctor who was criticised. Odette Surmont suspected that the former teacher had grown severely depressed since her retirement; Kaat Blum, from Kirchstrasse, maintained that Charlotte Maenhout must be abusing the children herself, and Rosette Bayer said it had to be jealousy, adding that the doctor would have to be vigilant, and make sure his babysitter didn't run off with his three sons. On one point, however, the ladies were all in agreement: Dr Hoppe ought to give Charlotte Maenhout her marching orders, and today wouldn't be soon enough.

At the Café Terminus, where every night booze worked to loosen the wagging tongues, René Moresnet talked his customers into wagering how long Charlotte would keep her job. And every time the date passed on which one of the regulars had bet some money, the loser, to great general hilarity, would bang on the café window and shake his fist when Frau Maenhout was seen leaving the doctor's house and crossing the village square for home. Father Kaisergruber kept his opinion on the whole affair to himself, but the very fact that he kept mum about it was proof enough, according to Jacob Weinstein, that his boss condoned the parishioners' behaviour, for he had certainly not forgotten that it was Dr Hoppe's miraculous potion that had cured his stomach ailment.

Frau Maenhout was not fired, however, and it was with growing disappointment that some of the ladies had to grant that her voice was heard ringing throughout the doctor's house with growing volume and self-confidence – almost as if she were rubbing it in.

Besides all the fuss over Charlotte Maenhout, there was a significant amount of talk about the doctor's children as well. Everyone wondered what was wrong with them, which led to more wild speculation. Léon Huysmans continued to maintain that it was elephantiasis, backing up his diagnosis with pictures from medical textbooks that showed people with disfigured features and disproportionately large bald heads. Some villagers even began to allude to the dreaded illness that was only referred to by its initial – 'the big C'.

Dr Hoppe stuck to his story, however, saying that there really wasn't anything to worry about; insinuating, even, that the flu virus that swept through the region practically every winter was considerably more dangerous than whatever it was that ailed his three little boys.

7

For four long months Frau Maenhout had hardly exchanged a word with Dr Hoppe. She had been meaning to talk to him about the children's tattoos on several occasions, but since he had largely left his sons alone after that episode, save for some routine treatments, she had not brought up the subject again. The boys' health did seem to be improving, and she was beginning to wonder if the doctor had been trying out new medications or techniques all this time. The children were still frequently tired, to be sure, and needed a lot more sleep than other children their age, but once awake they were far more communicative than before, as if they'd been shaken out of a persistent stupor. As a result, they were becoming ever more curious about everything that went on outside the four walls behind which, to all intents and purposes, they were being kept prisoner. But Charlotte always took care to keep her answers superficial, so as not to excite their longings too much.

'What's behind there?' they had asked her on several occasions, pointing at the houses across the street.

'More houses,' she had replied.

'Where are all those cars going?' they had asked when there was yet another traffic jam in their street.

'Up the mountain.'

'Where's the Netherlands?'

'On the other side of the mountain.'

'When are we going there?'

'Oh, some day.'

So their world view was restricted, in the literal as well as the figurative sense, to what they could see from their window: the church, the street, houses, some trees, cars and people. Frau Maenhout wished she could take them out some day – even if it were only to the opposite side of the street, or the village square, it would be a start. And so, when spring came, she decided to mention the idea to the doctor. She didn't think he would object, now that the children seemed to be doing so much better.

'I would like to take Michael, Gabriel and Raphael outside one of these days,' she told him.

'What for?'

'They have never been out of the house. In less than six months they'll be three, and they've never seen anything of the world.'

'Nor had I, at their age.'

His answer surprised her. It almost seemed as if he wished to impose his own childhood experience onto his sons. If that was the only thing stopping him from letting his children venture out, she really had to try to talk him out of such a silly idea. But it did make her wonder: why had the doctor not been permitted out of the house when he was little? But staring at his face, and – she couldn't help it – at his scar, a startling answer occurred to her. She did not push the thought away; she wanted to know if she was right.

'Are you afraid someone will see them?' she asked. 'Are you *ashamed* of your own children? Is that it?'

His reaction was almost imperceptible – for a split second he seemed to wince, as if he were biting down on something hard – but it was enough for her to know that she had touched a sore spot.

'Is that what you think? Is that really what you think?'

'I'm not the only one,' she bluffed. 'Everyone thinks so.'

He was quiet for a moment as he digested her words.

'I am *not* ashamed of them,' he then said. 'What makes you think that? Why should I be ashamed?'

Because of the way they look. It was on the very tip of her tongue.

But what she said was, 'In that case, there's no reason to keep them indoors, is there?'

'I don't want anything to happen to them. It is absolutely essential that nothing happens to them.'

Overprotective. Was that it? Was that why he was so strict? She had had to deal with this kind of parent before: parents who lived around the corner from the school but still felt obliged to drive their child right up to the school gate, for example, or who would not allow their child to go on a class outing, or sent in a note listing the activities their daughter was not allowed to take part in during break. But she didn't know any parents who kept their children at home all the time. Maybe the reason the doctor was so fearful was that he had already lost his wife.

She did not pose the question. It really wouldn't have mattered one way or another, at that point. What she said was, 'Then just let me take them out into the garden. Surely there's very little that can happen to them there? And I'll watch them like a hawk. I'll be with them every second.' Take it step by step, she thought.

'Well, perhaps, but only if the weather's good,' the doctor said, probably because he didn't want to give in to too much at once.

But to Charlotte, it was a victory of sorts.

Just as a fire will die out from lack of oxygen, so did the rumour epidemic that had kept the village abuzz for several weeks gradually peter out. There were still a few mothers who tried to keep at least a pilot light of gossip going, but even they were silenced when, on the first pleasant spring day of 1987, it was reported that the triplets had been spotted in the garden. Freddy Machon had discovered they were there when, walking his dog in the village square, he had suddenly heard children's voices on the other side of the high hawthorn hedge that enclosed the doctor's garden. He had crept closer and followed the hedge round until he found a gap through which he could peek into the garden. To prove it, he later showed the patrons of the Café Terminus the scratches on his hands made by the hawthorn's nasty barbs. He reported that the three boys had been sitting at a little table in the shade of the old walnut tree. Charlotte Maenhout had been with them, peeling potatoes. The brothers were playing a card game. After placing the cards face down, in columns and rows, on the table, they had taken turns turning the cards up two at a time, in search of pairs.

'Memory!' cried René Moresnet, as if it were a quiz. 'That's the memory game.'

'Could you tell if they were bald?' Jacques Meekers wanted to know.

Freddy shook his head and said that all three had been wearing hats, the brims pulled down over their ears, shading their faces.

'Naturally. Otherwise their heads would be terribly sunburnt,' Meekers said, rubbing his own bald pate. 'The sun can be treacherous this time of year. And what else? Did you see anything else?'

Freddy said that what had struck him most was the paleness of their skin. Their bare arms and legs – all three were wearing T-shirt and shorts – were as white as talcum powder. As if Frau Maenhout had rolled them in it before taking them outside.

'But did they seem animated?' asked the bar owner. 'They weren't in wheelchairs or anything, were they?'

'No idea,' Freddy finished. 'I didn't see any more than that, because Max suddenly started barking.'

'Well, what did you expect? – the poor dog probably couldn't believe his eyes either. I know what *I'm* going to do tomorrow. It's going to be another fine day, so they'll probably be sitting in the garden again. Come on, let's drink to the health of the doctor's sons. This round's on me.'

Over the next week or two, Freddy Machon's testimony prompted quite a few burghers to stroll past the house at number 1 Napoleonstrasse at a conspicuously unhurried pace. Nor were many of them disappointed, because when the weather was good, there were frequent sightings of Frau Maenhout and the children in the garden. One time the three boys were seen playing the memory-card game, the next they were listening to Frau Maenhout reading from a book, and over the course of several consecutive days they were observed working intently on a jigsaw puzzle, which according to Maria Moresnet had far more pieces than would normally be warranted for their age.

Indoors, the doctor's sons were also spotted more frequently. Several villagers had seen them peeking out round a door and heard them running off giggling the moment anyone tried to approach them. One evening, Rosette Baer had seen them traipsing down the hallway stairs one after the other, behind Frau Maenhout. They'd looked away shyly when they'd passed her on their way into the kitchen, but at least she had caught a glimpse of their bald heads. She had noticed, moreover, that they had bags under their eyes – pale-blue half-circles. Shortly afterwards she had casually asked the doctor how they were doing.

'They haven't been sleeping well, Frau Bayer. I think the mosquitoes are bothering them,' he had replied, and that had been all he would say about it.

'He doesn't want to admit the truth,' Rosette explained to Irma Nüssbaum. 'First the poor man loses his wife, and then it turns out that his children are suffering from some strange disease as well. Men don't know how to handle grief, you know. They just try to avoid it. It's much easier to pretend nothing's wrong.'

Julius Rosenboom had seen the boys at the doctor's house too; what was more, they had even exchanged a few words.

'I've talked to them! I've talked to them!' he shouted at his chums the next morning as he arrived in the village square. They were waiting for the bus that would take them to their school in Hergenrath.

'Who?' asked Lanky Meekers, poking Robert Chevalier in the ribs. The latter was making eyes at Greta Pick from the fifth form.

'The doctor's kids, of course!'

'What did you say?' asked Seppe the baker's son, who had also just arrived.

'I talked to the Hoppe brothers! Last night!'

'Tell us, tell us!' said Seppe the baker's son.

'I was alone in the waiting room when the door opened,' Julius began, after glancing at the doctor's house. 'It's probably that pain in the neck Frau Nüssbaum, I thought, so I kept my nose in my book. First it was quiet, but then I heard someone whispering. I looked up and there they were, right in front of my nose! All three of them! It had to be the doctor's sons. They were all totally bald, their heads as big as footballs, and they each had scar – you know, like this.' With his index finger he pushed a corner of his mouth up to his nose.

'And how tall were they?' asked Lanky Meekers.

'At least a head shorter than those two.' He was pointing at little Michel and Marcel Moresnet, who were waiting for the bus nearby, clinging to their mother's hands. He added in a whisper, 'And not nearly as chubby, either. They're really skinny, as a matter of fact.'

'And then? What happened then?' asked Seppe the baker's son.

'One of them asked me my name.'

'You didn't tell them, did you?'

'Of course I did. I was completely flummoxed.'

'Were they speaking German?' asked Robert Chevalier.

'Perfect German.'

'And what did their voices sound like?'

'Hard to understand. As if they could barely open their mouths.'

'Well, they can't, can they,' Lanky Meekers reckoned. 'Because of their scar. All that scar tissue.'

'It didn't look very nice, let me tell you.'

'And then?'

'The same kid asked me what I was doing, and I said I was studying, for school. "Where's school?" he asked. "In Hergenrath," I said. And then he asked, "Where's Hergenrath?" "Over there," I said, and I pointed somewhere. Then his brother asked, "Is it far away, over there?" "Just twenty minutes by bus," I replied. "Yeah," he said, "that's far." '

'I don't think they're all that clever,' Lanky Meekers remarked.

'No, they didn't seem too smart.'

'And then what happened, Julius?' asked Seppe the baker's boy.

'Nothing, because all of a sudden Frau Maenhout appeared in the doorway with her hands on her hips. She seemed cross, and told the boys they weren't allowed in the waiting room. Then they dashed out, but not before . . .'

'But not before what?' asked Robert Chevalier.

'Just before they turned to leave,' Julius continued, 'one of them stuck out his hand and touched my upper lip. He did! As if he wanted to see if it was real. I couldn't believe it!'

'Ha! The nerve!' Robert said indignantly. He glared at the doctor's house, then exclaimed, 'Well I'll be . . .' Keeping his eyes glued to the house, he tugged at Lanky Meeker's sleeve, pointing: 'There they are! At the window, on the first floor!'

The others looked round too and they all saw the boys' bald heads at the window. The little tykes had clearly been spying on them; they quickly ducked out of sight when Seppe the baker's boy shook his fist at them. A few seconds later, however, the heads popped up again, in unison, as if all three were attached to the same body.

8

Perhaps she shouldn't have taken such a big a step all at once, but Frau Maenhout began to nag Dr Hoppe, trying to persuade him to allow his boys to attend school after the summer holidays – they would be turning three in September. He came up with many arguments to put her off, but she was able to counter them, one after the other.

'They're too young,' he said.

She replied that in Belgium the minimum age for nursery school was two and a half.

Then he said that the boys weren't ready for school. She brushed that objection aside, informing him his sons had been ready for quite some time. In fact, she had never known any children who were as advanced for their age.

'Their health won't allow it. They tire too easily.'

She proposed that the boys start off with half-days. It was a perfectly normal thing to do.

The doctor went on to say that his sons might be exposed to infections at school, to which she stubbornly replied that they ran the same risk right here at home. He did not dispute that. But still he did not give his permission.

The next time she raised the subject, she stressed how crucial it was for their social development to have contact with children their own age.

'They have each other,' he answered, and then: 'When I was their age, I had no contact with children my own age.'

Once again he was comparing his sons to himself. It was almost as if he wanted the three of them to turn out just like him. So she asked him, point-blank, 'What do you want them to be when they grow up?'

He answered truthfully, and the fact that he did surprised her more than what he actually said. 'They'll have to continue the work I have begun. And take it to the next level.'

Just as you would expect. In that respect he was no exception. Many parents expected their children to attain what they had been unable to achieve for themselves.

'In that case you ought to send them to school as soon as possible,' she boldly pressed him.

But he stuck to his guns. 'When they are six, Frau Maenhout. As soon as they are old enough for primary school. Not a day sooner.'

Certain that the day would come when he would see for himself the advantage of allowing his sons to go to nursery school, she began to teach the three toddlers a few things through their play. They made such progress that it amazed her. The boys appeared to be even more intelligent than she had suspected. After just four weeks, despite a maximum of two hours per day to give them her undivided attention – the rest of her time was taken up with housekeeping – Michael, Gabriel and Raphael had already learned to read quite a number of words. It had not been her intention to teach them to read, but once she had shown them how letters could be linked together into words, the boys had taken it upon themselves to go hunting for words, and then tried to spell them out: in newspapers, magazines and books, on posters and folders, on paper bags, tins, cardboard boxes – in other words, anything that had letters printed on it. This had spurred Charlotte Maenhout to fetch from her old school some primers that she had used to teach reading. In no time at all the triplets had devoured the books. They played with letters the way other children their age played with building blocks or toy cars.

It was the same when they learned to count. Once she had taught them the numbers from one to ten, the boys began counting anything and everything as eagerly as they had hunted for new words. They counted the apples in the fruit bowl, the eggs in the fridge, the buttons on their shirts, the books in the bookcase, and soon they wanted to know what came next after ten, and after that, and after that, so that in no time at all they were able to count to one hundred.

There was no way that Dr Hoppe could have escaped noticing the progress they were making, but it was at least two months before he brought up the subject. Frau Maenhout had been assuming that he was angry with her, that he thought she was just trying to prove the need for Michael, Gabriel and Raphael to attend school. So his remark came as a surprise and at first she thought he was talking about her housekeeping.

'You've been doing some fine work there, Frau Maenhout,' he said.

She was standing in the hall, getting ready to go home. 'Thank you,' was the only thing she could think of to say.

'You are able to get more out of the children than I'd ever expected. Than I'd ever hoped for.'

'The credit is all theirs. They inspire each other. To them it's just a game.' She was tempted to add that they worked so hard in order to forget the tedium of their existence.

'Your modesty becomes you,' said Dr Hoppe.

'They'd have learned just as much with any other teacher. And just as quickly.'

'Not in a nursery school. They'd be wasting their time.'

His remark pulled her up short. It suddenly occurred to her that, thanks to her own efforts, the doctor now had a new reason not to send his sons to school. A possible solution presented itself.

'I could ask if they'd be allowed to begin in a higher class. We once had a student who was gifted, like them.'

She was thinking of Valerie Thévenet, from La Chapelle. The little girl had spent one term in a first-year class, and by the end of that time she was so far ahead of the others that the following term she had been moved up to be with the second years. Then she had skipped the third year. When she was ten, she had been sent to a boarding school in Liège, where she'd started the secondary school curriculum. The doctor's sons were even more advanced for their age than Valerie had been. Already they belonged with the six-year-olds. She actually had no idea if the advancement would be allowed, or even possible, but she wasn't letting on.

The doctor shook his head. 'That will always be an option, later on.' He paused and, after taking a deep breath, said, 'I should like you to continue teaching them.'

His request startled her, and at first she didn't know how to react. On the one hand she was flattered; on the other, she had the feeling she was being used.

'You would get a rise, naturally,' he said, confirming what he had in mind, as well as his determination to make it happen.

'And what if I refuse?' She wondered if he would look for someone else.

'I don't know. I want *you* to do it.'

She didn't know either, and was afraid to say the wrong thing.

'You've taken me by surprise, Doctor. I need a little time,' she said. 'I would like to think about it.'

'Please let me know by tomorrow. It's in the children's best interests, Frau Maenhout. And in those of others as well. Everybody's interests.'

She didn't understand. 'What do you mean? What others?'

'Mankind.'

She looked at him wide-eyed, but as always his eyes were glued to the ground. Never mind, she decided, he's just talking nonsense. The children – that's all that matters. It's in their best interests. Only theirs. He's right about that.

She had told him what she wanted. If he really wished to have her as the children's teacher, of course he could have her. On her conditions, however.

First, she had insisted that he arrange to have a classroom set up in one of the unused rooms on the first floor, to give the boys the sense that they were actually going to school, then going home when it was over. The fact that this would also give her far greater freedom, and especially privacy, than she enjoyed in the kitchen or the parlour was a factor as well, although she wisely kept that thought to herself. Furthermore, she asked that her working hours be extended, for she would never be able to cram both the housekeeping and the teaching into just four hours a day. She added that if he agreed to this proviso, she wouldn't ask for the rise he had first proposed – she was afraid that otherwise he wouldn't agree to her demands. Afterwards she regretted it, because he had said yes immediately, without even asking how much extra time she had in mind.

They decided that on weekdays she would be there from 8.30 until 11.30 a.m. and from five until eight in the evening, which gave her two more hours than before. How she arranged her time when she was there was entirely up to her. They also agreed that she would teach the children in French one week, and in German the next. 'Then if they also learn to speak English when they're a little older, they'll be able to communicate with half the world.'

Communication entails more than just language skills, Frau Maenhout thought to herself, but she didn't say it aloud.

Finally he too had a stipulation. It came as a total surprise. 'Could you please tell them about Jesus Christ?'

'Excuse me?'

'About Jesus. In the New Testament.'

'Tell them about Jesus,' she repeated, frowning.

'About Jesus, not about God,' he emphasised. 'Only Jesus.'

'Just about Jesus?'

'Yes, the New Testament, not the Old Testament.'

She couldn't believe her ears. In the first place she would never have taken the doctor for a religious sort, and in the second, she had to ask herself how she could possibly tell the boys about Jesus without mentioning God. She asked the doctor once more, just to be sure: 'So I'm to tell them about Jesus, but not about God?'

'That's right.'

'But it can't be done. It's impossible.'

'Nothing is impossible, Frau Maenhout. Difficult perhaps, but impossible, never.'

She decided not to pursue the matter. She was happy enough to have permission to give Michael, Gabriel and Raphael some religious instruction, even if it did come with restrictions.

She had one more thing to add, however: 'I didn't know you were religious, Doctor. You never go to church.'

The doctor answered, 'The church is the house of God. There's nothing for me there.'

'Then there's nothing for God here either,' she said – she meant it as a joke.

But the doctor remained grave. 'God is everywhere,' he said. 'In heaven. On earth and in all things.'

It was the catechism – the answer to the question 'Where is God?' She too had had to learn the catechism by heart as a child, and she had also never forgotten it.

'Where did you go to school?' she asked, because she was curious, but also because she wanted to change the subject. She didn't feel like discussing religion with him. There was little enough in the way of normal conversation anyway.

He pondered an instant before answering her. 'In Eupen.'

'At the Christian Brothers' School?'

He nodded.

'As a boarder?'

Again he nodded.

She knew the school, or at least its reputation. The students received a strict Catholic upbringing, and in the doctor's case it had clearly left its mark. She was curious to know what his experience of the school had been like.

'What did you think of—' she began, but he interrupted her.

'I have a great deal of work to do, Frau Maenhout. Another time.'

Just for a minute she had thought she might forge a crack in the wall he had built up around himself, but once again she'd been wrong.

'Another time,' she repeated.

Florent Keuning needed just three days to transform one of the first-floor rooms of the doctor's house into a functional classroom. He painted the ceiling and walls, scoured and polished the old floorboards, scrubbed the windows' rusty hinges and hung up the blackboard Dr Hoppe had ordered together with three wooden school desks and a teacher's lectern. To his chagrin, in all this time he had not seen the children, and had just about given up hope when on the last day they suddenly appeared in the classroom, no doubt lured there by his voice when he'd deliberately called out, 'Right, I'm done! The doctor's sons will be so happy!'

The boys made straight for the three desks, not even glancing in his direction. Each sat down at his desk although, being so small and slight, they could all easily have fitted at one. Their feet did not reach the ground, so that their short little legs dangled under the bench. They trailed their fingers across the wood as the handyman stared wide-eyed at the three bald heads. The blue blood vessels beneath the frail skin reminded him of the jagged veins running through certain types of marble.

The boys now turned their attention from the desk tops to the little hooks provided for hanging their schoolbags, then to the shelves underneath, where they would stow their books and notebooks, then to the grooves running along the backs of the desk tops.

'That's for your pencils and pens,' said Florent. At the sound of his voice, the three boys glanced up briefly. The handyman was shocked at what he saw. Only the scars on their upper lips and the flattened noses still conformed to the image he had carried around with him since the last time he'd done work for the doctor. Of course the children were two years older now, but even in that space of time there was no way they should have changed *this* much. They seemed to have grown much, much older, and that impression was caused not just by their baldness, but also by the big dark bags under their eyes, which made their faces look drawn, as well as the fact that they didn't have any eyebrows. It was as if all three were wearing masks, with just two round holes cut out for the eyes. This added to the impression that their heads did not really belong to their bodies. In spite of these changes, however, the three boys were still identical, and the handyman, even with his keen eye, so expert at telling if something was crooked or straight, was unable to detect the slightest difference. Since all three of them were gazing at him as if they hadn't understood what he'd said, he stepped forward, took the pencil from behind his right ear, and placed it in the groove in the middle desk.

'See, that's what I mean,' he said.

The boy sitting at the desk frowned. 'Well of course we know *that*,' he said, annoyed. 'D'you think we're stupid?'

Florent was startled again, this time by the voice, which sounded like the doctor's, except that it was much higher, and therefore had the unpleasant screech of someone scratching his nails down a blackboard.

'We already know how to read and write,' said one of the other two. He slipped off his bench and walked to the blackboard.

'There's some chalk in the tray,' said the handyman awkwardly.

The boy picked out a piece of blue chalk from the tray and, standing on tiptoe, began to write. A swollen vein ran right around the back of his skull from one ear to the other, like a cord for spectacles. The other boys also darted up to the blackboard to stand next to their brother, chalk in hand. They had the same large vein wrapped around the back of their heads. Florent noticed that all three were left-handed and were still wearing the coloured wristbands.

'Are you three upstairs?' Charlotte Maenhout's voice rang out suddenly.

There was no reaction from the toddlers.

'Yes they're up here,' called Florent.

'Just as I thought.' He heard her footsteps reverberating on the stairs. A moment later her large frame appeared in the doorway. She was carrying a cardboard box under one arm and a roll of paper under the other.

'Hello, Florent,' she said. 'I'm glad you're still here. Could you help me to hang up this picture?' She gestured with her head at the roll under her right arm.

The handyman nodded and hastened to the door. He look the paper from her, pointed his thumb at the three boys standing at the blackboard and whispered, 'They already know how to read and write.'

'They can count, as well,' she said briskly. 'So you'd better watch out when you make out your bill.'

He looked at her in dismay.

'It's a joke,' she said, tapping him playfully on the shoulder.

'What's it say?' cried one of the boys. He had turned around and was pointing his piece of chalk at the roll. His eyes bulged so dangerously they looked as if they might pop out of their sockets at any moment. The handyman looked the other way so that he wouldn't be seen to be staring.

'The map of Europe,' said Frau Maenhout.

'The map of Europe?' asked Florent.

'It was the only poster they were willing to part with at the school,' she confided to him. Then, turning to the children, she announced in a loud voice, 'And it's a good thing too, because the boys want to be world travellers – isn't that right?'

'Yeah, we're going ever so far away,' said Gabriel.

'Well then, I'd better hang this map up right away, so you can get started,' said the handyman, looking for a spot on the wall. 'Where do you want it, Frau Maenhout? By the window?'

'Yes, that's fine,' she said.

'Are you going to be teaching them?'

'The doctor wants me to. They'd only be wasting their time at nursery school.'

'He's right about that. If they're really so bright, it'd probably be counter-productive. Over here?' He pointed his drill at a spot on the wall. Frau Maenhout nodded.

He glanced at the doctor's sons. The sound of the electric drill didn't seem to bother them. He felt two conflicting emotions. On the one hand he was unsettled by the boys' physical appearance, but on the other he was glad to have seen them. Later, at the Café Terminus, the other patrons would hang on his every word. Still, he wished he had something more to tell them.

'Frau Maenhout,' he said softly, then went on in a whisper, 'is there something wrong with them? I mean, they look so . . . uh . . . different.'

Taking a deep breath, Frau Maenhout nodded coolly. 'The doctor says it has something to do with their chromosomes.'

'Chromosomes?'

'I don't quite get it either, but it's to do with their genes. Every human cell has a number of chromosomes – twenty-three, to be exact – and every time a cell splits, the chromosomes split as well – that's the way information is transmitted to the next cell.'

'You've already lost me, Frau Maenhout,' he whispered. 'But can't the doctor *do* something about it?'

'He's working on it, he says. It's going to be all right in the end.'

'Oh, that's good,' he said, with genuine relief.

He hung the map up on the hook, and was about to ask another question when Frau Maenhout called out to the little ones, 'Look here, it's the map of Europe!'

All three looked round and gazed at the map, which showed the countries of Europe in different colours, and the larger cities as red dots.

'This is where we are,' she said, tapping a finger at the spot where the borders of Germany, Belgium and the Netherlands converged.

'The three borders!' cried Florent enthusiastically, as if giving an answer to a difficult question. He glanced at his watch. The Terminus was about to open. 'I have to go, Frau Maenhout. I have to stop by Martha's shop before it closes. She has a job for me as well.'

'Oh, can't you please wait a moment? I've got another thing I'd like you to hang up.' She walked over to the teacher's desk, where she had deposited the cardboard box. She took off the lid, rummaged around in it and took out a cross.

'What's that?' asked one of the boys.

'This is Jesus,' she said.

'The son of a carpenter,' Florent added with a wink, waving his hammer.

'Why's he hanging on a cross?' asked the boy.

'I'll tell you another time,' said Frau Maenhout. 'Herr Florent is in a hurry.' She turned round and pointed to a spot over the door. 'Over there perhaps,' she said.

Florent nodded, moved his stepladder over to the door and began hammering a nail into the wall. 'Will you be teaching them religion as well?' he asked, over his shoulder.

'The doctor has asked me to.'

'Is that so? I didn't know the doctor was a religious man.' Another piece of news to tell the others. Everyone at the Terminus would be amazed.

'Oh, he is, Florent. Just because someone doesn't go to church, it doesn't mean he isn't devout.'

'He doesn't have the time to go to church, of course.'

'That's right, Florent.'

She handed him the cross, and he hooked it on the nail.

'There, that'll hold for the next thousand years,' he said, smiling, as he climbed down the ladder. He picked up his tool chest, and, sticking his other arm through the stepladder's treads, slung it over his shoulder. 'If you have any other job for me to do, Frau Maenhout, you just let me know.'

Nodding, he took his leave, sneaking one last look at the boys. Derelict. That was the word that suddenly came into his head. They looked derelict. Like an abandoned house that's gone to ruin after being battered for years by rain and wind.

The next day Frau Maenhout found the cross lying in the top drawer of her desk. Her eyes went automatically to the spot above the door, where even the nail it had hung from had disappeared. She had a hunch, which was confirmed at the end of the day, when she mentioned the incident to Dr Hoppe.

'Yes, I did that,' was his reply.

She immediately regretted having been so discreet with Florent Keuning the day before. When he'd started asking nosy questions, she had been tempted to tell him other, less flattering, things about the doctor. But she knew that the 'truth' as she saw it might very well be construed as slander, and that whatever she said would eventually reach the doctor's ears.

'Why did you take down the cross? I thought you wanted me to tell your children about Jesus.'

'About what he *did*. You have to tell them about his deeds. All the good things he did. Not about his death.'

'Death is a part of life,' she replied. 'Surely you know that?'

'True, true. But even if that's so, we don't have to be confronted with it all the time?'

'It's just symbolic.' Her voice had gone up a register.

'He was betrayed by God,' the doctor said abruptly. He hadn't even heard her remark. He hadn't even looked up.

'Excuse me?'

'God did nothing to save Him when He was on the cross. His own son. Is that really the image we want to preserve? Must we really be reminded of it?'

She remembered the discussion they'd had a few days earlier, when he had requested that she teach the boys about Jesus but not about God. So was that the reason? Because God had done nothing to save Jesus from the cross?

'You are wrong.' She said it adamantly, and was surprised at herself. It was the first time she had dared to contradict the doctor point-blank. She knew why she had suddenly found the guts to do so, as well: because she felt as if she were dealing with one of her pupils; a little boy, to whom she was supposed to teach certain things.

'You're wrong,' she repeated; 'the cross is a symbol of Jesus' suffering.'

'See? That's what I mean. Surely we don't need to be confronted with his suffering all the time?'

'Yes we *do*. So that we'll never forget that He gave His life for us.'

It was as if someone had grabbed the doctor by the hair and yanked his head up. Something in what she'd said must have hit home.

'In sacrificing His life,' she continued, 'He relieved man of his sins. And by ascending to heaven He demonstrated that He is beyond both life and death. And that He will be there for ever, for everyone. That is why we commemorate His death. That is why we are obliged to honour the cross.' Then she added emphatically, echoing what the doctor had once said to her, 'We. Everyone. Humankind.'

Her explanation was slightly simplistic, as if she were indeed addressing a little boy, but the doctor's reaction was childish too. He shook his head and then stomped off, leaving her standing there, speechless.

Charlotte Maenhout did not hang the cross back up. She didn't want to provoke the doctor, so she concentrated on the lessons instead. In fact, she'd much rather have seen the boys playing games or having fun with building blocks all day, as they were supposed to do at their age, but as they were so eager to learn, practically begging her to teach them more, she continued to do so, and with the utmost dedication, even though she realised that she was thereby furthering their father's ambition to turn them into some kind of prodigy.

Classroom time was largely taken up with reading and arithmetic, both oral and written, although it was clearly too soon for the latter – physically the triplets were still toddlers, and their motor skills were not sufficiently developed. She had not yet added religious instruction to the curriculum. The things the doctor had said to her over the past few days had made her hesitate. Anyway, the boys had more than enough to do with reading, sums and oral exercises – they couldn't seem to get enough. Still, there was one subject that captured their interest over anything else. The mere sound of it set their minds racing: world geography. At the beginning of the week she would let one of them point to a country on the map, and would then tell them a few facts about it, such as the names of the major cities and rivers. They would roll the names around their tongues as if they were sweets, committing them to memory. The rest of the week she would devote an hour every day to telling them about that country, showing them pictures or drawings of buildings like the Dom in Cologne or Paris's Notre-Dame, and the boys would stare at the pictures for a long time, fascinated.

She was, of course, only sharpening their longing to see more of the wide world in this way; but she was determined to take them outside, beyond the gate, beyond the village. Even though their father had yet to give his permission for such a venture, she still had hope. After all, the doctor frequently asked her about the progress his sons were making. With justifiable pride she would tell him about the new words the boys had learned, and then she would get them to read from one of the books she borrowed from the Hergenrath lending library every Saturday. The doctor expressed his satisfaction in his typical manner – that is to say, without much enthusiasm; but the fact that he did, at her urging, spend half an hour or so helping the children with their reading each day was a sign that she had his full support.

His reaction to the news that his sons had begun to do sums wasn't quite what she'd expected. 'Show me,' he'd said.

The boys had gone to the classroom to fetch the wooden blocks they used for counting, and he'd given them a few simple sums to do. As if performing some magic trick, Michael, Gabriel and Raphael pushed the blocks around, arranging them in different configurations, speedily arriving at the correct answer every time. It was the doctor's own idea to continue this little ritual each day after she went home, which came as a pleasant surprise to Charlotte. It seemed that he was finally trying to get closer to his children, as if he had finally acknowledged them.

'Some men don't know what to do with little kids,' opined Hannah Kuijk, with whom she was still in the habit of discussing such developments. 'They don't have the patience. To them children are little robots that produce nothing but noise and shit. It isn't until their children are a bit older and wiser – and so, in their eyes, more human – that they finally learn how to relate to them.'

Alas, Hannah's predictions were not borne out by what came to pass, and Dr Hoppe's involvement lasted only a short while. He kept it up for two to three months, working with his sons on a daily basis; but after that he began to skip a day here and there. The increasingly frequent excuse was that he was too busy. The boys would confirm this: their father had been poring over books with difficult words or long columns of numbers, or he had spent the entire time working in the lab, leaving them to do their homework at the desk in his office.

Over the next few weeks he even stopped apologising for his neglect, and Frau Maenhout had to find out from the children whether or not he'd had any time to read or do sums with them.

She was sorry that the doctor's interest in his sons' progress was abating; still, it did give her the freedom to do whatever she thought fit in the classroom. So one fine morning she opened a children's Bible and proceeded to tell Michael, Gabriel and Raphael the story of Creation, just as she had always done with her pupils at the start of the school year. She did not tell them about Jesus yet – not out of spite, but simply because she was following the order of the Bible. So the following day she continued with the story of Adam and Eve, and the next she told them about the Fall. Then came Cain and Abel, the Flood and the Tower of Babel. She read to the boys from the children's Bible for at most fifteen minutes a day, and sometimes even less than that, because if she heard Dr Hoppe's footsteps on the stairs, she'd clap the book shut and hastily put it away, even if Moses was on the verge of cleaving the Red Sea in two or Abraham was raising the knife in the air to kill his only son Isaac.

The boys listened just as breathlessly to the Bible stories as they had to the fairy tales she used to tell them, and couldn't stop talking about them afterwards. But Charlotte told them expressly that they must not talk about the stories to their father.

'A secret. We have a secret,' they cried, and Frau Maenhout realised that it was only a matter of time before they would shoot their mouths off. She'd have to see how she would talk herself out of that one.

The doctor's interest continued to flag, however, and in the end he no longer bothered to find out, either from his sons or from her, what went on in the classroom. When he did raise the subject with her, it was obviously more out of politeness than from any genuine concern.

She was increasingly getting the sense that he was leaving it all up to her, not because he thought she was so good but, possibly, because he was hoping to distract her so that she wouldn't notice what he was up to. For, after leaving his sons alone for a while, he had now gone back to putting them through all sorts of medical tests. Some new equipment had arrived, including an ultrasound and an X-ray machine, and more than ever he seemed to be treating his sons like guinea pigs. This in turn put a damper on his relationship with the children.

For this, Hannah Kuijk came up with yet another explanation. This time she was sure she knew what ailed the doctor: fear of commitment. 'Since losing his wife, he has grown fearful of putting his heart on the line again. He doesn't want to experience the same hurt all over again, if something should happen to one of his sons.'

It was a remark that kept preying on Frau Maenhout's mind.

It started when Raphael lost a tooth one day. There was nothing unusual about that, except that it was a little early for his age. He had been eating a sandwich and bit down on something hard. It turned out to be one of his milk teeth. Charlotte gave him a little glass jar in which to save the tooth, and later on he proudly showed the relic to his father.

The doctor reacted by collapsing into a chair and staring blankly into space for several minutes.

That was the turning point. Until then the triplets' condition had been fairly stable and it had seemed as if everything was truly under control. From that moment on, the triplets' health took a turn for the worse. Their joints ached. Their skin began to peel and brown spots appeared on the backs of their hands. They coughed a lot, and had frequent bouts of diarrhoea. And they were tired, even more than usual. Their minds were still as lively as ever. But how long would *that* last?

He doesn't want to experience the same hurt all over again, if something should happen to one of his sons. She couldn't get Hannah's words out of her mind. Was *that* why the doctor had stopped showing an interest in what the children were learning? – because there was no point to it?

For weeks she walked around, agonising over the possibilities. In the end she finally found the courage to speak to him.

She decided to come straight to the point. 'How old will they be, Doctor?'

She had given Michael, Gabriel and Raphael a project that would keep them occupied for a few minutes in the classroom. Surgery hours were over and the office door was ajar. The doctor was sitting at his desk, hunched over a pile of papers. He invited her to take a seat across from his desk, but she remained standing.

Her question took him by surprise. 'Who? The boys?'

She nodded.

'Why, they'll be four in a few weeks. But surely you know that?'

'That's not what I meant.'

'Then what *do* you mean?'

There was nothing guarded in his voice, which made her doubt herself for a split second.

'How long do they have left?' she asked. From his expression and the way he shifted in his seat, she could tell she'd been right to trust her intuition; yet he tried to keep up the pretence. 'How long do they have?'

Now she had to stand her ground or he'd simply fob her off with some evasive comment or other. She had no proof, only a premonition, but she mustn't let it show. 'They're aging very rapidly,' she said.

He did not reply.

'Much too rapidly,' she went on. 'It isn't normal. It's as if . . .' She had to search for the right words. 'It's as if every month they're another year older.'

'But I thought I'd explained it to you . . .'

'I don't need explanations!' she burst out suddenly. 'That's no help at all! And I don't want to hear that everything's going to be all right either. Because it isn't! Quite the contrary, it keeps getting worse. Surely you can see that for yourself!'

She was startled by her passionate outburst, but it did seem to have made an impact. Leaning back in his chair, the doctor raised his hand to his beard, inhaled deeply a few times and then exhaled through flared nostrils. His hand sank from his chin along his throat down to his chest.

'How long do they have left?' she asked again. She lowered her voice because she realised the children could have heard her.

The doctor leaned forward and folded his hands on the desk top. He must have had to break this kind of news before, to patients with some incurable illness.

'The way it looks now, which doesn't really mean much, because it could—'

'How long?'

'One, possibly two years.'

'One . . . two years?'

He nodded, no more.

'So they'll be lucky to reach the age of six,' she said, more to herself than to the doctor, as she collapsed into a chair. Conflicting feelings beset her: on the one hand there was the relief of knowing the truth at last; on the other, that truth made her break into a cold sweat. But now that she'd got him to talk, she had to go on.

'How long have you known?'

'Since shortly after their birth.'

'Why didn't you tell me?'

'Because it's going to be all right. The latest tests—'

'All your tests are useless! The only thing you've achieved with those tests has been to make your sons afraid of you!' She couldn't stop herself, but she saw no reason to rein herself in now. Her fury served as a release for the grief she did not want to show him.

'I am trying to save them,' said the doctor calmly. 'That is my goal. I want to cure them. Surely that's good.'

'They should go to hospital,' she said, after taking a few deep breaths – in, out.

'I know what is right,' she heard him say firmly. 'They are not going to any hospital.'

'You could get a second opinion,' she tried, pleading.

'They're all bunglers!'

That made her jump. It was the first time she'd ever heard him raise his voice. His exclamation was accompanied by a sudden movement of the arms and hands, as if he'd had an electric shock. All of a sudden she was afraid of him. That too was new. She had never felt comfortable around him, but she had never been scared of him before. Slowly she stood up.

He heard her push back her chair and said, without looking up, almost as if he were talking to himself, 'Time. I need time. That's all.'

She really wanted to leave without saying another word, but she couldn't stop herself from asking one last thing, even though she knew it was naive of her. 'What are their chances, percentage-wise?'

'I don't deal in probabilities. My starting point is the assumption that it will be all right. As it has always been.'

She went back to the classroom in a daze. There, she just about managed to keep herself together, even though every time she looked at one of the boys, she imagined she could see death in his eyes.

When she got home, she collapsed. She would have liked to ring Hannah for support and advice, but in the end she didn't. She wanted to keep the news to herself for now. Once she'd told someone else, it would all become so final, and then all hope of recovery would be lost. She vowed to herself that she would tell someone the moment she felt she could no longer bear it alone. And she also swore that in the meantime she would do everything in her power to make life as pleasant as possible for the children. Their fourth birthday was coming up in two weeks. And after that? After that, she had no idea.

9

Most of the villagers who had young children were understanding of the extreme measures the doctor took the morning after the birthday party. Some of the older ones brought up the death of Dr Hoppe's father, albeit in the most veiled terms, and suggested that the sad lot of the doctor's own sons provided the doctor with enough justification for his actions. Others weren't so sure, but the one thing they did all agree on was that the doctor's decision would only bring even more calamity upon the village. As for the events that had led to that decision, there had been several witnesses, and their testimonies were patched together to form a story.

Boris Croiset, who came by car on account of his sprained ankle, had been the first to arrive at the birthday party that day – 29 September 1988. He was one of five lucky children who had found an invitation from the brothers Hoppe in their postboxes a few days earlier. Six-year-old Olaf Zweste, of Kirchstrasse, and his neighbour Reinhart Schoonbrodt, the same age, were also invited, as were the five-year-old twin brothers Michel and Marcel Moresnet, who had proudly shown off their invitation to the patrons of the Café Terminus. Judging from the messy penmanship, in big block letters, everyone could tell that it had been written by one of the birthday boys himself.

That day, Frau Maenhout had led Boris into the kitchen, where the doctor's three sons, wearing gold paper crowns on their heads, were sitting reading. They had been told to close their books and put them away, and had done so with obvious reluctance.

'They were awfully big books,' Boris reported later, indicating with his thumb and index finger a girth of about five centimetres. Since he had only just started to learn to read, he was unable to provide titles, but had recognised the picture of a balloon on one of the covers.

Reinhart and Olaf had arrived together and had shaken hands with the birthday boys. Reinhart had noticed that all three had brown spots on the backs of their hands.

'Freckles, just like the doctor's,' his mother supposed.

They had given rather limp handshakes, too.

Those seeking further information about the triplets' appearance only heard what they already knew.

'They were short, and skinny. You could have knocked them over with a feather.'

'Their faces were very white, like clowns' faces.'

'Their eyes looked like frogs' eyes.'

'Their mouths were all crooked.'

By the time Michel and Marcel had arrived, Dr Hoppe had joined them too. It was the first time the children had ever seen him without his doctor's coat; around his neck, instead of the stethoscope, hung the Polaroid camera, for which Frau Maenhout had purchased several new film cartridges just the day before.

Next, the birthday boys had opened their presents, while their father had snapped pictures of them. Boris had given them a game of snakes and ladders, Olaf a set of dominoes and from Michel and Marcel they had received some colouring books; these the brothers had put aside indifferently. Reinhart, whose father was a lorry driver, had brought each birthday boy a *matrushka*, one of those wooden dolls with another little doll inside, which in turn hides another and another.

'Papa brought them back from Russia,' he had told them when they started opening his presents. The threesome had suddenly perked up.

'From Moscow?' one of them asked. 'Or from Leningrad?'

'No, Russia,' Reinhart said.

After presents it was time for cake, one that Frau Maenhout had baked herself. She came in with it singing 'Happy Birthday', and all the children sang along. The cake had twelve candles.

'Four for each birthday boy,' she said. 'You'll have to blow them out all in one go, boys.'

Michael, Gabriel and Raphael stood up and linked hands. The other children counted to three, and then the birthday boys tried to blow them out all in one go. More than half the candles remained lit.

'Is that the best you can do?' Michel Moresnet yelled, then blew out the remaining candles with one great puff.

'He just wanted to help,' Maria claimed in defence of her son later when she heard that the doctor's children had burst into tears.

The guests were then shown the classroom on the first floor. Frau Maenhout carried Boris up the stairs, on account of his ankle. After the children had been allowed to test out the desks, they split up into little groups. Gabriel and Raphael took Reinhart over to the map of Europe to show him where Russia lay. Then they asked him what other countries his father had been to, and told him that they came from Germany.

Michael showed Olaf and Boris their exercise books, every page filled with sums, and reacted with surprise when Boris told him he only knew how to count to ten. Boris slunk off and joined Michel and Marcel; Frau Maenhout had given them some chalk to draw on the blackboard.

Then Frau Maenhout had left to answer the telephone. At first she'd hesitated, listening to see if the doctor would answer it downstairs; then she'd gone to the top of the stairs and yelled down, 'Doctor!' but apparently he had heard neither the telephone nor her shout. So in the end she'd run down the stairs and answered the phone in the living room.

Nobody has ever come forward to admit they were the one who called the doctor's house and spoke to Charlotte Maenhout that day. The name of Irma Nüssbaum did come up, because she often rang Dr Hoppe for a telephone consultation, but she adamantly denied that it had been her. And Freddy Machon had seen Maria Moresnet making a phone call that afternoon from the Café Terminus, but Michel and Marcel's mum swore that she'd been on the phone to the brewery, and later proved it by producing the delivery slip with the date and time of her order.

It was only natural that nobody would admit to having made that phone call, because it was while Frau Maenhout was downstairs answering the phone that the drama took place on the first floor – a drama Michel and Marcel blamed squarely on the doctor's sons.

'Marcel saw there were nuts outside the window,' Michel told his mother afterwards. 'The whole tree was full of them. There were millions!'

The old walnut tree that grew right next to the house did bear an extraordinary crop that year. The branches groaned under the weight of the clusters of nuts inside their husks, some of them almost the size of an apple. The tree had not been pruned for years, and the loftiest branches had grown up past the roof. In the days before the birthday party, the first nuts had started falling onto the roof and from inside the house the noise sometimes sounded like gunfire, according to some of the patients.

'The three boys came and stood next to us,' Michel went on, 'and one of them said—'

'Gabriel – it was Gabriel!' Marcel piped up.

'Gabriel said he was going to pick us a nut.'

'We told him he mustn't . . .'

'. . . but then the other one grabbed a chair and put it under the window.'

'Gabriel climbed up on it and opened the window.'

'He reached out and . . .'

'. . . then the chair slipped under him and he . . .'

The doctor had been in the laboratory, and just before the crash he had seen a gold paper crown wafting down past his window. Then there was the loud crack of branches snapping, and in a flash he saw a body come tumbling down, followed by a dull thud. The doctor rushed outside, and Frau Maenhout must have heard it too, for she came racing out to the garden in a panic.

Irma Nüssbaum had stepped out of her house at practically the same moment – exacerbating the suspicion that it was she who had made the call – and understood from Frau Maenhout's reaction that something had happened.

'You could hear the branches snapping from right inside my house,' Irma asserted defensively, but no one really believed that the sound could have travelled as far as that.

In any event, she *was* able to testify truthfully that she had seen the doctor's two other sons peering anxiously out of the first-floor window.

'Inside!' their father had yelled. 'Get back inside!'

Irma had also heard Frau Maenhout's voice. First a shriek, and then: 'I'm calling the ambulance!'

'No, no ambulance!' she'd clearly and distinctly heard Dr Hoppe shout, and he'd had to repeat it twice, because Charlotte kept on insisting. Irma thought it was a shame that Charlotte seemed to have so little confidence in the doctor's abilities. Then the doctor must have picked the boy up in his arms, because she heard him say, 'Frau Maenhout, please hold the door open!'

At that moment Michel and Marcel had appeared at the window upstairs. 'He was trying to pick a nut, *Herr Doktor*! He just wanted to pick a nut!'

The doctor had ignored them, and the door had slammed shut behind him. A little while later Frau Maenhout had rung all the parents and asked them to come and pick up their children.

All day long, many of the villagers just happened to pass by the house at 1 Napoleonstrasse, and all gazed up at the big branch of the walnut tree that had snapped and was dangling down the trunk like a paralysed arm.

'I always said that tree was dangerous,' Irma repeated over and over again.

The next morning the sound of a chainsaw was heard in the doctor's garden, fifteen minutes after Florent Keuning had arrived.

'He asked me to,' the latter claimed afterwards. 'I couldn't really refuse, could I?'

Even from far away you could see every leaf of that walnut tree quivering, and the longer the sound of the chainsaw was heard, the more nuts fell onto the slate roof of the doctor's house.

'It's bad luck to cut down a walnut tree! Bad luck!' cried Josef Zimmerman, peering out of the Terminus window and seeing the broad crown suddenly disappear from the sky above the doctor's house.

Even inside the café, they could feel the thud of the tree as it crashed to the ground.

It had been her idea, of course. She had felt justifiably proud of herself for having arranged it. It had taken quite a bit of persuasion, but in the end the doctor had given his permission for a birthday party. One of the arguments she'd used was that it would be good for their health. The accident had shaken her to the core. But it hadn't ended there. Other things had come to light and shocked her even more. For instance, she later discovered that Michel and Marcel Moresnet had lied about the part they had played in the drama. As soon as all the other children had gone home, Michael and Raphael had told their version of the story. It turned out that Marcel Moresnet had crept up on Gabriel and had snatched the crown off his head.

'Hey, look, he's got no hair!' Boris Croiset had cried out. Michael, Gabriel and Raphael had tried to get the crown back, but the other kids had ganged up on them, passing the coveted headpiece from hand to hand.

It was true, she'd heard the commotion upstairs, but hadn't been able to get Irma Nüssbaum off the phone.

As soon as Michel Moresnet had the crown, he had flung it out of the window. The crown had landed in the walnut tree, and Gabriel, standing on a chair, had tried to grab it. But the thing had wafted down through the leaves and finally fluttered all the way down to the ground. The next moment, someone had pushed the chair out from beneath Gabriel and he lost his balance.

Frau Maenhout had wanted to tell the doctor the truth, but had not done so at first because she couldn't see the point. What was done, was done. On the other hand, had she told him, Dr Hoppe might have left the walnut tree standing. That had been the next shock. When she'd arrived at the house the next morning, the tree had already been cut down and Florent Keuning was busy sawing off the limbs.

So then she did tell the doctor after all, because Gabriel hadn't been trying to pick walnuts and therefore the tree had had nothing to do with his accident. She'd wanted to make the doctor feel guilty, possibly to assuage her own sense of guilt.

'Oh, that tree should have come down years ago,' he had replied, shrugging his shoulders.

For a moment it had seemed as if that was all that needed to be said, but then he had started venting accusations that had only increased her feelings of guilt. How *could* she have even *considered* leaving the boys by themselves? Didn't she realise that Gabriel might have been killed?

Did she understand that he'd be left with a scar, which meant that from now on he'd always look different from his brothers?

Dr Hoppe had said it all flatly, as a sort of recapitulation of facts, and it had hit her hard. She'd had no rejoinder, and had run away in tears. Only later did it occur to her what she should have said: that he too was to blame; that *he* should have answered the telephone; that it was even possible that he'd let it ring on purpose, to lure her away from the classroom, hoping that something bad would happen – something that he would then be able blame on her.

The next shock came when she saw Gabriel again for the first time, one week after the accident. All she knew was that he'd sustained some cuts and scrapes, a mild concussion and a head wound, which was now covered with a square of gauze. It had required seven stitches, and as long as he remained bald, the scar would indeed remain visible. But then it turned out that there was a dressing the size of a postcard on his back as well. The doctor hadn't said anything about that. Frau Maenhout and he hadn't spoken, however, since his outburst, and so she didn't have the nerve to come right out and ask him about it. Gabriel himself couldn't remember anything that had happened, from the time he fell from the window until he woke up in the darkened laboratory next to the doctor's office.

In the end she had carefully removed the plaster sticking the dressing to Gabriel's back. Underneath was a stitched-up incision at least ten centimetres long. She looked for the jumper Gabriel had been wearing the day of the accident, to see if she could detect any bloodstains on the back. She could not. There was some staining on the shoulders and on the front that had not come out completely in the wash. She couldn't stop wondering about it, but didn't want to go jumping to conclusions, so she mentioned it on the day he took out Gabriel's stitches.

'I wasn't aware that he'd hurt his back as well,' she said.

The doctor nodded. 'Oh, I removed a piece of one of his kidneys.'

'Why – was it damaged in his fall?'

'No. What makes you think that?'

His answer flabbergasted her. He wasn't even *pretending* – to him there clearly just wasn't anything wrong with what he had done.

'What makes me think that?' she said, trying to keep calm. 'You removed a piece of his kidney. Surely that's something you don't do for no reason.'

'No. I did have my reasons.'

'You had your reasons? That's it? Because you had your reasons? I don't believe you. There *was* no reason. I don't believe you any more.'

He didn't react the way she expected him to. She would have thought he'd either fire her on the spot, or to try to convince her he was right. But he seemed quite upset.

'You don't believe me, Frau Maenhout? Have you, too, lost faith in me? I have always trusted you and now you're telling me this? Why? Surely I've . . .'

He's wallowing in self-pity, she thought. He's trying to make me feel sorry for him. Don't fall for it.

'I refuse to listen to your stories any longer!' she said brusquely, although her legs were trembling. 'Everything you've tried – none of it has worked. None of it! It's about time that you faced the truth. You wanted to save their lives, but all you've done is push them closer to death. That's the only thing you've accomplished!'

She wanted neither to see nor to hear his reaction. She simply rushed from the room, afraid that she'd burst into tears right then and there, thereby showing him her weakness.

She did in fact burst into tears a little while later, in the bathroom, staring at herself in the mirror and asking herself why she had let him get away with it for so long.

10

Seven days. From Monday until Sunday. That was how long Frau Maenhout had given herself. To teach the children just a few more things. To enjoy being with them just a little longer. To say goodbye. Seven days. After that, she would go for help. Another doctor. A specialist. Perhaps even the police. She wasn't completely sure about that yet, but what she was sure about was that as soon as she did it she would lose the children.

Giving them up. Delivering them into good hands. That was how she qualified it to herself. It would make it easier to say goodbye.

In those seven days she would also have to try to collect some concrete evidence, proof that the doctor was abusing his sons. For it wasn't only his good name (to which many a villager would testify) she was up against, but also the doctor's own explanations, for he was bound to contend that every procedure and test had been necessary. For the sake of their health, he'd say. To save their lives.

She did not inform the boys. She just told them that by the end of the week their first year of school would be over and that she still had to teach them a few things.

'And what happens after this school year's over, then?' asked Michael.

She didn't want to lie to them, so she had to be careful what she said. 'The next school year will begin. I'm sure it'll be even more fun than this one. A lot more fun.'

One of the things she had yet to teach them was the Lord's Prayer. And she had not yet told them about Jesus. She hadn't found the opportunity.

The boys had no trouble learning the Lord's Prayer by heart – in both French and German. They did have some trouble mastering the sign of the cross, however. They couldn't remember the sequence of the gestures, nor whether they were supposed to start on the left side or the right.

She told them to cross themselves every night before bed, and to say the Lord's Prayer. The whole thing was exciting to them.

'And Father isn't supposed to know, right?'

She had told them he wasn't, but in fact it didn't really matter any more. She didn't want to confuse the boys, however, nor did she like to involve them in her quarrel with the doctor.

Also, since there was no way round the subject, she told the boys about death, despite the trouble and grief this cost her. 'Children who die', she told them, 'change into angels, and fly straight up to heaven.' And with an arm as heavy as lead she drew an angel on the blackboard.

'Where is heaven? What road do we take to get there?' Michael asked.

She thought it rather a sick joke that the boys were named after the archangels – as if the doctor had known, and had chosen the names on purpose.

'Heaven's up there.' She pointed at the blue sky. 'You just fly straight up, and you'll get there automatically.'

She also explained that heaven was like a country without borders, and that it had an endless river flowing through it. An enormous ship, with God at the helm, sailed along that river; and there was a seat reserved on it for everyone who got to heaven.

'Will we be allowed to steer the ship too, sometimes?' Gabriel asked.

'I think so.'

'I wish we were already dead,' he sighed, but fortunately she didn't have a chance to dwell on this because Raphael immediately came up with another question: 'How about grown-ups? Do they go to heaven too?'

'Only the ones who've been good all their lives.'

'Then you're going to heaven too,' Raphael said.

'And Father isn't,' Gabriel promptly added.

So they had got her to smile in the end.

For a moment she had felt envious of the fact that young children only see people as either good or bad, and wished that she were still at that stage herself. Then she could just have relegated the doctor to the bad camp a long time ago. As it was, she had been too considerate of his feelings, of his grief or despair or helplessness, even though he had never openly shown those feelings.

As the end of the week approached, she found it increasingly more difficult to see the boys without betraying her emotions. In the meantime, she had made a decision: she would call in the police. Any doctor or nurse would promptly be shown the door by Dr Hoppe, meaning that they wouldn't get to see the boys, and she thought it was crucial that they be seen by an outsider. Anyone who laid eyes on them would see that they urgently needed specialised help.

But then something intervened, something Frau Maenhout hadn't counted on. She had hardly seen the doctor all week. It was as if he had been avoiding her since their last encounter. When she arrived in the morning he would already be at his desk or in the lab, and he'd still be there when she left. On Friday morning, however, he suddenly appeared before her.

'I have to go away,' he said. 'To a conference in Frankfurt. I'm leaving tomorrow morning. A taxi is coming to pick me up at 5.30.'

That was all he had said. He hadn't even asked her if she would come and babysit, but she assumed that that was what he'd meant.

It was for the children's sake – that was what Frau Maenhout told herself. The boys had been dreaming for so long of seeing just a little bit of the world, and now that the opportunity had presented itself, since their father was going to be away for a few days, she would see to it that their dream was turned into reality: she would take them for a small outing, up to the three-border junction. It was the last thing she'd be able to do for them. If everything went off without a hitch, nobody need ever find out. At least Michael, Gabriel and Raphael would have something to remember in the time remaining to them. Besides, if the birthday party hadn't ended in disaster, she'd have sought the doctor's permission to take his sons to the three borders anyway.

She had not been up there herself since her retirement. Before that, she used to take her class on an outing to the top of the Vaalserberg every year, and before that, as a child, she had visited often. Back then it had never been very crowded – there had been no observation tower – but over the years the three borders had drawn more and more tourists, as evidenced by the traffic clogging Wolfheim's streets. Cars and coaches streaming through the village from morning till night had to squeeze under the narrow bridge at the end of Napoleonstrasse, and sometimes the traffic jam stretched all the way back to the doctor's house. After the bridge came the *Route des Trois Bornes*, which led the vehicles up a steep incline to the top of the Vaalserberg, the highest point in the Netherlands. Up there, a stone with the inscription '322.5 metres above sea level' was planted in the middle of a quadrangle of cobblestones. Just behind this, a row of ancient boundary markers sometimes led tourists to the erroneous conclusion that this was the site of the three-border junction. The actual intersection of the Belgian, Dutch and German frontiers was a dozen or so metres further south, marked by a small cement column in the shape of an obelisk. The letters 'B', 'D' and 'NL' had been carved into the sides of the column to show the tourists shuffling around it which of the three countries they were in at any given moment.

The Boudewijntoren was another big attraction. This tower, situated on Belgian soil but very close to the three borders, measured thirty-four metres high. A metal stair led up to the platform at the top, from which you had a great view of the entire region. The climb to the top had always been the highlight of the class outing. Unfortunately, since the tower would still be closed at such an early hour, Frau Maenhout wouldn't be able to climb it with the triplets. It was a shame, because the view from the top would finally have given some three-dimensional perspective to their map of Europe.

On the eve of the doctor's departure she worked into the night, rustling up a disguise for them. She didn't want the boys to be recognised if they happened to bump into anyone. The disguise was also intended to make them less nervous and boost their self-confidence. She had noticed that all three were much bolder when playing dressing up: they actually transformed themselves into the characters they were pretending to be. Which was understandable, since it was the only way of escaping their father's iron control.

Once in bed, she couldn't fall asleep. She kept rehashing the past: she had been with the boys practically every day for three years; and yet it seemed as if everything had happened in the space of just a couple of days. That was on account of the routine, she thought to herself. Many of the days had just blended into one another. Her forty-five years as a teacher were similarly compressed in her mind into just a few months. Still, just as she had missed the routine of teaching after her retirement, she was going to miss this routine as well. And of course she would miss the three boys.

She had come to love them, of that she was sure; yet she had never really come to *know* any of them. They had shown little in the way of a distinct personality in all these years. Not one of them – neither Michael, nor Gabriel, nor Raphael – had ever stood out from the rest by being particularly mischievous, or bashful, or cheerful. Hannah had once opined that their brains were probably connected to each other by some invisible thread, and that seemed to be the case with their personalities too. All three were introverts – quite curious, to be sure, about what went on around them, but on the whole they had remained largely withdrawn. Like their father, she thought ruefully – except that he had also lost his sense of wonder, or perhaps he'd never had one. Had she been given more time, she might have been able to get the three boys to blossom, to bring out what was hidden deep inside, so that they would not grow up to be like their father.

If she'd had more time . . . With that thought, she fell asleep.

When she arrived at the house the next morning, a few minutes before 5.30, Dr Hoppe was just coming out. The taxi had not yet arrived. She felt her heart pounding. The doctor did not greet her, but she decided to act as if nothing had happened between them, and asked, 'Are the boys awake?'

'I don't know,' he replied, opening the gate.

'May I go in to them?' she asked.

'If you like. You have the key.' He stood peering down the street.

'What time will you be back?' she asked. 'So that I'll know when to get dinner ready.' It was a crafty subterfuge, but his answer disappointed her.

'Don't worry about me for dinner.'

'Right, well then,' she muttered and without wasting another glance on him she walked up the path to the door as she heard the sound of a car approaching.

'Michael, Gabriel, Raphael, wake up!'

She flipped on the light in the bedroom. Other than some muttering there was no reaction.

'Wake up. We're going on a trip.'

Blinking their big eyes, the three boys immediately sat up in bed. She took a deep breath and scrutinised their faces one by one.

'What did you say, Frau Maenhout?' Michael asked, rubbing his eyes with the back of his hands.

'We're going on a trip. I'm going to give you a task.'

'A task?'

Then she showed them the costumes. Three capes, three hats and three cardboard masks. The capes and hats were in three different colours. Red. Green. Blue. She had painted the masks a silvery-grey.

'Today you're the three musketeers. Knights in the service of the King.'

'What king?' Raphael asked.

'King Boudewijn of Belgium. And he has given his musketeers a task. You're going to have to capture the three-border junction.'

The words were sinking in rather slowly.

'You'd better get up quickly, before the King changes his mind,' she added. And in the blink of an eye all three were standing to attention beside their beds.

As soon as they were dressed, she made them put on their masks. She had cut two slits for the eyes and a hole for the mouth. Next came the hats and the capes. They stroked the fabric as if it were rich velvet.

'There's still something missing,' Frau Maenhout said, and with a grand flourish she drew three wooden swords from her bag. 'First you'll have to be knighted.'

Three pairs of eyes stared at the swords through the slits in the masks.

'Get down on your knees,' she said.

She kept the ceremony short but solemn. The boys knelt down and bowed their heads, and she tapped their heads and shoulders with the sword: 'Raphael, on behalf of the King, I hereby name you Porthos, the cleverest of the musketeers. Gabriel, on behalf of the King, I name you Aramis, the noblest of the musketeers. Michael, on behalf of the King, I name you Athos, the bravest of the musketeers.'

She presented them with the swords, and they immediately took on the spirit of the musketeers. All three squared their shoulders, stuck out their chins and raised their swords high in the air, trying out the names she had just given them. She looked on, holding her breath, as they went to admire themselves in the bathroom mirror. Since their baldness and disfigurement were largely hidden, they looked, for once, like normal children. It almost seemed as if their real selves had been the disguise, since their features made them look stranger than the costumes they now wore.

At breakfast she taught the boys two more things. She had them form a circle and raise their swords in the air, so that these crossed above their heads, and said, '*One for all, and all for one!* That's the musketeers' motto. It means that you'll always be there for one another. No matter what happens.'

Their voices soared through the kitchen: '*One for all, and all for one! One for all, and all for one!*'

Finally she admonished them, 'Remember: musketeers answer only to God or the King. So you needn't be afraid of anyone.'

'God or the King,' the boys repeated, 'only God or the King.'

Then they set out to capture the three-border junction. It was Saturday, 20 October 1988: 5.50 a.m.

'We'll get there when the big hand points at 2.' Frau Maenhout pointed at the fluorescent-yellow hands of the clock on the church steeple. They had crossed Napoleonstrasse and were now walking past the terraced houses toward the Route des Trois Bornes. Twenty minutes to get there, fifteen minutes at the border, and twenty minutes to get back. Just in time for sunrise.

The boys were on her right. All three had their swords at the ready and kept looking over their shoulders, as if expecting an ambush at any moment. Wisps of fog trailed across the pavement, scattering like strays when one of the boys slashed his sword at the ground.

They halted before the bridge marking the beginning of the Route des Trois Bornes.

'We have go through that underpass,' Frau Maenhout explained, 'and then we begin the climb to the top of the Vaalserberg. That's where the three borders join. Are you ready?'

The boys nodded. Athos straightened his mask, Aramis clutched his sword even more firmly and Porthos tipped his hat. Frau Maenhout smiled, but the sick feeling she'd had all night did not go away.

'Excellent,' she said in a stage whisper. 'And remember: *One for all* . . .' She put her finger to her lips.

'. . . *and all for one*,' they replied softly.

The climb was longer and more difficult than she remembered. She never for a moment let the boys out of her sight. At the beginning the incline was gradual, but after the first hairpin bend it kept getting steeper. This was mirrored in the boys' progress. With the impulsiveness of little kids, they had covered the first hundred metres faster than their little legs could comfortably carry them, but then their pace began to slacken. After ten minutes or so they were scarcely making any headway at all. She had asked herself beforehand whether the boys would be robust enough to handle the walk, but was determined to carry them if necessary. When she had first come up with the idea of the outing, she had also considered asking Hannah Kuijk to drive them, but in the end she had decided that she wanted to do this alone. Just the boys and her. No one else.

In Wolfheim the clock began to strike six. The sound ascended swiftly out of the valley up the Vaalserberg. Frau Maenhout counted the chimes and at the last one she squared her shoulders, took a deep breath and announced, 'The musketeers will be riding the rest of the way on horseback.' Then she picked the children up in her arms, Michael and Raphael riding on one arm, Gabriel on the other. The boys promptly stuck their noses in the air and pointed their swords forward. She too stuck her nose in the air. Here we go, she thought.

It was tiring. Individually the boys weighed very little – just thirteen kilos each – but together they were quite a load. She soon broke into a sweat, and her arms felt like lead. She never for an instant thought of stopping, however. Every time she glanced at one of the boys and caught sight of the blue eyes through the slits in the masks, she found the strength to continue. Their breath on her face, and the warmth of their bodies against her chest, spurred her on. It was her last chance to feel that.

Finally the tower came into sight. It loomed up like some gigantic insect on tall, skinny legs, lit from below by the glare of floodlights. Open-mouthed, the three musketeers gazed up at it.

'The Boudewijn Tower,' said Frau Maenhout with great relief. 'Thirty-four metres high. When you're up on the top you can see Aachen and Vaals. And when the weather is clear, you can see as far as Liège. You can touch the sky up there.'

She shouldn't have said that. It was as if she'd waved a bag of sweets under their noses, then told them they couldn't have any.

'Can we go up there?' asked Michael. 'All the way to the top?' He pointed with his sword.

She shook her head. 'The tower is locked.'

She lowered the boys carefully to the ground and walked them over to the fence around the tower. A chained iron gate barred the entrance. Raphael and Gabriel gazed up, holding on to the railings. Michael did the same thing, only he was also trying to squeeze one of his legs and shoulders between the stakes.

'Look, I can get through! I can get through!' he cried.

Frau Maenhout, alarmed, yanked at his arm and pulled him down off the gate. Her fingernails dug deep into his skin.

'Ouch!' he cried, and for a split second she recognised the look they usually reserved for their father. It made her realise how rough she'd been.

'I'm sorry, I'm so sorry,' she said. She stretched out her hand to adjust his hat, but he pulled out of the way. 'We *will* go up the next time,' she promised him, knowing there would be no next time.

'Really?' he asked.

'Really.'

She took a deep breath and it struck her how nervous she was. She realised for the first time how impulsive her decision to come here had been. It was so unlike her. She turned her head towards a cement pillar bathed in a floodlight's yellow beam.

'Look, there's the three borders,' she said gently to distract their attention from the tower.

The boys instantly seemed to forget what had just happened. They glanced at the pillar, then at each other, back at the pillar, and began to run, their capes fluttering from their backs like brightly coloured plumage. They reached the pillar almost at the same time, and wrapped their arms around it as if apprehending a thief.

'We've got him! We've got him!' they shouted excitedly.

Frau Maenhout laughed. 'The King will be so pleased.' Walking up to them, she said, 'And now I think it's time for your battle cry.'

The three musketeers nodded and promptly raised their swords above their heads. It was 6.15, and at the three-border junction three little voices rose into the air: '*One for all, and all for one!*'

Frau Maenhout swallowed. She breathed in, out, in, out, then took a few steps forward and pointed at the ground. 'Each of you is standing in a different country. Just take a step back.'

On the pillar they could make out, in white paint, the letters 'B', 'D' and 'NL'. Frau Maenhout produced a piece of chalk and crouched down to draw the lines on the ground demarcating the borders. The boys followed her every move.

'*This* is Belgium. *This* is Germany. *This* is the Netherlands,' she said, walking around the column and the triplets. 'Belgium. Germany. The Netherlands. Belgium. Germany. The Netherlands. See?'

Three little heads bobbed up and down.

'OK, now it's your turn.'

She stepped back and, holding her breath, watched as the boys began moving round the column, slowly at first, then faster and faster. Each would yell out the name of the country he was in, and when at a certain moment all three turned their faces to her and she saw their eyes shining through the holes in the silver masks, she felt a flood of warmth. This was why she had done it, she now realised. For this.

'Come, Aramis, Athos and Porthos,' she said after a while, 'you have fulfilled your task. Now we must hurry back.'

'One more time, Frau Maenhout, just one more time,' Athos pleaded.

'OK then. One more time.'

Slowly, very slowly, they shuffled around the border junction, sticking out an arm or one leg as they went, so that each was in two countries at once. Her pupils used to do the same thing, she remembered. In that respect Michael, Gabriel and Raphael were no different from any other children. In that respect, at least. The thought came to her suddenly, and it brought back with it the queasy feeling she'd been having.

On their descent from the Vaalserberg, the queasy feeling would not go away. She was picturing what it would be like for her, later. Lonely. She'd be lonely. Just as she had been from the day she'd retired until the day she'd met the triplets. Lonely: she couldn't get the word out of her head.

'Come, boys, stay close to me.' They'd been walking for about five minutes and Raphael and Gabriel were already trailing a couple of metres behind. She turned round, looking for Michael, and felt her heart skip a beat. Michael was nowhere in sight.

'Where is Michael?' Her voice sounded squeaky. Gabriel and Raphael looked around. They hadn't noticed that their brother was missing either.

'Michael! Michael!' Frau Maenhout began to shout.

But there was no answer. She picked up Gabriel and Raphael and started to run back up the hill, back to the three borders. She had a bad feeling about this – a feeling that was all too justified. Michael was making his way up the tower. He had already reached the twentieth step and was climbing higher, his eyes fixed on the top. The harsh beam of the floodlight seemed to be following him up the tower.

'Michael, get down from there!' She lowered Gabriel and Raphael to the ground.

Michael, glancing over his shoulder, hailed his brothers with his sword. 'I'm gonna capture Aachen and Vaals! And Liège! And then I'm gonna climb right up to the sky!' Brandishing his sword in the air, he climbed on again as if nothing would stop him.

Frau Maenhout felt the world giving way beneath her feet. 'Michael, get down now!'

'I'm not Michael!' she heard. 'I am Athos, the bravest of the musketeers!' The cape danced up and down on his back.

'Michael, come back!'

'Athos! My name's Athos!'

'Michael, stop it, now! This isn't a time for games!'

But it wasn't a game to Michael. At that moment he *was* Athos, with all his being, the bravest of the musketeers. And it was only as Athos that he was brave enough to climb that high. Not as Michael, it suddenly dawned on her.

'Athos!' she cried. 'Athos! Stop it! Come down!' Her voice followed him up the tower.

There was just the slightest hesitation in his tread, then he called out, 'Musketeers answer only to God and the King. You said so yourself!'

Then, for a split second, he looked down. He was about ten metres above the ground, higher than he had ever been in his life. It gave him a shock, and he suddenly cringed, taking a step backward. Frau Maenhout saw it. His two brothers saw it. Then he lost his balance. Someone screamed. Instinctively he let go of his sword. It tumbled down and landed on the cement at the base of the tower. With a loud crack, the hilt and the blade split in two.

It was a quarter to seven when Felix Glück rang Otto Reisiger's doorbell at 17 Albertstrasse in Wolfheim.

'Herr Reisiger, there's a child stuck up on top of the tower!' he cried when a bulbous head appeared in one of the upstairs windows.

'What?' was the reply. 'How's that? Wait, I'm coming! Just a minute!'

That morning Felix Glück, garage mechanic from Aachen, had jogged to the three borders at sunrise and there, to his astonishment, he had come upon a lady and two children sitting on a bench next to the tower. All three had their heads bowed and their hands tightly clasped. They seemed to be praying. The middle-aged woman, her grey hair pinned up in a bun, had acted as though Felix had been sent by the Good Lord himself. 'Thank God!' she had cried, casting her eyes up to heaven. The two children beside her were wearing costumes. They had masks on their faces, and were dressed in capes and hats. Each had a wooden sword on his lap.

The lady, who had introduced herself as Charlotte Maenhout, had pointed out the little boy huddled motionless some ten metres up the Boudewijn Tower. She had begged him to run down to Wolfheim, to fetch Otto Reisiger, the tower watchman. He had the key and would be able to open the gate.

Felix Glück had made it from the three-border junction to Wolfheim in seven minutes, breaking his own record.

'Frau Maenhout?' exclaimed the watchman in surprise when Felix Glück told him the story.

'And her three nephews.' The mechanic nodded, staring at the man's pot belly.

'Three nephews? Oh, you must mean Doctor Hoppe's sons.'

'She said the boys were her nephews – her sister's grandchildren. I didn't see their faces because they kept their masks on. They were very young, anyway. Toddlers, I think. They only came up to here.' With his hand he drew an imaginary line about ten centimetres above his knee.

'Then it's the doctor's kids. There's no other explanation. What about the doctor – wasn't he with them?'

Garage man Glück shrugged his beefy shoulders.

'That's odd,' said Reisiger, 'very odd.'

Just a short while later the two men set off for the three-border junction in the watchman's old Simca. The car was making horrible noises.

'There's a hole in the exhaust,' remarked the mechanic immediately.

'I know,' replied Reisiger, shouting over the din. 'I've ordered a new car, but it won't be delivered until next week.'

He drove the car under the bridge in second gear. As he started up the Route des Trois Bornes, he asked the mechanic what Charlotte Maenhout had been doing so early in the morning at the three borders.

'No idea,' he replied. 'I asked her, but she didn't give me an answer. All she said was that she had to get back to the village, and soon.'

'She'll just have to be patient,' said Reisiger, switching into first gear because the old Simca could barely make it up the hill.

When they caught sight of the tower through the windscreen, Glück pointed up at the sky. 'There's the boy. Do you see him?'

The watchman nodded, pressing his nose flat against the windscreen.

The boy was hunkered down into a ball and seemed to have some sort of cloth draped over him. His arms were wrapped around one of the vertical banisters.

Frau Maenhout was standing by the gate, her face almost as white as the shawl around her shoulders. She was holding a child by each hand. The watchman couldn't tell if the children were bald because of their hats, but he did catch a glimpse of a scar through one of the masks' mouth holes.

As Otto Reisiger unlocked the gate, Glück the mechanic stared at the strapping woman. Her legs were shaking.

'I'm so sorry,' Frau Maenhout muttered several times. She was making a visible effort to fight back tears. But in spite of that, there was something hard about her. With a black habit on, she could easily have been taken for a nun, he decided.

'Wait here,' said Reisiger. He strode through the gate to the foot of the tower, but Frau Maenhout followed him at once.

'I'm coming with you,' she said, 'or he'll never come down.'

The watchman shrugged. Grabbing the handrail, he began to mount the stairs, with Frau Maenhout right behind him.

'Too bad this had to happen,' he said without looking back. 'The tower's going to be demolished soon. They're building another one in its place.'

Frau Maenhout did not respond.

'It'll be fifty metres high,' he said proudly, '*and* it'll have a lift!'

His words did not appear to be getting through to her. She could think of nothing but the boy, he realised; it was only natural. They had to be the doctor's sons – he was sure of it. He glanced down over his shoulder. The other two children were following his every move, their heads tipped back. He had seen the triplets once, when he had felt a sudden searing pain in his chest and had urgently rung Dr Hoppe's doorbell. The boys had been sitting at the doctor's desk in the office and they'd looked at him curiously. He had returned their stare. Afterwards he had invited the doctor to visit the three borders some time with the boys, but the doctor had never taken him up on the offer, at least until now.

Once they were at the top, the watchman saw that the boy's arms were tightly clasped around the banisters. Leaning down, he reached for the skinny arms, but the child began to yell, 'Don't touch me! Don't touch me!'

The shrill voice cut the air like a knife. Startled, Otto Reisiger took a step back, bumping into Frau Maenhout. As he made a grab for the railing, his free hand accidentally struck the child's hat, pushing it askew. What he saw then removed any doubt: a big bald skull with a network of inky veins.

'See now, it *is* one of the doctor's brats! I just knew it!' he exclaimed.

Frau Maenhout quickly looked the other way, turning to the boy. 'Let me try,' she said. She bent down and began talking to him in a soothing voice.

The watchman heard her say the name Michael a couple of times.

From down below, Felix Glück saw Frau Maenhout finally picking up the boy in her arms. She made an attempt to put the hat back on his head, but he slapped her hand away, yelling, 'No, no, I'm not a musketeer any more!' With his other hand, he pulled the mask off his face.

As if they'd been given a sign, his brothers both decided to follow his example. With a swift flourish they tipped the hats from their heads and ripped off their masks.

The mechanic caught himself staring, open-mouthed.

'They had the bodies of toddlers, but the faces of old men,' he later told his clients in the garage. 'They were sick. Very sick. That was as clear as day.'

When Frau Maenhout reached the bottom, Glück tried to see if the boy in her arms looked the same as the other two, but he kept his face buried in the woman's ample bosom.

'Look what I've found!' came the watchman's voice. He was standing at the gate, red-faced, waving a sword that was broken in two pieces. He laid the fragments of wood across each other and said, smiling, 'A couple of nails and some wood glue will soon fix that! Then you can play with it again!'

But the boys acted as if they hadn't heard him.

Reisiger shrugged his shoulders, tucked the smashed sword under his arm and locked the gate. 'Shall I take you back to the doctor's house, Frau Maenhout?' he asked.

She had been staring blankly into the distance, and it took her a while to turn her gaze towards him. She shook her head. 'No, no, it's not necessary, really.'

'But I insist, Frau Maenhout,' the watchman pressed her. 'The doctor would never forgive me if I left you here. And the boys would probably much rather go home by car than on foot – am I right?'

Again there was no response. Felix Glück stared at the boys. Little Martians, he thought – they look just like little Martians, only they aren't green. He heard the woman take some deep breaths. Then she assented.

Reisiger nodded. 'That's a wise decision, Frau Maenhout.' He walked to his car, opened the hatch and dropped the broken sword into the boot.

Meanwhile Glück the mechanic had gone to open the rear door. 'Please, why don't you take a seat in the back with the children, madam? That would be best, I think.'

She stepped past him and looked him briefly in the eye. 'Thank you,' she said. 'Thanks very much.'

Her eyes were soft. Suddenly she seemed much nicer than before.

The woman scooted into the back seat with the boys, and the watchman got in too. The car listed a bit to the side he was on.

'Herr Glück, thanks and see you around!' he cried, sticking his hand out the window.

'See you around!' said Glück, but his voice was lost in the car's deafening roar.

Five minutes later a group of people on the pavement in front of the Café Terminus watched as the car drove into the village.

'There's my husband,' exclaimed Frau Reisiger, waving at him.

From a distance he stuck his arm out the window and gave the thumbs-up.

'My God, all's well then,' she said, relieved.

The car rolled slowly past the onlookers. Otto Reisiger gestured that he would drop his passengers off at the doctor's house. But the villagers only had eyes for whoever was in the backseat.

Someone said, 'I *told* you so,' and that set the tone as the rest of the chorus joined in.

22

She had made a complete hash of it. That was the conclusion Frau Maenhout reached in Otto Reisiger's car. Not only had she got herself into a fine pickle, she had also disappointed the boys terribly. They didn't say a word, not even once they were home again. They were shattered, and she immediately put them to bed. Then she sat down at the kitchen table, and gave in to the emotions she had kept bottled up all this time. She could barely think straight. The one thing racing through her head was the question: how she could have been so *stupid*?

It was an hour before she was able to calm herself down, and the first thing she then asked herself was what to do next. She had boxed herself into a corner. How could she possibly accuse Dr Hoppe of neglect or abuse when she had shown such a lack of responsibility? The doctor would seize the opportunity to heap all the blame on her. It was more urgent than ever, therefore, to find some evidence that would prove the doctor's malevolent intent. Only then would she be able to take the next step.

So she began to search for evidence. She might have all day to do so, but then again, she might not. She had no idea where to look or what, exactly, she was looking for.

She began in the office. She had expected everything to be under lock and key, but that wasn't the case. When she opened one of the drawers, the patient files fanned out like an accordion. She limited herself to flipping through the Hs, however – she didn't want to be accused of anything more was than strictly necessary. If her search didn't turn up anything in the end, she would go through the rest of the files. Alas, the letter 'H' did not give her anything to go on.

In the other drawers she found nothing but medical implements – scissors, needles, bandages, cotton wool, rubber gloves. Gloves! It suddenly occurred to her that she had been leaving her fingerprints all over the place. It made her feel even more like an intruder. But she was doing it for a reason! – a triple reason, asleep upstairs. That gave her the courage to pursue her search. And that was how she came to discover something after all.

There was a pile of photo albums in one of the cabinets. Maybe she would find photos that would shed some light on the doctor's past? Photographs of the doctor as a child or teenager, photos of his mother, or his father, who had also been a GP; perhaps even a picture of his wife, the mother of Michael, Gabriel and Raphael! Who was she? What was she like? Charlotte had often wondered about her, especially since the boys were bound to start asking about her some day. Yet she knew very little. In all the years that she had been working there the doctor had only mentioned her once. Charlotte had questioned the doctor and he had replied that he knew very little about the boys' mother. That was all, but it had made Frau Maenhout wonder, naturally. Perhaps, she had thought to herself, perhaps Michael, Gabriel and Raphael's mother wasn't dead. Perhaps she and the doctor had never been married; perhaps the boys were the product of some sort of fling. At the time she had discussed the possibility with Hannah Kuijk, who had gone one further. 'Or a rape!' Hannah had suggested. Some hanky-panky between the doctor and one of his patients, perhaps. That would also explain, Hannah said, why he had been willing to trade a city like Bonn for a village like Wolfheim. The woman had lodged a complaint against him; his name had been dragged through the mud. And she'd probably not wanted to keep the babies, because they were so – 'Forgive me for saying it,' Hannah had said – *ugly*. So to the doctor the boys were a reminder of his disgrace, and that was the reason why he could not love them the way a father should.

Frau Maenhout couldn't help remembering that conversation as she stood at the consultation-room cabinet leafing through the photo albums, quite unprepared for what she was looking at. She had truly imagined something different.

It took her a while to understand. She had taken down the first album. It was marked 'V1' in the upper right-hand corner. She had no idea what that might mean. It was full of Polaroid pictures, probably taken by the doctor himself. Underneath each photo, in the white margin, was a caption written in felt-tip pen – another 'V1', followed by the date and the year; in this case 1984. The photos themselves were peculiar: just a hand, a leg, a foot, an ear or a navel. Opening the book at random, she saw that it was like that throughout. Then she went back to the beginning. The first page.

She recognised the baby immediately. In the first photo he was lying on his back, naked, on a bed or sofa, she couldn't tell which. She didn't know which of the three it was, there was no name, but there was a date: '29/09/1984'. The children's birthday. What struck her next was the cleft palate. Not the scar, because that didn't exist yet. This was something else. A wound. A gaping hole.

That it was definitely a gaping hole was confirmed on the next page. It gave her quite a turn. The doctor had photographed the cleft palate the same way that he had photographed the hands and feet and other body parts – close up.

She gasped, and snapped the album shut, but the picture stayed branded in her mind.

Then she took out the next album. 'V2' she read on the cover. Opening it at random, she realised at once that all the pictures were identical to the ones in the first album. Yet still she proceeded to take the third album down from the shelf, if only to find what she had expected on the cover: 'V3'. And that album, too, was the same: hands, feet, legs. But also the torso, the back of the head, the shoulders, the eyes . . . everything.

Everything.

She had to sit down on a chair by the desk. She felt dizzy.

A little later she started counting the albums from where she was sitting. She counted twelve. A simple sum. One album a year for each child.

It wasn't enough. What did it prove? Nothing. She came to that conclusion over the course of the morning. After her discovery she stopped searching and went up to the boys' bedroom. They were still asleep. She didn't stay upstairs long, as she couldn't think in their presence. Gazing at them, she kept seeing those pictures flash before her eyes.

Downstairs she walked towards the phone to call Hannah. But she kept procrastinating. She felt she had to make sense of it herself, first. But in the end she did dial the number.

No one picked up.

She made herself a cup of soup to force herself to think of something else. She did the washing-up. The ironing. Every so often she felt as if she couldn't breathe. What could she do? What *should* she do? She was distraught.

In the end she returned to the office. There had to be more. This time her gaze was immediately drawn to the door leading to the laboratory. That was where he always kept his children in isolation when they were sick. That door wasn't locked either, which was a bit of a let-down, because it meant there was less chance he was keeping something hidden in there.

She had not been in the laboratory very often. He cleaned this room himself, and the few times she had been inside she had seen that he did an extremely thorough job. No dust, no mess, no clutter.

It struck her again how clean the room was. No dust, no mess, no clutter. Yet it was different this time. All the glasses, all the jars, all the dishes – every piece of equipment, including the microscopes and monitors – looked pristine, as if they'd never been used. Each time she had peeked in here before, there had always been something bubbling or steaming somewhere; the tables or cabinets had held all kinds of Petri dishes or liquid-filled test tubes. But not this time. It was as if the room had recently been refurbished and was awaiting a new occupant. That was her first impression. But soon she arrived at a different conclusion: he's covering up his tracks. He's cleared everything away, thrown it out, destroyed the evidence.

She was too late. That, sadly, was the conclusion she had to draw.

She decided to look through the patient records once more, but first she returned to the cabinet with the photo albums. Overcoming her repugnance, she began leafing through all twelve albums, beginning to end, though in a cursory way. And even though she knew what she would see there, she kept having to swallow. She had hoped she might find a photo or a note stuck between the pages, something that would help her, but there was nothing. As she turned the last page, she had the sense that she was also closing the final chapter in the boys' lives.

At that point she gave up. She didn't have the strength or the courage to probe any further. She wanted to spend the time that remained with Michael, Gabriel and Raphael. Once the doctor was home again, she'd see what would happen. She'd just wait and see.

As she was returning the last album to the cabinet, her gaze landed on a pile of magazines lying on another shelf. They were all English-language journals with titles such as *Nature*, *Cell*, *Differentiation*. She picked up a few and flapped them around to see if anything fell out. But this final effort – she knew it was hopeless – also produced nothing. Until she started putting the magazines back on the shelf. As she was doing so, the portrait of a man caught her eye. It was on the cover of one of the issues *of Differentiation*. She recognised him immediately, from the red hair and the moustache camouflaging his scar. He didn't have a beard yet. Under the photo was a caption and one word immediately caught her attention: 'experimental'. She looked up the article. He had written it himself. It said 'Dr Victor Hoppe' above the title: '*Experimental Genetics of the Mammalian Embryo*'.

'Mammalian,' she said out loud; it made her think of the French word *mammalien*. From a mammal, then. 'Genetic experiments with mammalian embryos'. She shuddered involuntarily and glanced at the date on the cover. The issue was dated March 1982.

With growing astonishment she began to look through the other journals. Each had some mention of the doctor's name, and sometimes his photo. It was always the same photo: a simple passport picture. Some of the articles were written by the doctor himself, but most, it turned out, were about him. He was described as a 'famous embryologist' at the University of Aachen, where he had apparently done some remarkable experiments in the early eighties. The authors were all in awe of the doctor; many of them even applauded him. But then, suddenly, the tone of the articles began to change, as evidenced by the words that were used: 'investigation', 'falsification', 'fraud', 'chaos'. Those words shocked her. Especially the last two.

Finally, in the magazine at the very bottom of the pile, an issue of

Nature, she found one last article about him. It was short, but the title alone spoke volumes: 'University of Aachen: Victor Hoppe resigns'.

She felt another shudder running up her spine, and when she looked at the date of the journal, she gasped: 3 July 1984. Three months before the doctor had returned to Wolfheim.

On an impulse, she tore out the article.

Fraud and chaos. Chaos and fraud. She repeated the words to herself because she was trying to make some sense of them. The word 'fraud', in particular, set her thinking; indeed, it even gave her comfort. After all, it meant that the doctor had already deceived people in some fashion or other; that he had convinced people of things that were untrue. That was something she could use.

Suddenly some other words came back to her. How had he put it again? It was when she'd brought up the subject of the incision on Gabriel's back. She had said, 'I don't believe you,' or, 'I don't believe you any more.'

Have you, too, lost faith in me?

You, too. So she wasn't the only one.

She had a lead. That was all it was. But it was more than she had expected. She could look into this further. She would get someone to translate the article for her, contact the University of Aachen. But she wouldn't rush it. She mustn't make any mistakes. That night, when she got home, she would make a start. And then she'd have all of Sunday. She wouldn't have to defend her actions until Monday morning, when, she supposed, the first patients would inform the doctor about what had happened at the three borders. But by that time she hoped to have made some headway. And even if she hadn't, there was still time. All in all, she no longer cared if the doctor fired her.

Dr Hoppe came home that Saturday at half past five. Frau Maenhout was in the classroom with Michael, Gabriel and Raphael. After the boys had woken up at around two o'clock and had had something to eat, she'd taken them upstairs, but there hadn't been a lesson. The boys were distracted, and she too had been unable to concentrate. She had read to them, however. The story she picked from the children's

Bible was that of David and Goliath. About how a simple shepherd slew a giant.

'If you aren't big and strong, you have to be cunning,' she told them when she came to the end of the story. Then she told them to make a drawing of it.

'Just how big was the giant exactly?' Gabriel wanted to know.

'Three metres tall. Even taller than this.' She stretched her arm up in the air, as high as she could reach.

'He won't fit on my page.'

'You have to draw it to scale. You have to make everything smaller than it is in the real world.'

That was a difficult concept for them to understand. They didn't know how to turn something that was life-sized and real in their heads into something reduced and two-dimensional. For some reason she couldn't make them see it; they could only envisage what was real.

She drew a picture of David and next to him a giant four times his size.

'But that isn't a giant. He's much too small!' Gabriel yelled.

'All right, but just go ahead and copy it.'

She realised that she was a bit short on patience that afternoon. She was nervous, of course. She kept glancing at her watch. She bit her nails. She opened the window a crack and held her breath every time a car drove past.

At around five o'clock she couldn't keep it inside her any longer. She made the triplets pay attention, and started asking them questions. She wanted to prepare them. She didn't say, 'In case someone asks you . . .' She simply posed the question: 'What do you think of your father?'

'He's bad.'

'Why?'

'He does bad things.'

'What kind of things?'

'With needles. He sticks needles into us. Long needles . . .'

'Is that all?'

After thinking it over for a while, they couldn't come up with anything else. Which made her realise that there had been nothing else. Of whatever she thought the doctor guilty, very little could be proven. What it boiled down to in the end was that he had acted irresponsibly towards his children. Inhumanely, even. But he had never blown up at them. He had never hit them. All that he had done, in fact, was subject them to medical examinations, even if excessively so. He had kept them indoors. But was that a crime?

She gave a deep sigh and tried to compose her thoughts. Fraud and chaos. That was what she should be concentrating on.

When, at 5.30, the taxi stopped in front of the house, she walked over to the window, her heart beating loudly in her chest. The doctor got out and instinctively she stepped back so that he wouldn't see her.

'Your father is home,' she said to the children. 'You'd better tidy up. He'll be up in a minute.'

But he did not come upstairs.

She waited five minutes. Ten minutes. She heard him down in the office. She fervently hoped that he wouldn't discover she'd been snooping. She tried to remember if she had put everything back the way she'd found it.

Why wasn't he coming upstairs to check if everything was all right?

She decided to go downstairs herself, with the boys, and then leave. She walked over to the window to shut it, but a sound from outside caught her attention. She looked up. The sky was quite blue, aside from a few high wisps of cloud, yet it sounded as if a thunderstorm were approaching from some distance. She opened the window a little wider and leaned out. The rumbling came from the other end of Napoleonstrasse and was getting louder. She had heard the sound before, but at first was unable to place it. It sounded like a large convoy of automobiles. But that wasn't it.

Suddenly she knew what it was and grew pale as a sheet. When she turned round, she could tell from the way Michael, Gabriel and Raphael cocked their heads that they too had recognised the sound.

'The car,' said Gabriel. 'That's the car of that mister.' His voice could barely be heard over the sound of the car, which was now very close.

Frau Maenhout didn't say anything, but listened intently. She glanced at her watch. It was almost 5.45. Otto Reisiger was probably returning from the three borders, where he had kept the Boudewijn

Tower open until five o'clock. He's on his way to Albertstrasse, she thought; he won't stop.

But he did stop. The deafening noise of the damaged exhaust continued for a few more seconds, then suddenly it went quiet. Frau Maenhout swallowed and looked out of the window. The watchman had parked his Simca in front of the house. He leaned across the passenger seat to pick something up, then got out and slammed the door shut. In his hand he held the little wooden sword, which, by the looks of it, he had repaired. Frau Maenhout, slapping her hands to her mouth, saw him ring the bell. He pushed open the gate, which wasn't latched, and walked up the path.

She turned and looked at the children. 'Have we said our prayers yet today?' She just blurted it out. She didn't know why. Well, she did, but she refused to acknowledge it. She was afraid.

She walked up to the three school desks where the three brothers sat. They had folded their hands together obediently. From downstairs in the hall came the sound of voices.

'Our Father . . .' she began.

'The sign of the cross,' Raphael interrupted her, 'first we have to cross ourselves.'

'You're right,' she said, and raised her right hand to her forehead. 'In the name of the Father . . .'

Half-whispering, the boys said the prayer after her, the way she had taught them to. She closed her eyes and listened to the boys' sing-song voices.

'Our Father who art in heaven . . .'

She wouldn't take it lying down. She was determined not to. She would defend herself. She would say that it was his fault. Wasn't it?

'Forgive us our trespasses . . .'

'Thank you, Herr Reisiger!' came the doctor's voice. 'Goodbye!'

The children calmly continued their prayer.

'Lead us not into temptation . . .'

Downstairs the front door slammed shut.

'. . . but deliver us from evil. Amen.'

Then she heard the doctor ascending the stairs. She hastily decided to go and meet him halfway. She didn't want a scene in the children's presence.

'I'll be back in a jiff!' she told them. She walked to the door. The stress manifested itself in her hands, which she couldn't keep still. Outside Herr Reisiger's car started making its noise again. Not a loud grumbling or rumbling this time, but a high-pitched screech that lasted just a few seconds. She opened the door and stepped out onto the landing.

The doctor had just arrived at the top of the stairs. He was holding the wooden sword. She glanced at his face to weigh his mood, but his features, as usual, betrayed no expression.

'Herr Reisiger,' he began.

The deafening racket of the car outside suddenly returned. The doctor paused, then began again, 'Herr Reisiger returned the sword. He told me—'

'It's all your fault,' she broke in. She was wringing her hands together convulsively. She would remain on the attack.

'What?'

He's just pretending, she thought. He's trying to play innocent.

'It's your fault that it has come to this,' she said.

He bowed his head.

'That isn't true,' he said. 'It isn't my fault.'

'Excuse me?' she said, startled and furious at the same time.

He started to shake his head but his eyes remained fixed on the floor. 'I've done good. I have only done good. I didn't want this to happen.'

He's talking gibberish, she thought; it's almost as if he's drunk. He kept wobbling his head strangely from side to side. Outside the car began shrieking again, but the doctor's voice carried over it.

'*He* wanted it this way. He's the one. I tried to stop him. I did try. But . . .' He ran his hand over the sword's wooden blade and took a step forward, but appeared to stagger.

'I wanted to do good. I have always wanted to do good.'

Chaos and fraud. The words sprang to her mind again, and she said them out loud: 'Chaos and fraud!' She sidestepped to get away from him. 'Chaos and fraud. That's what they accused you of. You tricked everyone. Before. And now.'

Just then there was a loud bang outside. It made her jump, but the noise did not seem to register with the doctor.

'You mustn't say that!'

He had taken another step in her direction. She took another step backwards. Sensing she had found a sore spot, she went on: 'You can't take the truth. You haven't the guts to face it. You overestimated yourself.'

'You mustn't say that,' he repeated. He was shaking his head even more vehemently than before, like a child caught doing something he shouldn't be doing, who refuses to own up to it. The doctor made a sudden lunge forward. Charlotte Maenhout was caught completely off guard and instinctively took another step back. Only then did she realise that she was standing right at the edge of the stairs. But it was already too late.

'Doctor ? My car won't start. Could you . . .'

The watchman, who had entered the doctor's house, froze. 'Oh my God!' he cried.

Dr Hoppe was kneeling next to Frau Maenhout, who was sprawled at the foot of the stairs. He pressed his index and middle finger to her throat, waited a few seconds, then looked up.

'The Lord giveth and the Lord taketh away,' he said.

Otto Reisiger slowly crossed himself.

He hadn't meant this to happen. Victor Hoppe hadn't wanted this. He had simply wanted to give the sword back to her. That was all. But then she had said things. Alleged things. And something had got into him that was more powerful than he was. Evil had got into him. He knew it. And what was evil had to be vanquished. That he also knew.

II

In the scientific literature, Victor Hoppe's career is usually summed up as follows:

The German embryologist Victor Hoppe received his doctorate from the University of Aachen in the sixties with an outstanding thesis on cell-cycle regulation. He spent several years in Bonn working as a fertility specialist, and in 1979 he astonished the scientific community by producing mouse offspring of single-gender parentage. He held a research chair at the University of Aachen and in December 1980 he astonished the scientific community again by cloning mice. He was the first scientist to successfully apply the cloning technique to a mammal. Three years later he was accused of fraud by his colleagues. It seemed that his experiments could not be replicated using his data, and Dr Hoppe refused to give a demonstration of his methods. In June 1984, after an investigation by an independent commission, he ended his research at the university and turned his back on academia. Some scientists later expressed some regret about the entire episode, suggesting that with the removal of Dr Hoppe a great talent had been lost, whereas others continued to maintain that his work was just amateur bungling.

That is how it is still characterised, even today. Except for the doctor's nationality, everything else is true. But it's only half the truth. Examine it under a microscope, and quite another story will emerge.

In London on Tuesday, 16 December 1980, at half past four in the afternoon, the editor-in-chief of the science journal *Cell* received a phone call from Dr Victor Hoppe. The name sounded familiar to the editor, but he couldn't immediately place it. Speaking in English with a German accent, the doctor asked him when the deadline for the next issue of *Cell* was. Excitedly he added that he had some important news. His voice sounded muffled, as if he were holding a handkerchief over the mouthpiece.

The editor informed him that the deadline for the January issue had been a week earlier, and he was expecting the proofs on his desk any moment now. Articles for the February issue were still being considered.

Dr Hoppe did not want to wait that long. 'It's too important,' he said.

Warily, the editor asked him what it was about. There was some hesitation on the other end of the line. Then he heard a very self-assured, 'Cloning. I've cloned some mice.'

That made the editor sit up. If true, this was indeed important news. The announcement also jogged his memory, and he suddenly knew who Victor Hoppe was: the German biologist who had published a significant article in the journal *Science* some years before, on mouse-embryo engineering.

'Well! That truly would be a first,' said the editor.

'I would like to publish a report on my experiments as soon as possible, you understand.'

'I quite understand,' the editor replied, suddenly most accommodating. 'I may be able to arrange something for the current issue. Could you fax me the article today?'

'No, not until tomorrow.'

'That's going to be tight. I'll need it by twelve o'clock at the very latest. Is that possible?'

There was actually another day's leeway, but the editor did not tell him that. The more time he gave the doctor, the greater the chance that other journals would find out about it and might try to get the scoop.

'Twelve o'clock. I think I can do that.'

'Excellent. How many mice have you cloned, if I may ask?'

'Three. Three in all.'

'That's fantastic. I'm looking forward to reading your account.'

'Just a few minor details and it's finished. You can count on it.'

When Victor Hoppe, in Aachen, put down the receiver, he had not actually put down on paper very much of the article he was supposed to deliver the next day. He did have an outline in his head, and had jotted down the data every step of the way. He had also taken some photos, but that was all he had. He knew that it was his technique, in particular, that he had to emphasise. Most of his colleagues used viruses as vectors in cell hybridisation, whereby they forfeited the process most important to cloning. He, on the other hand, used a method developed in the seventies by Professor Derek Bromhall of England, which Dr Hoppe had then refined: using a microscopic dropper, or pipette, he would insert a foreign nucleus into the cell and, keeping the micropipette *in situ* would then suck out the cell's original nucleus. That way the cell membrane needed to be pierced only once, making for swifter healing. The recently discovered agent cytochalasin B, with which he then treated the cell, worked to keep the cell supple, encouraging it to fuse with the new nucleus.

It was all very simple in theory, but in practice this method required a great deal of expertise and a thousand times more dexterity than you'd need to thread a needle. Many of his attempts failed, either because the cell membrane was too badly damaged, or because too much cytoplasm was sucked out together with the nucleus. The fusion of the nucleus and the new cell was also seldom straightforward, and the chance of a re-engineered cell developing into an actual embryo was completely down to luck. The data Dr Hoppe had recorded didn't lie. Of the five hundred and forty-two selected white mouse cells, less than half survived the microsurgical intervention in which the nucleus was replaced with another harvested from a brown mouse. Of the remaining group, only forty-eight cells successfully fused with the new nucleus. These were cultured for four days, at which point it transpired that only sixteen of the cells had developed into tiny embryos and were therefore suitable for implanting into the uteri of some white mice. Despite the low numbers – less than three per cent of the cells had made it to the penultimate stage – it was a great achievement for Victor Hoppe, an achievement to which his colleagues had never even come close, because to date all their attempts had come to naught at the Petri-dish stage.

Then he'd had to wait three weeks until the embryos were fully gestational and could be born. He had used that period to start a new series of cells. To his dismay, of these not one survived the culture stage, which meant that he was forced to pin all his hopes on the implanted embryos. The young mice would be born hairless; the doctor would find out if his cloning experiment had been successful only three days later, when the pelts began to grow. The sixteen doctored cells would have to produce brown mice, while the fifteen control eggs that had been fertilised normally, which he had implanted into various uteri at the same time as the others, would be expected to produce mice with their mothers' white pelt.

The mice were born on 13 December 1980, in a University of Aachen laboratory. As a precautionary measure, they were taken out by Caesarean section. The procedure was a simple one compared to the microsurgery required to substitute the nuclear material of the cells. Still, he had to concentrate with all his might, because he was so nervous that his hands were shaking.

The first of the five white mothers – in order to tell them apart he had marked them with ink, from one to five dots each – did not provide the hoped-for result; indeed, of the eight neonates, all of them stillborn, only three were physically recognisable as mice. Of the other five, two were as wrinkled as raisins and the next two looked more like some shrivelled three-month-old human embryo. The skin of the last deformed mouse was thinner than crêpe paper, so transparent that you could see all its innards. Dr Hoppe was disappointed, but after dunking his first mouse's offspring in formaldehyde, he proceeded to cut open the second mother with fresh hope. In this case too, four of the five implanted embryos were stillborn; they had fused together in pairs. One of the pairs shared a spine, the other pair had just one set of hindquarters. But his attention was immediately drawn to the fifth specimen, which was twice as big as the others, and not just that, it was alive! But that was as far as it went. The little creature was scarcely moving – the only evidence of life was some twitching of the hind legs – so the doctor quickly grabbed a tiny pipette and began pumping air into its minuscule mouth.

'Breathe! Breathe!' he cried as if addressing something human.

* * *

'Breathe! Breathe!'

Dr Karl Hoppe's distorted voice rang through the house at 1 Napoleonstrasse in Wolfheim, where he had just helped to deliver his wife of a son. It was a Monday morning, 4 June 1945. The pains had started two days earlier, although the actual labour had lasted nine hours.

So it was a boy. In that case his name would be Victor. That was something they had decided on beforehand. However, the child's sex wasn't the first thing the father had looked for. His gaze had initially gone to his child's face. Through the veil of slime and blood over the mouth, nose and cheeks he had immediately seen that his fears had come true: the boy had the same harelip that he had inherited from his own father.

In the village, many people thought that, if a child was born with that particular deformity, it was because the mother had seen a dead hare when she was ten weeks pregnant. Even his own wife believed the old wives' tale, although he had warned her that it was something that ran in the Hoppe family, as did red hair. She had nevertheless shunned the butcher's shop for the entire length of her pregnancy, and whenever she was forced to walk past the shop window, with its display of meats, she had taken care to stare straight ahead.

It hadn't helped. The child was born with a harelip. It was the first thing his wife had asked him. Not if it was a boy or a girl, but if it had . . . With a trembling hand she had pointed at her own mouth, which was slick with sweat. He had merely nodded and then announced that it was a boy, hoping that would take her mind off it. She had closed her eyes and sighed.

The boy's breath was coming out ragged, and so an oxygen mask was immediately clapped onto his impaired mouth. Dr Hoppe began squeezing a black balloon at three-second intervals to pump air into his son's lungs.

'Breathe! Breathe!' he cried.

If he stopped the artificial respiration, the child might die before it had properly lived. As he automatically went on squeezing the balloon, however, the doctor did ask himself whether it might not be best for the boy if he did not make it. He had assisted in the birth of several disfigured babies before this, children with impairments far more dire than a cleft palate; yet this question had never even occurred to him then. He had always made every effort to save the child's life, as he had been trained to do, but now, in the case of his own son, his very first child, he was plagued with doubt. Memories of his own childhood suddenly gave him pause. Every squeeze of the balloon felt like a stab in his gut. When he abruptly stopped pumping, telling himself he was only checking to see if his son was able to breathe on his own, it felt as if a heavy load had been lifted from his shoulders.

'Is he alive, Karl?' he heard behind him. 'For God's sake, tell me he's still alive.'

His wife's pleading shook him out of his stupor and he went back to pumping air into his son's lungs with all his might.

The screeching that started up some moments later furnished the mother with the answer to her question.

* * *

The mouse did not make it, notwithstanding Victor's best efforts. Thirteen dead mice and not a single live specimen. That was the result halfway through. It gave the doctor a sense of doom, which turned out to be premature, however, because half an hour later he extracted six live young from the third mouse. Two of these were conjoined at the skull, to be sure, and expired almost instantly, but the other four looked perfect. Each mouse was the size and shape of a child's pinkie, but with a tail, four legs and two ears. The skin was hairless and pink. The eyes were closed and bulged out. The mouths immediately started opening and closing, rooting for a nipple. Victor gave a sigh of relief. Of these six implanted embryos, three were reconstructed ones. So there had to be at least one cloned specimen among these four survivors. The doctor's hands shook as he deposited the four nurslings into a box of shredded paper, which he then placed under a heat lamp. He would feed them some milk with a dropper the first day, and then each would be put in with one of the adult mice that had given birth the natural way a few days earlier. Inexperienced mothers sometimes ate their own newborn offspring.

He extracted four more live specimens from the fourth mouse, and the last one also brought more hope than disappointment, for five of its seven implanted embryos had developed into live mice, so that the total offspring came to thirteen: a result that was far beyond his expectations.

Three nights later, on 16 December 1980, Victor discovered that three of the eleven remaining young – two more had inexplicably died a day after their birth – were beginning to grow hair of a tawny hue, whereas on the other eight white bristles were clearly showing up against the pink skin. All the stress that had been building in him over the past seventy-two hours suddenly melted away. It was replaced with a sort of daze, and it was in this zombie-like state that he stared at the three brown mice for a full half-hour as they sucked their fill at their mothers' teats. Every now and again, he'd stroke the back of one with the tip of his finger.

* * *

Johanna had expected her son's harelip to look quite different. The worst she'd expected was a surface wound just a couple of centimetres long, which would be gone with a few stitches. She had only ever seen her husband's scar and had never tried to imagine how he might have looked before it was stitched up. So when he deposited the child in her arms, she was so taken aback that she promptly pushed it away.

'Get it away from me!' she cried, raising her arms in a gesture of revulsion, so that the baby rolled down her chest and landed face down on her naked belly.

Karl, hesitating, didn't know what to do. He had never yet experienced a situation like this in all his professional life. Every woman he had ever delivered of a baby had always wanted to hug the child to her chest immediately, even if there was something wrong with it. Some wouldn't even let you prise the child away from them.

'Get it away from me, Karl!'

Johanna thought she could feel the child's mouth stuck to her skin like a suction cup, and when her husband finally picked it up and took it from her, the sensation wouldn't go away, so she peered anxiously at her stomach to see if the child was really gone. A little trail of blood from the umbilical cord was left on the spot where it had been lying. But she thought it was blood from her son's split upper lip, and so she started screaming in horror.

Just a few days after his birth, Victor Hoppe was admitted to the Clare Sisters' convent of La Chapelle, a few kilometres from Wolfheim. The child had been bitten by the devil – according to his religious mother, at least. For hadn't she avoided all contact with hares, both dead and alive, and not only at the beginning of her pregnancy but for the entire nine months? And yet the boy's face had still been besmirched. So there must have been other forces at work.

Father Kaisergruber, who had come to christen the child, confirmed her suspicions. '*Mon Dieu!*' the curate had cried when he first set eyes on the child, and instinctively made the sign of the cross.

This had not escaped Johanna's notice. 'It's the devil's work, isn't it?' she asked him. She was hoping for an affirmative answer, so that she could then consider herself blameless; and affirmation was what she got. It wasn't more than a nod, but it was good enough for her. In the short interval between her question and his response, the priest had glanced out of the corner of his eye at the doctor, who was standing in a corner of the darkened room with his hand over his own deformed mouth.

It's all his fault. He has passed on the evil. He should never have been allowed to bring any children into this world. That was what Father Kaisergruber was thinking, but he did not say it out loud; he still had respect for the doctor, even so. That was why he had just nodded. Upon which the mother let out a deep sigh.

The convent of the Clare Sisters at La Chapelle had always been an institution for mentally and physically disabled children, but during the war Sister Milgitha, the abbess, had decided to open the convent doors to well-to-do burghers from France and Belgium who had had to flee their homes. When the war ended, the convent was compelled to open as an asylum once again. Victor Hoppe was its first new patient, and since his physical impairment didn't amount to a real disability, the sisters noted in his patient file that he showed some signs of retardation. No other particulars were recorded. The file was signed underneath by both parents.

Sister Milgitha had based the steep monthly fee for Victor's care and upbringing on the doctor's conjectured income, and increased it again when she saw the baby. She told the parents that the supplement was to cover extras, such as special dummies and disinfectants. She told one of the other nuns, however, that the reason she had asked for more money was that she was convinced that Dr Hoppe and his wife would pay any price to be rid of the child. She had also gathered as much from Father Kaisergruber.

It was he who had suggested to the parents that they might want to entrust the child to the care of the Clare Sisters for the time being. Sister Milgitha had just a week earlier summoned him to tell him that she was reopening the institution. She had asked him to try to find her some 'unfortunates' – those were her actual words. Naturally he would be rewarded for his efforts. Wasn't he waiting to be promoted from curate to pastor?

The curate had never expected to find his first 'unfortunate' so soon.

'The evil must be driven out,' he told the doctor and his wife after the christening. He had surreptitiously pinched the baby's bottom during the proceedings, so that it had started screeching like a banshee when the holy water was poured over its head. The mother had clapped her hands over her eyes; the father had looked the other way. Then the curate had done it again, twice more.

Pinch. Dunk.

Pinch. Dunk.

He had finished all of the holy water and little Victor was shrieking bloody murder.

'The evil can only be driven out with the help of God,' he'd said, stressing his words one by one. He had put the howling child back into the cradle without bothering to dry its head. The sparse red hair clung to the little skull and the swaddling cloth was soaked through.

Gazing into the mother's eyes, the curate had casually mentioned: 'The sisters at La Chapelle have reopened the mental institution.'

He didn't look at the doctor, deliberately. He had no idea what he would think of the idea. As for the mother, he was almost certain that she did not want this child. She had refused to hold it during the christening ceremony and one could scarcely help noticing that she did her best not to look at it at all.

The mother turned to her husband. The curate, discreetly averting his gaze, inclined his head towards the cradle, where Victor was still bawling at the top of his lungs. With a theatrical flourish, he brought a hand up to his forehead, peered down at the baby from beneath that hand and shook his head gently to show how concerned he was. He waited with bated breath for a response, but it did not come.

'I could,' he therefore began, turning back towards Johanna, '. . . make an appointment for you, if you wish, to see Sister Milgitha.'

'We'll think about—' the doctor said, but his wife broke in abruptly.

'I want it gone, Karl!' she said vehemently.

'Johanna, we have to—'

'He has the devil in him!' the mother cried out, practically hysterical. 'Surely you can see that for yourself!' She whipped her head back around towards the curate.

From her look, he understood that he was being asked to intervene. 'Doctor,' he said calmly, 'I do think it would be best, for the child.'

Something in the doctor's expression suddenly changed. First came a startled look of surprise and then, for just a split second, his eyes went glassy, as if trying to remember something.

The curate deduced that his words had touched a nerve, and so he deliberately went for the doctor's sore spot a second time. 'You have to think of the boy's future,' he said, holding the father's gaze.

Slowly Dr Hoppe turned to stare at the cradle. The howls came in waves, with brief lulls as the baby gasped for air with a nasty squeaking sound.

'Think of the boy, Doctor.'

The curate watched the father take a deep breath, and then heard him say, 'All right then, why don't you make the appointment. Today, if at all possible.'

Then the doctor scurried out of the room.

From the years 1945 to 1948 the convent of La Chapelle was home to seventeen nuns, and in that period the asylum had an average of twelve patients. Victor Hoppe was the youngest patient there, Egon Weiss the oldest. Egon was twenty-seven when he was admitted a month after Victor, and according to the accepted diagnostic definitions of the time, he was an idiot – the severest form of retardation. He spent most of his stay in the asylum shackled to his bed, where he kept up a stream of animal noises day in, day out. He had the devil in him, no question about it.

Egon Weiss's preferred mode of communication was to howl like a wolf, or growl like a mad dog, and it drove the nuns and the other patients crazy. Victor, however, was fascinated by it. The shrill sounds Egon made were a welcome change from the rather monotonous hymns and prayers the patients were subjected to, which the sisters considered more beneficial than any medicine.

Most of the patients idled away the days doing nothing. In the morning some would move from their bed to a chair, others would stand up and remain on their feet until it was time for bed again. Once a day all the patients had to go to chapel. If they could not walk by themselves, they were rolled there in wheelchairs; Victor was carried. The hymns were in Latin, the prayers in both French and German, in the hope that the patients would at least understand something. One nun sat at the front leading the prayers and hymns, the other sisters were spread out among the patients, most of whom sat compliantly through every service. A few even muttered along with the Our Fathers or Hail Marys.

Only Egon Weiss went on wailing, and was often taken back to the main hall before the end of the service. Barbiturates were of little help in his case, for even in his sleep he went on making a racket as if there were a pack of dogs on his heels. The only thing that made him shut up was when he was dunked into an ice-cold bath, then a scalding hot one, and then back into the freezing cold again. Then he'd be quiet for almost an hour, the time it took him to dry off.

Victor didn't talk for the first three years. In the first year of his life it was assumed that he couldn't make any sounds on account of his deformity, but once his cleft palate was surgically repaired and he still wouldn't say a word, the nuns surmised that he wasn't intelligent enough to learn to speak. A few additional tests, during which he showed no reaction, substantiated this assessment.

His father had at first still harboured the hope that the problem would resolve itself. When that turned out not to be the case, it did somewhat ease his conscience, since it had now been positively established that his son was at the asylum because he was feeble-minded. The thought that it was the cleft palate that had been the deciding factor had caused him many a sleepless night. He used to visit the mental institution on a weekly basis over the first year, and every time he saw that sorry group of idiots and imbeciles, he had the feeling his son did not belong there. But fortunately now it turned out that the boy was mentally disabled as well.

His mother never went to see him, not even once. She never even asked her husband how he was. He therefore kept quiet about the child, except on that one day.

'He's been diagnosed as retarded,' he said. 'The tests have officially confirmed it.'

Johanna blinked. That was her only reaction to his announcement.

'He can stay there', Karl went on, 'as long as we like.'

His wife gazed at him expectantly.

'I told them that we would be most grateful if the sisters could go on taking care of him. That's best, for the boy. Sister Milgitha thinks the same thing.'

His wife nodded. That was all. Until he turned and was about to walk out of the room.

'Why is this happening to *us*, Karl?' she said, her voice tinged with despair.

This time it was he who fell silent. He didn't have an answer. Except perhaps that they should never have considered having children. But they had never discussed it. And now it was too late.

* * *

Louise Brown was born on 25 July 1978, in England. She was the product of the successful collaboration of the zoologist Robert Edwards of Manchester and the gynaecologist Patrick Steptoe of Oldham. Edwards had started experimenting with *in vitro* fertilisation in the 1960s; in the seventies, Steptoe had discovered a method of extracting egg cells through the vaginal canal and then reimplanting them via the same route. In the autumn of 1977 Louise Brown was conceived when an egg cell from her mother was artificially combined in a Petri dish with a sperm cell from the father, and the resulting embryo returned to the mother's womb. The news of Louise Brown's birth, which was announced in the summer of 1978, caused a worldwide sensation; it was received everywhere with feelings of both revulsion and admiration. For Victor Hoppe, who had been working for years towards the same goal, the birth of the first test-tube baby meant a shattering end to his own research.

Victor had started experimenting with amphibian and mouse eggs whilst doing his doctoral research at the University of Aachen, and it was in 1970, when he was an associate at a fertility clinic in Bonn, that he had first attempted to fertilise a human egg outside the womb. He had obtained the human eggs from the hospital in Bonn, harvested from ovaries that had been taken out for gynaecological reasons. The sperm he used were his own. After five years of experimenting, he had finally stumbled upon the right combination of method and medium to promote the fusion of the egg and sperm in a Petri dish. He then left the fertilised egg in another culture to develop into an embryo, as he had done with the mouse eggs. It had taken him another year before he had quite mastered that procedure, but all in all it was a relatively speedy result.

In the spring of 1977, on the strength of these results, he persuaded several couples to take part in an experiment taking his research one step further. He found couples in which the woman was unable to produce mature eggs as a result of some ovarian abnormality. Dr Hoppe told them that it was possible to have a donor egg fertilised with the husband's sperm, and then, after three days, when it had split and multiplied into sixteen cells, to have it implanted via an abdominal incision into the wife's uterine wall. Over the following year and a half he performed this procedure nine times, on four different women. Their bodies invariably rejected the foetuses within three weeks. The last time this happened was two days after the birth of Louise Brown. When the news broke, Dr Hoppe took the reams of data he had gathered over the years, and filed it all away for good.

Victor Hoppe was in the habit of jotting down his data on any old scrap of paper that happened to be within reach, whenever or wherever inspiration struck: stationery, used and unused envelopes, pages torn from periodicals, scraps of newspaper, calendar pages, bread bags turned inside out or other packaging that came with groceries or medication. The data itself might be in the form of words, sentences, formulas or sketches – scribbles that often filled every inch of blank space on the page. Notes were scrawled horizontally, vertically or diagonally, in the margin or squeezed in between headlines or columns of other text. The handwriting was messy, to say the least.

To an outsider – and that meant everyone else – this data was quite worthless at first glance, except to show how chaotically or amateurishly Victor Hoppe went about his work. With great difficulty, and some prior knowledge, one might have succeeded in linking one or two of the formulas or sketches to one of the many experiments the doctor had carried out, but even then it was impossible to find any further connection or logic to the hundreds and hundreds of jottings.

And indeed there wasn't any, at least not on paper. The context was all inside Victor's head. He needed only a single word or formula to summon up, in a split second, every bit of information connected with it. To him, the notes were simply keys to doors that gave him access to a vault crammed with information. The way his brain worked was a blessing in his line of work, because it spared him constantly having to look things up, saving him a lot of time in the process. In his personal life, this gift was more of an impediment, since every word he saw or heard might evoke a slew of useless associations or unpleasant memories.

In today's world, Victor Hoppe would probably have been diagnosed as having Asperger's syndrome. Dr Hans Asperger, paediatrician at the University of Vienna, described this mild form of autism in his thesis *Die Autistischen Psychopathen im Kindesalter*. He had studied children with severe deficiencies in socialisation, imagination and, above all, communication skills. Although their language ability was intact, they often came across as pedantic or mannered. These children appeared to have no sense of humour at all and showed very little emotion. They also took practically everything that was said to them literally. On the other hand, they were all exceptionally intelligent, and capable at an early age of remembering the most complex, but frequently also the most banal, things, such as the Vienna tram schedule in its entirety, or the names of all the parts of the internal-combustion engine.

Dr Asperger published his findings in 1944, but it was not until the 1960s that his study drew the attention of other academics, and even then it took until 1981 before it was officially recognised as a syndrome. It is now thought that both Leonardo da Vinci and Albert Einstein suffered from Asperger's syndrome.

* * *

The Clare Sisters of the La Chapelle institute had never heard of Asperger's syndrome. Even the term 'autism' was unfamiliar to them. They were only aware of three previously established classes of psychiatric aberration: idiocy, for an IQ of between 0 and 20; imbecility, in the case of an IQ between 21 and 50, and feeble-mindedness, between 51 and 70.

Victor Hoppe was therefore categorised as feeble-minded. Since he didn't speak a word, the sisters assumed that he didn't know any words or understand them. His behaviour, too, bore that out. He scarcely betrayed any reaction or emotion to what was being said to him. The only thing that seemed to fascinate him was Egon Weiss's animal braying. He could sit for hours staring at the young man and listening to him. He was also the only patient who could sleep in the bed next to the idiot without being driven totally round the bend by him. This led the sisters to suspect that Victor Hoppe's condition might be even worse than was feared, and that he might in fact be an imbecile or even an idiot, although he was too young for them to know for sure.

When he was three, Victor finally began to speak. All of a sudden. It happened one night during the sweltering summer of 1948. The near-tropical heat that had gripped a great portion of Europe for weeks had penetrated even the thick walls of the cloister at La Chapelle and caused the temperature in the normally chilly building to rise dramatically. With the heat came the flies and the mosquitoes. The flies were attracted by the smell of rapidly spoiling food, the mosquitoes by the sweat of the patients, who even in these circumstances were bathed only a couple of times per week.

If at night the heat did not prevent the patients from getting any sleep, the buzzing of the flies and whining of the mosquitoes would. Egon's screams, too, had become quite unbearable. The weather conditions had exacerbated his own condition dramatically. The heat squeezed the sweat from his pores, the flies crept up his sleeves and trouser legs, and the mosquitoes sucked his blood right through his clothes. But he was unable to swat them off, for he was tethered to the bed, tied down by the ankles and wrists. His own stench, the tickle of flies crawling on his skin and the itch of the insect bites were driving him into a mad rage.

None of the other patients was able to get any sleep. They became irritable. Rebellious. One afternoon, Marc François, imbecile, aged eighteen, tore off all his clothes and began running through the building in search of somewhere cooler, somewhere Egon's voice would not reach. It took eight sisters to catch and restrain him.

Fabian Nadler, likewise imbecile, aged fourteen, smashed a windowpane with his bare fist and started trying to corral the flies towards the opening. Other patients joined in to help. They leaped and darted through the ward, chasing visible and invisible flies. Angelo Venturini, feeble-minded and a partial cripple, aged twenty, took advantage of the commotion to pick up a shard of glass, and headed over to Egon Weiss's bed. He was presumably on his way to cut the demons out of Egon's body and chase them out the window with the flies. But he tripped before reaching Egon's bed and slashed his own thigh instead.

Victor Hoppe, feeble-minded, aged three, was not ruffled by any of this. The heat and the din did not seem to affect him. He did not even appear to notice Angelo Venturini's assault. He sat in a chair beside Egon's bed and the only thing that interested him was the bugs – not the ones on his own body, but the ones crawling over his neighbour's face. Whenever a fly or mosquito landed there, Victor would shoo the insect away with a sweep of the arm. He kept it up all day long. It did seem to calm Egon Weiss somewhat, and every once in a while he'd turn and stare at the toddler with hollow eyes. His gaze was blank, but the very fact that he was looking at the child at all was a triumph over his usual feral skittishness. If Victor had been given the chance, he might even have succeeded in taming Egon.

But each night he had to go back to his own crib. The night sister would raise the side rails so that his arms could no longer reach far enough to swat at the flies and mosquitoes. In the faint glow of the night lights over each bed he saw the insects buzzing round his neighbour's head and heard his voice escalate to a bellow once again.

Then Angelo Venturini decided to make a second attempt at silencing the demons inside the idiot's body, and this time he succeeded. He couldn't remember a thing about it afterwards and, since he had been afflicted with somnambulism ever since childhood, the nuns thought that he had acted unconsciously.

Nonsense. In order to walk in your sleep, you have actually to *be* asleep. And no one could sleep that night – including Venturini. So when he got out of bed, he was wide awake. In order to keep up the pretence while making his way down the narrow aisle between the beds, he kept his head cocked sideways, with a pillow wedged between cheek and shoulder. His genuine sleepwalking episodes had never involved a pillow.

Sister Ludomira, who was on night duty, glanced up through the window of the screened-off cubicle at the end of the ward, recognised Angelo Venturini from his hobbled walk, and went back to the prayer book in front of her. She knew from experience that he would walk up and down three times, and then get back into bed.

That night, however, Venturini did not walk up and down three times. He limped straight over to Egon's bed. Perhaps Egon did not see Venturini's shadow as he leaned over him. Perhaps he did not recognise the danger. Perhaps he just wanted the itch to stop. In any event, Egon did not put up a fight when Venturini pressed the pillow to his face. He did not shake his head. He did not try to yank his wrists or ankles out of their restraints. He just tried to continue screeching. But his voice now sounded muffled, the way it occasionally did even when he didn't have a pillow pressed to his face. That was why Sister Ludomira did not immediately look up.

She only looked up when Egon Weiss suddenly fell completely silent. Angelo Venturini was just lifting his pillow off Egon's face. Tucking the pillow back on his shoulder and snuggling his head against it, he walked down the aisle, back to his bed.

Across the aisle, Marc François was sitting up in bed, swaying jubilantly from side to side, clapping his hands, and braying with laughter. Sister Ludomira sprang into action. She flipped on the overhead light, pulled on the cord that rang a bell somewhere in the convent and rushed to Egon's bedside. Venturini crept into his bed, stretched out and promptly fell asleep, in spite of the buzzing of the flies and mosquitoes.

Sister Ludomira could only confirm, from Egon's vacant eyes, that he was dead. She crossed herself. Then she heard an unfamiliar voice behind her. She turned round, and, covering her mouth with her left hand, crossed herself again with her right.

Victor was on his knees in his crib, hands folded over the bars, his head resting on his hands. A stream of sound was coming from his mouth, which at first Sister Ludomira thought was just gibberish, but which, it suddenly struck her, had a distinct rhythm. That was when she realised what the boy was babbling in his shrill little voice – in German:

> *'Holy Joseph, solace of the wretched, pray for us.*
> *Holy Joseph, hope of the sick, pray for us.*
> *Holy Joseph, patron of the dying, pray for us.*
> *Holy Joseph, terror of demons, pray for us.'*

Egon Weiss's death certificate ascribes his death at age thirty to asphyxiation, caused by swallowing his own tongue.

An interim report on Victor Hoppe, from around the same time period, notes, 'Speaks. Unintelligibly, alas.'

* * *

The two women had come all the way from Vienna. They had a specific request and had already been turned down by several other physicians. Almost all of these had told them that their wish was beyond the realm of possibility – for the foreseeable future, anyway. The ladies themselves, however, were convinced that these days, ever since Louise Brown's birth, anything was possible, and that the doctors' objections were of an ethical rather than a practical nature.

'Is it because we are a same-sex couple? Is that the reason? Is that why you won't do it for us?' was the question they kept asking.

'No, it's impossible. It's simply impossible.'

One doctor had said, 'It isn't allowed,' which had made them all the more determined.

In the end they had crossed the border. Perhaps it was permitted in Germany.

The consultation took place on 11 November 1978. 'We want a child,' one of them said to Dr Hoppe.

'From both of us,' the other clarified.

They both sensed that the doctor thought they were talking gibberish. All the hope that had been building up in them on the train ride to Bonn promptly vanished into thin air. They felt both ridiculous and naive, and had already half-risen from their seats when the doctor had curtly said he could do it.

They were astonished at this, and reiterated, adamantly, that they wished the child to be from both of them – the way it was with a man and a woman: with physical characteristics inherited from both.

'I can do it,' the doctor said again, 'but not right away.'

'We have all we need with us,' one of them said, while the other took a portfolio from her bag and shoved it ostentatiously under his nose. 'Here are the results of our Pap smears and blood tests, and a schedule of our menstrual cycles. We are both fertile right now.'

'Our menstrual cycles are in sync,' the other said proudly, giving her girlfriend a fond look.

'Nuns in a convent tend to menstruate at the same time of the month,' the doctor responded dryly.

The ladies were briefly taken aback. The doctor had opened the portfolio and was leafing through it.

'What are our chances, Doctor?'

'I don't believe in gambling,' he replied.

The ladies felt uncomfortable in his presence. But the discomfort they felt was far outweighed by the happy tidings that followed.

'Come back tomorrow,' he told them after examining them. 'Then we'll begin.'

He had wanted to send the women packing. He *should* have sent them packing. But as usual, he had blurted out things he had not meant to say, expressed thoughts that had suddenly popped into his head.

'I can do it,' he'd said. By the time he heard himself say it, it was too late. The women had misunderstood him when he'd added that he couldn't do it right away. Or perhaps it was he who had failed to make himself clear, as usual.

When they had told him what they wanted, he had seen in a flash how he would go about it. It was possible, in theory. He would have to take nuclei from random cells taken from each woman, and fuse them together inside a fertilised egg whose own nucleus he would have removed beforehand. It was an experiment he had performed several times as a student, albeit on frog or salamander eggs, not human ones.

So he had said, 'I can do it.'

But in the next instant the practical obstacles had occurred to him. Human egg cells were a thousand times smaller than amphibian eggs. And his experiments with the latter had never actually produced an embryo capable of developing into an adult. That was why he had added that it wouldn't be possible immediately. He needed more time, was what he'd meant. Months, perhaps years.

But his first words had given the women hope, and they had latched on to that hope. At that point he had felt he couldn't disappoint them, which had made him say even more things that had stunned them.

Then he had examined the women. One of them had suggested that perhaps they could both become pregnant at the same time. She may have meant it as a joke, but the doctor had not taken it as such. Indeed it had set him thinking, and it occurred to him what a unique chance these women were offering.

When he had said that he would begin the next day, he knew it was too soon. He had to practise first. With other animal cells – mouse cells; or rabbit cells. But he hadn't told them that. If he had asked them to come back in six months, they might have changed their minds.

They returned the next day at the appointed time and he performed the procedure. But unknown to them, he used unfertilised eggs. At least that way he'd gained another month.

The women were both a week late. In those seven days they had become convinced they were pregnant. This they had told him with great excitement. And then the embryos must have somehow been rejected by their bodies without them noticing it. The doctor did not deny their theory, even though he knew there had never been an actual embryo. Then he proceeded to implant another set of unfertilised eggs into both women, since he was still experimenting.

This was how far he had got by this point: he had managed to grow mouse embryos from two female eggs, but none of the embryos had developed into live mice. As for human cells, he had progressed no further than the nuclear-fusion stage. However, even this was an exceptional result.

Then he had shut himself in his laboratory for days at a time. He was working on several experiments at once, starting a new one before the previous one was finished. He jotted down the data only sporadically – too sporadically, in fact, even for him. I'll get to it later, he kept thinking; his mind was already on to the next step. His thoughts were like domino pieces: as soon as one toppled over, all the others followed automatically.

On 15 January 1979 the women once again came to his office. He had wanted to postpone their meeting since he needed another month. But they had insisted, and he'd given in because he didn't want them to go elsewhere.

'Is it going to work this time, Doctor?'

'Time will tell.' He had been expecting the question, and had prepared an answer.

'And if it doesn't . . . ?'

He'd been hoping they would ask that. 'Then I'd like to try one more time. If you'll agree, of course.'

The women looked at each other. One said, 'So you think it won't work this time either?'

Her remark was a reproach, but his response was the same nonetheless. 'Time will tell.'

'We have been discussing it . . .' the woman continued after a short pause. 'Maybe we should stop. We are—'

'You don't have to pay me,' he said quickly.

'It's not about the money. We no longer trust that it's possible.' Her words made it sound as if she were breaking up with someone.

Her friend concurred. 'People have told us that what we want is impossible.'

'Who are these "people"?' he shouted, louder than he'd meant to. It made the women jump. For a moment he feared they were slipping through his fingers like sand, but then it occurred to him that they wouldn't have come back if they had given up hope completely. He just needed to convince them. So he took them to see his laboratory.

'Sometimes what may seem impossible is merely very difficult,' he told them.

The three mice he showed them were five days old, the size of an infant's little finger. Their skin was covered in fine hairs, brown in the case of two of the mice and white in the case of the other. They were tucked in a box of shredded paper, being suckled by a black mouse.

'That isn't the biological mother. She merely carried them to term.' He picked two adult mice, one white and one brown, out of another cage. 'These are the mothers. The babies are their offspring. No male mouse was involved.'

The women looked on open-mouthed.

He did not try to deceive them this time. He told them that he needed to carry out a few last experiments on human eggs but was certain that it would work after that. He spent an hour and a half lecturing them on how and why it would work this time, and they never interrupted him once. So in the end he managed to convince them to wait another month before the next attempt.

That very day he wrote down everything he had told them. Now that the women had seen the mice, he anticipated that the news would spread quickly, so he would have to make his methods public, before other scientists cried foul and accused him of spreading lies. He'd have preferred to wait until the women had actually given birth, but he no longer had that option.

The article practically wrote itself. He only had to consult his scarce notes a couple of times. He sent it the very next day to *Science*, the journal that years ago had published some extracts of his thesis. He had taken Polaroid pictures of the mouse young and their female progenitors, and also included microscope slides or sketches of each stage of the division process. Then he shut himself in his lab once more.

* * *

Lotte Guelen had entered the convent of the Clare Sisters at La Chapelle a year after the end of the Second World War. Her father,

Klaas, was from Vaals in the Netherlands, and in 1928 he had moved to Liège in Belgium to work in the coal mines. He had met a nurse at the hospital a year later, Marie Wojczek, the eldest daughter of strict Catholic immigrants from Poland. Marie was nineteen years old. They'd married after they'd known each other only six months. That was in March of 1930. Marie was three months pregnant with Lotte. She had hidden the slight bulge of her belly under her wedding dress by means of a corset. No one had noticed a thing – not until six months later, that is, when anyone who bothered to do the maths came away frowning. But that was as far as it went. Even her parents never mentioned it. It may have been precisely for that reason that Klaas and Marie never stopped feeling guilty about it.

Sixteen years and three daughters later, their guilt was assuaged by sending Lotte to the convent at La Chapelle. Lotte did not put up any resistance. She wanted to become a teacher and thought that the postulancy would be her first step towards that goal. Her parents, however, had failed to tell her that there was no school attached to the convent of La Chapelle. She found out soon enough, when the nuns put her to work in the asylum. As a postulant, she had to change the cotton nappies of patients who were incontinent, and empty and rinse out the chamber pots of the rest. Her tasks also included changing soiled bed linen and cleaning festering wounds. During the year of her postulancy she was not allowed to speak to the patients.

That probationary year was extended to almost twenty-one months, at which point her parents insisted that Sister Milgitha allow Lotte to become a novice; on her visits home their daughter had twice told them that she refused to return to the convent.

The habit Lotte was given to wear as a novice finally made her feel worthy, even though she had to sweat through the leaden heat of the summer of 1948. Her tasks remained the same, because she was still the youngest nun in the order. Her name did change, however. From then on she was known as Sister Marthe, a convent name the abbess had picked for her. St Martha was the sister of Mary Magdalene, and had always faithfully taken care of the household chores while her sister went to listen to Jesus. According to Sister Milgitha, the convent name was a reward for Lotte's hard work.

For herself, the greatest reward was that she was now allowed to talk to the patients. She was informed of this the day after Egon Weiss was silenced for good. Undoubtedly the two were connected, since permission to talk to the patients involved being discreet and not passing on what the patients said. Or what they blathered: that was the word Sister Milgitha had used. Which led Sister Milgitha to dismiss everything the patients said as nonsense. What Marc François had blathered, for instance. The imbecile had waved Sister Marthe over a few days after it happened and whispered in her ear that Egon had been murdered. He illustrated his words by slashing his forefinger across his throat. She then asked him who had done it. Tucking the same forefinger behind his ear, he had pointed furtively at Angelo Venturini. When she reported this to the abbess, Sister Milgitha took her to have a look at Egon's corpse. The abbess pointed out the unblemished throat of the deceased.

'You see, Sister Marthe,' she said, 'it's all nonsense, the patients' blather. That's why it's dangerous to pass this sort of thing on.'

Sister Marthe understood, perfectly.

Since Egon's death, his howling at night had been replaced by Victor's sing-song voice. As soon as the overhead light went out, the boy would start on a string of litanies and not stop until daybreak. His voice had no intonation or feeling. It was nothing more than an incessant mumbling and so did not disturb the other patients. On the contrary, the monotone sound seemed to calm them down and lull them to sleep.

Victor slept during the day, or perhaps he was just pretending. Whatever the case, it was as if he'd erected a wall around himself. Neither the voices of the nuns, nor the din the patients made, seemed to reach him. The sisters soon gave up trying to have any interaction with him; the patients, on the other hand, persisted, in some cases only because they'd forgotten they had already tried before. Jean Surmont sat down on the rails at the foot of Victor's bed and crowed like a rooster; Nico Baumgarten stood next to the bed imitating the sound of a trumpet; and Marc François, sneaking up to Victor, proceeded to empty a round of imaginary machine-gun bullets into him.

Since Egon's death Victor had refused to eat; he would only drink. His plate would be left on the table by his bed, and if he hadn't touched it by the time the other patients were done with their meal, it was simply cleared away. Sister Milgitha said that he would eat when he was hungry, but when the boy still had not eaten anything after three days, even she began to worry.

'He is mourning for Egon,' said Sister Marie-Gabrielle.

'He's much too young,' said Sister Milgitha. 'It's just a prank. We'll teach him not to try that sort of thing with us.'

That afternoon, with the assistance of three other nuns, she stuffed his mouth with food, pinching his nose shut until he swallowed it. She forced his entire meal down his throat that way.

Less than a minute after he'd gulped down the last mouthful, Victor threw it up again – all over Sister Milgitha's habit.

Marc François, across the room, howled with laughter. To restore her own dignity, the abbess gave Victor such a box on the ears that it made everyone gulp.

Victor didn't cringe or move a muscle. Even though they could all clearly see Sister Milgitha's handprint reddening on his cheek, the boy remained completely impassive.

'There truly is evil inside that boy,' the abbess declared, and she decided to post a sister by his bed, to read to him from the Bible, day and night. That way, she hoped, the devil inside Victor would never get any sleep, so that in the end, desperate for peace and quiet, it would leave the boy's body.

Victor's bed was moved to a separate room, and the sisters took turns reading to him, in two-hour shifts by day and four-hour shifts at night.

Sister Marthe was assigned to read to him for a portion of the night; she didn't mind this too much, because it meant she was allowed to sleep in the next morning, and skip matins.

The first night, she watched Victor as he lay in bed, eyes closed. She stared at the scar over his mouth, which ruined the symmetry of his face, and at his flattened nose, seriously disfigured by the deformity. The scar pushed the wings of his nose upward, causing the right nostril to gape open much wider than the left.

'That's how you can tell he's retarded,' Sister Noëlle had explained.

She also stared at his hair, at how red it was; but she didn't find anything devilish about it, as the other nuns so loudly maintained. She even leaned forward and cautiously touched it. Nothing happened. Her hand had not been singed. She wasn't struck by lightning. Nothing.

Yet perhaps something did happen . . . because when she placed her hand on his forehead, the boy stopped talking for an instant. Then the unstoppable stream of words started up again. Her own voice was supposed to drown his out as she read to him, but she couldn't do it. His voice hypnotised her.

The boy spoke poorly. The sounds found their way out through his nose, lending his voice a wooden, mechanical tone. But since it was litanies he was reciting, it was possible for a careful listener to translate the noises into actual words.

There had been some debate among the sisters as to the boy's intelligence. Some maintained that anyone who knew such lengthy verses by heart could not be retarded. Others said that even a parrot could be taught to recite them. Sister Milgitha had intervened, saying that the noises the boy was producing weren't real litanies, but the ravings of the devil within. With that, the abbess had put an end to the discussion.

But Sister Marthe definitely recognised the prayer of St Joseph, and also that of the Holy Ghost. Never stumbling or stopping, Victor would rattle off the entire sequence, sometimes in French and at other times in German; he even did a better job of it than she ever had. She'd been having a hard time mastering the litanies, and every time she had to recite them for Sister Milgitha she would falter halfway through, or skip a few lines. It was her inability to perform this task adequately that had given Sister Milgitha the excuse to postpone her noviceship. True, she *had* in the end been promoted, but the abbess had warned her that she would not be allowed to take her vows if she did not know her litanies by then.

That was why, starting that very first night, Sister Marthe began repeating the litanies after Victor. She spoke in a whisper so that her voice would not be heard in the hall. And if she heard a sound anywhere in the building, she would stop and go back to reading aloud from the Bible, as she was supposed to do.

The next afternoon she read aloud to him from the Bible for two hours in Sister Noëlle's stead. When she had finished, she whispered in his ear that she was looking forward to practising with him again later that night. She received no reaction.

The second night went off just like the first night.

'Irit-uf-is-dom-an-un-ner-an-ing,' said Victor.

'*Spirit of wisdom and understanding*,' Sister Marthe recited.

'Irit-uf-oun-sel-an-orri-tude,' said Victor.

'*Spirit of counsel and fortitude*,' Sister Marthe repeated.

At the end of the night, stroking his red hair again, she asked him, 'Are you praying for Egon?'

He nodded, but showed no further emotion.

'That's good. It will surely help him to find peace,' she said.

He did not respond. But a little later, as she walked away, she felt his eyes on her. She glanced over her shoulder and saw him look quickly the other way.

'You *have* to eat something,' said Sister Marthe. She held a bar of chocolate under his nose.

He brusquely twisted his head away.

It was the fourth night that she had sat with him. The previous night had been quite extraordinary. Victor had been playing a game with her. At least, that was what it seemed like. He kept breaking off in the middle of a litany, leaving her to continue it. A few verses later he would join in again. They had repeated this a few times. But when she made a mistake he had shaken his head and corrected her. That was when she realised that he was testing her. She, a twenty-year-old woman, was the pupil of a child of three.

They had kept the game up for two hours, with three short breaks, during which Victor would involuntarily drop off to sleep. He hadn't eaten in a week and hunger was taking its toll. The abbess had said that she would give him an injection of undiluted glucose if he continued to refuse to eat. This wasn't without its risks, Sister Noëlle blabbed, but she hadn't explained what kind of danger the injection entailed. Sister Marthe had therefore decided that she had to convince Victor to eat.

'You *have* to,' she tried again.

Victor kept his lips clamped shut.

'If you don't eat, Sister Milgitha will hurt you again.'

No reaction whatsoever, as if she were talking to a wall.

'If you don't eat, you will die.'

Even those words did not elicit any emotion on his pallid little face.

'Once you're dead, you won't be able to pray for Egon any more.'

A frown passed over Victor's face – just fleetingly, but it was enough.

'Nobody else will pray for Egon. The sisters won't do it.'

Now Victor began to pluck nervously at the bed sheet that came halfway up his chest.

'Nor will the other patients,' she went on. 'Nobody. Not Marc François. Not Angelo Venturini. Not Nico Baumgarten. Nobody.'

She saw his pupils swivel in her direction.

'No, not even I, Victor. Because if you die, I'll be praying for *you*.'

Logically, it didn't really make sense, but Sister Marthe had instinctively invoked the only reasoning young Victor Hoppe was able to understand.

If . . . then. One thing led to another, in his mind. A chain reaction.

If . . . then. That was the way his brain worked.

Sister Marthe broke off a piece of chocolate and held it to Victor's mouth. The boy parted his lips and allowed her to place the chocolate on his tongue.

'Maybe you should sit up a bit,' she said, 'or you might choke.'

He lifted his head and looked round in a daze, as if he had only just realised that he was no longer on the main ward. It did her good to see Victor starting to suck on the chocolate. Without a word he accepted another piece and stuck it into his mouth. Then another one, and another. He began wolfing down the chocolate greedily, as if he'd suddenly realised how ravenous he was.

'Now you'll probably want a little water as well,' she said as the boy started on the last piece.

He nodded and said something she did not understand.

'What did you say?' she asked. It was the first time he had actually used his voice to communicate.

'Yeah-sis-ter,' she heard again. And then, 'P-ease.'

She was stunned. None of the sisters had ever taught him to say those words. They had never taught him anything, in fact, except how to walk. Yet all the time he had been mute he must have been watching and listening, filing it all away somewhere in his head; filing it away for a day when he might have a need for it; or the desire to use it.

'Then I'll just go and get you a glass of water. I'll be back in a moment.'

She walked to the bathroom. She wished she could go straight to Sister Milgitha to tell her the news. 'Victor's eating!' she wanted to say. And, 'Victor can talk!'

But the abbess was to be woken only in cases of dire emergency. And Sister Marthe didn't think this was an emergency. It certainly wasn't. This was good news. Not only for Victor, but also for her. She had proved herself as a novice. She, Sister Marthe, Lotte Guelen in another life, had succeeded in persuading Victor to eat again, something none of the other nuns had been able to do.

When she returned with the glass of water she found Victor lying down again, reciting yet another litany.

'Victor,' she said quietly, 'Victor, I've got some water for you.'

The boy went on praying as if he hadn't heard. She started to feel uneasy. Had she dreamed the whole thing? She glanced at the crumpled chocolate-bar wrapper on the bedside table, and frowned.

'Victor? Didn't you want some water?'

She listened to his voice. He was saying the litany of Divine Providence. He was almost finished with it.

She decided to join in for the last few lines. '. . . *no matter how little we may deserve this grace, grant us, we beseech Thee, the mercy to submit to all the decrees of Your Providence over the course of our lives, so that we may come into the possession of the heavenly goods. Through Christ, our Lord. Amen.*'

She had just finished crossing herself when Victor sat up again. Not looking at her, he reached out to take the glass from her hand. 'Ac-k-you,' he said.

'You're welcome,' she replied, and let out a sigh of relief.

'Shall we pray some more for Egon?' she asked next.

Victor nodded. She noticed that he continued to avoid all eye contact. She might finally have got through to him, but he was still keeping his distance.

They recited the litany of St Joseph together, and then Sister Marthe suggested that Victor just close his eyes for a bit. It was 4 a.m. She saw that he was hesitant.

'I think Egon would want it,' she said. 'In fact I'm sure of it.'

That seemed to reassure the boy. He closed his eyes, and she began to sing to him softly.

> *'The little flowers dropped off to sleep.*
> *Their fragrance had worn them out.*
> *They nodded their little heads at me*
> *As if to say good-night.'*

She paused, then said, 'That's a Dutch song, Victor; my grandmother used to sing it to me all the time.'

But Victor, it turned out, was already sound asleep.

The next morning Sister Milgitha witnessed Victor eating his bread. Hunched over, his head lowered, he sat cross-legged on his mattress and, holding the bread up to his mouth, nibbled at it with tiny bites. His eyeballs kept swivelling from side to side, as if he were afraid someone would come and take his food away from him.

Sister Marthe was standing next to the abbess. Her eyes were shining. She'd got up that morning at the same time as the other nuns, even though it was her prerogative to sleep in, and had immediately gone to tell the abbess the great news. The abbess had been incredulous and announced she wanted to see it for herself. Just as St Thomas would not believe that Jesus Christ was risen until he had touched Christ's wounds with his own finger, Sister Marthe thought to herself.

For a minute she was worried that Victor wouldn't want to eat in Sister Milgitha's presence, but when she handed him a piece of bread, he took it from her.

'Here you are,' she said.

'An-k-you,' was his reply.

She felt as if she'd won a glorious victory.

'Reading to him has helped. The evil has been driven out,' Sister Milgitha said. 'I knew it would work. The sisters have done good work.'

Sister Marthe couldn't believe her ears. She blinked, and when she saw the abbess looking at her, she didn't know how to hide her disappointment.

'You too, Sister Marthe,' the abbess said dryly.

She felt Sister Milgitha's hand lightly touch her shoulder.

That was all.

Sister Milgitha had decided that Victor would continue to be read to for two hours a day, just in case the devil tried to return. That task was given to Sister Marthe, not because she had forged a relationship with the young patient, but because – so said the abbess – she'd be able to study her Bible texts at the same time that way.

Sister Marthe didn't really care what reason was given. She was just glad to be allowed to spend two hours a day alone with Victor. At ten in the morning and three in the afternoon she would fetch the boy from the main ward and together they would retreat to a little room at the far end of the convent, where the sound of the other patients would not disturb them. Sister Milgitha often happened to pass that way, and would peek in through the door's stained-glass window. Occasionally she would come in and, nodding to Sister Marthe to continue her reading, would stand motionless in a corner of the room, listening. Then she'd walk out again without a word.

'She's keeping an eye on me,' Sister Marthe said to Victor, not just to reassure him, but also because she was certain that was the case.

So she obediently did what was expected of her, reading aloud from the Bible for an hour without a break. Victor, hands folded on his tray, his head slightly bowed, sat across from her in a high chair without moving a muscle for the entire hour. She wasn't sure if the Bible stories interested him, or if he understood much of the lofty language – 'It doesn't matter,' Sister Milgitha had told her – but he did seem to be following attentively. So attentively, even, that when she asked him if he remembered where she had left off the last time, he promptly rattled off the last sentence word for word. Here was further proof of what an extraordinary memory he had. In her opinion, it was also a sign of intelligence, but the nuns she discussed it with said that the one had nothing to do with the other.

'He is feeble-minded, Sister Marthe, remember,' said Sister Noëlle.

'Once feeble-minded, always feeble-minded,' said Sister Charlotte.

Sister Marthe refused to believe it, but to her chagrin she couldn't come up with any further way of proving that Victor really was intelligent. Until, that is, the boy himself provided her with the proof one day.

Several weeks had passed since the first reading session, and Sister Marthe had arrived at chapter 25 of the Book of Exodus. When she asked for the end of the previous chapter, Victor said, 'An-fo-ty-days-an-fo-ty-ights-Mo-hes-wa-on-e-ount.'

'Moh-zzes, Victor,' she said. 'With a zzzzz. As in ro-ses.'

She had been working on his pronunciation without the abbess's knowledge. If he mangled a word, she'd often say it again slowly and ask him to repeat after her. He would try his utmost, but some sounds were simply beyond him. He was improving by leaps and bounds, however, although she wasn't sure if she could offer that as proof of intelligence.

'Mo-shes,' Victor repeated.

'That's better,' she said, even though it wasn't a great improvement. She did not like to push him too much, as he might give up and refuse to continue.

She opened the Bible to the page she had marked with a ribbon, the last page they'd read, and put it down on the table. Victor stretched out his hand across the table. He touched the gilt edge of the book with the tip of his finger.

'You want to hear more, don't you?' she said.

'Mo-shes,' said Victor.

He evidently hadn't understood what she'd said. Every once in a while he would react quite differently from the way she'd have expected him to, and it sometimes made her feel, however briefly, that she should just stop wasting her energy.

Reaching over, he planted his index finger on the open page. 'Mo-shes,' he said again.

'That's right, Victor,' she nodded, 'that's where we left off last time. At Moses on the mountain.'

'*Mo-o-shes!*' he said insistently, moving his finger across the page to another spot, and stiffly keeping it there.

It suddenly dawned on her: his finger was pointing at the name

'Moses'! She glanced from the boy's finger to his face. His eyes, too, were raptly focused on the word.

'Moses,' she said, trying to keep down the excitement in her voice. 'It says Moses. You're right. That's very good, Victor. And does it say Moses anywhere else?'

His finger moved to another spot. His hand was now more relaxed.

'Mo-shes,' she heard him say again. Again he pointed to the name Moses, which appeared twice more on that page.

'Good, Victor, that's excellent! And where else?'

Again he moved his finger. Again he pointed at Moses.

He can read, she thought. Thank God, he can read!

She had been a bit premature in jumping to that conclusion, she realised when she tried pointing out some other words on the page. Victor didn't get a single one. He had probably recognised the name Moses from the identical look of the characters, and the unmistakable capital M (which from where he was sitting actually looked like a W), but that was as far as it went. But still, at least he *had* worked out that every word she read corresponded with a set of characters on the page. That, in her eyes, was a remarkable achievement – he had only just turned three, after all – and to see if her guess was right, she decided to settle it beyond all doubt. Pointing to the word 'the' on the same page, she said it aloud at the same time. He then promptly pointed out every single 'the' on that page, and waited impatiently for her to teach him another word. That was when she decided. She would teach him to read, in order to convince the other nuns that he was not feeble-minded.

* * *

On 14 February 1979 – the two women were just delighted with that date, convinced that it would bring them luck – Victor Hoppe implanted a three-day-old hybridised embryo into each of their wombs. He had removed the nuclei of two eggs culled from an anonymous donor and injected the nuclei from the women's own eggs in their stead. Once the nuclei had fused, the cells had begun to divide, producing, three days later, an embryo sixteen cells strong. Even at that stage, it was still smaller than the head of a pin.

Two days before the implantation procedure, he had received a letter from the editor of *Science*. It said, among other things: 'We congratulate you on your groundbreaking research and the attendant results, which have astonished every one of us [. . .] Your findings could be the start of a new era [. . .] We would be most delighted to publish your work, were it not for a few points that still require some clarification. In the enclosed report you will find a number of questions and comments [. . .]'

Perusing the enclosed report, he'd shaken his head. He found most of the comments irrelevant. He had been asked to provide further explication of procedures and methods that, to him, seemed self-evident. What irked him most was the question pertaining to references, which they clarified by writing, '[. . .] names of colleagues who have been witness to some or all of the experiments, or of (academic) institutions under whose supervision the research was carried out.'

They don't believe me, he'd thought to himself. He felt offended. And humiliated. Disappointed, he had filed away both the letter and the report. And it was on that very day that he succeeded in hybridising the two women's eggs in a Petri dish.

The report's last question was, 'Have you managed to replicate the experiment yet?'

He had not. After the mice were born, he had concentrated solely on adapting his method to human eggs.

The penultimate question asked, 'Are the hybridised mice themselves fertile?'

He couldn't have answered that one even if he'd wanted to. All three mice had died quite suddenly – one after ten days, the other two within three weeks. He had dissected them, but found nothing out of the ordinary.

As it turned out, one of the two women did become pregnant. The other embryo had probably failed to attach itself to the uterine wall. There was great rejoicing, however, and an even greater fear of a miscarriage. On his recommendation, the women decided to rent a flat in Bonn for the duration of the pregnancy, within walking distance of his practice. A first ultrasound would be done when the foetus was six weeks old. At that stage it should be possible to detect the beating heart and the spinal column.

In the meantime he rewrote the article on his experiment with the mice for *Science*. The success of his experiment with human embryos impressed on him the need to get his first report out of the way before he could consider publishing his next.

He didn't include the fact that the mice had died. Not yet. First he wanted to have a chance to repeat the experiment with some fresh mice, so that he'd be able to answer in the affirmative the question of whether he had been able to replicate the experiment, as well as the one about the hybridised mice being fertile. But this time the experiment failed. He did succeed in starting several new embryos, but none of them developed to maturity in the womb of an adult mouse.

He had no idea where exactly the experiment had gone wrong. Or perhaps he did, but would not acknowledge it.

Luck. That was bottom line. His technique with the micropipette, in which the nucleus from a cell was removed and replaced with another, demanded the utmost dexterity. The slightest wrong movement would damage the cell membrane or the nucleus. Another problem could arise if too much cytoplasm was sucked out. Was his technique at fault, then? Surely not, since his method is the one that has now been adopted by researchers the world over. However, the equipment they use is far more refined, eliminating the danger of an accidental jostle. So Victor Hoppe was ahead of his time. And since he did not have recourse to today's more advanced equipment, a great deal of luck was needed to accomplish what he was attempting.

But to Victor, luck was not the issue. He ascribed his failures to lack of concentration. He didn't really see the point of experimenting on a new set of mice, now that he had achieved positive results with human cells. It was like being asked to go back to working on toys instead of getting on with the real thing.

In the revised article he made no mention, therefore, of repeating the experiment, or of the question of the hybridised mice's fertility. Nor did he name any references. But he did conscientiously answer all the other questions and comments, and wrote up his methods in greater detail. It was enough to convince the majority of the scientists on the *Science* editorial board. They argued that Dr Hoppe's findings were so revolutionary that they simply *had* to be published, if only to open up the topic for discussion. Those opposed to publishing the article wished to forestall such a thing. They maintained that a single successful attempt wasn't a reliable result, but an accident. In the end, however, they yielded to the majority opinion.

* * *

Sister Marthe taught Victor to read during the winter of 1948. Since she did not want to be caught doing it, she taught him only when she was on night duty. Once everyone else was asleep, she got the boy out of bed and led him to the screened-off cubicle that overlooked the general ward. She had with her a number of letters and sounds that she'd written on separate cards beforehand. With these she taught him to spell out his first words. He turned out to be a voracious student, and each lesson again reinforced her hunch that he was intelligent. She had only to give him a couple of examples with a few letters and he would swiftly spell out the series of words she gave him. His progress was so rapid that she was forced to bring him a new letter or sound to work on almost every lesson.

He was also starting, for the first time, to show some signs of having feelings. This was largely manifest in his eagerness to move the letter cards around the table. She was at times more astonished by his excitement, especially in light of all those years of passive behaviour, than by the spectacular strides he was making in learning to read. He wouldn't stop, not even for a short break. She often ended up having to force him to stop by grabbing his wrist, and even then his eyes would continue scanning the letters in search of the next combination.

She always ended the lesson after an hour to an hour and a half, because Victor had to get up for Mass the next morning with all the other patients. Clinging to her hand, he would reluctantly trundle back to his bed, where he would recite another litany for Egon Weiss as she waited beside the edge of his bed.

'Sleep tight, Victor,' she'd whisper when he had finished. 'Tomorrow we'll learn another letter.'

'W-ich-un?' he'd ask.

'The "B", as in "boy",' she would tell him. Or, 'The "C", as in "cat".'

Teaching Victor rekindled Sister Marthe's desire to become a real teacher. The brief time she spent alone with the boy was so much more precious to her than any other hour of the day. Victor made her feel that she was doing something useful, and his rapid progress persuaded her that she was cut out for the job. If she could just show Sister Milgitha how good she was at teaching, then perhaps the abbess would finally see that she was capable of more than changing nappies or emptying bedpans. Perhaps the abbess would even consent to her pursuing her novitiate at another convent, where she might study for her teaching qualifications. If the abbess gave her consent, her parents would surely have no objections either.

In order to convince the abbess, Sister Marthe had to finish coaching Victor, and so she began to step up the pace. She took over the night duty of some of the other sisters, and sometimes she made the boy practise non-stop until 3 a.m. She taught him to read not only new words but also simple verses, which she would print in her best handwriting. In the daytime she also managed to squeeze in some reading practice during the Bible sessions, making him search the Bible for recognisable words. Every once in a while he even managed to read a complete sentence.

As the intensity of the lessons grew, so did her carelessness. One day she was abruptly spoken to by Sister Milgitha.

'Sister Marthe, what have you been up to at night in the sisters' quarters?'

She felt her cheeks promptly turning red.

'Excuse me?' she asked, stalling. One of the patients must have seen her with Victor and informed the abbess; it was the only explanation.

'I know that Victor comes and sits with you at night,' the abbess said sternly. 'Might I ask why?'

She considered telling her the truth right then and there, but if she did, the abbess would in all probability want to test Victor immediately, and Marthe was sure he'd just clam up.

'Victor suffers from dreadful nightmares,' she said quickly.

The abbess gave her a quizzical look.

'If I don't take him out of the ward,' the novice added, 'he'll scream and wake everyone up.'

'What kind of nightmares?'

'I don't know, Sister Milgitha. He won't tell me.'

She thought it sounded plausible. She started feeling a little calmer, especially when she saw the look of accusation vanish from the abbess's eyes.

'I was worried,' said Sister Milgitha.

'Oh, don't be. Victor is—'

'Not about Victor, Sister Marthe. About you.'

That she had not expected. She gazed at the abbess, frowning.

'You have been looking rather pale these days.'

'I—' she tried, but the abbess immediately interrupted her.

'It might be best if you skipped night duty for a while. And reading two hours a day, I think, is also tiring you. Sister Noëlle will take over from you.'

Excuses! She felt that she was being given excuses. The abbess simply wanted to separate the two of them, Victor and her. That was the reason!

'I – I feel quite well, actually,' she said, her voice trembling. 'There's nothing wrong with me.'

'I think it would be for the best. That way you'll be able to concentrate fully on your other tasks.'

Sister Marthe felt cornered. And she knew that arguing wouldn't help. There was nothing else for it. 'Victor can read,' she said sheepishly. She had always thought that one day she would say those words with well-deserved pride, but now it felt more like a confession of guilt.

'Victor can *what?*'

'He knows how to read. I've taught him to read, Sister Milgitha.' Her voice sounded reedy.

'Sister Marthe, do you realise what you are saying? The boy isn't even four yet!' The abbess paused. Then she added emphatically, 'And he's feeble-minded.'

Sister Marthe shook her head. 'He isn't retarded. He really isn't . . .'

'That is not up to you to determine, Sister!'

The abbess stuck her nose in the air and was already turning on her heels when Sister Marthe cried out, 'Please, let Victor prove it to you!'

The abbess did not respond, but she didn't walk away either.

'Won't you let him prove it to you?' said Sister Marthe, practically pleading this time.

'Fine, let him prove it. Right now! Then we'll know, one way or another, won't we, Sister Marthe?'

'Oh, not right now. Please . . .'

It was even worse than she'd expected. Sister Milgitha didn't give him a chance. Five nuns, including the abbess, came and stood around him in a circle, the way they did when they were about to wrestle a patient into a straitjacket. Of course he was scared.

She was told to stand behind him, and was only able to catch a glimpse of his face when Sister Milgitha briefly stepped aside. The abbess pointed at her and said, 'Victor, Sister Marthe claims that you can read. Won't you show us?'

From somewhere Sister Marthe summoned up the courage to interrupt the abbess. She took the sheet of paper out of her sleeve with the verses that he had read the night before – all the way through, and without a single mistake.

'Sister Milgitha, this is—'

The abbess made a broad dismissive gesture with one hand, and took the Bible from Sister Noëlle in the other. She opened the book to a random page and shoved it under Victor's nose. 'Read something to me,' she said.

Now's your chance, Victor, Sister Marthe thought. She knew he could do it. Even if it was just one sentence.

But Victor didn't open his mouth.

And the king said, Bring me a sword. And they brought a sword before the king. And the king said, Divide the living child in two, and give half to the one, and half to the other. That was what it said. Black on white. His eyes had fallen on that passage, and it had flustered him so much that he had been unable to utter a word.

* * *

'Will we be able to tell if the child is from both of us?' one of the women asked.

The doctor had just finished carefully spreading the clear gel over her stomach and was ready to perform the first ultrasound. He shook his head. 'Not from the scan.'

'I mean later, when it's born.'

'It will definitely be a girl,' he replied. 'It has to do with the chromosomes. Women have a sex chromosome of the double-X kind, which is why—'

'But will we be able to tell any *other* way?' she broke in.

He had already gone into great detail about the baby's gender, but now he started again from the beginning, as if he wasn't even aware that he was repeating himself. She hadn't understood very much the first time, but what she did remember was that its being a girl did not necessarily mean that it had come from both of them. The uncertainty had festered, even though the doctor had shown them pictures of nuclei taken from their cells fusing together, and then the egg splitting, first into two, then into four, next into eight and finally into sixteen cells. To the woman, however, it had just looked like pictures of bubbles suspended in water. There was nothing to convince her that what she was seeing had come from both of them. Her girlfriend had told her not to be so suspicious and had asked, with a giggle, if she wanted to see her name etched on the cells or something.

'Just as you would expect in the case of a normal child,' said the doctor, switching on the monitor, 'it is likely to take after one parent more than the other. Or it may even end up looking like one of the grandparents.'

His answer still did not satisfy her. She couldn't shake the feeling that she was carrying something foreign in her belly.

She squeezed her girlfriend's hand as the icy probe came pressing down on her stomach. There would not be much to see yet on the ultrasound, according to the doctor; but she was still hoping, somehow, that it would give her more certainty.

The doctor silently moved the probe across her stomach. The screen showed white, grey and black specks, with no discernible structure. It was like the faint beam of a flashlight flickering across the rough walls of a cave.

She turned her gaze from the screen to her naked stomach. It wasn't any bigger. She hadn't felt nauseous yet either. Maybe she wasn't pregnant at all.

'There it is,' said the doctor.

'I don't see anything,' she said.

'This,' he said, pointing with the tip of his finger. 'This curved white line. That's the spinal column.'

The line was even thinner than his finger. It was the only thing not moving on the screen, like an animal frozen in a hunter's rifle sight.

'Seven point eight millimetres,' he said. 'It's 7.8 millimetres long. Now we'll try to find the heartbeat.'

Keeping the probe in the same spot, he ran his other hand across the ultrasound's keyboard. 'There it is!'

She didn't know where to look, or what she was supposed to see.

'Where?' said her friend, in a whisper, as if afraid that the sound of her voice would disturb it.

The doctor was pointing at the screen with the tip of a pen. It looked like a little light flickering on and off. A blinking black-and-white light.

'It's as if she's winking at us,' she heard her girlfriend say.

Suddenly she felt at peace. The realisation that there really was something alive inside her promptly changed her entire attitude. The questions she'd been asking herself no longer needed an answer. There was a baby growing inside her belly. That had always been her most fervent dream. And it might even turn out to be their joint biological offspring, which would be great, but suddenly didn't seem so important any more.

Her girlfriend's quiet sobs roused her from her musings. The sight of her teary eyes and her blissful smile made her suddenly aware of how selfish she'd been. She was shocked at herself, but did not let on, and took both her girlfriend's hands in hers.

The doctor, twiddling the monitor's knobs, was avoiding looking at them, as if he were afraid of being confronted with their feelings. The soft hissing sound they'd been hearing in the background was suddenly louder. Now a different sound was heard coming from the speaker: a dull, irregular tapping, like someone testing a microphone with their finger.

'The heart,' said the doctor. 'Listen, you can hear the heartbeat.'

Indeed, the sound did seem to be more or less in sync with the blinking light on the screen, but it was fading in and out.

But there was more. Every so often, they could hear a second ruffle of beats, like an echo of the first heartbeat, but it couldn't be, because the rhythm was different.

She looked at her girlfriend and tapped at her own earlobe, to draw her attention to the other sound. Her friend nodded. She had heard it too.

'We can hear another heart,' she said to the doctor. 'Is that possible?'

He did not respond. He was peering at the screen and pressed the probe more firmly against her stomach. He was frowning.

Now the double beating could be heard even more clearly, but the blinking light had vanished. The doctor moved the probe hastily around the gel on her stomach. His head seemed to be following it, in nervous circles. She glanced at her girlfriend again, who said, more insistently this time, 'Doctor, we can hear another heartbeat!'

He remained silent.

'Doctor!' she herself now cried.

Startled, he looked up.

'*Was* there another heart?' she asked.

The doctor shook his head. 'Your own heart. It was your own heart.' He said it in a neutral tone of voice, yet she still felt ridiculous. Apparently she'd been making a fuss over nothing.

The doctor put down the probe and began wiping the gel off her stomach.

'I'm sorry,' she stammered. 'I thought . . .'

'No matter,' said the doctor.

It *had* been her own heartbeat. It hadn't been a lie. But there was something else as well. Should he have told her? – that there was something strange going on? It would only make her fret, and that could lead to further complications.

There had been two foetal heartbeats – clearly audible. But he hadn't been able to see the second one. Nor had he discovered another foetus. He had studied the photos carefully afterwards, and not a single scan revealed a second spinal column.

It could be that the second foetus was completely hidden by the first one. Possible. But most unusual.

If there were two foetuses, then the egg must have split again inside the womb, and each half had begun to develop separately. In that case, it would be twins. Identical twins.

The second ultrasound, two weeks later, provided the definitive answer. The pregnant woman seemed very calm – calmer, at any rate, than the first time, when she'd expected him to be able to tell her, at this early stage, what it would look like when it was born. The only way he might have been able to tell that the child took after at least one of them would have been if one of them was known to be the carrier of some genetic defect. But neither of them was aware of any such defect. Too bad, he even caught himself thinking; it would have given him some concrete measure of proof, for all the sceptics out there.

He had decided that if the second ultrasound showed two foetuses, he would tell the women. At eight weeks they ought to be clearly visible, even if they measured no more than two centimetres each. Their minuscule size notwithstanding, the foetuses would already show definite human characteristics. Head, arms and legs would be recognisable, and the face would already have two eyes, a mouth and two nostrils. It was most unlikely at this stage that the other foetus would still be invisible.

Proceeding with the second ultrasound, he tried sneaking up, as it were, on the uterus. Instead of zooming in on it directly, he took a detour around the liver, the stomach, the pancreas, the bladder and the appendix – coming at it in a pincer movement.

The women were watching the screen with bated breath. Every now and again they looked at him questioningly. He didn't say a thing.

He soon found the first amniotic sack inside the uterus. A black spot, the size of an apple. There was no second amniotic sack, however. The foetus was lying at the bottom of the sack like a pebble.

He zoomed in on it. There *were* two foetuses, after all! He started counting: two heads, four arms, four legs. And two beating hearts.

Right next to each other. And in between, like a curled forefinger: a single spine.

The blood drained from his face.

'What's the matter, Doctor?' both women asked.

He could no longer pretend. But he still couldn't bring himself to tell them the whole truth. 'Twins. You're going to have twins.'

* * *

One day Sister Marthe did not return to the convent at La Chapelle. This occurred after she had gone home to stay with her parents for the five-day holiday novices were allowed to take once a year. At first her parents had reacted with surprise when the abbess gave them the bad news. They told her that they had seen their daughter off in person when she'd boarded the bus back to La Chapelle. It wasn't until Sister Milgitha told them they might have to report this to the police that her father confessed they had quarrelled over Lotte's decision to leave the convent.

Sister Milgitha, in turn, was greatly astonished at this piece of news. She told the parents that she hadn't had any inkling that Sister Marthe was making plans in that direction. According to the abbess, she had seemed quite content since becoming a novice almost a year ago. She'd comported herself as an able nun since then, and had she continued on the same path, she would soon have been ready to take her temporary vows. The abbess was confident that Sister Marthe would be back, and suggested that they refrain from informing anyone of her disappearance for the moment. Lotte's parents were of the same mind, since if the news got out, it would only make people talk.

Sister Marthe did come back. But not until three months had gone by. After she'd been gone one week her parents did receive a letter. It said she was doing well. And that she needed some time, to think things over.

'She is back, and she is sorry,' read the telegram that Sister Milgitha sent to Lotte Guelen's parents on 12 November 1949.

At first it was as if she'd just been gone on some errand. Her habit was immaculate, and her black cap fitted her head like a glove, or as a horseshoe fits a hoof. The gold cross on her chest had not lost any of its lustre.

In the bright light you could tell that she was more tanned than before – her face; the backs of her hands. Sister Milgitha noticed the colour of her arms and neck at once, but she didn't mention it. She just asked if Sister Marthe was sorry, and she said that she was. Then the abbess said that she was welcome, and cited the parable of the Prodigal Son.

And that was where they had left it. At the time the abbess thought it was the best thing to do. She would cross-examine the girl some other time.

Victor noticed immediately that there was something different about the way she carried herself. She now went about slightly hunched over, and her back had a slight sway to it, which made her usually flat stomach stick out a bit. There was also something defiant about her demeanour. It was quite a change from the way she used to be before her disappearance. Before, she used to walk with drooping shoulders, her eyes downcast, and her pace had been so slow that it was almost as if there'd been someone clinging to her habit, holding her back. Anyway, Sister Marthe barely spoke to him any more, ever since the time Sister Milgitha had asked Victor to read something and he'd refused. He thought she was angry with him. He'd never seen her at night after that, and she had never come for the daytime Bible-reading sessions either. And then she was gone, just like that.

But now she was back. And that very first day, she whispered to him, 'I've missed you.'

I've missed you too, he wanted to tell her, but the words wouldn't come.

Later, when she had another opportunity to speak to him, she said, 'I'll be leaving again soon. For good this time.'

He did not know what to say. The news gave him a sinking feeling, a feeling he had never had before.

The sickly smell would come, and then it would go again. Victor had been aware of it since he was young. And when the smell was there, all the sisters smelled of it at the same time. Every time one of them leaned down over him, the smell was unmistakable. It rose from their clothes, from their hands. Their breath reeked of it. And it smelled the way the cold bacon fat tasted that he sometimes had on his bread.

The sisters seemed to be aware of it too, because while the smell was on them, they had even less patience than usual. Even Sister Marthe. Every time she'd smelled that way, she'd been more impatient with him during their reading sessions. Irritable. But whenever she caught herself, she'd apologise.

'I'm sorry, Victor. It will pass.'

And it would also return, he knew.

But ever since Sister Marthe had come back, the smell was no longer on her. The other sisters had had it twice, but she hadn't. When the other sisters had the smell, being washed and tucked in by Sister Marthe was like a breath of fresh air. But the fact that she did not reek of it was just something he'd noticed; he drew no further conclusions. Therefore the thing she confided to him one day came as a complete surprise.

She was drying him off with a towel in the bathroom.

'They'll start noticing fairly soon,' she began. 'You can already see it. And feel it.' She took his hand in hers, and placed it on her stomach.

He could feel nothing but the soft fabric of her habit.

'There's a baby growing inside my belly,' she whispered.

She moved his hand up and down, and he felt the roundness of her stomach; there really was something hidden underneath her habit.

'As soon as Sister Milgitha finds out, I'll have to leave,' she went on. 'First she'll scold me until she's blue in the face; but I don't care, because once she's finished yelling at me, she won't have a choice. And my parents won't be able to send me back ever again.'

She sank to her knees and took his hands in hers. She looked him straight in the eye, but he looked away. 'If it's a boy,' she said, 'I'll call him Victor. Is that all right with you?'

It was all right with him.

As soon as Sister Milgitha began to suspect something, she started checking Sister Marthe's underwear for bloodstains each washing day. She took out a calendar and calculated when it might have happened and how far along she might be. She began keeping a close eye on the novice, taking notice of how often Sister Marthe stroked a hand over her slightly swollen belly.

'Do you have a stomach ache?' she once asked her, waiting to see her reaction.

But Sister Marthe was not flustered. She shook her head innocently, then shot the abbess an indignant look, as if wondering what had given her that idea.

When five weeks had gone by and Sister Milgitha had not discovered any evidence of blood in her underwear, she decided to have Sister Marthe examined. Since she was not versed in that sort of thing herself, she approached Dr Hoppe one day when he came to visit his son. She occasionally consulted him on medical matters when her expertise or that of the other sisters wasn't up to scratch, but this time she was vaguely embarrassed. She did not let on what she was really after, but simply asked him to give his medical opinion on a sister who had been complaining of a stomach ache for several weeks.

She took him to the room where Sister Marthe was engaged in private Bible study. On the way, he asked her about his son.

'No improvement,' said Sister Milgitha, 'alas.'

She heard him sigh.

'Do you think he's happy?' he asked.

'I am sure that he is, Doctor.'

'I hope so, Sister. I do hope so, for his sake.'

When the abbess and the doctor entered the room, Sister Marthe, looking up from the Bible on the table before her, immediately pushed her chair back, rose to her feet and nodded politely.

Sister Milgitha had expected that the novice would refuse to be examined, or at least that she would first ask questions, but to her surprise the girl said nothing. In fact she lay down on the bed when Dr Hoppe invited her to do so with a gallant flourish. Even when he asked her to pull up her habit, she did so without hesitation. The abbess, standing in a corner of the room, took a furtive peek at the novice's bare stomach. It was unmistakably swollen.

The doctor placed his right hand on the stomach. 'Tell me where it hurts,' he said.

He moved his hands all over her stomach, pressing the tips of his fingers into her flesh. 'Does that hurt?' he asked several times.

She shook her head.

Now he began palpating the pelvic area. From time to time he would press his thumb deep into her flesh. It did not escape the abbess's notice that he frowned as he did so.

'May I please have the stethoscope?' he said.

She handed him the stethoscope.

'Could you hold your breath for a few seconds?' the doctor asked the young nun.

The abbess couldn't help holding her breath too. We'll know soon enough, she thought.

The doctor listened intently, frowned again, moved the stethoscope and listened. Now and then his gaze would travel to the novice's face, but she kept her eyes fixed on the ceiling. Finally, exhaling deeply, he lifted the stethoscope off her belly. He asked the abbess, his face betraying nothing, 'Would you be so kind as to let us have a moment in private?'

She caught his eye, saw that he meant it, and left the room.

Sister Marthe, relieved, pulled her habit back down and perched on the edge of the bed.

The doctor had taken a seat at the table. He picked up the Bible and started turning it round and round in his hands nervously. 'I want you to know, before I tell the abbess,' he began. 'You may need a little time to digest this. I myself don't quite understand how—'

'I already know, Doctor,' she broke in. She didn't want to make it difficult for him. 'The stomach aches were a fabrication of Sister Milgitha's. If I felt anything, it was the baby kicking. He's rather . . . lively.'

The doctor moved his head up and down and pursed his lips, causing the scar over the right side of his mouth to pucker. 'How long has it been? Do you know approximately?' he asked.

'Four months.'

'Yes, just as I thought. Otherwise you wouldn't have been able to feel the baby kicking.' He glanced at the Bible and looked at her again. 'How old are you?'

'Twenty.'

He nodded.

'And a half,' she added.

'And you wish to keep the child?'

This time it was she who nodded. 'Yes, very much, Doctor.'

'You understand that you will in all likelihood have to leave the convent? I expect that Sister Milgitha will not allow you to stay.'

'I do know that. Could I ask you to stick around for a short while after informing her? I'm not sure how she'll . . .'

He nodded sympathetically.

'I'll give her the news in your presence. Is that what you want?'

'Yes, please, Doctor. Thank you.'

He placed the Bible back on the table, ran his fingers over the cover and then stood up.

'Dr Hoppe?'

He turned towards her.

'You're Victor's father, aren't you? Victor Hoppe? You . . . I've seen you sitting with him a few times.'

'That's right. Victor's father – yes, I am.' Avoiding her gaze, he fixed his eyes on a spot somewhere above her head.

'Doctor . . .' She had a moment's hesitation. 'Doctor, Victor is not feeble-minded. He really isn't at all.'

The abbess asked him if he would help get rid of the child, if that was what Sister Marthe's parents wished. Her request did not register straight away, because he was busy struggling with some questions of his own. Was it true, what Sister Marthe had told him? – that Victor could speak? that Victor knew how to read?

On the way to the abbess's office, striding through the convent's hollow corridors, he tried to decide whether the girl had spoken the truth. The conclusion he came to was that she had no reason to lie, especially now that she was about to be expelled. He had asked her how it was that he had never noticed any of this, and she'd explained that it was difficult to get through to Victor – that it was a matter of trust. That had felt like a dagger to his heart.

When the abbess repeated the request, and her words finally sank in, he objected immediately. 'She wants to keep the child. Whatever the consequences.'

'She is too young to make that decision herself.'

'She is twenty years old!' he shouted, louder than he'd intended.

'She is still a novice, Doctor. Her parents aspire to her becoming a fully fledged nun. That is why I am asking you again: can you help us?'

He shook his head, slowly at first, then more and more vehemently. At the same time he decided that he would not mention what Sister Marthe had told him about his son.

Trust. The word came into his head again. The abbess had never managed to win Victor's trust; nor had he. That was the conclusion he arrived at as he stared at her. And listened to her. That was why Victor had never spoken. And because he hadn't spoken, he had been classified as feeble-minded. Just because of that.

He pushed his chair back and stood up, still shaking his head. He wanted to rail at the abbess, to vent his intensifying anger, but he couldn't, because his rage was aimed, above all, at himself. How in God's name could he have committed such a great wrong, and done this to his son?

The grey woman and her helper were from Aachen. They were instructed not to ask any questions and just get on with the job. That was the arrangement Sister Milgitha had made with them. They were paid more money for their silence than for the task they had been assigned.

Lotte Guelen, quite unaware, was sitting in her cell in her underwear. A few minutes earlier, the abbess had ordered her to take off her habit and hand it over. It had felt as if she were taking off a heavy yoke. It's finally over, she'd thought to herself. Sister Marthe was dead and Lotte Guelen had been resurrected in her place. Sister Milgitha had left the room without saying a word. Lotte expected the abbess had gone to fetch her street clothes and asked herself if they'd still fit.

When the abbess returned, she wasn't alone. She was with two other women, one of whom was grey from top to toe. The apron. The eyes. The hair. And the face. As if she had smeared her skin with ashes beforehand.

Lotte caught sight of the grey woman, and she knew. She screamed. But Sister Milgitha immediately clamped a hand over her mouth. With the other hand she gave Lotte's chest a push, so that she landed flat on her back. The two women then tied her to the bed with a leather strap. She tried to resist, but it was three against one. Her wrists were tied down too. The grey woman yanked her legs apart and the other woman tied her ankles to the sides of the bed. Then they propped a pile of plump pillows under her bottom, so that her pelvis was pushed upwards. Her knickers were cut away with a pair of scissors. She shut her eyes. She didn't see the long needle the grey woman took out of her bag.

'Do it quickly,' Sister Milgitha had instructed the grey woman at the outset.

As the needle was inserted, Lotte bit into the towel covering her mouth to take the edge off the pain. The abbess's fingernails dug deep into her right cheek.

The grey woman held apart the novice's labia with one hand, and with her other hand she prodded the needle about. Luck was on her side. It took only a couple of pokes to hit the mark. She nodded at her assistant, who held out the towel to receive the bundle.

Sister Milgitha caught a fleeting glimpse of the foetus, which was much larger than she'd expected. But what startled her even more was that it already looked so *human*.

When she saw the grey woman gazing at her, she quickly looked away. 'Take it and bury it somewhere,' she said.

At the end of that day Lotte came to see Victor. She was wearing her habit again and whispered something in his ear. Then she pressed her lips to the top of his head and said a few more words. She left without looking back.

'It's gone, Victor. The baby's gone. I'm sorry.'

That was the first thing she'd said. And then, after the kiss, she'd said, 'God giveth and God taketh away, Victor. But not always. There are times when it's up to us. Remember that always.'

Those were the last words he ever heard her say. The next morning, his father took him home.

The date was 23 January 1950.

* * *

He had two options: either give two lives, or take two lives away. That was the dilemma Victor Hoppe was wrestling with during the month of April 1979, as congratulations from his fellow researchers, who had read his article in *Science*, came pouring in by post and telegram.

Either he could allow the foetuses to develop, or he could abort the pregnancy. That was something he had never done before. He had never taken a life. That was why he was so desperately torn. From the moment he had started on his doctoral research, his mission had always been to create life. That had always been the challenge. That he might make the ultimate decision about life. Not about death.

The envelope with the University of Aachen logo caught his notice. The card inside was from a professor he did not know, a certain Rex Cremer, dean of the Faculty of Biomedical Studies. The message was also one of congratulations, but it was different from the others. There was one line that had caught his eye:

You have certainly beaten God at his own game.

Rex Cremer had meant it as a joke. The divine comparison was supposed to be a way of snagging Dr Hoppe's attention. He'd assumed that his colleague would understand he was being ironic. Not for a minute did he think that he might take it any other way.

The telephone conversation he had with him on 15 April 1979, caused him to rethink that assumption.

'Dr Hoppe, this is Rex Cremer from the University of Aachen.' Here he paused deliberately, to give the doctor time to recognise the name.

His reaction, however, was instantaneous. 'Dr Cremer, thank you for your card.'

He was pleasantly surprised. 'You're welcome. You deserve it.'

'But it isn't really true,' he heard the doctor say, almost as a reproach.

'What isn't really true?'

'What you wrote. That I've beaten God at his own game.'

'Oh, that? It was only—'

'God would never have done it.'

Rex was confused. It was as if he had dialled the wrong number, but the person on the other end of the line wasn't aware of it.

'I don't understand what you mean.'

'Just that your comparison does not apply here. You have arrived at the wrong conclusion.' The doctor was speaking in a rather patronising tone, which made the dean feel as if he were a student again. A mediocre student, at that. Victor was often to make him feel that way.

'God would never have attempted such a thing,' Dr Hoppe continued in the same tone of voice, 'He would never have tried to create offspring from two female or two male animals. Therefore I have not beaten Him at his own game.'

There wasn't a shred of irony in his voice, and that, too, irritated Cremer. 'I hadn't really thought of it that way,' he said, careful not to betray his annoyance. 'But the reason I was calling—'

'Of course, we should not *over*estimate Him, either,' Dr Hoppe brusquely interrupted.

'No, of course not,' Cremer responded diplomatically, wondering if the doctor was drunk.

'Because if we overestimated Him, we'd be underestimating ourselves,' Dr Hoppe went on, imperturbable. 'That is the mistake a great many researchers tend to make. They impose limits on themselves. They decide before they even start what can and what can't be done. And if something is deemed impossible, they simply accept it as such. But sometimes that which appears to be impossible is merely difficult. It's just a matter of persevering, isn't it?'

'And that, happily, is what you have done.' The dean had finally found an opening that let him get to the point he had wanted to make from the outset. 'That, among other things, is why I would like to invite you to come and talk to us. The university would like to offer you a research chair, for an indefinite period. We would very much like you to continue your research under our roof, in the Embryology Department, where you earned your doctorate.'

There was silence at other end of the line.

'Your former professors still sing your praises. They would very much like to see you return. We also have several excellent new biologists on our staff, and I'm sure you will find some splendid collaborators among them.'

'I prefer to work alone,' was the curt answer.

Cremer thought for a moment. 'That could certainly be taken into consideration. The most important thing is that you agree to come and work for us. Could we make a date to meet?'

'Now is not a good time. Please give me a while to think it over. I'll give you a ring later in the week. Is that acceptable?'

'That's fine. Let me give you my direct line.' Rex repeated his phone number twice, and ended the conversation by assuring Victor that he would look forward to his call, even though he wasn't entirely certain of that.

She thought she was having a chorionic-villi test. At least, that was what Dr Hoppe had told her. The test would allow him to see if the twins in her stomach had Down's syndrome. If they were mongoloid. She'd never heard of this test before, but he told her it was relatively new.

The doctor had carefully explained that he would pass some narrow tongs through the vagina and cervix to take a sample of placental tissue. She might feel a little pain, but he would mitigate that by administering a topical anaesthetic. By examining the tissue sample's chromosomes he would be able to determine whether both children were healthy. Or not.

'And if they aren't . . . ?'

'In that case we'll see,' the doctor had replied, and quickly changed the subject. He talked about the risks associated with the test. There was a small chance of a miscarriage. Later on. A very small chance. Nothing to worry about.

The woman remembered all this as she lay down on the examination table, slipping her ankles into the stirrups. At the doctor's request, her friend had stayed in the waiting room. It wouldn't take long, he had reassured her. They would have preferred to be together during the procedure, but neither had the nerve to protest.

'You'll just feel a little pinch,' she heard him say.

She could not see him. Her stomach and nether parts were hidden by a green sheet; the doctor was parked on a stool on the other side.

The sting sent a mild shock through her entire body. When it eased, she gave a sigh of relief. Then, suddenly, she felt something cold on her stomach. The gel for the ultrasound, she realised. She couldn't see the ultrasound's screen either. But she didn't mind, because she didn't really want to see what was happening inside her. The sounds she heard were bad enough: the buzzing and clicking of the ultrasound, the clatter of the doctor rummaging through a drawer of metal instruments, the creaking of his stool, his breath.

Now he was moving the probe across her belly. When he stopped at a certain spot and held it there, she wanted to ask him if he could see them – the twins. And if they were OK. But before she could say anything, he said, 'Please hold your breath for a few seconds. It won't take long.'

She took in a few gulps of air and clamped her lips shut. Notwithstanding the local anaesthetic, she could feel something cold entering her. She balled her fists and dug her nails deep into the palms of her hands.

He began moving the probe over her stomach again, in small, circular motions. His breathing was agitated. He was inhaling and exhaling through his mouth, which made it sound as if he were panting after some exertion. Then his hand stopped again.

It's going to happen now, she thought, and clenched her jaw.

Nothing did happen, however. Perhaps she simply hadn't felt it, she thought at first. But a few seconds later, when she finally had to gasp for air, it occurred to her that she couldn't even hear him panting any more. She waited a few seconds more, not wanting to startle him, and then asked hoarsely, 'Doctor, is something wrong?'

There was no response.

'Doctor?'

Then suddenly everything happened at once. She heard a stool creak, and at the same time the probe was lifted from her stomach and the cold instrument was pulled out of her. There was some clattering of dishes, and then she saw the doctor rush out of the room.

He couldn't do it. He had been *this* close. But just as he'd been about to cut the conjoined foetuses apart, in order to pull them out of the womb piece by piece, something had stopped him – as if someone had grabbed his wrist and yanked his arm away.

Then he had stormed out, mortified, leaving the woman lying there in that uncomfortable position. He darted into the bathroom, peeled off his latex gloves and washed his hands for a long time. He stared into the mirror. Because he had not taken the time to shave all week, his jaw sported a sparse beard and he was suddenly struck by how much he looked like his father.

He went on staring at himself in the mirror. At the red hair. At the nose. At the scar on his upper lip.

And it was then, in that very instant, that the idea must have sprung into his mind. It wasn't more than a flicker, but it was enough to spark the fire that would shortly turn into a blaze.

When he finally returned to the woman's side, he had no idea how long he had left her lying there. She had stayed in the exact same position, as if she'd been afraid that if she stirred, even slightly, it might somehow harm the twins.

As soon as he walked in, she asked him what was going on. He answered that he had felt faint. It wasn't even a lie.

Then she asked him if everything was still all right. And if the procedure had worked. He lied twice in reply.

Helping her off the table, he told her to expect the results in a week. He had already told himself that at that point he would tell her the truth about what was growing inside her. Not about what he had been on the point of doing. That didn't matter any more. He was already beyond that, in his mind. Way beyond that.

The women returned three days later, visibly shaken, and after another ultrasound there was nothing he could do but confirm their worst fears. One of them burst into tears, and the whole story came pouring out in one breathless rush, to make the doctor understand that there was nothing they could have done to prevent it.

It had started with a bad stomach ache, and she had sat on the toilet and started straining, she said. She had not had a bowel movement in days and her intestines had suddenly just let go, in one lengthy, drawn-out convulsion. There had been a stench she had never smelled before, which had made her gag, and before wiping herself she had flushed the toilet, to make sure whatever had been inside her was expelled down the drain as quickly as possible.

Did he understand?

Afterwards she had wiped herself and flushed the toilet a second time, still without looking, her eyes clenched shut, because she was so disgusted at herself. Then she'd stood up, and the pain in her belly had been as bad as before, and that was why she thought her bowels weren't quite empty yet, and so she had pushed again, because she thought the pain would go away if she just managed to . . .

Did the doctor understand?

And she had had another bowel movement and, again, the overpowering stench, and in the end, in the end, it was possible she might have felt something else leaving her body, out of another orifice, but then, everything down there hurt so much that she really didn't know *what* was coming out of *where*, and so she had flushed it all down the drain, because she never thought that there could have been . . .

'Do you understand what I'm telling you, Doctor ?'

Again she had cleaned herself with reams of toilet paper, and she had flushed all the paper in several batches too, with her head turned away, still revolted at herself, and then she had stood up to pull up her pants and had noticed that the pain was gone, and it was only then, *only then* that she'd seen the blood pouring down the insides of her thighs, and had looked down at the toilet bowl where everything that had come out of her with such force had now vanished.

Did he . . . ?

He *did* understand, he assured her.

Who had been deceived, when all was said and done?

Victor did not ask himself that question. It was no longer of any importance to him. The women had scarcely left his office when he took the first step to set his next plan in motion. He picked up the phone and dialled Rex Cremer's number.

'Dr Cremer, this is Victor Hoppe. I promised I would call you back.'

'I am happy you called, Dr Hoppe.'

'Do you remember that we talked about God, the last time? You said that I had beaten God at his own game?'

'Certainly I remember.'

'Well, I have changed my mind.'

'So you think you have?'

'I mean that I would like to try something else.'

'Something else than what?'

'Than creating offspring of exclusively female or exclusively male parentage. In order to truly beat God at his own game, one has to break entirely new ground.'

'How do you mean?'

'God created man in his likeness.'

'Right, and from Adam's rib he created woman . . .'

'Quite so. It is eminently possible to create a woman using a man's rib. Perfectly possible. That doesn't strike me as such a difficult thing to do. If you took a bone cell, sucked out its nucleus and replaced it with the nucleus of—'

'Dr Hoppe, I was only joking. Where are you headed with this?'

'. . .'

'Dr Hoppe?'

'Cloning.'

'Cloning?'

'Cloning. Creating an identical genetic copy of—'

'I know what is meant by "cloning", but what would you want to clone?'

'Mice. For example.'

'That's impossible. It's impossible to clone mammals, from a biological standpoint.'

'It's just a question of technique. It *has* to be possible, with the right equipment. It ought to be even simpler, in principle, than my last experiment.'

'I don't know about this. You are springing something on me I wasn't prepared for. We'll have to discuss this another time. Let's set a date, shall we? Then—'

'Tomorrow. I'll come by tomorrow.'

'As you like. Ten o'clock? Is that convenient?'

'Ten o'clock.'

* * *

One day Johanna Hoppe would not get out of bed. She refused to eat and left her bed only to go to the toilet. She refused to get up the next day too, and the ones after that. Her husband, who did make some attempt to talk her out of it but was ordered to leave her alone every time he tried, finally gave up, and two friends who stopped by on the third day had also left tut-tutting. At first there were frequent bouts of weeping, but these gradually petered out as the light in her eyes began to dim. There was just one final flicker of animation: a temper tantrum of sorts, when she just laid into herself, pummelling her head with her fists. After that came a permanent collapse. All trace of emotion vanished from her face, and nothing moved except the beating of her heart.

It didn't really surprise anybody in Wolfheim.

'She's never got over it.'

'The child's lunacy has been working its way back into her own blood.'

'After the kid was born, she never allowed Dr Hoppe to touch her again.'

'She bathed five times a day.'

'The light was never turned off at night.'

'The devil takes his own.'

'Let us pray.'

Nor did it surprise anyone that the doctor had taken his wife's care upon himself, instead of putting her in a nursing home. After all, he was the one best qualified to assess her condition, best equipped to dispense medication and to give her a blood transfusion if necessary.

'And it's what's best for her,' he said over and over again, just as he'd always claimed that it was best for his son to be with the Clares.

Many of the villagers were surprised, therefore, to find out one day that the doctor had brought the child home.

'Surely he's got enough on his hands, taking care of his wife?'

'*She*'d never have stood for it, anyway.'

He made no effort to keep his son hidden from the villagers, however. He took the boy along when he went shopping, had him wait in the car when he made house calls and occasionally took him for a walk in the village, nodding at everyone as if nothing were amiss.

Of course everyone was immediately struck by the uncanny resemblance between father and son – the hair, the mouth, the eyes – so that people had to wonder if the boy had inherited any traits at all from his mother. But what struck the villagers even more than the resemblance was that there was something so obviously wrong with the boy.

'He doesn't speak.'

'He doesn't laugh.'

'He's a simpleton.'

Nor did most people understand why the doctor had taken him out of the mental institution, especially after Father Kaisergruber, who had just been appointed pastor of Wolfheim that year, let slip that there was still evil in the boy. He understood that to be the case from talking to the abbess of the cloister. Whenever anyone discreetly questioned the doctor about it, however, the answer was always the same: 'It was a mistake. Victor did not belong there.'

The villagers would nod sympathetically to his face, but no one really believed him. And the more frequently the boy was seen in public, the more people became convinced that there was definitely something about the boy that was more evil than good.

Karl Hoppe was aware that people were talking and would have liked to show them that there was nothing wrong with his son, but unfortunately there wasn't much to show. Not only did Victor not speak a word; he seldom showed any emotion. Nevertheless, he took the boy with him everywhere he went, in the hope that contact with normal folks would make Victor open up. What it really came down to was that Victor would have to be reborn. That was how he pictured it.

Of the reading ability Sister Marthe had told him about there was still no sign. Victor would leaf through the picture books his father gave him, but that was all. When asked a question, the boy would just shrug his shoulders or else not react at all.

Karl remained convinced that one day he would see a change. It's a matter of trust, he kept repeating to himself. That was what Sister

Marthe had urged him to remember. After all, how could he expect the boy to forgive him straight away, after what he had done to him for almost five years? That was another reason why he persisted in talking to his son as if nothing were wrong. As he had also been talking to his wife, ever since her descent into a permanent catatonic state. Even though he never got any response, in the past few months he had told her more than he'd ever done in all the preceding years.

But he did not tell her that he had brought Victor home. He didn't lie about it; he simply didn't volunteer the information, afraid that, if she knew, his wife would curse him for all eternity. And that was the reason, the only reason, that it suited him if Victor's voice was never heard.

He had had a hopeful sign one day. He had left Victor in his wife's former sewing room while he saw patients. He'd parked him in front of the half-finished jigsaw puzzle she had begun a few days before taking to her bed for good.

'Why don't you finish this puzzle?' he had said to Victor, showing him what to do by fitting a couple of jigsaw pieces together.

He didn't expect much, because it was a two-thousand-piece puzzle, a picture of the Tower of Babel. But it was the only thing he currently had in the house to stimulate his son's mind, and at La Chapelle he had occasionally seen the patients working on puzzles. According to Sister Milgitha, it could be quite therapeutic in imparting some structure to their addled brains. When Johanna had suddenly come home with this puzzle some six months earlier, it had surprised him. Was she reverting to a second childhood, or was it her way of trying to revive the lost child inside her? One of his colleagues had suggested that it was Johanna's way of filling up some emptiness, piece by piece. It still didn't seem very likely to him, but he did come to regard the puzzles as good therapy, because they had a calming effect on his wife. Perhaps *too* calming, as it later turned out.

When the surgery hour was over, he returned to the sewing room and stood watching his son from the doorway. He saw how the boy was intently sorting through the loose pieces, choosing one and then slotting it confidently into place without trying it out first to see if it fitted. Walking up to the table, he saw to his amazement that Victor had already finished more than three-quarters of the puzzle.

So he isn't retarded after all, he told himself excitedly.

But he was forced to revise his opinion a little while later. He had been observing his son doggedly at work on the puzzle for about fifteen minutes. Doggedly – that was what struck him the most. There was something mechanical about Victor's actions. The boy's eyes skimmed the pieces; he pounced on one, then popped it into place. And again. The same way of searching, the same way of choosing, the same way of slotting it into place. And then again. Searching, choosing, slotting into place. And again. But Victor's face remained impassive and blank the entire time.

Compulsive behaviour. That was the thought that popped into Dr Hoppe's mind, and his fears were confirmed when he snatched a puzzle piece out of Victor's hand. Victor didn't even attempt to resist. There was no sign of annoyance. No puzzlement or anger.

Come on, *say* something! Show some reaction, for God's sake! he wanted to yell at the boy, but he kept a lid on his anger. Shaking his head, he stared at his son, who seemed to have frozen in mid-action, his hand hovering in the air, his thumb and forefinger pinched together as if still clutching the puzzle piece. He waited in that rigid attitude until his father finally gave the piece back to him. The boy slotted it into the exact spot where it was supposed to go, then doggedly moved on to the next piece.

Compulsive. The word stuck in the doctor's mind, and continued to haunt him. He couldn't help thinking of the place from which he had rescued Victor.

It had come to his attention that, ever since he'd brought his son home, people had begun to shun his house. Father Kaisergruber was the first one he noticed keeping his distance, for in the past the priest used to stop by practically every week to read to Johanna from the Bible. The doctor had taken over this task, but only because he thought that was what his wife would have wanted. Personally, he would never have started on the Bible readings in the first place, because he was far less religious than his wife. Less fanatical, he sometimes thought to himself, although he never actually said so aloud.

It was beginning to dawn on him that his patients had also started staying away. The waiting room often used to be quite crowded, but since Victor's return this was no longer the case. Week by week, the number of patients dwindled, until one day not a single person showed up.

He was reminded of his first months in Wolfheim, some ten years ago. A recently qualified physician, he and his wife had arrived from the nearby village of Plombières, which was already served by two GPs. And even though Wolfheim had had to make do without a doctor for years, to begin with the villagers would have nothing to do with his practice. There was great distrust of outsiders, and it had taken months before he and his wife were accepted by the community. It never occurred to him that his physical appearance might have had something do with the initial scarcity of patients, but he did realise that the villagers' change of heart had had more to do with Johanna's piety and her selfless devotion to the Church than his own medical skills.

He didn't know how to turn the tide this time, without his wife's help. Actually, he *did* know – it was quite simple, really – but he was absolutely determined not to send Victor back to the asylum. He would just have to make it clear to the villagers, as well as to Father Kaisergruber, that there was nothing evil or stupid about Victor; that the harm and the stupidity lay largely in the superstitions they clung to. In his role as physician he had often had to contend with these, but this time it would be quite a different sort of struggle – a more difficult struggle. He was convinced of it.

In spite of his father's best efforts, Victor was often led to think of the institution. For there were so many things in his new house to remind him of the place: the cross hanging on the wall in every room, the font of holy water in the front hall, the statuette of St Mary and dried palm fronds on the mantel, and the framed prints everywhere cautioning *God is watching you* and *Here people never swear*. The smells coming from the surgery and waiting room also brought back memories. One time it might be the smell of ether or disinfectant; another, the odour of sweat and unwashed bodies.

But what transported him back to the convent more than anything else was the words he heard every night when he was in bed. In the room next door, his father was reading from the Bible. The words were difficult to make out, but since he knew them anyway, it wasn't hard to follow. It often made him think of Sister Marthe.

There was a patient in the room next to his. That was what his father had told him. His father had also said he wasn't allowed in there – that it was forbidden. But he didn't understand. The only rooms that were forbidden were the sisters' rooms. That was what he'd been taught. Patients were not allowed in the nuns' rooms, but patients were allowed to visit each other. That had always been allowed.

And so he'd crept into the patient's room anyway. Once. And another time. And then many times. But only when he heard his father sleeping. His father made this grunting sound when he slept, the same kind of sound the other patients used to make.

The first time he'd gone to see this patient he had noticed, from a distance, that her hands were folded in prayer and there was a rosary looped around her hands: he recognised it; it was the same kind of rosary all the sisters had. So maybe the patient was a sister after all, and that was why he wasn't supposed to go into her room.

He crept a little closer and in the light from the candle that was always lit he stared at her face. The face looked like a sister's face, but without the cap and veil. So then she must be a patient after all – a quiet patient. Not at all like Egon Weiss; more like Dieter Lebert. That one was always flat on his back, with only his chest moving, up and down. Up and down. Lebert is a vegetable, Marc François had once told him, but Victor didn't believe him.

On his visits to the patient next door he would go and sit by the bed and watch the chest going up and down. Sometimes he'd read the Bible that was on the bedside table. He usually stayed there for as long as he heard the sound of his father sleeping. When the grunting stopped, he'd sneak back to his own room.

But then, suddenly, the patient was dead. He could tell immediately, because the chest stopped going up and down. He could tell by the smell, too. He knew that smell. It smelled as if someone had pooped in their pants. And another smell, too, that he couldn't place.

When someone died, you had to pray. That was what you were supposed to do. Pray for the soul of the deceased to find peace, the sisters used to say. And so he folded his hands together and began reciting the litany of the Holy Ghost. Out loud. Because the sisters always had to be able to hear the patients praying.

Karl Hoppe's first thought was that he was dreaming. Then he thought someone had broken into his house. But as soon as he realised that it was a child's voice, he remembered Victor, and leaped out of bed.

He raced to his son's room, but slowed down when he reached the door, so that he wouldn't alarm the boy.

'*Spirit of mercy and compassion. Spirit, who in our weakness giveth us succour and affirmest that we are God's children . . .*'

He wasn't listening to what was being said, but to the way it was being said. He heard nasal sounds. He also noted that the 'p' and the 'b' were barely pronounced. A speech impediment. It *had* to be Victor's voice; it could not be otherwise. He could speak! The joy of that realisation, however, was promptly checked by the realisation that the voice was coming not from Victor's bedroom but from Johanna's.

'. . . *Who leads us on the right path. Highest spirit, who enlivenst and fortifiest* . . .'

A shudder ran up his spine. He reached the bedroom in two strides and there he saw his son sitting at his wife's bedside. Victor's ginger hair glinted in the candlelight as he sat with his head bowed and his hands folded, droning his monotone utterances over Johanna.

She mustn't find out, Karl Hoppe thought, darting forward in a panic. Grabbing his son just above the elbow, he dragged him roughly off the chair. The boy let out a scream, and in the space of that scream the doctor glanced at his wife. And in that split second he knew, from the colour of her face and the way her mouth hung open, that she was dead. He let go of his son, pressed his index and middle finger to his wife's carotid artery, felt that her body had gone cold and her heart had stopped and, although he knew it was pointless, started calling out her name over and over again.

Then he looked at his son, who had been silent for three months and who had just been talking. Then he glanced at his wife, who was dead. Talking, dying – all of a sudden he was convinced there must be some connection there, between his son's talking and his wife's dying – that the one thing had led to the other. And even though he had never really believed the story about his son having the devil in him, in that instant, with the candlelight casting long shadows on the walls, he did believe it. And that recognition, that painful recognition, made something inside him snap. It was as if a handle had been twisted, causing all the fury and all the grief and all the disappointment that had been locked away for years to come pelting out, not via his mouth, in the form of curses, nor via his eyes, in the form of tears, but through his right hand, which suddenly shot forward and, with a loud smack, collided with his son's cheek.

Karl Hoppe had always told himself that he would never do what he had just done. Ever since his teenage years, when it had first occurred to him that he might one day have children of his own, he had decided never to do to his own children what his father had done to him. But the slap he had given Victor made him recognise with some consternation the trait he had always deplored in his father: a violent nature.

The impulse had simply been too strong to resist. If anyone had the devil in him, it was he, Karl Hoppe, when he slapped Victor. He really regretted doing it, but he couldn't take it back. So then what was the point of being sorry? When his own father had shown remorse while he was still smarting from the sting of his blows, he had never set much store by it. For he had known that no matter how sorry his father was right then, he would surely give him another beating some day.

No, he would rather think of a way to make up for it. What would it take for Victor to forgive him? How would he ever be able to win his trust now?

The new jigsaw puzzles seemed like a good place to start. In between receiving condolence calls – the villagers seemed to have been reminded all of a sudden that he lived there – the doctor paid a visit to the toy shop on Galmeistrasse, and bought the three puzzles they had in stock. He'd been afraid Victor might refuse anything he offered now, but the boy tore open the packages without hesitation, and immediately began working on one of the puzzles in the sewing room, isolated from the stream of visitors.

By the end of the day he had completed all three. The doctor had actually been hoping that those three puzzles would keep his son occupied right up to the funeral. But after finishing a puzzle Victor refused to break it up and start over again.

Karl Hoppe therefore had to make a decision. 'Here,' he said, 'I think it's what *she* would have wanted.'

By 'she' he meant his wife, but as he handed the Bible over to Victor, he was also thinking of Sister Marthe. She had told him, during their brief conversation in the convent, that Victor enjoyed reading from the Bible. But he had wanted his son to forget his years in the asylum as quickly as possible, and so he had deliberately kept the book from him. The fact that his son had prayed for Johanna – a realisation that occurred to him only some time later – made him reconsider that decision. Perhaps this was the way to win his trust. He was doing it not just for Victor, but also for his wife, because he was certain that she would have wanted it, as he had already said to Victor. And finally – although he would not admit this to himself – he was doing it for his own sake; for his own peace of mind. It afforded him some measure of relief, like finally being in a position to pay off old debts.

He had no great expectations and was most surprised when, as soon as the Bible was in his hands, Victor immediately began to read. Even though he wasn't reading aloud, the doctor was sure that that was what he was doing. He could tell from the way Victor was moving his finger across the page below the words.

Verse 1. Verse 2. Verse 3. Verse 4. Verse 5.

'Why don't you read it out loud, Victor?' he asked, wondering if he wasn't expecting too much.

But Victor did read out loud. '*And the evening and the morning were the first day*.'

The doctor was amazed. You see, he thought, I always knew it.

'Go on, go on, Victor.'

'*And God said: Let there be a firmament in the midst of the waters, and let it divide the waters from the waters . . .*'

He was only half-listening, wondering what his wife would have thought of the scene.

He tried once more to concentrate on what Victor was saying.

'*And God said: Let the waters under the heaven be gab-dered together unto one—*'

'*Gathered* together,' he corrected him automatically, but immediately regretted it, because with a shock he was again forced to recognise his father's ways in his own behaviour. No, even worse, it was as if he were hearing his father's voice.

'You have to learn from your mistakes,' his father used to tell him constantly, which meant that the only thing his father ever noticed was the mistakes. His father had never praised him for the things he'd done right, because that was what was 'expected of him'. Those, too, were his father's exact words.

'Gaddered,' said Victor.

'Gathered, Victor, *gath*-ered,' he said, even though he had meant to say it was just fine like that.

A few days after Johanna's funeral, Karl Hoppe paid a visit to Father Kaisergruber. The doctor had come to settle up what he owed him for the funeral Mass, and he asked him point-blank just before he left, 'Do you still believe that my son should be in an institution?'

'I do think that would be for the best,' was his honest answer.

'But he is not retarded.'

That's not the only reason, the priest thought.

'I can prove he isn't retarded,' the doctor went on. '*Victor* can prove it.'

'Well now, that's something I'd like to see,' responded the priest, although he didn't really mean it.

'Not yet. He's still practising. Soon. You'll be amazed.'

Even then Father Kaisergruber already suspected that Karl Hoppe was desperate. At the doctor's house, a few weeks later, his guess was confirmed. He had tried to wriggle out of the doctor's invitation but had not managed to do so.

The doctor first showed him into a little room where a number of jigsaw puzzles were displayed on the table and on the floor. 'Victor completed them. All of them. And all by himself, without any help,' he said proudly.

The priest nodded, wondering if that was the only thing he was required to come and see.

But then the doctor asked him to follow him into the living room, where Victor was seated at the head of the long dining table. The doctor invited the priest to take a seat at the table and he did as asked, although he did leave one empty chair between himself and the boy.

The last time he had seen the boy had been in the asylum, just days before Dr Hoppe had taken him home. Afterwards Sister Milgitha had told him that the doctor had made quite a scene, along with some disparaging remarks about the institution. In his role as shepherd of Wolfheim he had felt compelled to make excuses for the doctor. He'd said that the doctor's wife was poorly; the doctor must be suffering from stress.

'In that case he should go and see a doctor himself!' Sister Milgitha had exclaimed indignantly.

The abbess had asked him if he didn't agree it would best to give the doctor the cold shoulder for now. Not to punish him, she said, but merely to give him time to reconsider. Her question of course provided its own answer.

That had been four months ago and the priest had not seen Victor since then. But nothing about the boy's appearance had changed. He saw that at once. His bearing. His appearance. His gaze. As if only the decor had changed and Victor was still sitting in the very same spot. A bulky tome lay open on the table in front of the boy; the priest presumed it was the Bible.

This was confirmed by Dr Hoppe, who had taken a seat across from him on the other side of the table. 'Victor reads the Bible,' he said.

The boy remained impassive, but his father seemed very nervous. He kept rubbing his hands, and when the priest looked at him, he would hastily look the other way.

'Well! That's excellent,' said the priest. He glanced at Victor, whose eyes were indeed fixed on the Bible, but in such a way that it looked as if his father had made him sit like that and warned him not to move. How old might the boy be now, he wondered. Almost six?

'But he can do other things as well,' said the doctor, stressing the word 'other'. Can't you, Victor?'

Still no response from the boy. The priest did not know which of the two deserved more pity.

'Father, give us a verse from Genesis.'

'What do you mean?'

'Just the two numbers. Chapter 12, verse 7, for instance.'

The priest shrugged. 'Chapter 7, verse 6, perhaps.'

He had to think for a moment to remember what was in that verse, but before he had a chance to do so the doctor indicated with a nod of the head that it was Victor he should be addressing. He looked at the boy and repeated, 'Chapter 7, verse 6.'

As he said it, it came back to him; *And Noah was six hundred years old when the flood of waters was upon the earth.*

The room was silent. The only sound was the ticking of the clock on the mantel. The priest let his gaze wander. Next to the clock was a statuette of Mary under a glass dome and above it, on the wall, the palm fronds from last year.

'Victor, chapter 7, verse 6,' he heard the doctor say.

Out of the corner of his eye the priest stole a glance at the boy.

The doctor urged his son again, insistently, 'Victor, Father Kaiser-gruber has asked you to read something.'

I ought to put an end to this painful spectacle, thought the priest. 'Why don't you just let him read whatever he likes from the Bible,' he proposed. 'Surely that's—'

'No, no, he can do it! He's done it hundreds of times. But he simply won't! Chapter 7, verse 6, Victor!'

He misses his wife, thought the priest. She'd never have allowed it to come to this.

'Doctor . . .' he began.

'You don't believe me, do you?' the doctor broke in abruptly. 'You think I'm making the whole thing up. You think Victor is retarded, don't you!'

'Doctor, there is nothing wrong with that. Your son is retarded. You don't have to be—'

'*Show* him, Victor! Show him he's wrong!'

'You don't have to—'

'*Quiet!*'

The priest was visibly shocked, which made the doctor realise he was making a scene.

'Victor *must* speak,' he said in a calmer voice. A voice that hid his anger, but not his despair.

But Victor would not speak, and the priest could tell from the doctor's reddening face that he was making an effort to control himself. He considered suggesting that there might still be room for Victor at the institution at La Chapelle, even though he wasn't at all sure that was the case; but he thought it wiser to keep his counsel.

He pushed his chair back and stood up. 'I really do have to go now, Doctor. I'm so sorry.'

The doctor did not even get up to say goodbye. He only nodded, and went on nodding his head.

Father Kaisergruber wondered if he should say anything else. He looked at Victor one last time and thought, I've tried to save him, I can do no more than that.

'Amen.'

That was what all the patients said when they got something from Father Kaisergruber. Marc François sometimes said, 'Amen and out!' but that was wrong. Sister Milgitha would punish him, later. But all the others always said, 'Amen.' They said it after they got the body of Christ from Father Kaisergruber. And if you didn't get anything from him, you had to shut up. Sister Milgitha said so.

Doesn't my father know that, then? Victor wondered. Didn't Sister Milgitha ever tell him?

Karl Hoppe thought things had been proceeding quite well until then. From the moment he had given his son the Bible the boy seemed to have changed – as if opening the Bible caused Victor to open up as well.

Sometimes he thought that it had been the slap that had done it. That hitting him had released whatever had been stuck fast inside the boy. But he preferred to suppress that thought. No, it was the Bible. In giving him the Bible he had won his son's trust.

It was not as if they'd been having any real conversations since then, Victor and he; no, it was more a matter of monosyllabic exchanges. He would ask something and Victor would answer 'Yes,' or 'No,' or 'I don't know.' What the boy was really thinking was anyone's guess. Even when he told him something important, Victor showed no reaction.

'You know the lady who used to lie in the bed upstairs?' he began one day.

Victor nodded.

'That was your mother.' Victor didn't even look up. The doctor might as well have been talking about the weather. 'She was ill,' he added, nonetheless.

And that was all he ever told him about her. Nor did Victor ever ask for more. He was as frugal with his questions as he was with his answers.

Just once, Victor had asked him, 'How do I get to become a doctor?'

'By studying hard and reading a lot.'

'Is that all?'

'You also have to be good to people. And to do good.'

'Be good. Do good,' Victor had repeated after him.

It was a lame answer, but for Victor it was enough, apparently, because he had nodded and gone back to whatever he was doing. Which was reading, usually. And his reading material was almost exclusively the Bible.

Victor read, and his father corrected the mistakes he made. As soon as Victor could read flawlessly, he would show Father Kaisergruber: that was what the doctor had resolved soon after his wife's funeral, and it was the reason he had taken the trouble to stir up the priest's curiosity beforehand. He regarded it as a challenge.

When one day he noticed that Victor could not only read the Bible but also recite long passages by heart, he raised the bar even higher. Father Kaisergruber would be flabbergasted.

Victor didn't seem to find it difficult. He probably regarded it as a game, although he never gave any indication that he might actually be enjoying it. He never gave any indication of anything, in fact. That had not changed. And to the doctor it was a constant irritant.

However, showing off how intelligent Victor was should be enough to make the priest sit up.

But what should have been a triumph ended instead in a humiliating defeat. And after the priest had left, the doctor set about hammering the verse in question into Victor's head, syllable by syllable – No. Ah. Was. Six. Hun. Dred. Years. Old. When. The. Flood. Of. Wa. Ters. Was. Up. On. The. Earth – and had Victor cried, had he dis-solved into a flood of tears, his father might possibly have come to his senses in time. But Victor bore every blow with passive resignation. Right until the very last syllable.

* * *

When Rex Cremer contacted Victor Hoppe in April 1979, many of Victor's former professors were still teaching at the university. The dean, who had only held that post since 1975, had asked several of his colleagues beforehand to tell him about Victor Hoppe. Some professors, especially those who taught the purely theoretical subjects, such as the social sciences, policy or ethics, remembered seeing little of him in class – and when he had shown up, he had stood out largely on account of the way he looked – but said that in the exams he had consistently demonstrated a thorough knowledge of the subject. The professors who had supervised him in the lab, however, still had vivid memories of Victor Hoppe as a student. They all concurred that his physical appearance and his voice made him memorable, naturally; but it was chiefly his enthusiasm, or, as one professor described it, his obsessiveness, that truly made him stand out. He could spend hours at a time on a single experiment without ever showing any impatience or irritation, and his diligence often led to extraordinary results.

'He was one of the most gifted students I have ever had,' was the unanimous consensus. Some of the professors did add that this applied only to his intellectual gifts and not in any way to his social or communication skills.

'A loner,' one of the professors said. 'I don't think he had much contact with the other students.'

According to his former supervisor Dr Bergmann, who had since retired, Victor possessed a staggering store of theoretical knowledge, which enabled him to pursue ideas that were so revolutionary that they could never be realised in a practical setting, at least not in this century.

At a meeting convoked to decide on Victor Hoppe's appointment, another professor, Dr Maserath, said, 'He made me think, sometimes, of Jules Verne, who wrote about space rockets before the invention of the fuel engine.'

'But there is a difference,' Dr Genet, Victor's erstwhile genetics professor, had astutely commented: 'Jules Verne restricted himself to writing books and never tried to put his ideas into practice.'

He came back to that point later, when Rex Cremer told him that Victor wanted to try cloning mice.

'See, that's what I mean!' exclaimed Dr Genet. 'We've only just learned to stand and already he's wanting to run!'

'It *is* raising the bar rather high,' said Dr Maserath, 'but I don't know if that's such a bad thing.'

'That's exactly what he said to me on the phone,' Cremer agreed: 'that we scientists impose limits on ourselves; that many of us make that mistake.'

Dr Genet reacted as if he'd been personally attacked. 'But it's also our job to be realistic! At this point in history his ideas are pure nonsense! Surely you must know that too!'

'Nonsense has led to a lot of new discoveries,' said Dr Maserath light-heartedly; but when he saw Dr Genet turning his head away in disgust, he quickly added that it was, indeed, rather too early for that kind of experiment.

'There you go, passing judgement on him before you have even given him a chance to explain it to you,' said Cremer, nettled. 'It may be that he's already much further along than we think. Didn't he surprise everyone with his last experiment as well? Which, incidentally, was the reason for bringing him here. Do you really want to tell him to put the brakes on?'

'I am surprised that he is willing to accept a chair,' said Dr Maserath calmly. 'He was offered a teaching position here before, after he got his PhD, but he turned it down.'

'He'd had a lucrative offer from the fertility clinic in Bonn,' said Dr Genet. 'They offered him the freedom to do independent research.'

'What he really wanted to do was to turn theory into practice,' Dr Maserath added. 'How did he describe it again?'

'I want to give life,' said Dr Genet. 'We laughed about it afterwards. Especially the *way* he said it: without a trace of irony. And now he wants to take it even further. I don't know if—'

'Let's wait and see what he has to say, tomorrow,' Cremer broke in.

'I can't wait to find out,' said Dr Genet. 'I really can't wait.'

Victor Hoppe had been talking for almost three hours without interruption. It made him feel as if he were sitting an exam again. There were five biologists at the table, including two of his former professors. He had twice mixed up their names when answering a question, though not on purpose.

One of the five was Rex Cremer. The dean was friendly. Not pushy. Not wary. Nor overly ingratiating.

The two professors he hadn't met before had shaken his hand politely. They didn't ask any questions but simply listened, spellbound.

His two former professors, on the other hand, were very critical, but that did not bother him one bit. He was able to answer every question at length, and explained in detail how he was hoping to clone the mice – within a year, he boldly claimed. He declared that in his view the current method of hybridising cells using the Sendai virus was already out of date, and that *his* method, using the micropipette, had a much greater chance of succeeding. It was simply a matter of technique, he had stressed.

When he had finished, one of his old professors had one last question. It was one he'd been expecting. Was it his intention, if it were ever to become possible . . . uh . . . would he ever consider – cloning humans?

He had been ready with his answer, but it left the biologists none the wiser. '*Come, make us gods, which shall go before us*,' he'd said. He had always thought that it was a lovely line.

And then he had stood up and left.

Victor Hoppe's project was approved by a vote of three to two. He started working at the University of Aachen on 1 September 1979. He was given his own laboratory and a generous budget for the purchase of technical equipment. A room with a desk and a pull-out sofa was also put at his disposal, so that he would not have to commute from Bonn to Aachen every day. He was expected to report to the dean once a week, and there was a conference with the other biologists every other month at which he was to bring them up to date on his experiments.

He did not have much news to report for the first few months. He told them he was practising his technique. The egg cells were still too frequently and too severely damaged by the micropipette, with harmful consequences. He was asked what kind of consequences he was referring to. He replied that the egg might tear further at the site of the puncture, which could lead to its splitting into two distinct entities that did not completely separate.

One of the biologists said, 'Siamese twins?'

Indeed, replied Victor Hoppe.

Hoppe's research project had failed to deliver any concrete results by the end of the year. Dr Genet felt vindicated in his belief that the university would have been better off investing its money in some other project.

Three months later, Rex Cremer made a discovery that would turn out to be of great importance to Victor Hoppe's experiment. He was successful in producing the agent cytochalasin B from a mould. This mycotoxin acted on the cytoskeleton, impeding its protein molecules from multiplying. This allowed the cytoplasm surrounding the cell nucleus to remain soft, resulting in a smaller likelihood of damage when the egg cells were pierced with the micropipette, and greatly increasing their chances of survival.

At the next review session Victor announced that the blocking agent that Dr Cremer had discovered did make a big difference and that a breakthrough would not be long in coming now. Nevertheless it took close to eight months before any clones were born. For Victor had failed to take yet another factor into account. The chances of success may have increased, but they were still so minimal that luck continued to play an essential part.

In the end, this it what it boiled down to:

542 cells were microsurgically implanted with a foreign nucleus.

253 cells survived the procedure.

48 cells fused with the new nucleus.
16 cells developed into minuscule embryos.
3 embryos grew into cloned mice.

* * *

On 31 August 1951 Dr Karl Hoppe drove his son to the boarding section of the Christian Brothers' School in Eupen, a town some twenty kilometres south-east of Wolfheim.

'It's the best thing for you,' he told Victor as they waited outside the monastery's wooden gate.

The thought that it might be the best thing for himself no longer even crossed his mind. Once he had made the decision, he had convinced himself that he was doing it for Victor's sake. Besides, Johanna would have insisted on it, he reminded himself more than once, thus downplaying his own role in the decision. So he didn't feel at all guilty when the time came to send Victor to the boarding school. He felt nothing much, in fact, as they stood there by the gate. He might as well have been delivering a package.

He had not warned Victor beforehand. That too had seemed to him to be the best thing. He had just told the boy that he'd be going to school. It wasn't until they were in the car on their way to the monastery that he informed him that he would be a boarder for a little while.

The little while ended up being ten years. Victor came home only for the Christmas, Easter and summer holidays.

'I'll write to you,' was the last thing Karl Hoppe said to his son before he disappeared through the entrance.

He never wrote, not even once.

All in all, boarding school did turn out to be the best thing that could have happened to Victor. Living at the school, which most of the boys considered a kind of hell, was a breath of fresh air to him after a year and a half of living with his father. The strict rules and the rigid schedule gave him the structure he had missed at home, and which was necessary for him to function. The hymns and prayers, the monks in their habits, the echoing corridors, the cavernous dormitory and the nightly weeping of the homesick boy in the bed next to his –

all of this was familiar to Victor. It was as if he were being given a custom-made suit to wear that was a perfect fit after a year and a half of clothes that had hung on him like a sack. As a matter of fact, on his first day at school he'd experienced this in a literal sense, having been made to trade in the clothes he'd been wearing for a school uniform. All the other first years were being fitted for the same apparel as well, and whereas the rest of them sniffed and tugged at the stiff new fabric, feeling uncomfortable, Victor just sat there calmly. He felt he had come home again. Every once in a while he'd glance at the door of the great hall, expecting Sister Marthe to materialise any minute.

It was lucky for Victor that he was placed in Brother Rombout's class, a young monk who had taken over teaching the first and second years from Brother Lucas just the year before. Brother Lucas had viewed the students as lumps of clay to be kneaded harshly into the shape he had in mind for them, whereas Brother Rombout preferred to take each boy's individual talents as a starting point, and then stimulate those talents and make them blossom.

The young brother had delicate features, which, with his long eyelashes and thin eyebrows, gave him a rather feminine air. He also had a pleasant voice, the boys found out when he recited the Lord's Prayer the first morning of the new school year, after which he told them a story from the Bible. Brother Rombout's looks and his voice, the prayer and the Bible story all pleased Victor very much. And when the brother asked if any of them knew how to read, and fingers went up in the air to the right and left of him, he too, after a brief hesitation, stuck his finger in the air. And that was how it all began.

More than Brother Rombout's looks and personality, it was his teaching method that greatly influenced Victor Hoppe's development. While studying to become a teacher, the monk had developed an educational method of his own, which he proceeded to test on his pupils. His novel approach, which would eventually attract quite a following, consisted of tackling arithmetic and the natural sciences, in particular, in a controlled progression, from the concrete to the schematic, and thence to the abstract. This method simulated the way young children's brains process information. In Victor Hoppe's case it suited the way his brain worked seamlessly. The monk found in Victor proof positive that his was the right approach, but in actual fact it may have been the other way round: Victor was just the right boy for the brother's method.

During the 1951–2 school year Brother Rombout had charge of the first and second years, a class composed of boys who were six, seven and eight years old. Subsequently, at the start of each new school year, he would take his best students with him to the next two-year stage, giving him a chance to adapt his method progressively to the next age group and allowing him to put his theories into practice. Victor Hoppe was the only boy in the first-year class who made it to the seventh, and top, level in just three years. Brother Rombout had promoted him to the next stage every year, in spite of the growing age gap between Victor and the other boys in the class. When after three years he attained the seventh level, Victor was nine; the oldest students in his class were thirteen.

A year later, on 30 June 1955, Victor graduated from primary school. It had taken him just four years.

These facts, recorded in the annals of the Christian Brothers' School in Eupen, attest to Victor Hoppe's intelligence, the boy who'd started life condemned as a half-wit. But what they don't show is how Victor's attitude towards God was shaped at this school, or, rather, *mis*shaped. This is to a certain extent clear from the report cards that have survived and in which Victor's grades are recorded in Brother Rombout's elegant handwriting. Year after year, Victor earned 10s, 9s, or very occasionally an 8, in every subject – in every subject, that is, except religious instruction. The first year he still had a 10 for religion. That was to be expected, since he had startled and delighted many a monk with his biblical knowledge. But it was no more than superficial knowledge. He had no real understanding of what he was reading or reciting. The second year he received an 8 in religion, and the next year only a 7. In his last year, Brother Rombout gave him a 4; it was the only time he had failed a class. The brother's accompanying comment was: 'Victor will never become a priest.' He probably meant it ironically, because had the brother known what was really going on inside Victor's head, he would never have written anything so flippant.

Discipline flowed forth from a healthy dose of fear. That was the way it was, not only at the monastery school in Eupen but at many other Catholic schools as well. Fear was created not only through the threat of corporal punishment but also by presenting God as the Almighty who would condemn all sinners.

Wrath. That was a word that was frequently invoked. The wrath of the Lord shall come down upon the sinners.

The sinners were the students, and most of the monks acted as if they were God, or at least God's representatives on earth.

Brother Rombout was an exception to this, and yet he too, albeit indirectly and unconsciously, contributed to Victor's aversion to God. Five times a week, when the other students in his class were introduced to the Bible through simple stories and pastel illustrations, Victor was given permission to go and sit at the back of the classroom and read the Bible for grown-ups (as Brother Rombout called it) in peace. In his teaching method, that was called differentiation: assignments adjusted to each individual's level of mastery.

And Victor would read. Of course Victor would read. He buried himself, he plunged in, he disappeared completely into the formal language, which, as he grew older, he increasingly began to understand. And the more he understood, the more he realised that the picture of God that most of the monks liked to paint was quite in accordance with what was written about Him in the Bible. And that picture was, to put it mildly, not very positive.

Until about the age of four, children generally see people as either exclusively good or exclusively bad. Nor was it any different for Victor – except that in his case this perception never changed. Other children gradually learn to detect shades of grey in the black or the white. They discover that there is some good and some bad in everyone, in ever-changing proportions, depending on the situations in which they find themselves.

Victor had trouble with nuances. Unable to show much emotion himself, he was likewise unable to distinguish it in others. To him everything was either black or white. He couldn't help it: because of his Asperger's he didn't even know it wasn't supposed to be that way.

But had somebody – a father or a mother, for instance – given Victor more individual attention, he might gradually have been taught or have discovered for himself that every human being is made up of an entire palette of feelings. In that case he might have started to blossom himself, in the widest sense of that word; because, when all was said and done, Victor never got beyond the bud stage. But at boarding school his conviction that there were only good people and bad people was reinforced over and over again. Certainly his lack of intimacy with others played a role in this, but the monks contributed as well. They were masters at hiding their true feelings from one another as well as from the students; indeed, they were expected to do so. Even Brother Rombout. His goodness was certainly apparent, but that was all that he would reveal. What went on inside him, what brooded and seethed there, what he might be feeling or longing for – none of that was made public. So how could Victor be expected to discover that there was more to life than just good or bad?

The more experience Victor had under his belt, the more he came to associate the good or the bad in a person with either that person' s voice or the kind of physical contact he had with them. For he couldn't tell anything from reading someone's face.

First, the voice. The volume and the vibration. A loud volume usually came with a heavy vibration. That was bad.

Brother Rombout always spoke in a soft voice, and when he sang, he sang in a mellifluous voice, not like the dull drone of many of the other monks' voices. Listening to Brother Rombout was a pleasure.

Brother Lucas, the third- and fourth-year teacher, and Brother Thomas, the first-year teacher, had voices that sounded like the lowest notes of the chapel organ. But they could do what the organ couldn't do: they could let out all the stops and still make the sounds vibrate. Their voices were never actually directed at Victor, but he could hear them through the classroom walls. They sounded like a thundercloud passing overhead, and Victor pictured God hurling bolts of lightning at the students, because when the brothers raised their voices, they usually did so in the name of God.

'The wrath of the Lord shall smite you.'

'Fear the Day of Judgement, for God will know how to find you then.'

'God's vengeance will be implacable.'

Father Norbert, who usually supervised evening study, likewise had a voice with the bad sound in it. Victor had once experienced it himself. He didn't know why, but Father Norbert had shouted at him. He was always shouting at the other boys, in fact, but never at him. 'Look at Victor – he should be your example.' He often shouted that at the other boys. But this time, this one time, he had shouted at Victor.

'Look at me, Victor Hoppe! *Look* at me when I'm talking to you!'

But he couldn't. He didn't look up at Father Norbert. He wanted to, but he just couldn't do it. It was as if his head had been nailed fast to his neck. Then he'd felt a box on the ear.

'God will punish you for this, Victor Hoppe!'

The physical contact: touch. That too was either bad or good. Hitting someone was bad. Besides the floggings, Father Norbert was also bad when he pinched a student's ear between his thumb and forefinger and twisted it until the boy had tears in his eyes. Victor had often seen him do that. And whacking someone's fingers with a wooden ruler was bad too. Brother Lucas and Brother Thomas did that. The students in their classes would show off the black-and-blue marks across their fingers.

In Brother Rombout's touch Victor recognised goodness. That sort of touch was gentle. A hand on his shoulder. A pat on the head. The way the brother leaned over him and guided his hand to help him write. That was all good.

And what about God? The image Victor came to have of Him was largely formed by the pronouncements of Brother Thomas, Brother Lucas and Father Norbert. Since they were always presenting God as threatening, as the one who excoriates and punishes, all-powerful, omnipotent and all-knowing, Victor, who was himself powerless and could barely tell the difference between abstract and real, concluded that God *had* to be the source of all evil.

And that image of God, that terrifying image, was underscored for him by what he read in the Bible, the Bible that Brother Rombout allowed him to read in peace, never realising what exactly Victor was getting out of it. What he got out of it was: God unleashed wars, God destroyed cities, God sent down plagues, God punished, God killed.

God giveth and God taketh away, Victor. Remember that.

God gave, it was true, but for all that God gave, he took away just as much, and more.

Jesus was good, however.

The New Testament came as a revelation to Victor when he was in the fifth- to sixth-year learning group. He had read that part of the Bible before, but now he came to it with the insight he'd gained from more than two years in boarding school.

Victor read about how Jesus fed the hungry; how Jesus calmed the storms; how Jesus healed the sick; how Jesus raised the dead.

Victor discovered that Jesus did not raise his voice, nor hit people, nor punish people.

Therefore, Jesus was good.

It was not only a revelation to Victor; it was also a comfort. Jesus was the Son of God, after all. The Father did bad things; the Son did good things. It was a familiar scenario, and it comforted him. It was no exaggeration to say that he saw a friend in Jesus. Jesus was also more *real* to him than God – more physical; more human. In that respect it was easier for Victor to imagine what He was like.

Besides being a friend, he soon came to see Jesus as a fellow sufferer – not little by little but quite abruptly, when he came to the end of the Gospel according to St Matthew. '*Eli, Eli, lamma sabaktáni*: that is, "*My God, my God, why hast Thou forsaken me?*"' That sentence struck him like a bolt of lightning. God had deserted his own Son. He had abandoned Him to his fate. This was only too familiar to Victor. Hadn't his own father likewise abandoned him?

Did Victor imagine himself to *be* Jesus? Certainly not, because, first, he possessed no imagination. Secondly, he did realise that Jesus and he were two separate beings. It would be more accurate to say that Victor thought that he was *like* Jesus. They shared the same fate and therefore they were both good. Jesus had done more good than Victor, to be sure, but Victor still had plenty of time to catch up. If he became a doctor, then at least he'd be able to heal the sick. That's the way he thought. If . . . then.

There was one thing he just couldn't understand: how had his own father ever become a doctor? Doctors were supposed to do good, weren't they?

Over time, Karl Hoppe's medical practice began to thrive once more. The doctor had seen the error of his ways – in the opinion of the villagers, anyway; though they did ask themselves what on earth his son was doing at that school. But at least Victor was now safely in God's hands again. Which was how Father Kaisergruber put it.

The doctor himself, however, was not doing so well, his patients noticed. It was difficult to draw him into conversation. He seldom laughed any more. He was losing weight. He did continue to practise medicine, and to do his job well, which was the most important thing, wasn't it?

He doesn't even look me in the eye – that's how far it's gone; that's how far I've allowed it to go. That was how Karl Hoppe put it to himself whenever his son was home for a few days, after months away at school.

It also struck him that Victor's intelligence seemed to be progressing in leaps and bounds. His homework, in grammar as well as arithmetic, was increasingly difficult. And Brother Rombout confirmed this. He said that Victor was his best student, head and shoulders ahead of the other boys.

The doctor always had to swallow when he heard that. He never let on that Victor had once been declared feeble-minded.

He wanted to know if his son was as silent in the classroom as he was at home.

'Yes,' the brother affirmed, 'Victor is rather introverted. A lot goes in, but not much comes out.' Then he added: 'He doesn't have any friends.'

There's another thing Victor and I won't ever be, thought the doctor: friends.

Later he again made a mental list of all the things his son might hold against him. There were times when he was ready to discuss these things with Victor. He wanted Victor to know what his mother had been like and why the two of them had decided to send him to the institution. He also considered giving Victor the patient file the sisters had kept on him – he had never been able to bring himself to throw it out, perhaps because he wasn't quite ready to pretend that that chapter in Victor's life had never really happened. He also intended to explain to Victor some day why he had hit him. What he wanted to say was that something had just come over him, something more powerful than he was. Finally, he would like to ask Victor to forgive him.

But every time he made up his mind to talk to him, he would decide at the last minute that it was better for Victor to forget rather than forgive. The blows he had dealt him would probably be the hardest thing for his son to forget, but the years the boy had spent in the mental institution were bound to fade from his memory in good time. He had been so young, after all. And who remembers what happened before their fifth birthday anyway?

* * *

The seventeenth of December 1980, early morning.

'Done it.'

'Victor?'

'Yes, it's Victor.'

'Victor, it's four-fifteen in the morning!'

'Done it,' he said again.

'What have you done?' asked Rex Cremer, annoyed.

'The mice. The clones.'

'Excuse me?'

'I've cloned the mice.'

The dean was dumbstruck. Victor's flat tone of voice, as if he were simply reporting something routine, was completely at odds with the bombshell he'd just delivered.

'Victor, are you serious?'

'Yes.'

'How many are there?'

'Three.'

'Where are you? Are you at the university?'

'I'm here, yes.'

'I'm on my way.'

On the way to the university Rex Cremer tried to work it out in his head. Fifteen months had gone by since he had recruited Victor and in that time Victor had not produced anything remarkable. The other biologists had urged Rex to put an end to the experiment, but he had stood his ground and backed Dr Hoppe. His stance was informed not so much by hope as by the fact that he was not yet ready to admit that he'd been wrong about Victor. When he had been woken by the phone call that morning, he had just come back from a week's holiday. He had spoken with Victor just before he left. If what Victor had told him on the phone was true, then at the time they'd spoken the embryos had already been implanted, the birth of the mice imminent. Yet Victor hadn't breathed a word – as if he had been reluctant to say anything until he possessed some concrete proof.

When the dean arrived on campus, he went straight to the lab, where he found Victor hunched over a microscope.

'So where are they, Victor?'

Without raising his head Victor pointed at a table in a corner of the lab. It held a Plexiglas cage half-filled with shredded paper. Rex leaned down and counted seven young mice and one grown white mouse. He immediately saw that the half-naked mice were several days old; he had assumed that they'd just been born. So Victor had kept quiet about this even longer than he'd thought.

'How old are they?' he asked.

Victor wagged four fingers above his head.

'In that case why did you wait to call me until now?'

'Because I couldn't be sure until I could tell what colour they were,' Victor replied, sliding another Petri dish under the microscope. 'I had to wait until the hair started growing in.'

The dean leaned down closely over the cage, and now he noticed the barely detectable colour difference.

'White and brown mice?'

'The ones with the brown coats are the clones,' Victor informed him. 'The white ones are normal mice. The clones are from the eggs of a black mouse; the eggs' nuclei were replaced with nuclei from five-day-old embryos from a brown mother. And the surrogate birth mother was a white mouse.'

It took some time for his words to sink in. Rex tried repeating to himself what Victor had said. So Victor had removed the nuclei of the eggs of a black mouse and substituted donor nuclei from developing embryos that he had taken from a brown mouse. The three brown mice in the glass cage, therefore, had to be clones of mouse embryos; they weren't the product of normal cell division. Victor had therefore succeeded, for the first time in the history of science, in cloning a mammal. Rex was flabbergasted.

'By Jove, you did it!' he cried.

But Victor did not respond. He was adjusting the microscope with his left hand while jotting something down on a sheet of paper with his right.

The dean turned back to the mice. 'Victor, this is a world first,' he said emphatically. 'Do you realise?'

'The world will know about it soon enough,' Victor replied flatly.

'What do you mean?'

'I've already written the report and sent it off, to the editor of *Cell*.'

'But you can't! You mustn't. I mean . . . You should have presented it to us first, or to me, at the very least. That's not the way we do things here. Certainly not in this case.'

'It had to be done quickly,' Victor replied.

Rex took a deep breath, his eyes fixed on his colleague's back.

'And why *Cell*?' he asked. 'You gave your last article to *Science*. It has greater impact, surely?'

'They ask too many questions.'

'But they have to! That is why they—'

'There are times when one should simply accept the facts.'

'Victor, you are extremely accomplished, but that doesn't mean that you don't have to account for what you do.'

'I don't have to answer to anyone,' Victor answered sullenly. Pushing his stool back, he stood up and strode over to the table. He picked up one of the cloned mice, set the little animal on the palm of his hand and pointed it at the dean.

'*This* is my answer,' he said.

Rex stared at Victor in astonishment. It wasn't his words or his anger that surprised him, but his altered appearance. He now sported a carroty beard, something Rex had never seen on him, and there were heavy blue bags under his eyes, setting off the paleness of the skin on his forehead and cheekbones. He must have gone without shaving for at least a week and probably hadn't slept much in all that time either.

'Victor, how long have you been at work?'

Victor glanced at his watch, and then looked away, as if trying to count how many hours he'd been awake. He shook his head. 'I don't know.'

'Victor . . .'

Victor was stroking his beard absent-mindedly.

'Victor,' Rex said again, 'perhaps you should go and rest for a few hours. I'll stay here and cover for you in the meantime.'

Victor nodded and stared at the mouse on top of his hand. He cautiously ran his finger a few times down the animal's spine, as if wanting to reassure it before he left. Then he put the mouse back in the cage with the other mice, turned on his heel and walked to the door.

'Victor, where can I find your report?' asked Rex. 'I'd like to read it.'

'By the fax machine,' he replied, circling his left hand in the air.

Rex Cremer wondered what all the fuss had been about, for the article was exceptionally explicit and clear. Victor had described the method he'd used thoroughly, step by step. After each step, moreover, he had evaluated the results, and had even posed a few critical questions at the end, as if to involve other scientists in the quest for answers. Furthermore, he had stressed the importance to his method of cytochalasin B, the agent about which Cremer had already published his own article. Finally, he had been able to support all of the results with data that would have been inconceivable before.

When the dean gave the other biologists at the university the news, they were quite indignant at first, but after reading the report they too were forced to admit that the method he described was indeed revolutionary – and, on first perusal, so simple that it was really a wonder nobody had thought of it before. They looked forward to hearing the reaction from the scientific community when the article was published.

That happened on 10 January 1981. *Cell* published a full-page photo of the cloned mice on its cover, and Victor Hoppe's piece was the lead article. The reaction was overwhelming. Prominent scientists from all over the world were filled with astonishment, but gave generous praise – the word 'genius' was touted more than once – and the news was written up in both national and foreign newspapers. Requests for interviews with Victor Hoppe came pouring in, but he turned down every one, nor was he prepared to pose for any photographs with his mice. After much persuasion he finally did give in somewhat, granting the university permission to circulate the passport photo taken of him when he had been hired, the same one he had on his ID badge. At the time that photo was taken he hadn't yet had the beard, which he was never to shave off again.

Rex Cremer was the university's spokesman and, as one might have expected, he was asked by the members of the press if this meant that cloning humans was now a possibility and if Dr Hoppe, or any other scientist, might venture to do so. Rex told them that it was too early even to think about walking on two legs when the science had only just begun to crawl. He also stressed that these clones were clones grown from embryos, and that the cloning of adult animals would be quite another story. For that to happen one would have to use the nuclei of mature cells, cells that had already developed some specific function. We certainly won't see it happening in this century, he declared, and he believed it too.

Strictly speaking, Victor ought to have repeated his experiment, even if only once, because reproducibility is an essential scientific principle. But his mind didn't work that way. It told him he had to go on to the next step. If he managed to achieve one thing, then he would have to start on the next. If . . . then. That was what he knew. Not if . . . if. But Rex Cramer, who had tried several times in vain to get Victor to repeat the experiment, didn't know that.

'Victor, you *must* repeat the experiment. You can't just assume that it will work a second time. Besides, there are a number of questions unanswered. Do cloned mice live as long as other mice? Can they reproduce? Are the offspring fertile? These are points other scientists have already been raising, Victor, and I find myself unable to give them any answers.'

'Time will tell,' said Victor.

'But even *then* you'll have to show that your experiment wasn't just a fluke,' Rex said, raising his voice. 'There's no way round it.'

'Only circus animals repeat their tricks over and over again.'

'OK, then what do you want to do, Victor?'

'I want to clone adult mammals.'

The dean sighed.

'If I succeed,' Victor went on, 'that will be proof enough that my technique works. Isn't that what they want?'

'But they won't wait. It'll take years.'

'It won't take me years.'

'Victor, be sensible, just this once. I know your abilities, but—'

'It is feasible, if the donor cells can be deprogrammed,' Victor broke in. 'If we can return them to their elemental stage. Back to G0. Another possibility is to alter the programming of the receptor eggs. That can be done by electrical stimulation. Anyway, the cycles have to be synchronised at the moment of fusion, because if not you'll get abnormal chromosomes.'

For a moment Rex wished he could tell Victor that he was wrong, but he couldn't. What Victor was saying made eminent sense, and the way he described it made it seem so straightforward that it was almost as if all he had to do was pour some liquids into a bottle and shake them up a bit.

'Victor, the faculty will never approve . . .'

'I'm doing it anyway.'

'That's not the way we work here. I've already told—'

'If I can't do it here, then—'

'Goddamn it, Victor, you're not making it easy for me! You're lucky that I've always stood by you so far, I hope you realise that!'

'I've never asked you to.'

'That is true,' the dean was forced to admit, with a sigh. He realised he was facing a serious dilemma. If he forced Victor to play by the rules, Victor would leave. And that, naturally, would mean a great loss to his department, which had just been given a large grant by the university to continue the research. But if he were to give Victor carte blanche, the other biologists, who *did* have to be accountable for their work, were sure to raise a ruckus. It might just have been possible to indulge Victor in this if he had shown a little more team spirit and openness with his confrères, but that had not been the case. He was not in any way cut out for teamwork. He would not listen to authority, never took other people into account and never showed appreciation for anything or anyone else. His talent did make up for that to some extent, but for how much longer?

'Victor, give me some time to think it over.'

'There is no time.'

'What difference can a few days make?'

'God created the world in a few days.'

'Victor, you're driving me insane! Listen . . .'

Suddenly Rex pulled himself up short. Once again, Victor had mentioned God, and something clicked in Rex's mind. He had always considered Victor's allusions to God as some sort of joke, but suddenly he wasn't so sure. In the fifteen months that he had known him Victor had never once told a joke. He'd never even laughed at anyone else's jokes; he took everything seriously. The dean hadn't really thought about this until now, but it was possible that Victor was entirely serious when he talked about God. Rex did not believe in God himself, he had not been raised religious. His parents were free-thinkers and had always left it up to him whether to believe or not.

'You don't have to answer this, but . . .' he began, and perhaps he was even hoping he would not get an answer: '. . . do you believe in God?'

'As the creator of all living things – yes, I do,' answered Victor, as if it were a given.

'And then who created God?'

'Man.'

For a moment the dean was rattled, not only by the sincerity of Victor's answer but equally by the response itself. God had made man and man had made God – that was what it boiled down to. The one led to the other, and the other led back to the first. It was extraordinarily simple, as simple as all of Victor's explanations. It made Rex think of the snake that bites its own tail, devouring more and more of itself until there's nothing left. It made sense in a logical way, but from a practical standpoint it was impossible. When Rex taught a genetics class, he often used the snake example to demonstrate the difference between religion and science. In religion, proof was immaterial; in science, proof was all that mattered. He had always regarded religion and science as being completely separate things. An unbridgeable chasm lay between them. But evidently that chasm did not exist for Victor; or perhaps it did, but there was a bridge spanning it – with Victor standing on the bridge. Which would also explain his behaviour, and especially his mindset. As he had once said, some things simply had to be taken for granted. That was the religious man speaking, not the scientist. So, in that sense, a single positive result was all the proof Victor needed; and that was why, in his view, further testing was unnecessary.

'I think I'm beginning to understand, Victor, but that doesn't mean I agree with you. I'll have to think it over.'

Victor nodded.

'I'll let you know as soon as I can,' Rex finished, adding, 'If the world hasn't come to an end by then.'

Now Victor frowned. Rex stood up with a smile and reached out a hand to touch Victor's shoulder. 'Just kidding!'

Rex Cremer thought that he had finally worked out what made Victor Hoppe tick. But if Victor's nature consisted of many layers, Rex had only scratched off a sliver of the surface. The example of the snake devouring itself was a good one, but that was as far as it went. He was assuming that Victor possessed some measure of self-awareness, but that wasn't the case. It was much simpler than that, in fact – more logical. The answer lay in the snake itself. Victor was both the head *and* the tail. He devoured and was being devoured at once. That was it. He had no choice.

Victor did not wait for Rex Cremer to make a decision. He had already started experimenting on adult mammalian cells. He had scraped off a square centimetre of epidermis from his own thigh and had begun culturing the live cells in a number of different mediums. He had done the same thing with the liver cells of an adult mouse as well as some cells that came from the stomach of a bull. He did wonder if he was obliged to inform the dean of his exact plans but decided that it was too soon. He would just tell him that he wanted to clone adult mammals. That was all. At least he wouldn't be lying.

The solution Rex Cremer came up with, which was approved by the faculty, was that Rex himself would try to reproduce the cloned-mice experiment. That would allow Victor Hoppe to forge ahead with his own experiments. Cremer also arranged it so that Victor would report only to him and that he would then give a full account to the other departmental scientists. The dean thought that in this way he would be the one pulling the strings, but in truth he had hitched himself to the wagon whose course was set by Victor.

* * *

In his last year of primary school Victor ended up with a 4 for religion, and even there Brother Rombout had been generous, for Victor had shown very little interest in the subject all year. At least, that was how Brother Rombout interpreted the fact that Victor refused to open a Bible any more and had left the exam sheet blank. The monk had tried to bring his pupil round, but none of his talks had helped. A great shame, he thought, because he would have liked to send Victor to the junior seminary, where the boy might have trained for the priesthood.

But Victor wanted to be a doctor. He had mentioned this several times in passing and had demonstrated a great interest in the natural sciences. He is turning his back on the dogma of the Father, thought Brother Rombout, and opting for the practical laws of Mother Nature instead. Faithful to his own teaching methods, he encouraged Victor's interest by giving him books and assignments in his chosen field.

That was how Victor escaped being sent to the junior seminary. But he very nearly failed to be offered a place at the normal secondary school of the Christian Brothers' School. It had nothing to do with his intelligence but everything to do with the spectacle he made of himself during the last week of primary school.

A crazy spectacle – that was what the other students called it; they couldn't stop talking about it, unanimous in their opinion that they'd never have expected such a thing from Victor, the model student.

A display of blasphemy! That was how the abbot of the monastery described what Victor Hoppe had done. It was an unfortunate choice of words, thought Brother Rombout, since there had certainly been no blasphemy involved; although he had not raised that point in Victor's defence when he'd gone in to bat to keep his best pupil from being kicked out. He had stressed Victor's intelligence. He had said that it would be a shame to lose Victor's talent on account of a single transgression. He did call it a transgression, but only because he couldn't immediately think of a better word. He had considered using 'peccadillo' or 'slip-up', but those words didn't quite seem to fit the bill.

'*Egregious!*' was Abbot Eberhard's own term for it.

'Egregious,' Brother Rombout repeated after him meekly, although he strongly disagreed. But he had to kowtow to the abbot, pay him lip service.

In the end the abbot imposed reams of extra homework on Victor, and then gave him one more chance. One more egregious transgression and he would automatically be expelled.

Brother Rombout was relieved and, in hindsight, agreed with the students that what Victor had done might indeed be called a spectacle. Like them, the monk would never have thought Victor capable of making such a scene.

It happened during the last week of June 1955. The exams were over and, following school tradition, the students in the senior class (Brother Rombout's class that year) were going to visit Calvary Hill at La Chapelle. The monks described it as a school outing; the students termed it a pilgrimage, a word they spat out as if it tasted revolting.

The seventeen students of the seventh year were accompanied not only by Brother Rombout but also by Father Norbert, who was to lead them on the Stations of the Cross. The Road to Calvary was situated on top of Altenberg Hill. It had been built by the Clare Sisters of La Chapelle in 1898 to express 'their adoration of the Cross'. The convent, also the asylum in which Victor had spent the first five years of his life, was situated at the foot of the Altenberg, from which a narrow stone staircase ascended up to Calvary Hill. Since the patients were never allowed to venture outside the convent walls, Victor had never visited it when he lived there. Consequently, he had no clue that he was so close to his former home that day, but then he did have other things on his mind.

You could say that it had all started with the jeering. That he had recognised the jeering for what St Luke the Evangelist had described in the words: '*They will mock him and insult him.*'

Victor didn't know how to ride a bike.

The monk, the priest and the seventeen students were to make the journey from Eupen to La Chapelle by bicycle, a trip of about fifteen kilometres. Most of the boys had their own bikes; the boarders were to borrow theirs from the younger students. Victor was lent a bicycle belonging to a boy in the fourth year.

As the group set off with Brother Rombout in the lead and Father Norbert bringing up the rear, Victor Hoppe just stood there, one leg on either side of the bike, clutching the handlebars.

'Come on, Victor Hoppe,' Father Norbert urged him with a two-fingered rap on the back of the head.

But Victor stayed put, his head hung low.

'Victor, if you're expecting the Lord to do the pedalling for you, you're sadly mistaken!'

Father Norbert was still in a jovial mood. But when he realised that Victor still had not budged, he shouted at Brother Rombout to wait and clamped the rebel student's ear between his thumb and fore-finger.

The other students began to laugh. It was just a snigger at first, because they were happy it wasn't their turn to be singled out as the victim.

It may have been that that was the point when the priest realised something was amiss, because in spite of the increasing pressure on his pinched ear Victor still hadn't begun to move. Or it may simply have been a ruse on his part, to prod Victor into action. Whatever the reason, he said, loudly and with a touch of scorn in his voice, '*I* think Victor Hoppe doesn't know *how* to ride a bicycle.'

The giggling grew louder. A grin spread across the priest's face.

Meantime the high priests and the elders stirred up the multitude.

Brother Rombout had jumped off his bicycle and was walking back to Victor. Father Norbert went on, now shouting, 'Well, if Victor Hoppe doesn't know how to ride a bicycle, he'll just have to make his own way to Calvary Hill!'

Some of the boys started jeering.

But they shouted even louder.

Brother Rombout scowled at the students to be quiet. Father Norbert finally released Victor's ear and moved out of the way with his bike.

Brother Rombout leaned over Victor, placing a hand on his shoulder. 'Victor, have you ever been on a bike?' Softly.

Victor shook his head. The laughter that followed halted abruptly when the brother raised his head and sent his pupils a withering look.

'Oh, let's just leave him here then,' said Father Norbert brusquely.

Brother Rombout shook his head. 'He can ride on the back of my bike.'

All the students saw the other priest raise his eyebrows, but Brother Rombout ignored him. 'Just wheel your bike back to the rack, Victor. And then you'll come with me.'

And so they rode to La Chapelle, Brother Rombout at the head of the pack with Victor Hoppe sitting on the back of his bicycle, gripping the saddle for dear life. He looked neither right nor left, but he knew that his fellow students were staring at him derisively, making faces at him.

Mocked him and insulted him.

That was how it had started.

Jesus condemned to death. First Station.

That was what the sign said underneath, in three languages: in German, French and Dutch.

Victor stared at the sculpture and he recognised the scene.

The high priests. Who stirred the crowd.

The multitude. That cried, 'Crucify Him!'

Pontius Pilate. Who washed his hands.

And Jesus. Who was bound and silent. Submitted to his fate.

The scene was carved out of white sandstone and crowned an altar of black marble. The altar and the relief carving were set inside a grotto, behind a cast-iron fence. The grotto was made of pumice from the Eifel region, Brother Rombout told them.

Then it was Father Norbert's turn. Before starting on the first prayer he reminded the students that they weren't allowed to talk for the entire Way of the Cross, all fourteen stations of it. Their voices were only to be heard in prayer.

'This holy place will tolerate only holy words,' said the father.

Holy place. Holy words. It made Victor's head buzz.

Then the priest opened his prayer book and intoned, '*We worship Thee, O Christ, and praise Thee.*'

And all the students responded, '*Because by thy holy cross Thou hast redeemed the world.*'

Then Father Norbert recited the prayer of the first station, and when it was over all the students said the Lord's Prayer.

Next they strolled down a twisting paved path to the second station, with Father Norbert reading non-stop from the prayer book, which he carried before him on outspread hands as if it were a dead bird.

Jesus takes the cross upon his shoulders. Second Station.

Again Victor stared, overwhelmed. The grotto. The fence. The altar. The sign. And above all of that, the sculpture.

The three-dimensional relief carving was so lifelike that the stone figures looked as if they might step out of the scene at any moment – as if they were only posing while there were people looking at them. But Victor knew the figures couldn't actually be real, because they were too small. They were even smaller than he was, in fact.

'*Amen.*'

Yet as he followed his class to the next station, he couldn't help glancing over his shoulder, and he kept looking back until the sculpture was out of sight and he was sure that the figures hadn't moved.

So he walked from station to station with the rest of the group, and three times he saw Jesus fall. And three times he had the urge to help Him to his feet again.

But that was what the fence was for, thought Victor to himself – so that no one would help him.

'*We worship Thee, O Christ, and praise Thee.*'

'*Because by thy holy cross Thou hast redeemed the world.*'

They had arrived at the eleventh station.

Jesus is nailed to the cross.

'*Drawn by thy wounds*,' Victor heard the priest pray, as he stared at the raised hammers that were poised to drive the nails through Jesus' hands and feet. For once, Victor was relieved that the figures did not come alive. But that didn't mean that at the next station Jesus would not be hanging from the cross. Victor knew that he would be, and that was why he did not say the Lord's Prayer, because it was God's fault that Jesus had ended up on that cross. He had abandoned his Son to his fate.

'*Amen*.'

This time Victor did not look over his shoulder as they walked on. If he looked back, he knew he would see the figures starting to move. They really would this time, and then the hammers would come down with a wallop. He didn't want to be a witness to that.

He hung back a bit, because he had no desire to see Jesus hanging from the cross either. But Brother Rombout's hand on his shoulder gently pushed him forward.

The path took a sharp turn, and they arrived at the large clearing in front of the twelfth station. Victor's mouth fell open.

There was Jesus on the cross, large as life. Not inside the grotto, but on top of it. Not as part of a relief, but all by Himself, as if He really had been dragged out of the sculpted scene and hung on the cross. As if he had only just died up there, on the hill.

And to the left and right of Jesus were two other crosses, with equally life-sized, crucified men. And at the foot of Jesus' cross, just as large and real, were four people Victor could easily have recognised had he been paying any attention.

All he did see, however, was Christ on the cross – large, and grey-looking; as if dust had drifted down from heaven and settled on Him.

The thought that had first taken hold of Victor a while ago, when they had mocked and jeered at him, now grew more insistent. Each line led to the next.

Thou that destroyst the temple, and buildest it in three days, save Thyself. If Thou be the Son of God, come down from the cross. Likewise also the chief priests mocked him, with the scribes and elders.

A rosary of words unfurled itself.

They said: He has saved others; Himself He cannot save. If He be the King of Israel, let Him now come down from the cross, and we will believe Him.

Victor disengaged himself from the group, and neither Brother Rombout nor Father Norbert saw him go because they had their eyes closed while reciting the Lord's Prayer. Just a handful of students, squinting through half-closed eyes, saw Victor leave.

He trusted in God; let Him deliver Him now, if He will have Him: for He said, I am the Son of God.

He disappeared into the pines that grew on either side of the cave. The students began nudging each other.

The thieves also, that were crucified with Him, cast the same in his teeth.

He emerged from the side, like someone entering from the wings. Hurrying beneath the cross of the murderer, past Mary Magdalene, past the Roman soldier, he halted at the foot of Christ. He stood with his back to the cross, pressing his spine up against it. The top of his head came up to Christ's navel.

Now from the sixth hour there was darkness over all the land unto the ninth hour. And about the ninth hour Jesus cried with a loud voice.

Then Victor stretched out his arms like Jesus Christ above him, opened his mouth and cried, 'ELI, ELI, LAMMA SABAKTÁNI!'

His shrill voice soared into the sky and everyone looked up to see Victor as his head sank slowly down.

* * *

A few weeks after Victor Hoppe's article was published in *Cell* a treacherous wind came blowing in from the west, from across the Atlantic. At Philadelphia's Wistar Institute for Anatomy and Biology the biologists David Solar and James Grath had pored over the article shaking their heads. The two scientists had been working on cell-nucleus transplantation for many years, and had built up an impressive and unassailable reputation in that field. Victor Hoppe's account immediately raised many questions in their minds. Professional jealousy no doubt played a part, but that never came up for discussion. What mattered was that they had questions. And that was why they decided to undertake what Victor had consistently refused to do: repeat the experiment.

They didn't take any short cuts. Their experiments took them three long years – three years of hovering over the same little spot, like wide-winged vultures coasting on a breeze.

If anyone could have felt that wind coming, it ought to have been Rex Cremer. In those same three years he too had repeatedly tried to duplicate Victor Hoppe's experiment, yet not once had he managed to clone a mouse embryo. Something always went wrong. One time the embryos died when they were still in the growth medium, another time they failed to implant in the uterus, and on those rare occasions when the experiment actually did result in a birth, the mice were either stillborn or had severe birth defects. You just have to keep trying, Victor insisted, but he had never shown him how, or given him a helping hand.

Notwithstanding his optimistic predictions, Victor had not managed to clone any adult mice in those three years either, so that Cremer was beginning to doubt that his technique was viable. Victor maintained that in his own case it wasn't the technique that was the problem but the fact that he wasn't having any luck deprogramming the cells. He did grant that he was finding it more difficult than he had expected – it was the first time he'd admitted to any such thing – and when one day he finally did achieve a breakthrough, he acknowledged, moreover, that luck had played a significant part. He explained that, after abandoning a certain experiment, he had left the used cells in their Petri dish and forgotten about them. Under normal circumstances he would have added some supplemental serum to the growth medium to keep the cells alive, but he had not done so this time, so that the cells had literally been starved. A few days later he happened to come across the same Petri dish again and decided, just out of curiosity, to examine the cells. He saw that some of them were dead; but others were still alive, although so badly weakened that they had lost their specialist function. These cells had therefore reverted to the elemental phase, as if they had not divided more than once or twice – the exact stage Victor had been attempting to arrive at for almost two years. All that was left was to deduce the quantity of serum needed to ensure that the cells would not have sufficient nourishment to thrive but would be kept just alive, frozen in the G0 phase.

Rex heard Victor's story with growing astonishment, and when he had finished, he told him that all scientific discoveries hinged on such flukes: quirky coincidences that then had to be turned into verifiable fact.

Victor replied, 'I've got the hang of it now. It won't be long.'

'How much longer, Victor?'

A firm date would help the dean to placate the other members of the faculty, who were running out of patience.

'Before the end of the year.'

It was July 1983.

'That's just six months from now.'

'Six months from now,' Victor echoed, and from his tone it was impossible to tell if he considered that to be plenty of time, or not.

Victor, in the meantime, had contacted the women again. But before ringing them he'd put down on paper what he wanted to say. Literally. Word for word. He had even read the sentences aloud to himself, to try to make them sound as natural as possible.

He would like them to come to Aachen. Just to talk. More than that he would not say. Of course they were bound to ask him what he wanted to talk about. About the past, he would answer them. But also the future. He would tell them that science had made great strides in the past few years. He would not mention the part he had played in it. He would also tell them that what used to be quite impossible was now merely difficult. And what had proved to be difficult before, was now much easier. He thought that sounded quite good.

One of the women answered the phone, and he told her his name and asked how she was and how her friend was doing. The whole thing was written down on the slip of paper next to the phone. But then she gave an answer that didn't fit in with his scenario. Her friend had run off with someone else. Not too long ago. It had only been a month or two.

He had no idea what to say. He couldn't think of the right words. Fortunately for him, she immediately started pouring her heart out.

She rambled on for quite a while, and so all he had to do was make sympathetic noises.

Finally she stopped in mid-sentence and apologised – said that she shouldn't be bothering him with this. And then she asked what she could do for him. She probably just meant to ask about the reason for his call, but Victor Hoppe did not interpret it that way. He took it literally. So, apparently *she* wanted to do something for *him*. The very thing he wanted, in fact.

'I want you to come here,' he said. It wasn't a question and sounded more like a demand.

She replied that she was experiencing financial difficulties, that she couldn't afford the trip; and a hotel room was out of the question.

He told her that he would reimburse her for any expenses. Money was no object.

Then she asked what he wanted to talk to her about, which finally gave him the opportunity to consult his notes.

He had no trouble persuading her. There was her injured self-image. There was her jealousy. And her loneliness. All of it had been fermenting inside her for the past two months. As it happened, his proposal had come at a very good time. A baby would re-establish her womanhood. It would be a thorn in her ex-lover's side. And it would put an end to her loneliness. What's more, it was going to be a girl – a girl who would look just like her.

The wind that had sprung up in Philadelphia three years earlier and that had, over time, increased to hurricane strength reached the European mainland at the end of February 1984. That was when an article appeared in the journal *Science* entitled, 'Instability of mouse blastomere nuclei transferred to enucleated zygotes to support development *in vitro*'. The authors were David Solar and James Grath, and their article discredited Dr Victor Hoppe's findings. Solar and Grath had followed his method of cloning mouse embryos to the letter, and they had not once succeeded in culturing an embryo that survived. They had gone over Victor Hoppe's report with a razor-sharp knife and mercilessly eviscerated almost every point he had made. Their conclusion was as terse as it was unequivocal: 'The cloning of mammals by transferring a cell nucleus to an egg is impossible from a scientific standpoint.'

Even more important was what could be read between the lines. The article suggested that Victor Hoppe's work was worthless and, even worse, that he had committed fraud.

Rex Cremer barged into the lab without knocking. He was holding the issue of *Science*, and from a distance waved it at Victor, who was seated at his desk.

'Have you read it?'

'They're incompetent bunglers,' Victor said quickly.

'That's what they are accusing *you* of.'

'Oh, who cares what they say?'

'They have a reputation, Victor! And they are leaders in the field!'

'It doesn't mean a thing.'

'It means everything, because what they say is immediately taken as gospel.'

'They're bunglers, nevertheless.'

'I've never managed to repeat your experiment either,' said Rex dryly. 'Not once, in three years.'

This time there was no response. Victor would not look up.

The dean continued. 'I've always backed you', he began calmly, 'and I would like to come to your defence again, but this time you'll have to cooperate. The rest of the faculty is furious.'

'It's no business of theirs,' Victor muttered into his beard.

'It certainly is very much their business. The entire department is affected. Even the vice chancellor has had to field unpleasant questions. It is urgent that we come up with a response.'

'I won't respond to slander.'

'This isn't slander! Can't you get that through your head? It's the result of years of research by two highly respected scientists. If you won't defend yourself, then it's over.'

'What is over?'

'All of it. The entire experiment. The subsidies will dry up and the department will be cut back, perhaps even eliminated.'

Still Victor wouldn't look up. He was breathing heavily. 'There's more,' he said finally.

'What did you say?'

'That there's more.'

'What do you mean?'

'I can prove them wrong.'

'Then you should do just that.'

'It's too soon.'

'You promised you'd be finished in six months. It's been seven months now. I was really hoping you'd have come up with something, Victor.'

Rex sighed. He realised that he had been much too trusting and that he would end up having to pay the price for his naivety.

Behind the desk Victor folded his hands and lifted his head. 'I *have* finished,' he said. 'But now I've got to wait.'

'What do you mean, Victor? Stop speaking in riddles. This really isn't the time.'

'I'll show you.'

He stood up and walked over to the table that held the binocular microscope used for the cell-injection process. Surrounding it were piles of papers and journals and racks of empty test tubes. A quick glance told Rex that there was notepaper everywhere, all over the lab, but apart from that there was no other sign of Victor's work. He saw no test equipment, no Petri dishes nor mouse cages anywhere. It did indeed look as if Victor had completed his experiment, as he claimed, and that he was now killing time reading magazines, like a watchman on the night shift.

Victor returned with a stack of cards and started flipping through them. As though getting ready for a round of poker, he removed five cards from the stack and placed them on the desk top, under Cremer's nose. Five identical photographs, each marked with the same date and a different three-digit number. They were pictures of microscope slides. Not providing any explanation, Victor next slapped down another five photos on the desk top. These too were identical, and were barely different from the first five pictures. Each photograph showed the tip of a pipette piercing a cell wall. Just above this row of ten images Victor spread another series of five pictures, each showing a cell after the first cell division – the date was one day later than the previous photos. Not saying a word, he went on to a fourth, then a fifth set of images, each showing the next stage in the growth process of an embryo.

So far Rex was not particularly impressed. What Victor was showing him was no different from photos he'd taken himself. The next series too, with eight-cell embryos – at the stage, therefore, when they were ready to be implanted into the uterus – wasn't anything new.

'What do you want—' he began.

'Wait,' said Victor, dealing out another couple of series of five pictures, planting down his thumb hard on each photo, as if stressing its importance. Rex now saw that in every new set of pictures the embryo seemed to be growing. From eight cells to sixteen cells to thirty-two cells. That, as far as he knew, had never been accomplished artificially without resulting in all kinds of abnormality. By the next set, you couldn't even count the cells with the naked eye, but there had to be sixty-four, and when Victor spread out the last set, so that the entire desk top was covered from corner to comer, the dean knew that the embryo in the photo had grown into one hundred and twenty-eight cells.

'How did you do it?' he asked excitedly. 'And why let them grow to this stage?'

'When a fertilised egg travels in the normal way down the Fallopian tube to the uterus,' Victor explained, 'it arrives when it has grown to the size shown in this photo. Five or six days after conception.'

Tapping his finger on one of the photos in the last series, he continued, 'The chances of an artificially fertilised egg implanting itself in the uterus are likewise greatly increased if it is transferred at a much later stage than has been done before now.'

'But no one has ever managed to produce embryos this far along.'

'Sometimes what seems impossible is merely difficult,' Victor said, almost mechanically.

'But then how, Victor?'

'It's just a matter of discovering the right equation. It's chemistry, that's all it is. I'll write the whole thing up for you.'

'Well, you'd better do it quickly,' said Rex, who was starting to feel hopeful again. He picked up one of the last photos and read the date:

10 February 1984. Counting on his fingers, he said, 'It's been nearly three weeks. So you should be expecting the mice to be born any time now?'

He saw Victor shaking his head.

'Did it go wrong?' he asked. 'Did they abort after all?'

Again Victor shook his head.

'What, then, Victor?' exclaimed Rex impatiently.

'It's going to take about nine months,' said Victor, staring into space.

About nine months. The words swam around in Cremer's mind. Nine months. He gulped, hoping that the thought that had just come into his head was wrong. With a sick feeling he turned to look at the photograph in his hand, even though he knew it wouldn't make him any the wiser. Most mammalian embryos looked almost identical at that stage.

'Are they . . .' he began, but could not get the words out.

'Human embryos,' Victor asserted.

Rex buried his head in his hands.

If anyone actually did commit fraud in this whole affair, as was the charge, it was Rex Cremer, when he found out that Victor was in the process of cloning a human being. He certainly knew what he was doing, but felt he had no choice. It was the only way he saw left to him to rectify the situation. His decision may have been overly short-sighted, or coloured by self-interest; perhaps it was pure panic, but in any case it was his own decision. It was true that Victor had presented him with a fait accompli, but the scenario that came next was all down to Cremer. He prevailed upon Victor to go along with it, though he did have to resort to a stratagem to make him come on board. For starters, he told Victor to clone some adult mice as quickly as he could, since that was the experiment he was supposed to be working on. Victor might consider it a step in the wrong direction, but at least he'd be able to rebut Solar and Grath's criticism that way and, even more important – and Rex said this with great emphasis – he would also convert the rest of the unbelievers. Besides, it would give Victor a chance to prepare people for the news about the human cloning, which would otherwise smite mankind like a thunderbolt out of a clear blue sky.

Convert the rest of the unbelievers. Prepare the people. Smite mankind. A thunderbolt out of a clear blue sky. Rex Cremer used those words deliberately, and they did not fall on deaf ears. The dean also suggested that they pretend the photos he'd just seen were of mouse embryos rather than human ones.

'I've got to show the others *something*,' he explained. 'That's the only way to convince them at this stage.'

'Of what?' Victor asked.

'Of the righteousness of your work.'

Again he had been deliberate in his choice of words, but he also meant what he said. He sincerely believed that Victor had achieved as much as he claimed he had, although he was somewhat dubious about the experiment's eventual outcome – more dubious, in fact, than about the experiment itself. For the moment, anyway. He was secretly hoping that the embryos had not implanted themselves in the woman's womb, or that they would still end up being rejected. It would spare him a good deal of guilt, although that wasn't his first concern.

'What if they want to know where the embryos are?' Victor asked.

'Then we'll tell them that they were aborted. I can show them some abnormal embryos from my own research.'

'We? You're saying that "we" will tell them . . .'

'Yes, Victor, that's right: we. You and I. We'll have to get our story straight. Later, when the time is ripe, we'll tell them the truth. And then they'll understand. Right now we're just playing for time. We must prepare the world for what is to come.'

Victor nodded, and Rex had the feeling that he had convinced him. He'd been right to think it was possible to steer Victor in a certain direction by using the right words. Victor could be influenced through rhetoric. He seemed to hold the word in greater esteem than he held knowledge. Or perhaps he considered the word to be the higher form of knowledge – Rex wasn't quite sure which, but it didn't really matter. Either would suffice to explain why Victor did not attach much importance to scientific papers, for papers were about data, less about words, and bombastic language was totally taboo. It was the content that mattered, not the aesthetics.

A little while later Rex put his theory to the test once more by asking Victor another question. He was so convinced that he had worked Victor out that he thought he already knew the answer.

What he asked was why Victor had chosen to clone himself. He was certain he would again say something about God creating man in his own image.

But this time Victor's answer was quite different. The first thing he did was point at his mouth – at the scar over his upper lip, half-hidden by his moustache. 'Because of this,' he said. No obfuscating words. No rhetoric.

'What do you mean?' Rex asked, his voice wavering.

'This will be the proof. Just like the colour of the fur in the case of the mice.'

Rex immediately saw what he meant. All of a sudden it was about science again. About the substantiation of it. The proof. What had happened to the word?

'So you mean,' he began, with some hesitation, 'that if the baby, when it's born, also has . . .' – he pointed awkwardly at his own upper lip – 'then that would be the physical proof that the baby is your clone.'

Victor nodded.

'But it can also simply run in the family, be passed on from father to son, can't it?' Rex had no idea of how close his remark was to the truth. 'It can be inherited. It's a genetic defect, isn't it?'

Victor nodded again, but was ready with his answer. 'Every cleft palate is unique,' he said in a professorial voice. 'Its position, form, depth and width. Therefore if I can show that the child's cleft is identical to mine . . .'

'But how are you going to do that?' Rex interrupted him. 'Yours has been . . .'

He wasn't able to come up with the right word, and therefore made another awkward gesture.

Victor pushed a cardboard file towards him. 'With this,' he said.

Rex opened the file and stared open-mouthed at the pictures, all in black and white, in stark focus, so that each photo mercilessly displayed what the scar had kept hidden all these years. He couldn't tear his eyes away from it. From the missing tissue, and the skull showing beneath. And the longer he looked at the pictures, the more he felt something inside him was being ripped asunder – as if what he was looking at were contagious.

'And the woman, Victor?' he managed to say. 'The woman. Does she know?'

Victor did not reply, and Rex understood.

Victor had not told her. He had tried to, but had not been able to do it. He had started to tell her, and at first it had gone well, the way he had planned it. He'd said that the baby would come from her own egg cells and that there would be no sperm involved. That much was true, and so he'd been able to say it without any qualms.

She had repeated his words to herself. *Own egg cells. No sperm.*

Her enthusiastic reaction made Victor realise at once that his words had given her cause to assume something he had never intended her to think.

She'd exclaimed, 'So the child will look exactly like me!'

He was going to tell her that the child she would give birth to would not look like her – not remotely like her. He was going to add that he would make her a child that looked like her the *next* time.

He was going to tell her. But then she said it.

She said, 'A child that looks exactly like me. Now *that* would be a gift from God.'

Her words had cut him to the quick.

* * *

At the secondary level of the Christian Brothers' School Victor was given many nicknames that made fun of the way he looked. Even the teachers, both the monks and the laymen, would sometimes refer to him as 'Red in Form 2B', or 'Harelip in Form 4A'. Victor heard it all, especially when the students yelled all sorts of nasty things behind his back, but he didn't let it bother him. There was very little, in fact, that bothered him. Which was fortunate, for in those years there was no one to stand up for him the way Brother Rombout had stood up for him in primary school.

His indifferent demeanour led people to say that Victor had erected a wall to protect himself from whatever was thrown at him –

sometimes literally, when they pelted him with wads of paper or balls, or figuratively, when the other kids jeered at him or called him names.

Since he never showed much reaction, the teasing didn't go very far. At the beginning of each school year, when the presence of new boys in the class meant that his classmates had to prove themselves all over again, Victor was always seriously tormented, but after just a few weeks they would start leaving him alone again.

In the dormitory, too, he did not attract much attention, especially since he always had his nose in a book. Victor read and read, always and everywhere. He read textbooks, he read encyclopedias, he read journals, he read reference books.

The list of books he borrowed from the school library was impressively long, but also limited, for Victor was only interested in books that touched on the natural sciences. Not once did he ever take out a book on any other subject, or read something just for fun.

His extreme fixation estranged Victor even further from those around him. For when Victor did speak, it was always about the wonders of the human body or about the workings of the X-ray machine or about some new drug that had been developed to combat an exotic disease. And once you got him talking, he'd drone on and on with such pedantry that there were few who were able, or even wanted, to follow what he was saying. He wasn't conscious of this himself because nothing ever seemed to get through to him. It was only when the teacher shouted at him to wrap up his monologue that he would stop.

It was also during Victor's years at the secondary school that his supposed 'sloppiness' grew more pronounced. At least that was how the teachers interpreted his habit of handing in incomplete assignments. Some teachers called it laziness, and as a matter of fact they were the ones who came closest to the truth. For Victor simply didn't bother to do many of his assignments, because he did not see the point of repeating the same thing over again once he knew how to do it, or of writing something down on paper when it was all already imprinted on his brain.

Owing to his purported sloppiness and the limited scope of his interests, Victor was only a middling student. He received high marks for physics, chemistry and biology; in Latin and languages he was about average, while in geography, history and maths he usually just skated by. He almost always failed religious studies, music and art, but never badly enough to keep him back a year. Skipping a form, as he had done in primary school, was out of the question in the light of his unimpressive grades. Victor therefore took six years to complete secondary school, like most of the other students, but since he had already been advanced for his age when he started, he was still, at sixteen, the youngest boy to graduate on 30 June 1961, and heading straight for university.

In those six years he had never had another outburst, or made a spectacle of himself. It has to be said that Victor had found peace in his own set of beliefs – peace in the sense that he was not troubled by any new insights. God did bad, evil things, and Jesus only did good.

Jesus had been punished for it, too, in the end. Victor had seen that with his own eyes. If you did good, you were punished for it. This had been confirmed on Calvary Hill, when Father Norbert had dragged him away from the cross and boxed his ears, like a thunderstorm breaking out overhead.

'God will punish you for this, Victor Hoppe!'

The bad would always try to vanquish the good. Again and again and again.

Notwithstanding all that he was up against, Victor was determined to continue to do good. It was still his goal in life to become a doctor, and as long as he had that goal, and was working towards it, nothing could make him change his mind.

But he did have to remain on his guard against the bad. It was always lying in wait for you. He could tell that from looking at his father. As a doctor he did good, but as a father he did bad. And the bad was getting worse. Even though Victor was seldom home, his father always found some reason to get angry with him. Then he'd yell louder and louder, and sometimes it would come to blows.

'*What have I done to deserve this, for Christ's sake!*' That was a frequent cry of his, and Victor knew that he was referring to the evil that had taken possession of him.

Even the people in the village said so. His father had not yet returned from making house calls one day, and there were people waiting for him at the gate. Victor was in his room and could hear their voices outside his window.

'The doctor isn't doing too well, is he?'

'It's going from bad to worse.'

That was what they'd said. And that had been enough for Victor.

Victor was fifteen when he found out that the mental institution where he had spent his early years was in the village of La Chapelle. He had never given the institution much thought while he was at school. It wasn't as if he had forgotten it, but it had been a long time since anything had triggered the relevant cogs in his brain to set his memory in motion. Anything that used to do so no longer held that power. The weekly Mass and daily prayers just rolled off his back. He had permanently packed away the Bible he used to read so avidly, just as he would pack away his old textbooks at the end of the school year. At the secondary school he never again had a teacher like Brother Rombout, who with his gentle mien and mellifluent voice had kept alive the memory of Sister Marthe, and ever since he had moved to a new dormitory, even Father Norbert, whose stentorian tones sometimes reminded him of Sister Milgitha, had disappeared from his immediate radar.

All in all, besides finding some peace in his belief system, Victor actually found some peace of mind at the school. But then something happened to jog his memory, not suddenly, but bit by bit – as if someone had started plucking the strings inside his head, and the sequence of sounds turned into a recognisable melody.

It happened, as before, on the occasion of the annual class outing. The students in fifth-form Latin always took a trip to the three-border junction, and from there on up to Calvary Hill at La Chapelle. Victor had never been to the former but was all too familiar with the latter. Yet he did not raise his hand when the students were asked if any of them had already followed the Stations of the Cross. Nor was he looking forward to it much. He had no interest in seeing the three-border junction, and as for Christ's Road to Calvary, he didn't need to be confronted with that again.

This time the students went by coach. There were twenty-one of them, and none of the boys would sit next to Victor. He didn't care.

He didn't even notice. There were boys seated in front and behind him, however, and one of them, Nico Franck, a gangly seventeen-year-old, tapped him on the shoulder just as the coach was leaving.

'Victor, you know we're going to be right by the mental institution.'

The boy sitting next to Nico Franck, promptly added, 'Yeah, and you'd better make sure the nuns don't catch sight of you, or they'll come and get you.'

'And then they'll put you back in with the idiots, where you belong,' said Nico.

The laughter that followed did not bother Victor. What did bother him was the words: *Institution*. *Nuns*. *Idiots*. Three memory strings that were plucked.

Victor stared out of the window, but he barely noticed what he was looking at. He didn't even notice that they drove right past his house.

'That's where Victor lives, during the holidays. His father is the local doctor,' his Latin teacher, Brother Thomas, said.

'I thought he lived in a mental institution!' Nico Franck jeered, jumping up and tapping Victor on the top of his head.

'Franck, sit down and behave!' shouted Brother Thomas sternly.

The laughter continued a while longer.

Mental institution. That string being plucked again. The start of a melody.

When the coach reached the top of Mount Vaalserberg, everyone got out. Victor was the last one to exit the bus. As Herr Robert, the geography teacher, explained what they were here to see, Victor looked about. It was crowded. Dozens of tourists wandered around the summit, which was furnished with a kiosk and a few benches.

'They're going to build a new tower up here, one that'll be even taller than the Juliana Tower,' said the teacher. 'The old tower is over there – in the Netherlands. Have any of you ever been to the Netherlands?'

Victor didn't hear the question. He was thinking about the institution. About the nuns. About the idiots.

Imbeciles. *Retards*. The two words spontaneously popped into his head.

'Victor, let's go!'

The troop of students had already set off in the direction of the three-border junction. Victor trotted after them.

A cement column. That was all it was.

'Belgium, the Netherlands, Germany,' said Herr Robert as he paced around the column, sticking his arms out at right angles.

Victor did not get what the teacher was trying to show them. It was too abstract for him. Brother Rombout would have made it easier for him to visualise; he'd have taken a piece of chalk and drawn some lines on the ground, and then Victor would probably have been able to see it. His mind was elsewhere, anyhow. And it didn't improve matters when something Brother Thomas said triggered something else inside Victor's head.

'This is the geographer's golden calf,' said the monk. He placed one hand on the stone and the other on his fellow teacher's shoulder. 'The physical representation of something that is in fact invisible. Just like God, in other words.'

Victor did not hear the irony in the monk's voice. What he heard was 'golden calf'. And 'God'. Which suddenly made him recall another voice: '*Moh-zzes, Victor. With a zzzzz. As in ro-ses.*'

He felt a shudder running up his spine. From there on, nothing registered. He didn't see the boys in his class pacing around the three borders, scissoring with their arms and legs. He did not hear the geography teacher asking him if he didn't want to go 'abroad', like the other boys. Nor did he hear Brother Thomas say, 'Victor is dreaming about travelling much further. He's dreaming of the seven seas.'

After the class had wandered over to the highest point in the Netherlands, where, according to Brother Thomas, the three border posts represented people's desperation for something to hitch themselves to in life, they climbed back into the coach.

'Now we'll be driving to La Chapelle,' said Herr Robert. 'To Calvary Hill. Brother Thomas will give us its history.'

'At the end of the eighteenth century', began the monk, 'a boy named Peter Arnold lived here. He suffered from epilepsy and one day he bought a figurine of Mary in the market and hung it from an old oak tree . . .'

'Victor, are you paying attention?' Herr Robert, who had taken a seat beside him, nudged the boy.

'Hung it from an old oak tree,' Victor answered mechanically.

The geography teacher nodded and went back to listening.

'. . . was cured of his epilepsy. That is why the Clare Sisters had a chapel built right beside that oak tree. A few years later another miracle occurred. Frederik Pelzer, a boy about your age, was abruptly cured of his insanity after his parents went to the chapel to pray for him. The nuns then decided to build a convent and a mental institution next to the chapel, to save even more unfortunates.'

Unfortunates. Most of the words had gone right over Victor's head, but that word snagged him like a fish hook. He hadn't heard it since he had left the institution.

Let us pray for the unfortunates. That was the way Sister Milgitha would begin the prayer when they were brought to the chapel. The unfortunates – that was them, the patients.

The cogs in his brain began to turn, in the cadence of a litany.

Marc François.

Fabian Nadler.

Jean Surmont.

Every name called up a face.

Nico Baumgarten.

Angelo Venturini.

Egon Weiss.

He saw Angelo Venturini placing the pillow over Egon Weiss's face.

Let us pray for Egon Weiss, who has exchanged the temporal for the eternal.

So that his soul may find peace.

Are you praying for Egon? That's good. Then he's sure to find peace.

God giveth and God taketh away, Victor.

He saw Sister Marthe turn her back and walk away. She walked as if she were bearing a heavy cross.

Victor was found in the convent's churchyard. He was on his knees before a headstone, hands folded.

It was at the Sixth Station of the Cross that it had dawned on Herr Robert that Victor was no longer with the other students. Nobody knew how long he'd been gone. Nobody had missed him.

Brother Thomas and Sister Milgitha were the ones who found him.

The convent's abbess clapped her hands to her mouth when she caught sight of the boy.

'Do you know him?' the monk asked her.

But she shook her head.

'No, I don't know him,' was her reply. 'I've never seen him before. He must have been lost.'

Then Brother Thomas took the boy by the arm and led him away. Victor meekly went with him.

He hadn't been lost. The place where they found him was simply as far as he'd got.

Dr Karl Hoppe was reading the newspaper after breakfast when his son came into the kitchen. The boy poured himself a cup of milk and stood hovering by the sink.

'When did you take me out of the institution at La Chapelle?'

It was a double whammy: the very fact that Victor had suddenly asked him a question, and then of course the question itself.

'What did you say?' the doctor asked, outwardly unruffled. He turned a page of the newspaper and hoped Victor would not have the guts to ask the question again.

But he did.

'Institution?' the doctor heard himself say. 'What gave you that idea? You've never been in an institution.' He did not look up as he said it.

'But wasn't I . . .' began Victor. 'The sisters . . .'

'No, Victor, you were not!' said the doctor, raising his voice. Slapping his paper down on the table, he jerked up his head. 'If I say you weren't, then you weren't! I'm the one who should know!'

His son dawdled a bit longer, evidently mulling it over, and then turned on his heel. As he did so he let go of his cup of milk. He didn't hurl it down on the floor; no, he simply turned round, let the cup fall from his hand and walked away.

Karl Hoppe sat there for a moment, frozen, as if nailed to his chair. Then he jumped up and ran after his son.

When Victor returned to his boarding school a few days later, he found, unpacking his suitcase, a file with his name on it. In the upper right-hand corner was printed 'Sanatorium of the Convent of St Clare', followed by an address in La Chapelle. The file didn't contain any letters, just an index card with some dates on it and a couple of black-and-white photographs.

Victor stared at the photos dispassionately, as if seeing them through the eyes of a doctor who has already seen this many times before.

Then he studied the card. Each date was followed by one or more words. 'Feeble-minded,' it said in a couple of them. 'Can speak. Unintelligibly, alas,' he read. Then he read the last line. 'Discharged,' it said, preceded by a date: 23 January 1950.

Seeing that date did shake him, however.

* * *

Rex Cremer immediately sensed something was afoot. Prior to the meeting his colleagues on the faculty had started avoiding him, and whenever he tried to engage anyone in conversation, the answer was curt or unresponsive. They'd have to change their tune soon enough, he thought to himself.

When the vice chancellor had called the meeting to order, Rex took the floor and passed around the photos of the six-day-old embryos. He felt slightly uncomfortable claiming they were mouse embryos, and his discomfort grew when nobody said a word. He noticed some of the faculty looking at the vice chancellor, who cleared his throat and said, 'We cannot take anything for granted any more. We understand that you want to support Dr Hoppe, but there is too much at stake to let matters simply take their course.'

'But . . . the photographs speak for themselves, surely?' said Rex, hearing Victor's voice in his own.

'This isn't about the photographs,' said the vice chancellor, 'Not in the first instance.'

Rex swallowed. He wondered if the vice chancellor knew he was lying about the photos. The thought made him shudder. It was just beginning to dawn on him that he had made a terrible mistake. The events of the past few days had disconcerted him. He had started doing things he'd never have done before; things that would never even have occurred to him.

The vice chancellor took advantage of Cremer' s silence. 'There is going to be an inquiry. We have set up an international scientific commission, which is to investigate whether Dr Hoppe has . . .' – the vice chancellor hesitated briefly – 'whether Dr Hoppe has been making things up.'

Making things up. It was one of the worst things a scientist could be accused of. And the very fact that an investigative commission had been set up without Rex's knowledge meant that they were having doubts about him too. That set his mind reeling. Could it be that it was all indeed a sham and that he hadn't been able to see it because he did not think Victor capable of such a thing? Could it be that Victor had taken advantage of his belief in him? Rex tried to sort it out in his head, but the vice chancellor was still droning on, as if reading a declaration.

'The investigation will focus, first and foremost, on the cloned-mouse experiment that is being disputed by Dr Solar and Dr Grath. Dr Hoppe will have to give a demonstration of his method, and the commission will check to see if the claims he makes in the article in *Cell* are corroborated by his actual research data.'

The research data were a muddled labyrinth in which only Victor would be able to find his way – Cremer knew that. Besides, Victor would refuse to demonstrate his technique, for he was bound to consider the entire investigation a waste of time. Rex knew that too. And yet he made a split-second decision not to say anything. The commission members would just have to see for themselves how difficult it was to work with Victor Hoppe. Then they would understand that even he, as dean, had had no say in the whole affair. It might even be to his advantage if the commission did conclude that the whole thing was a sham. Then he could simply make it plain that he'd had nothing to do with it – that Victor had planned and executed the entire thing all by himself.

'What do you say, Dr Cremer?' asked the vice chancellor.

The dean was still staring at the photographs, wondering how he could ever have allowed himself to be swept along like that. He remembered his excitement when Victor had shown him the photos, but also how shocking it had been to find out that they were human embryos. And he had done nothing – taken no action. Not even when Victor had shown him what the child would look like at birth.

'Dr Cremer?' The vice chancellor's voice startled him out of his musings.

Rex looked up and, putting one hand to his chin, said, 'Yes, I do think it's important for us to find out if anything has been misrepresented.'

When Victor found out that there was to be an investigation into his activities, he went straight to the vice chancellor to submit his resignation. The vice chancellor told him that that would be interpreted by the outside world as a confession of guilt. If Victor was convinced that he had done nothing wrong, then it would be best to wait for the outcome of the investigation. To Victor, the very fact that there was to be an investigation was a sign of their lack of confidence in him, but the vice chancellor assured him that the probe was not intended so much to uncover lies as to shine a brighter light on the truth, and so refute Solar and Grath's criticism. Once Victor had thought it over, he decided he could live with that, and said nothing more about resigning.

He did insist on absenting himself while the investigation was being conducted, because he couldn't bear to watch strangers messing with his life's work. When the vice chancellor asked him if he wouldn't agree just once to give a demonstration of his methods, he replied that it was all clearly described in his article, and that the rest was a question of technique, which meant practice, practice, practice. He considered himself entitled, therefore, to keep his technique a secret, in order to prevent others from taking credit for it. The vice chancellor objected, saying that he was not making the commission's task any easier. But Victor craftily turned the tables on him by answering that it would give them the opportunity to demonstrate their own competence.

In his conversations with the commission members Rex Cremer minimised his own role in the affair. He granted that as dean he should have exerted more control, but in his own defence he argued that, when he had been hired, Dr Hoppe had insisted on complete independence. He had made frequent attempts to find out more about Dr Hoppe's methods, but the latter had never agreed to divulge details. If that was so, the commission wanted to know, why had Cremer not asked more questions? Cremer told them that Dr Hoppe had managed to fob him off each time with his claim that it was just a matter of technique. One of the commission members asked if he still believed that was true. 'No,' he said. And reiterated it.

The inquiry had been in full swing for a month when Cremer received a phone call at home from Victor, who had been staying away from the university and had returned to Bonn in the interim. He wasn't particularly surprised that Victor was calling him out of the blue; he expected that Victor wanted to find out what progress the commission had made with their investigation.

'Victor! It's been a while,' he said in a neutral tone. He was determined to keep his distance.

'I need your help,' said Victor, coming straight to the point.

'Victor, the commission is still investigating. I can't tell you anything. I don't know anything. They're just doing their job, and—'

'It isn't about the commission,' Victor replied firmly. 'I'm not bothered about that.'

Rex was startled, but also wary. He wasn't about to let himself be talked into anything again. 'What's it about then?' he asked, trying to keep his voice as light as possible.

'The embryos,' said Victor.

Rex let out an audible sigh. 'OK, what's the matter with the embryos?' he asked, but quickly caught himself. 'Which embryos?'

'The clones. My clones.'

'Victor, I don't know if I can—'

'Rex, I need your help!' was the desperate cry.

Rex was flabbergasted. He had never heard Victor sound like this. He was always so self-confident, and had never even asked for advice, let alone help.

'What's the matter, then?'

'There are four of them . . . There's going to be four . . .' Victor blurted out. He was talking so fast that it was even more difficult to understand him than usual. 'Four, don't you understand? It's too many! It wasn't what I—'

'Calm down, Victor!' shouted Rex, but then was appalled at his own tone. Taking a deep breath, he said, 'I'm trying to follow what you mean.'

He knew perfectly well what Victor meant, but had no idea what he thought of it, nor if he ought to believe it. When Victor had shown him the pictures of the five embryos six weeks ago, he had told him that he'd introduced all five into the woman's womb in the hope that at least one would implant itself. Rex had thought it rather a large number – standard procedure was two to four embryos, at least in the case of *in vitro* fertilisation. Now it looked as if only one of the embryos had been rejected, and the other four had implanted themselves and begun to develop. If it were true and everything took its normal course, then there would be a quadruple birth. Four clones in one go. If it were true. But he didn't believe it. And, what was more, he wanted to have nothing to do with it.

'I don't see the problem, Victor,' he said dismissively. 'Four out of five embryos. I'd call that a success.'

'It's too many.'

'Couldn't you have foreseen that? Or perhaps you underestimated yourself?'

He was conscious of the derisive tone, and wondered if Victor would notice.

'I wanted to be certain,' said Victor.

'So, now you are.'

'But there's four of them. I don't know if she'll want them. If she'll want to raise—'

'So? In that case you can take a couple of them yourself.'

'I can't. I don't know how—'

'Well, then you will have to face up to your responsibilities,' said Rex, in a rather paternalistic tone of voice. 'It goes without saying. If you decide to bring children into the world, you have an obligation to look after them.'

Amused, he waited for an answer, which failed to come.

'Victor?'

But the phone had already gone dead.

The commission completed its inquiry in two months. In the report that was delivered to the vice chancellor on 30 May 1984 there wasn't a word about fraud, or deception, or fabricated data. The independent investigators had found no proof of any such thing. In no way, however, did this mean they endorsed Victor Hoppe's experiments or imply that his results could be accepted as genuine. On the contrary, the commission had determined that Victor Hoppe's notes were 'riddled with deletions, illegible passages, muddled statements and contradictory data'. Consequently, the commission had concluded that 'even the most elementary scientific guidelines had not been followed' and it therefore arrived at the verdict that 'the value of Dr Victor Hoppe's entire inquiry must be brought into question'.

* * *

I'm proud of you, Victor. I'm truly proud of you.

That was what his father had wanted to say, on the phone, when Victor told him the news. He had been prepared to say it.

But the tone in which his son had informed him that he had passed his medical degree held him back. It was a tone of complete indifference. As usual. And he thought, Can't you just be *proud* of yourself for once, Victor? Shout it to the rooftops, for crying out loud!

He did not voice those thoughts. He simply said, 'That's very good, Victor. Excellent.' As if someone had asked him how he liked some culinary dish.

And when he hung up, he cursed himself. Also as usual.

He started the letter with 'Dear Victor', but immediately crossed that out. Then he tried 'My son', and 'Son', but went with a simple 'Victor' in the end.

The vice chancellor of Aachen University summoned Victor Hoppe to his office in the early afternoon of 27 June 1966. He glanced at the young man and asked himself if they had ever met before. Probably not, or he would doubtless have remembered him.

The vice chancellor had been informed by Dr Bergmann, the dean of the College of Biomedical Sciences, that Victor Hoppe had graduated *cum laude* the previous day, and that he had always been a quiet, hard worker, his innate talents boosted by his extraordinary persistence – a young man of few words but abundant results. Promising. Dr Bergmann hoped that Victor Hoppe would pursue his doctorate in one of his college's departments.

'Is he emotional? Will the news . . .' the vice chancellor had enquired at the end of the conversation.

The dean had been unable to say.

The young man sat there rather stiffly. His head was slightly bowed, arms and legs crossed. A defensive posture, the vice chancellor knew, indicated shyness, fear, but also reticence.

'Victor,' the vice chancellor began after sitting down behind his desk.

The young man shifted in his seat, but did not look up.

'Victor, allow me first to congratulate you on your diploma. Your professors have sung your praises.'

'Thank you very much,' was the polite response.

The nasal voice took the vice chancellor aback for a second. It required some effort to remember what he had been intending to say.

Congratulations. Condolences. Those were the words.

'But I am so sorry to have to offer you my condolences as well,' said the vice chancellor.

Victor Hoppe still did not look up.

'Your father has passed away,' the vice chancellor went on. He tried to inject some sympathy into his voice.

The announcement did not seem to startle the young man. He just nodded a couple of times. Perhaps he had felt it coming. Or perhaps his father had let him know what he was planning to do, or had already made earlier attempts. The vice chancellor wondered if he should tell him anyway.

'You are not surprised?' he tried.

Victor shrugged his shoulders.

'You did see it coming, then,' the vice chancellor concluded.

Now Victor shook his head.

'What was I supposed to see coming?'

The vice chancellor folded his hands together and he sighed. 'Your father made his own decision,' he said slowly. 'About dying. He took his own life.'

This did not evoke any emotion at first.

'How?' Victor finally asked. 'Do you know how?'

He knew how, but should he tell him? Was that his job? If the boy wanted to know, he had that right, of course. But how to tell him?

'From a tree,' he said, hoping that that would make it clear enough.

The boy nodded and then said something the vice chancellor didn't quite follow.

'Like Judas, then.'

'What did you say?'

Victor shook his head and remained silent.

'Is there anyone who can come and pick you up?' the vice chancellor asked, concerned. 'To take you home? Can I call someone for you?'

'No, Vice Chancellor, thank you,' Victor answered. And after a brief pause, letting his hands fall into his lap, he asked, 'Do I have to go home? Is that really necessary?'

'I should think so,' said the vice chancellor, with a frown. 'The police will want to ask you some questions. Nothing out of the ordinary. It's standard procedure, in the case of . . .' He couldn't get the word out, so quickly changed the subject.

'Do you know what you are going to do? I mean, what's next for you? Now that you have graduated.'

Victor shrugged.

'I haven't thought about it yet.'

'Your professors would very much like you to pursue your doctorate here at the university. You could go far, with a talent like yours. It would be a shame to waste it.'

The vice chancellor thought he caught just a flash of something that might have been a reaction, but it was so faint that he could easily have imagined it. He decided to return to the subject some other time.

'Shall I ask someone to take you home?'

Victor shook his head and stood up. 'No, thank you. I'll manage.'

'I hope so. But if there is anything I can do, please don't hesitate to come and see me.'

'I'll do that, Vice Chancellor. Thank you.'

'You're welcome, Victor. And again, my condolences.'

Someone from the police social-work department gave Victor the letter. The envelope had been opened. To rule out foul play, the man explained. He said he was sorry.

When the man had gone, Victor read the letter. He wasn't really hoping to find any answers in there, since he didn't have any questions. It did shock him, nevertheless.

Victor, inside every person there are hidden forces that are stronger than either willpower or reason. You can do as much good as is in your power, yet in the end you'll still have to atone for the evil that you have done. To do only good, therefore, is not enough. You must also vanquish the evil. And I have done too little of that. Alas, for me there is no way back.

You are not to blame. Remember that. You have done better than anyone ever expected of you. You ought to be proud of that.

Your mother would have been proud of you too. She was a good and devout Christian. That is another thing you must always remember. I know that she would have liked to give you all her love, but inside her, too, there was something that was more powerful than she was. I hope that you can forgive her.

You don't need to forgive me. I do not deserve it. I should have accepted my responsibility, but I never did. That sort of thing is unforgivable. If you bring children into the world, you have an obligation to look after them. Never forget that.

Speaking of which: everything here is yours, naturally. The house, the furniture, the money, and of course the practice. You have always wanted to become a doctor: now there is nothing and nobody standing in your way.

I do wish you much success and happiness. Your father.

His father's words had shaken Victor. Not what he had done, or his death, but his words. They shook the very foundation upon which

Victor had built his world. He had always assumed that doing good was sufficient, and that evil needed only to be avoided. After all, evil was out to crush anyone who attempted to do good. But now it seemed that it might be the other way round. It was an entirely new insight for him. It set him thinking, but more than that: for the first time in his life he began to have doubts. About what he knew. About what he had done. And about what he was going to do. And Father Kaisergruber's visit that same afternoon only made matters worse.

Father Kaisergruber had gone to see Victor Hoppe about the funeral arrangements with a heavy heart. He wanted to keep the visit as short as possible, and therefore came straight to the point.

'I'd prefer to keep it understated, I hope you understand.'

'No, I don't understand,' answered Victor.

'It's not permitted. It isn't really permitted.'

'What isn't permitted?'

'A church service, for your father.'

'But I don't want one in any case.'

'It is what *he* wanted.'

'What he wanted?'

'He left instructions. For the undertaker. Haven't you seen them?'

Victor shook his head.

'He wanted to be buried next to his wife, your mother. He wanted it for her sake. It's not really allowed, but we'll just let that slide. But it has to be done quickly, and it has to be low key. No choir, no eulogies. Restraint.'

'Why isn't it allowed?'

'Because of . . . you know. Everyone knows about it. Everyone could *see* him.'

'But because of *what*?' Victor persisted, to the priest's annoyance.

'God will not permit it.'

'What won't God permit?'

He was arguing like a child, thought the priest, every answer met with another question.

To head off further discussion, he decided to make it quite clear. 'Suicide,' he said flatly.

'Where does it say that?'

'In the Bible.'

'Where in the Bible?'

The priest began to feel a bit hot under the collar. Rarely did anyone contradict him. And the worst thing was that he didn't have an answer, because he didn't know where in the Bible it was written that suicide was not permitted. He mentioned a verse nevertheless. At the end of the Gospel according to St Matthew, referring to Judas's suicide.

'Matthew 27, verse 18.'

'*For he knew that for envy they had delivered him*,' responded Victor, to the priest's amazement, adding, 'It isn't in the Bible. There's nothing about it in the Bible.'

The priest was momentarily thrown off balance, but he quickly recovered.

'The Church won't allow it!' he declared categorically. 'Life is a gift from God. We are not permitted to take it into our own hands. It is not up to us to make decisions about life or death. He is the one who decides! God giveth and God taketh away, none else but He.'

'Who gives Him that right?' Victor raised his voice. 'Why should we deliver ourselves to his will? He is evil, and evil must be striven against.'

He truly has the devil in him, thought Father Kaisergruber; I always knew it. 'You ought to be ashamed of yourself for saying such a thing! Didn't they teach you anything at that school? Your father took you out much too soon! Sister Milgitha was right: the evil was never driven out of you!' Then he brusquely stood up and began to walk away. He had gone only two steps when he halted and turned back. Victor was sitting there as if the hand of God itself had smitten him.

'Your father's funeral is on Saturday, at half past nine. A quiet and understated Mass. And then he'll be laid to rest in your mother's grave. The way he wanted.'

Victor did not attend his father's funeral. He had returned to his room at the university campus some days earlier. He seemed to have lost his footing and his direction. He was completely adrift, his head all abuzz with voices and words.

Your father took you out much too soon.

You can do as much good as it is in your power to do, yet in the end you'll still have to atone for the evil that you have done.

Evil must striven against.

The evil in you is never vanquished.

God giveth and God taketh away, none else but He.

He was in such a state that he hardly dared leave his room.

The vice chancellor and the dean of the College of Biomedical Sciences came looking for him. It was the middle of August. The dog days were making a last effort to push up the temperature above thirty degrees and everything was blistering in the sun.

The vice chancellor knocked, but nobody came to answer the door, although both he and Dr Bergmann could hear a voice inside. It sounded as if a tape was being played at slow speed.

'Victor!' the vice chancellor shouted.

The sound stopped, but still no one came to open the door.

The vice chancellor went to fetch the spare key from the concierge, hoping that Victor had not succumbed to despair the way his father had.

When he opened the door, a blast of heat hit him in the face, immediately followed by a stench – the stench of rotting flesh. His mind had made the association with rotting flesh even before he noticed the flies, which came swarming out of the room. Dozens of them. Green and glinting. Buzzing loudly.

The vice chancellor took a step back in alarm, and bumped into the dean. In an unconscious reflex both men pinched their noses with one hand. They were thinking the same thing. Both were hesitant to go any further.

But what about the voice? Where had the voice come from?

The vice chancellor, arm outstretched, pushed the door all the way open and glanced inside the sweltering room.

The young man was seated at a desk, hunched over a book, his elbows propped on the desk top, hands cupped over his ears. The desk was in a corner of the room, to the right of the window, and the window-sill was littered with empty food tins. To the left of the window was a small counter with a gas burner and saucepan, also cluttered with tins. There were flies crawling in and around the pan.

The vice chancellor, gasping for air, said, 'Victor? Victor Hoppe?'

The boy did not look up. There were flies dancing above his head and crawling over his freckled forearms.

The dean had also sidled closer and was staring over the vice chancellor's shoulder into the room. Taking a deep breath, he stepped inside and made straight for the window, which he threw wide open. The tins on the windowsill clattered to the floor and Victor looked round, startled. Dr Bergmann could barely recognise him. The pale face was even paler than usual, the eyes bloodshot, and little tufts of red hair sprouted from his chin, too sparse yet to amount to a beard.

'We thought there might be something wrong with you,' said the dean quickly. 'How are you?'

'I'm searching for answers,' Victor said in a hoarse voice, gazing at the open window.

The dean pursed his lips and exchanged looks with the vice chancellor. 'All of us, Victor, are searching for answers,' he said.

'How long have you been in here?' the vice chancellor asked.

Victor turned his face towards the door. His eyes landed for a moment on the vice chancellor's tie. Then he looked down and shook his head.

The vice chancellor spoke again. 'You may want to freshen up a bit, Victor. Dr Bergmann and I would like to have a word with you – about your future, and so on. Shall we say, half an hour from now in my office?'

The young man nodded without meeting their eyes. He is embarrassed, the vice chancellor thought, and, trying to put him at ease, said, 'We quite understand that you are having a hard time. That's normal. Anyone would, in your situation. We're going to see what we can do to help you. You mustn't worry.'

The vice chancellor gestured at Dr Bergmann, who said, 'See you later, Victor.'

'He's desperate,' said the vice chancellor a little later, when they were out of earshot. 'He doesn't know how to handle his father's death.'

'Yes, I'd say so. Did you see what he was reading?'

The vice chancellor shook his head. 'No.'

'The Bible.'

'The Bible,' the vice chancellor repeated. 'In that case he definitely is desperate.'

Dr Bergmann laid out for Victor the different directions he might follow in his doctoral research, or, as the dean put it, which department might be the best fit for his particular skills.

He might choose oncology, and specialise in cancer research. Or geriatrics, where he could work on the prevention of infectious diseases in the elderly. But Dr Bergmann could also see him doing excellent work in the embryology department, where they were just starting an experimental project on *in vitro* fertilisation, spearheaded by the dean himself.

The vice chancellor watched Victor Hoppe closely while Dr Bergmann was talking. The young man showed no enthusiasm, asked no questions, but simply nodded now and then – almost, it seemed, out of politeness.

'It's quite simple really, Victor,' the vice chancellor interjected. 'If you would like to go for your PhD – and of course we hope that you will – you have a choice of oncology, geriatrics or embryology; or, put another way, of saving lives, extending lives or creating lives.'

He tapped his forefinger on the names of the three departments Dr Bergmann had written down. Then he repeated both the gesture and the words once more: 'Saving life. Extending life. Creating life.'

'Creating life,' said Victor, but it wasn't clear if he meant it as a question.

'Making new lives,' the vice chancellor explained, happy that at least he'd managed to capture Victor's attention. And then he said, remembering the Bible Victor had been reading, 'Bestowing life. Just like God.'

Bestowing life. Just like God.

Victor saw it as a gauntlet thrown down at his feet. A challenge.

God giveth and God taketh away, Victor. But not always. Sometimes we have to do it ourselves. Remember that.

All of a sudden he understood. And suddenly he had a goal in life once more.

* * *

Rex Cremer drove to Bonn on 15 June 1984. Victor Hoppe had had a phone call the day before from the vice chancellor, requesting that he return to the university because the commission's report was in, but Victor had refused. 'Just send it to me,' he'd said, without even bothering to ask what it said.

This had put the vice chancellor in a fix, but then Cremer had volunteered to pay Dr Hoppe a visit and deliver the findings in person. It gave him an excuse to talk to Victor again, finally, after two months.

He parked his car in front of the terraced house that still sported a sign proclaiming that Victor Hoppe was a fertility specialist. He had not told him he was coming, and hoped Victor was at home. Whether Victor would let him come in was another matter.

As he rang the doorbell, he noticed that his hand was shaking. He heard noises on the other side of the door and when he caught sight of the doctor, he saw that he had let his beard grow.

Victor glanced at Cremer, then peered down the street, as if to see if he had brought anyone else with him.

'I have the commission's report with me,' said Rex. 'The vice chancellor has asked me to go over it with you.'

The doctor did not respond.

'Perhaps we should go inside,' the dean tried. 'I don't think we ought to discuss it out here.'

'Do you still believe me, Dr Cremer?' Victor asked abruptly.

Rex was caught off guard, not only by the question but also by the formality. They had been on a first-name basis almost from the start, but now he had become 'Dr Cremer' again, as if to underscore the fact that there was a new distance between them.

'The commission's report doesn't state that they don't believe you,' he answered with some hesitation. 'It's just the standards you have set for your research that are in question.'

'I am not talking about the commission. I'm talking about you. Do *you* still believe me?'

The directness of the question left him no option. 'I must confess that I have my doubts.'

'Do you want to see her? Will you believe me then? When you *see* it?'

It almost sounded as if he were reciting a poem. He spoke in a kind of stiff, monotone cadence, but devoid of any emotion. Then the doctor turned and went back inside.

Rex stood there nonplussed. *Do you want to see her?* Did he? he wondered. Of course he wanted to see her, but he was afraid of becoming involved in something he really should keep clear of. But he did want some clarity. That was what he had come here for. So he decided to follow Victor inside.

The doctor had gone upstairs and was waiting outside a door. When Cremer joined him he knocked, but there was no answer.

'She may be asleep,' said Victor, turning the handle. 'The pregnancy is wearing her out. And there have already been some complications.'

The chamber was in semi-darkness. In the middle of the room stood an old-fashioned metal hospital bed surrounded by all sorts of equipment. Rex recognised an ultrasound machine and a heart monitor, its screen lit up. There was an intravenous drip hung on a stand, its tube connected to the arm of the woman in the bed. Under the sheets her stomach already showed a distinct bulge. Cremer had worked out beforehand that she must be about five months pregnant by now.

Victor waved him over to the head of the bed. Cremer shuffled forward cautiously and caught sight of her short black hair. Then he looked at her face. It was rather plump. Her eyes were closed, her mouth half-open. She was breathing peacefully, in and out.

Victor gestured that they should leave the room. Rex took one last look at her face. At her stomach. Did she know what was growing in there? He bumped into the bed, on purpose, making it move a few inches. The woman woke up, startled. Her eyes were large and dark. Physically, Victor and she were as different as day and night.

Victor immediately turned back to reassure her.

'This is Dr Cremer,' he said. 'He is dean of the University of Aachen.'

Rex had seen her hands fly instinctively to her stomach, as if to protect what was inside.

'How do you do?' he asked automatically.

'It's very tiring,' she said in faintly accented German. 'But the doctor says it will be fine.'

Her response sounded rehearsed, but perhaps she'd been telling herself that for all these months in order to sustain herself. Rex couldn't help feeling that she barely knew what was happening to her. There was something naive about her, something childish, even though she looked to be well into her late twenties.

He stared at her stomach again and wondered if he should ask about it. But he didn't. He did not want to provoke Victor. Not yet.

'If the doctor says it will be fine,' he said, 'then it probably will be fine.'

Then they left the room and went to Victor's office.

'Does she know?' he asked straight out.

'What?'

'That she's having four babies. Four boys. Clones.' *Your* clones, he meant.

'There's just three of them now,' Victor replied. 'One died in the womb. It's still in there, but the heart has stopped.'

'Does she know?'

'No.'

'She still thinks she's having a girl?'

Victor nodded and Rex thought, He's mad. It was the first time that he actually believed it, too.

But still he didn't say anything. I have to remain detached, he thought, and began telling Victor about the report.

'I don't want to know,' Victor said quickly. 'Anyway I'm not coming back.'

That was precisely the solution suggested by the vice chancellor. The academic year was over, and so he had asked Cremer to convince the doctor not to come back to work. Then there would be no need to fire him.

As there was no need to convince him, Rex got up again almost immediately. He left the report on the desk.

Victor walked him to the front door. Rex wanted to know one more thing. 'When are they due? Approximately?'

'The twenty-ninth of September,' Victor had answered without faltering.

[illegible] Germany. For the doctor says a [illegible].

Her response [illegible] perhaps [illegible] telling herself [illegible] could [illegible]. There [illegible] something [illegible].

[illegible]

[illegible]

"Do you know [illegible]?"

[illegible]

"Do you see [illegible]?"

[illegible]

"She still thinks she's [illegible]."

[illegible]

But she didn't [illegible] anything [illegible].

I [illegible] to know [illegible].

[illegible]

[illegible]

[illegible]

III

2

Rex Cremer crossed the summit of Mount Vaalserberg at a snail's pace. His car drove slowly past the crowds of tourists who were visiting the three borders. As a child he too had come here, and he vividly remembered having climbed the Boudewijn Tower, which now rose up before him. He leaned forward so that his chest almost touched the steering wheel and gazed up. On the platform at the very top he saw a group of children, some of them pointing at something in the distance, others waving at their family or friends down below.

Thirty-four metres. That was how high the tower was. That was another thing Rex remembered. He'd always had a good mind for numbers.

The former dean crossed over from the Netherlands into Belgium without noticing. He was on his way from Cologne to Wolfheim. After passing through Aachen and Vaals, he had followed the signs for the three borders.

'After the three borders you head down the Route des Trois Bornes,' Victor had explained. 'At the bottom of that road, you go under an arched bridge, and then you'll see the house straight ahead of you. A villa, behind a gate. Just past the church. Number 1 Napoleon-strasse.'

The Route des Trois Bornes with its hairpin bends required all of Cremer's concentration. This gave him a few minutes' relief from the jittery feeling that had accompanied him the entire trip. But as soon as he caught sight of the bridge, he started feeling on edge again, even worse than before.

He had bumped into Victor at a medical-equipment fair in Frank-furt the week before. It had been over four years since they had last seen each other or spoken. He had deliberately not stayed in touch with Victor, even though there were still so many questions left unanswered.

For the first few months after seeing him in Bonn, Rex had kept a careful eye on the medical journals and newspapers, and to his relief had never found an article by or about Dr Victor Hoppe. So he had come to assume that the cloning experiment had failed – presuming it hadn't been a downright fabrication to start with. More and more scientists were beginning to come to the conclusion that it just couldn't be done; in all this time no one else had succeeded in cloning a mammal. To Cremer, however, it was still a mystery: had Victor actually made the whole thing up? and had he, as dean, been made a fool of by Victor Hoppe? As far as his colleagues at the University of Aachen were concerned, there was nothing to be done over the matter, which had made it difficult for him to continue working with them. He had stayed on as department head after the hullabaloo had died down, but he had found that he no longer had his colleagues' respect. A year later he had accepted an offer from a bio-tech company in Cologne, where he had taken over as chief of the new stem-cell research and DNA technology department.

It was in that capacity that Rex Cremer had travelled to the fair in Frankfurt on Saturday, 29 October 1988, to view and order new equipment. He had only just walked in when he'd spotted Victor. Right away, from afar. He felt a shock go through him.

He did not go over to Victor, at least not at first. He wandered through the fair for two hours, and kept catching sight of him, but their eyes had not met. Then he started following Victor. What sort of apparatus caught his eye? What kind of questions was he asking?

His voice! When Rex got close enough to hear that unmistakable voice, he suddenly remembered the things Victor used to say.

That's the mistake they make. They set themselves limits.

God created man in his image.

There are times when one should simply accept the facts.

There's four of them. It's too many.

He walked past Victor deliberately, in the hope that Victor would be the one to recognise and hail him, as if he wanted to provide himself with an excuse in case anyone should spot them together. But

Victor did not approach him. His former colleague didn't even seem to recognise him when he gave a quick nod as they passed each other.

In the end his curiosity won out. He turned round and said something to him. Victor looked as if he'd just been woken from a trance.

'Hi! It's me. Rex Cremer. From the University of Aachen.'

'You have changed,' Victor answered dryly.

He hadn't thought about that. He'd assumed that he was easy to recognise, but in the intervening years he had taken to wearing glasses and had grown his hair.

'Good observation,' he answered, instinctively straightening his glasses. 'But tell me, how are you?'

Victor shrugged his shoulders non-committally. It wasn't clear if he just wasn't in a mood to answer, or if the shrug was meant to be the response. He didn't ask Rex anything in turn, so again it was up to Rex to say something.

'And what are you up to now? It's been so long . . .' He kept the question deliberately neutral. He remembered how evasive his former colleague could be.

'I'm a GP,' Victor had said.

'A GP,' Rex echoed, rather startled. To cover his surprise, he quickly added, 'Where?'

'In Wolfheim.'

'Wolfheim?'

Victor nodded. That was all. He didn't bother to explain where that might be. It wasn't that he was being mysterious or reticent – no, it was more a matter of indifference, as if he and the man facing him had no history together. But his attitude changed when Rex told him that he too had left the University of Aachen. That did seem to surprise Victor. He looked up, very briefly, as if he were about to say something. But there was still nothing forthcoming until Rex let slip a remark that he knew would not leave the doctor cold.

'I had lost their trust.'

However, his confession had a somewhat different effect from what he'd intended, because Victor, not bothering to lower his voice, said, 'As *I* lost *yours*.'

Rex looked round, embarrassed. Best just to ignore that, he thought to himself; it would only lead to a pointless argument.

'How did it all come out, in the end?' he asked. He was expecting an evasive answer, and would have been satisfied with that. It would have put his mind at ease. Yet the answer only raised more questions.

'It isn't finished yet.'

He felt a shudder of apprehension. 'What do you mean?'

'I'm starting over again.'

That answer was more reassuring. So the previous experiment had failed. And evidently it hadn't been a complete fabrication either. It had, simply and logically, ended in failure. Thank God.

And yet he asked one more question. He wanted to have it from the doctor's own mouth that the experiment had failed. Victor waited, staring at the ground – and then Rex asked the question.

Originally, they had made a date for the day after the technology fair, but Victor had cancelled that morning because something had happened. He had sounded confused; from what Rex was able to gather, something had happened to his housekeeper – an accident or something. Could he possibly come a few days later? Rex had agreed, even though it meant he'd have to curb his impatience a while longer.

What did he know, as of now? That three boys had been born four years ago, and that the fourth embryo had failed to thrive and died. He also knew that all three were clones of the doctor, and that they looked exactly alike, down to the most minute detail. Finally, he knew that the boys were still alive.

All of this he had found out from talking to Victor that morning at the fair. And he, Rex Cremer, had listened open-mouthed.

'May I see them?' he had blurted out.

He would be allowed to see them.

He'd had one more question. And the reply to that, too, had startled him. No, had shocked him. He had asked the names of Victor's children.

Rex Cremer parked his car in front of the villa. He saw the sign on the gate, with Victor's name and the hours of surgery. As he got out he heard the village clock strike two. He was right on time. Across the street a woman was sweeping the pavement. He nodded at her amicably, but she barely acknowledged him. Victor came out of the house, greeted him with a nod of the head and unlatched the gate.

'Follow me,' he said. He was already halfway up the garden path.

Rex felt as if he was just another patient coming for a check-up, a feeling that was reinforced when he saw that he was being shown into the examination room. Victor sat down behind his desk and invited Rex to take a seat across from him. Rex immediately noticed the framed photograph on the corner of the desk that was half-turned towards him, almost as if it were on purpose.

'Is that them?' he asked.

Victor nodded.

'May I?' He stuck out his hand.

Victor nodded again and said, 'It's an old photo.'

Rex picked up the frame and noticed that his hand was shaking. He was still somehow hoping that the whole thing had only been a figment of Victor's imagination, and even though just a glance at the photo clearly showed the uncanny resemblance between the three boys, he was still not completely convinced they were indeed clones. They could be a set of identical triplets, and had simply inherited Victor's characteristics: the red hair and . . .

Every cleft palate is unique.

He could still hear him saying it, although it had been several years ago. He stared at the mouths of the three children in the picture, but the print was not clear enough to make out fine details. Besides – this was something he *was* able to see – the upper lips had been repaired. But the doctor would certainly have saved photographs of the children prior to surgery, even though that kind of proof was no longer necessary. A British scientist had recently found a way to dissect and read the genetic code unique to every human being. A DNA test would determine unequivocally if the children were indeed identical copies of Victor Hoppe.

'They must have changed quite a bit,' Rex began, as neutrally as he could. 'How old are they in this picture? About one?'

'Just a year old,' the doctor replied. 'They have changed – you are right.'

'I can't wait to see them.'

He was eager to see the children straight away, but when Victor began speaking again, he realised that his patience would be put to the test.

'I have tried to slow it down.' It didn't sound like a justification. Victor was simply giving Rex a piece of information.

'What have you tried to slow down?'

'It's been too rapid.'

'What . . . I don't follow.'

'The telomeres on some of the chromosomes are much shorter than normal.'

Rex looked at him nonplussed, but the doctor took his look to mean something else.

'You do know what telomeres are, don't you?' he asked.

'Of course I know what telomeres are. I just don't know what it has to do with all this.'

But as he said it, it did begin to dawn on him. Telomeres were long chains of building blocks at the end of every chromosome in the nucleus. These telomeres were somehow responsible for providing the energy required for cell division. With every division, a number of these telomeres disappeared for good, because the cell could not manufacture replacements. The more frequently a cell split, the fewer chromosome telomeres were left; in short, the older the person, the shorter the telomere chain.

'Soon after the boys were born,' Victor explained, 'I discovered that the telomeres of the fourth and ninth chromosome were much shorter than those on the other chromosomes.'

Rex didn't really want to hear the rest. The more he found out, the more involved he would be. But he already had a strong suspicion that he knew what the doctor was trying to tell him. One of the questions biologists frequently asked themselves, a riddle that hadn't yet been solved, was what the actual age of the clone would be. Since the cell providing the donor nucleus had come from an adult, the clone's cells would, by definition, be much older than the cells arising from normal insemination. Was that it? Had something gone wrong on that front?

He felt his anxiety rise. 'Does that mean—' he began.

'I have tried to slow it down,' the doctor interrupted, raising his voice slightly. There was despair in that voice. It was the first time

Rex had noticed anything like that in Victor. Or . . . perhaps not: it had happened once before, when Victor had begged him on the phone for his help because it turned out that as many as four cloned embryos had implanted themselves.

'But I'm not giving up,' he heard Victor declare stubbornly, all trace of despair gone. Then he fell silent again.

'Dr Hoppe, you mentioned the telomeres of the fourth and ninth chromosomes,' he began. 'You said they were much shorter. How much shorter?'

Victor stared at the photograph Rex was still holding.

'Less than half,' he said mechanically.

'Less than half. That is . . . Were there any consequences, for the children?'

'They are ageing very rapidly.'

Rex's worst suspicion had been confirmed, although he wasn't sure what this meant on a practical level.

'Was it obvious?' he asked. 'I mean, could you tell just by looking at them?'

He hoped that the doctor would now suggest that they go and see the children, but Victor just nodded, staring at the photo.

'There didn't seem to be anything wrong at that stage,' he said. 'But then . . .' He was quiet again.

'Then what?'

'They suddenly went bald. That was the start of it.'

Rex looked at the picture. The boys' red hair was already thinning at that stage, so it wasn't hard to imagine the hair completely gone.

'Was there nothing you could do?' he asked.

'I tried.'

'And what about now?'

'The telomeres of the fourth and ninth chromosomes are all used up.'

That made Rex sit up, startled.

The doctor confirmed his fears: 'Since then the cells have stopped dividing, and the cells that are left are slowly dying.'

'Which means that the ageing process has become irreversible?'

Victor nodded. 'But all's not lost,' he said, finally. He straightened himself, his hands on the armrests of his chair, as if he were about to stand up.

'Not lost?' asked Rex, surprised.

'It was a mutation. Simple as that. Now that I know about it, I can look out for it the next time, in the embryo-selection process.'

Rex didn't know where to look.

'It is our task, after all,' Victor went on stolidly. 'It is up to us to correct the mistakes which He in his haste has wrought.'

Rex's eyes were almost popping out of his head by now.

'A mutation is nothing more nor less than an error in the genes,' Victor went on in a monotone. 'Just as *this* was an error in the genes.' Raising his hand to his upper lip, he ran his finger over the scar.

Rex did his best not to stare.

'And by correcting those congenital errors, we correct ourselves,' said Victor firmly. 'That is the only way to beat God at his own game.'

This startling pronouncement transported Rex back in time, back to the day when he had written to congratulate Victor Hoppe on his article, before they had even met.

You have certainly beaten God at his own game.

And as he thought about it, it dawned on him that it was he, Rex Cremer, who had set the whole thing in motion with that one ostensibly innocent phrase.

'Shall we?' Victor had pushed back his chair and was getting to his feet. 'You wanted to see the children, didn't you? Come with me. They are upstairs.' Not waiting for an answer, he walked to the door.

Rex stayed in his seat a few seconds longer, completely flummoxed. When he stood up, he felt dizzy. He blinked his eyes a few times and took a deep breath.

'Dr Cremer?' he heard from the corridor.

'Coming,' he replied. As he followed Victor up the stairs, he tried to focus his mind on what he was about to be shown, but the words he had just heard kept spinning round in his head.

It is up to us to correct the mistakes which He in his haste has wrought.

This isn't possible, he thought. He's just provoking me. Victor Hoppe is trying to get my goat. He is pulling my leg. Next he'll probably tell me that he made the whole thing up; that he just wanted to see how I'd react. That's the reason he asked me to come. So that he could make fun of me. Because people used to make fun of *him*.

As Victor opened the door, Rex was still hoping that the whole thing was an elaborate sham. Even when Victor stepped into the room and Rex heard him say, 'Michael, Gabriel, Raphael, there is someone—'

The voice broke off in mid-sentence. Rex, hearing it from the stairs, cleared the last three treads in one stride. Two more steps and he was standing in the doorway, peering inside.

He didn't immediately realise that it was a classroom. His glance was first drawn to the blackboard, where Victor was heading with long, rapid strides. Storming up to the board, he snatched the eraser and began wiping the surface clean. Rex just caught a glimpse of a drawing the full height of the blackboard. It was a drawing of a person – a man or a woman. With one swipe the doctor had already erased the face. What was left was the hair, pinned up in a bun. So then it was a woman. The bun was white, and was surrounded by a yellow radiance. That was next to go – the knot and the yellow glow around it, which Rex suspected was supposed to represent a halo, because the woman had also been endowed with a pair of wings. White wings, depicted as large oval shapes on either side of the torso.

It was a child's drawing, with simple lines, but that made it instantly recognisable. It was erased in a trice.

The doctor then turned his attention to the remaining half of the blackboard, which was covered in scribbles. The single phrase Rex managed to decipher before it was obscured by the doctor's hand told him what the rest of the text had said: . . . *who art in heaven* . . .

Victor put down the eraser and turned round. He rubbed his hands together, and dust flew into the air. Then he wiped his face. His fingers left white tracks in his red beard.

For a split second Rex had forgotten what he'd come for, but Victor's glance reminded him.

There were three of them. Three, but it might as well have been two, or four. It wouldn't have made the slightest difference, for he saw it immediately. He saw that it wasn't a sham. Victor Hoppe had made nothing up.

2

When, in the autumn of 1988, the walnut tree in the doctor's garden was cut down, there were few villagers who really believed that the event would bring bad luck to Wolfheim, as Josef Zimmerman had predicted. Not one year later, however, even the greatest sceptic was forced to admit that the old man had been right. Jacques Meekers had come up with his own theory by then: that the calamity had been spreading through the village the way the roots of a tree spread under the earth. If anyone happened to express doubts about his theory, he would unfold a topographic map of Wolfheim and its surroundings, and spread it out on the counter of the Café Terminus. He had marked every spot where the calamity had surfaced with an X. Each cross was given a number, and was connected with a jagged line to the mark where the walnut tree had once stood. In the map's margins, Meers had jotted down the details of the accidents relating to each X, including victim and date. He had strengthened his case by including even run-of-the-mill mishaps that had had negligible consequences, and was able to refute the objection that there was no way the tree's roots could have spread all the way to La Chapelle by showing that the distance between La Chapelle and the tree's core was less than five hundred metres as the crow flies.

The onslaught of the calamities, everyone agreed, had started with Charlotte Maenhout's accident on 29 October 1988. Her funeral had lured many folks to the church, most of them probably hoping that Dr Hoppe and his three offspring would attend the service. The doctor had not made an appearance, however, either at the Mass or at the graveside. Jacob Weinstein reported afterwards that the doctor had rung shortly before the funeral to excuse himself: the children were very sick. Sick with grief, of course, he'd supposed, but when some days later the details of Charlotte's will became known, he was forced to revise his assumption, as were many of the other villagers.

Father Kaisergruber personally heard the news from Notary Legrand of Gemmenich. The notary told him that Charlotte Maenhout had left all her money – he didn't say how much, but it was a hefty sum – to a children's cancer foundation. That piece of news needn't necessarily have raised any red flags, but Notary Legrand added that Frau Maenhout had had her will changed just two months prior to her death. Before that, the doctor's children had been named as her beneficiaries. They were to have received the money on their eighteenth birthday.

But there was more. Irma Nüssbaum had seen a big box being delivered to the doctor's house, marked with a large radioactive warning, and the next day he'd had a visitor from Germany who had told Irma that the children were not doing so well.

'He was in there for over an hour,' Irma said, 'and when he came back out he looked as if he'd seen a ghost. He got into his car, but then got straight out of it again. I went over to him and asked him what was the matter – was it the children? He gave me this guilty look, and that told me enough. They aren't doing too well, are they? I asked. I saw him hesitate, but then he shook his head. No, he said, not really. In a tone as if someone – well, *you* know. Then he asked if I knew a certain Frau Maanwoud. Frau Maenhout, you mean, I said; she was the doctor's housekeeper. He wanted to know what had happened to her and I told him that she had fallen down the stairs at the doctor's house the week before. She had died instantly. I asked him why he wanted to know. Oh, no reason, he said, no reason; he'd just heard something about it. He was definitely distraught, because he got back into his car without saying another word.'

The doctor's absence at the funeral, the news of Charlotte's Maenhout's inheritance, Irma Nüssbaum's story – all led to the same conclusion.

'The doctor's sons are dying.'

'So it must be – *you* know . . .'

'It's probably leukaemia,' said Léon Huysmans. 'It's fairly common in young kids. And fatal.'

'You could see it coming.'

The villagers grew even more convinced of their theory over the following weeks, when they saw that Dr Hoppe's surgery was shut more often than not. No one answered the telephone, and the gate remained locked, so that several of his patients were forced to find another doctor. There was some grumbling, but for the most part people were understanding.

'He has to look after his children.'

'They must be going downhill fast. That's why you never see them outside any more.'

'How awful: first his wife, and now . . .'

From all quarters came offers of help, both from the ladies, who offered to take care of the housekeeping, and from the men, who wanted to mow his lawn. Dr Hoppe thanked them all but turned them down. The only offer he did take up came from Martha Bollen, who told him he could order his groceries over the phone and have them delivered to his house.

'He wants to spend as much time as possible with the children, naturally. It goes without saying,' said Martha, who delivered the groceries herself and always threw in some treats for the kids.

Once, when making a delivery, she just couldn't keep it in any longer. 'Doctor, is it true—?' She deliberately broke off in mid-sentence because she assumed he would know what she was talking about.

'What?' he asked. 'What's the matter?'

'You know, about the children?' she tried.

She could tell from his expression that he was startled. Yet he still pretended that he had no idea what she was talking about.

'What about the children?'

With the utmost reluctance, she uttered the name of the illness that had taken her own husband's life ten years before.

The doctor frowned and shook his head. 'Cancer? No, not as far as I know.'

His response sounded forced, so she did not pursue it. It was quite obvious to her that he did not want to talk about it.

'He isn't ready to face up to reality yet,' she explained afterwards, in her shop. 'He has to learn to cope with it first. When my husband fell ill, it took me three months before I could bring myself to tell my customers.'

For two weeks the sad news about the doctor's sons was practically the only topic of conversation in the village. Then suddenly, literally in the blink of an eye, it was eclipsed by another tragedy that caused even greater consternation.

'Here, see this X, halfway down Napoleonstrasse, a stone's throw from the doctor's house,' Jacques Meekers would explain years later at the Café Terminus. 'That's where the second accident happened. Not even *two weeks* after Charlotte Maenhout died! The victim was Gunther Weber – you know, the deaf kid. It was 11 November 1988: Armistice Day. So it was a public holiday.'

Gunther Weber and five other boys had been playing a game of football on the village green. It was a peaceful autumn day, and since early morning cars and coaches chock-full of Belgian tourists had been snaking through the village on their way to the three-border junction. A traffic jam had soon clogged the narrow underpass leading to the Route des Trois Bornes. By lunch time the traffic jam stretched all the way past Dr Hoppe's house. With so many people stuck inside their cars, and therefore so many eyes on them, the boys were encouraged, as usual, to show off. Fritz 'Lanky' Meekers, thirteen years old by then and just shy of two metres, had never given up the hope that one day a football coach would jump out of his car and offer him a contract to play for a top club, a dream shared by the other boys as well, though it was, as a rule, crushed by Meekers.

'You, Gunther, *you* – picked for a top club? You can't even hear the referee's whistle!' It was a remark he would regret for the rest of his life, since it was the constant teasing that goaded Gunther Weber into being even more of a show-off than the others, because he wanted to be considered as good as the rest of them.

Gunther was goalie as usual, because from between the goalposts he had a view of the entire field. Julius Rosenboom had just kicked the ball wide of the goal and Gunther had gone to retrieve it. As he picked up the ball, he felt all eyes in the traffic jam upon him, and it made him puff up with pride. Pushing out his chest, his nose in the air and the ball under his arm, he marched back to the goal. He placed the ball on the ground, repositioned it a few times with a great deal of fuss, turned the ball over one more time and nodded theatrically when he was satisfied that it was just the way he wanted it.

'Gunther, don't be such a show-off!' yelled Lanky Meekers. 'OK, we've all seen you!'

It may have been those very words that encouraged Gunther to stretch out his one-man show even longer. He tapped one of his ears, pretending he hadn't understood. Then, raising his hand to his eyes, he peered in the direction where he was intending to kick the ball. He stretched his arm high up in the air and waved it back and forth.

'Gwo-back, gwo-back,' he shouted at his mates. 'I'm-gwonnah-kick-de-bwall-erry-fah!'

And as the other boys started walking backwards, Gunther also took several giant paces back, to give himself a running start. *Look there – what's that boy doing?* he could sense the people behind him wondering, and he imagined them nudging each other. He took yet another couple of steps backward, rolling his shoulders demonstratively. *He's going in for the kick. That boy's going to kick that ball clear up into the sky! Just look at how far back he's going!*

He was some twenty feet from the ball when he saw his mates starting to wave and shout at him. But he was too far away to read their lips. Keeping his eyes on the ball, he took another step back and then pitched forward slowly, like a runner waiting for the starting shot. In his mind he could hear the shouts of encouragement behind him: *Gunther! Gunther!*

Oh, he was going to give that ball such a kick! Just one more step back and then . . .

Gunther Weber landed under the 12.59 p.m. bus that had come swerving into the bus stop on the green. The boy was killed instantly, it was determined by a physician in one of the stationary cars who had immediately rushed to his side. That news was his parents' only consolation, although it did not bring them much comfort. They had lost their only child.

Victor Hoppe, standing at a first-storey window, watched people rushing to the scene. It was as if they were all pouncing on some quarry sprawled in the middle of the street, except that they all hung back a bit, leaving an empty circle around it. Peering through the glass, Victor could just make out their stricken faces, discreetly averted, yet sneaking covert glances at what was lying there. A man, shouting, was elbowing his way through the crowd, which fell back to make way for him. The man had to be a doctor, Victor guessed, and the quarry was the victim of an accident. Then he made the connection between the sounds he had just heard and the bus drawn up close to the victim.

He recognised the gestures the doctor was making. A life had been taken. That was easy, taking a life. There wasn't anything to it. It was much easier than creating a life. Taking a life was easy, even if you hadn't meant to. That was something he'd learned just the other day.

Victor Hoppe looked on, fascinated, his hands behind his back.

The doctor's announcement caused a stir amongst the crowd. Heads were shaken or bowed; people buried their faces in their hands. A small group of boys stood huddled together, sobbing.

One boy detached himself from the group and walked away. Victor Hoppe saw that it was Fritz Meekers. The kid was screaming and yelling, and was running towards the village green, where two stacks of coats had been piled on the ground about three metres apart. The goal. And a ball lay on the ground beside the goal. Fritz was racing towards the ball. He seemed to be skating across the tarmac; it almost looked as if he were floating, as if his screams were making him levitate above the ground. Using all the pent-up force of his run, he gave the ball a vehement kick. A long-drawn-out wail followed the ball as it soared into the sky. Fritz didn't watch where it went. His long legs buckling under him, he sank to his knees and his shoulders began to shake. People began walking over to him.

Victor turned away to stare at the victim again, who, he was certain, must be one of the kids from the village.

Someone came over with a blanket. The physician flung it over the victim so that the body was no longer visible. Death has to be erased as quickly as possible, thought Victor. Erased, like a mistake on a blackboard.

He saw that people were already starting to leave. The show was over. They returned to their cars or their coach and went back to being ordinary tourists again, on their way to the three-border junction. It was not a real place, Victor knew: only an arbitrary figment of the human imagination. Not real, yet it did exist. They all wanted to see it with their own eyes, even though there wasn't really anything to see. And even though there wasn't anything there, it did give them something to believe in. The three-border junction was like God. People were attracted to it, but at the same time they were being deceived.

Suddenly people were getting out of their vehicles again. Something new had caught their attention. Victor blinked. The little group of people still hovering around the victim broke apart, this time to make way for a woman who had come running over. It was Vera Weber. Now he knew who the victim was. The doctor had stood up, and was trying to restrain the woman. Shaking his head, he grabbed her by the shoulders, but she shook him off.

Victor gazed at Vera Weber in astonishment. The woman was yelling. The woman was screaming. Victor lifted his hand to the window to open it, resting his finger on the latch. A gentle breeze carried the eerie sounds inside. He had heard those sounds before. Long ago. They were sounds of grief. Of despair. And of madness. The sounds touched off something inside his head and he shuddered.

The woman knelt by the blanket and pulled it off. Her voice had stopped. In the breathless silence, she cradled the boy's head in her arms, lifting it onto her lap. She stroked his hair. She was talking to him. Didn't she know he was dead?

God giveth and God taketh away, Victor. Remember that.

The woman understood. Suddenly she did understand, because she stopped talking to the boy. Lifting her head, she gazed up at the sky, stretched her arms into the air and clutched at something that wasn't there. And as she tried to grab the something that wasn't there, she started screaming again.

Victor closed the window, shutting out the noise. What he'd been hearing was strange to *him*, but the sound itself wasn't strange. It was only strange to someone who wasn't familiar with it. Because he didn't know. He didn't know that a mother could be so grief-stricken about her child.

Gunther's parents were startled when Dr Hoppe paid them a visit. Their son was lying in an open coffin at home, for people to come and pay their last respects. The doctor was one of the first to drop by.

'My condolences,' he said. 'I know how you must feel.'

His visit and his words moved them. Lothar and Vera Weber thought that he showed great courage in coming to express his sympathy when he was going through such a hard time himself, and would shortly be losing not one child but three. That was why they did not have the heart to ask him if he would like to go and say goodbye to their son in person. They thought it would bring up too many emotions for him. But then he himself asked to see the boy.

'Would you like me to come with you?' Lothar suggested.

But that wasn't necessary. Dr Hoppe went in by himself, disappearing behind the heavy dark drapes that screened off the coffin. The doctor did not stay long, but the parents quite understood. They offered him coffee, but he politely declined.

'If ever I can be of assistance,' he said finally, 'please do not hesitate to contact me. You need not abide by God's will.'

Then he left, leaving Gunther's parents somewhat bewildered.

He had used the scalpel to make a quick incision in the scrotum, about two centimetres long. The scrotum was shrivelled, stiffened, as when a boy is dunked in icy water, an instinctive somatic reaction to protect the testicles. It worked to keep the temperature constant a little longer, which meant that some of the tissue might possibly still be viable. It was a gamble, but a reasonable one. And if not, at least he'd have some sperm to work with.

The two testicles were the size and shape of dried white beans that had been soaked in water too long. Working quickly, he snipped them free of the sperm duct and then slipped them into a jar filled with cotton wool. The jar disappeared into the breast pocket of his coat.

He zipped up the boy's trousers again without making a sound.

Now he'd have to be quick.

We must abide by God's will.

That was what was written at the top of the mourning card Victor had found in his letter box that morning, before setting out to see the Webers.

He had taken it as a fresh challenge. As if someone had thrown down the gauntlet again.

It made everything that had gone before seem quite irrelevant.

3

Seeing them for the first time was a tremendous shock. The boys looked old, terribly old, largely on account of their skin, which seemed to be made of dried-out leather. They were emaciated, truly skin over bone. Rex took it all in at a single glance; he tried to look away, but he found his eyes were drawn back irresistibly. And it wasn't as a scientist that he was staring at them, but as a voyeur.

Victor, for his part, was every inch the scientist when it came to the children. He talked about them as if they were research specimens, even when they were standing right in front of him. It was dreadful, and Rex felt very uneasy the whole time. The doctor lined up the three boys in a row and then pointed out the details of their physical similarity: the shape of the outer ear, the position of the milk teeth, the pattern of veins on the skull and the misshapen nose and upper lip.

Next he showed Rex the variations, but stressed that these had arisen at a much later date. There were wrinkles and grooves in the parched skin that were not exactly alike, and there were brown spots on the back of their gnarled hands that differed in size and shape. Victor didn't explain this, but Rex assumed they must be age spots.

He noticed, moreover, that one of the boys had more of these liver spots than the other two, which made him wonder if the ageing process might be more rapid in this boy's case. The same boy also had a scar on the back of his head, which according to the doctor was the result of a fall, and another on his back, the result of a surgical procedure on one of his kidneys – an experiment that had not proved conclusive, Victor admitted.

But prior to that, before the ageing process had really set in, he repeated emphatically, you couldn't tell them apart at all. Indeed they were so alike that he'd had to tag them. The way we do with mice, he added without even a grain of irony in his voice, as if it were the most normal thing in the world. Lifting up the boys' shirts, he showed Rex the dots tattooed on their backs: one dot for Michael, the firstborn, two dots for Gabriel and three dots for Raphael.

'Otherwise known as Victor One, Victor Two and Victor Three,' he added.

Cremer's eyes were drawn to the boys' chests. Even from far away he was able to count the ribs; the thin skin was stretched over them like a garment draped over a coat rack. Later he found out that the boys weighed just thirteen kilos each. Thirteen kilos for a height of 1.05 metres; but even that dimension was rapidly dwindling, for the children's spines were becoming more and more crooked.

V1, V2 or V3. That was how the Polaroids in the photograph albums were labelled. Rex was shown these when he and the doctor returned to the consultation room. Twelve albums filled with photos. Beneath each photo a date, and, again, V1, V2 or V3.

Three children's lives, meticulously recorded. No, that was wrong: it wasn't about the children's lives, because the photographs bore no resemblance to family snapshots. These were pieces of a jigsaw – a jigsaw showing parts of the children's bodies, to demonstrate the similarities between the three boys at every stage of their life. But as he leafed through the endless series of pictures, what struck Rex was mainly the boys' senescence, rather than their resemblance, as if the albums spanned not four, but eighty, years.

Actually, he wished he could leave, but Victor just went on talking and explaining non-stop, repeating himself more than once. He told his story soberly and without a trace of emotion, and Rex listened to him with astonishment. Victor told him about the boys' intelligence, about their talent for languages, and their memory. In all those things, said Victor, he recognised himself. He had made sure their talents were encouraged, so that they too would later be able to use their knowledge and insight in the service of humanity. That was how he'd phrased it: 'in the service of humanity'. And, moreover, he had said 'they *too*'.

Rex shuddered, but held his tongue, because the doctor wasn't finished. He had started telling him what the next steps would be. In order to solve the telomere problem, he was considering using nerve cells as the donor material instead of skin cells. Nerve cells split far fewer times than other cells; this should automatically solve the telomere problem. Bone cells would do as well, since those grew more slowly than other cells. The same held true for the sex organs, because their cells only began to divide at a later stage, at puberty, meaning the cells were younger, and their telomeres longer. The simplicity and logic of his reasoning again reminded Rex why he had given Victor carte blanche in the past. He was, and remained, far ahead of his time.

Rex felt himself getting sucked in again, slowly but surely. Victor's nasal drone seemed to be having the effect of making him even more receptive to what Victor had to say. I *must* get out of here. The thought suddenly popped into his head. I've got to get out of here, before I become even more involved.

He stood up promptly and said, 'I can't stay any longer; I have to get back.'

He knew it sounded like a fib. It was obvious he was looking for a way to escape.

But Victor did not try to detain him; on the contrary, he stood up and walked him to the door. Rex was outside before he knew it, but once the gate had shut behind him and he was sitting in his car, he didn't drive off immediately. Something was stopping him. Not what Victor had told him, but what the children had said: a few words that had upset him more than all of Victor's assertions combined.

'Dyou-know-whey-frow-mai-wood-is?'

One of the boys had spoken up. Rex had been about to leave the classroom after Victor had suggested they continue their discussion in the office. The three boys, who had patiently submitted to the doctor's humiliating prodding and probing, stayed behind. Were left behind. Victor had left the room without another glance, not even a word. Cremer was hanging back for one last look at the boys, as if to convince himself that what he was seeing was real. Then one of the boys said something, but Rex was so taken by surprise at first that he didn't quite catch what he had said.

‘Dyou-know-whey-frow-mai-wood-is?’ The boy’s voice was as nasal as Victor’s but his articulation was better.

‘What did you say?’

‘Dyou-know-whey-frow-mai-wood-is?’ the boy said again, staring straight ahead as if he were speaking to someone else.

Did he know where Frau Maiwood was. He didn’t know any Frau Maiwood.

‘No, I don’t know,’ he had replied.

‘Shees-wiv-God-in-eav-ven,’ he heard, but this time it wasn’t the first boy who spoke up. One of the others had answered, although the voice was identical.

Rex did not understand what they meant. It wasn’t until the third boy spoke that it became clear to him.

‘Shees-dead-fad-der-did-it.’

This all took place within the space of a few seconds, but at the time it seemed much longer, and he was surprised that Victor hadn’t rushed back to tell the children to shut up. When the doctor did come back, he didn’t even act surprised or angry. He simply ignored the children, and again asked Rex to follow him to the office.

As Victor went on jabbering, the boys’ words went round and round inside Rex’s head.

Shees-dead-fad-der-did-it.

It wasn’t until he was sitting in his car that the significance of the words really hit him. He felt so nauseated that he had to get out again. Leaning against the open door, he gasped for air. A woman walked up to him and asked him what was the matter, and then she began talking about the children. ‘They aren’t doing well, are they?’ she said. He couldn’t deny it; perhaps he didn’t *want* to deny it. He asked her if she knew who Frau Maiwood was, and what had happened to her. Frau *Maenhout*, she said, Frau Maenhout, the doctor’s housekeeper. She fell down the stairs. An accident.

That did reassure him somewhat. Yet the boys’ words stayed with him all the way back to Cologne. He tried to recall everything that had happened, from start to finish, and the more he tried to piece it all together in his head, the more far-fetched it all seemed. As if he’d been watching a film. Characters on a screen. In the end he wondered if he might not just have imagined the whole thing.

4

Lothar Weber had phoned Dr Hoppe behind his wife's back. She wasn't in agreement with him.

'Why? I'm not sick,' she had answered when he had suggested going to see the doctor.

But she was sick – sick with grief. Lothar saw it day after day. It was the little things he noticed. The way she dragged herself out of bed and trailed around, the way she ate her food more slowly than usual, the laundry and ironing piling up, his shoes never getting polished, the drawn-out silences.

Lothar was suffering too, as never before, but he was still able to concentrate on his work at the foundry. Vera was at home by herself all day long.

He had been hoping that the pain would level off at a certain point, but it seemed to him that her sorrow was growing more intense, week by week. When one morning she decided not to get out of bed at all, he rang the doctor. It was the run-up to Christmas, and he thought that the holidays would only make her grief even worse. He had heard from someone at work that there were pills to make life a little easier to bear, and he wanted to ask the doctor if his wife might have some. He hadn't mentioned it over the phone, because he thought it wouldn't be proper; he'd just asked the doctor to stop by the house.

'It's Vera,' he said. 'She's ill.'

The doctor promised to stop by that very day. That had given Lothar hope, because Dr Hoppe seldom made house calls these days.

If ever I can be of assistance, please do not hesitate to contact me. He had not forgotten that, and the doctor was evidently true to his word.

He arrived at 3.30. Vera was still in bed. She hadn't eaten a thing all day. Nor had she spoken. When Dr Hoppe appeared in her bedroom, she sat up a bit, tugged at her nightie and glared at her husband. He made a helpless gesture, but was secretly relieved at her reaction; apparently her inertia had not quite gained the upper hand.

'Are you in pain?' the doctor asked.

Vera shook her head. Lothar saw that she was about to burst into tears. He also felt a lump in his throat.

'Are you sad?' the doctor asked next.

Vera promptly began to sob, so intensely that her shoulders heaved. 'I miss him so!' she cried. 'And it isn't getting any better! It won't go away! Gunther, my poor, poor Gunther!' She bowed her head and buried her face in her hands.

Lothar tiptoed closer. He looked at Dr Hoppe, who betrayed not the slightest emotion. As it should be, of course. That was why he had asked the doctor to come: because he would be able to judge things soberly, from a distance.

'You loved him very much,' said Dr Hoppe, and you couldn't tell from his voice whether it was a question or a statement.

Lothar frowned, but his wife did not seem surprised at the doctor's words.

'He was my only child, Doctor,' she sobbed. 'He was all I had. And now he is gone.'

Lothar looked at his wife, who had buried her head in her hands once more. He perched on the edge of the bed and awkwardly began rubbing his hands on his thighs. It made him feel guilty sometimes, that his wife seemed so much more grief-stricken than he. But then again her bond with Gunther had always been stronger, and she'd been far better at dealing with his congenital deafness. She had even taken a sign-language course. He, on the other hand, had seen Gunther's disability more as a burden, so he had always kept their exchanges short and businesslike. He regretted that now.

'Why don't you just have another child?' Dr Hoppe asked.

Lothar gulped. He saw his wife taking her hands away from her face.

'I'll be forty next month, Doctor.'

Her husband was thinking the same thing. Besides, she had been closed to him for years – from the moment she had heard that

Gunther was hearing-impaired, in fact, even though the specialist had stressed that it was not in any way a certainty that the next child would be born deaf as well. And now she was too old to get pregnant. Dr Hoppe had probably thought she was younger.

'Your age is no problem,' the doctor said, shaking his head, 'these days, that is. It's just a question of technique.' He said it with such conviction that that seemed to settle it.

Vera shook her head. 'I don't know, Doctor. I've never considered it. It is—'

'If you like, you could have another son.'

'A son?' asked Vera, swallowing.

'A son who would be the spitting image of Gunther. It can be done. Nothing's impossible these days.'

'But Doctor,' Lothar began hesitantly, 'will he then . . . will he . . .' He glanced at his wife, but she was staring straight ahead, bewildered. 'Would he be . . .' he said again, discreetly tapping his right ear.

'No, he won't be deaf,' answered Dr Hoppe firmly, whereupon Vera burst into tears.

Lothar gave a sigh, and considered for a moment. 'We don't have to decide this minute, do we?' he said, somewhat anxiously. 'Isn't that so?'

'No, I am just giving you the option,' said the doctor calmly. 'Take your time. Think it over. You too, Frau Weber. You really need not abide by God's will.' Then he turned round.

Lothar got up, but the doctor gestured to him. 'Stay with your wife, Herr Weber, I'll find my own way.'

Lothar nodded and sank back down on the bed. He watched as the doctor left the room, his back and shoulders squared. There was a self-assuredness in his posture that Lothar envied, but at the same time it filled him with awe. He heard his wife sobbing, and remembered that he had not even asked about the pills that were supposed to make life easier.

He sighed and turned to his wife. 'Vera . . .' he began.

His wife lifted her head. Her eyes were damp and red. She raised her right hand and then let it fall back into her lap. 'We didn't even ask how his own children are doing,' she sobbed.

The holidays ended up rubbing quite a bit of salt into Lothar and Vera Weber's wounds, and after Mass on the first day of the new year, seeking solace, they went to speak with Father Kaisergruber.

'Must we abide by God's will?' Vera asked him.

The priest then told them the story of Job, who was tested by God after the devil had challenged Him.

'*God deprived Job of all his worldly goods, and his children also. And still the poor man did not curse God. God giveth and God taketh away, he said. And then God smote Job with sore boils from his head to his feet. And Job said, "Shall we receive good at the hand of God, but shall we not receive evil?"*' The story was accompanied with much gesticulation, as was the priest's wont.

'Now, do you understand what Job means?' he said, turning to Vera. 'You have a roof over your heads, you drive a nice car, Lothar has a good job . . . surely you don't reproach God for granting you those things?'

'I'd trade all of it in just to have Gunther back,' Vera sighed.

'The story doesn't end there,' Father Kaisergruber continued. 'Because Job abided by God's will, he was rewarded by Him once more, in the end. Listen . . .'

The priest opened the Bible and read aloud, '*He received fourteen thousand sheep, and six thousand camels, and a thousand yoke of oxen, and a thousand she-asses. He also received twice seven sons and three daughters.*'

'What on earth would we *do* with all those animals?' Lothar demanded.

'You have to . . .' the priest began, but the smile on Lothar's face made him realise it was meant as a joke.

'Don't worry, I get it,' Lothar told him, and his wife nodded silently.

That night he reached for her, and for the first time in years he found his wife open to him. She was as unresponsive as a board, however, and after not even two minutes she pushed him off her.

'It's too risky,' she said. 'What if . . .'

'We must abide,' said Lothar.

'It's too risky. We mustn't provoke God, either.'

Lothar let out a sigh. He felt his penis shrivel up.

'What *do* you want, then?' he asked, even though he thought he knew the answer.

'We could at least talk to him.'

'To the doctor, you mean?'

The slight stirring he felt beside him told him that she was nodding her head.

'If it would make you feel more certain,' he said, turning on his side, his back to her.

'I think it would.'

Gunther Weber's parents came to see him, and the wife asked how likely it was that they would have a disabled child if they tried to conceive naturally.

'The normal way, she means,' her husband added.

He had replied that it was quite a big risk that way, but that there were other methods to mitigate such a risk. A question of technique, he assured them again.

'But if there's such a big risk,' she said, 'surely it means that God does not want us to do it? So then we do have to abide by his will.'

That gave him pause. But then he said, 'Well, and what about Sarah?'

'Sarah?'

'Abraham's wife. In the Bible, the Book of Genesis.' He proceeded to recite the pertinent verses by heart: '*Then He said, "When I return to you about this time next year, Sarah your wife shall have a son." Sarah stood behind him, listening at the entrance to the tent. Now Abraham and Sarah were already old and well advanced in years, and Sarah was past the age of childbearing*.' He was able to recall the words effortlessly, and out of the corner of his eye he could see the wife listening to him breathlessly, which was reason enough for him to continue. '*And Jahweh visited Sarah as he had said, and Jahweh did unto Sarah as He had spoken. For Sarah conceived, and bore Abraham a son in his old age, at the set time of which God had spoken to him. And Abraham called the name of his son that was born unto him, whom Sarah bore to him, Isaac.*'

The doctor paused, feeling himself break into a sweat. The wife and husband were both staring at him wide-eyed, waiting for him to go on, and then he said, even though he knew he was cutting it very close, 'If you want, you can have a son by this time next year.'

That was on 20 January 1989.

It was cutting it very close, because most of the cells that Victor had harvested – that was the word he used – had already died. So he would first have to culture the few remaining live cells until they multiplied by cell division, although that would involve a further loss of telomeres. It couldn't be helped, but at least there were many more telomeres left this time, compared to four years ago when he had cloned himself. He had again starved the newly formed cells and left them hovering between life and death, until they reached the G0 stage. It was like saving someone from drowning over and over again, only to throw them back into the water each time.

At the same time he had to decipher the genetic code stored in each nucleus. That was more difficult than he had anticipated, because it turned out that the DNA in many of the cells wasn't intact, so it was like having to decipher fragments of text scattered on little snippets of paper.

When he had promised Gunther's parents that he would help them, a little over two months after their son's death, he had not yet deciphered the code. And once he had, he wouldn't even be halfway there. The next step was to find the error in the code that had caused the boy's deafness, and then try to erase that error. It wasn't until he'd completed that stage that he'd be able to start culturing the embryos. And only then would he be able to make Vera Weber pregnant. If, that is, she was able to produce enough viable eggs in the interim, for that was another question mark.

To complete all of this, he had given himself four months, with the assumption that the pregnancy would last just eight months. That was cutting it very close. He was aware of that. But it was part of the challenge. He thought it was still doable, in any case. More than ever, he was sure that he had everything under control.

5

On Saturday, 1 April 1989, Rex Cremer's telephone rang.

'Are you Dr Cremer? Of the University of Aachen?'

'I am no longer employed there, madam. It's been quite a few years.'

'Do you happen to know where Dr Hoppe might be? At the university, I was told . . .'

'I don't know that name, madam.'

'But you came to see me, in Bonn. It *was* you, wasn't it?'

'I don't know what you are talking about.'

'At Dr Hoppe's. You came to see me there, when I was pregnant.'

'You must be thinking of someone else.'

'I'm trying to find the children, sir! I want to see them. I want to know how they are. You *have* to help me.'

'I don't know where he is, madam. In Bonn, perhaps.'

'He hasn't lived there for a long time. I've been there. I went there a month ago.'

'I'm sorry, I can't help you.'

'If you do see or hear from him, please tell him I am looking for him. Tell him I wish to see the children. That I have the right.'

'You have the right?'

'I'm their mother! Surely that gives me the right to see them!'

'You are their mother?'

'Of course I'm their mother!'

'Please calm down, madam. You've caught me off guard. The children, you say. What do you know about the children?'

'Nothing. Only that they were boys. Three boys! But I've never seen them.'

'Never?'

'On the ultrasound, sir, only on the ultrasound. I was asleep when he took them out.'

'And then? What did he . . .'

'He'd promised me a girl! One girl! And then all of a sudden he informs me it's boys. Three boys! Actually, four . . . because one . . . one was . . .'

'When did he tell you that?'

'The day before their birth. He showed it to me! On the ultrasound. I was – I was in shock! I didn't want them! Not back then. Do you understand? Can't you understand that?'

'I understand, madam, I do understand.'

'But now I want to see them. I want to know how they are doing and tell them I'm sorry. I want to explain to them why I wasn't there for them – why their mother wasn't there for them. They must have been asking themselves that question, don't you think? Maybe they don't even know I'm alive. My God, imagine if—'

'Madam, I don't know. I have had very little to do with Dr Hoppe.'

'But have you seen him? Have you ever heard from him?'

'. . .'

'Sir?'

'I heard that he had moved to Belgium.'

'Belgium?'

'Just across the border. A village called Wolfheim, something like that.'

'Wolfheim, did you say?'

'Something like that.'

As if he'd simply passed the ball on to someone else. It was that simple, really. For five long months Rex had been carrying around a terrible sense of guilt, and suddenly it was gone. In those first days after his visit to Wolfheim, the guilt had haunted him constantly. He had tried to sort it all out in his mind, first from a rational scientist's point of view, just as Victor Hoppe had done, and then from an outsider's moral perspective. And so his sense of guilt had kept on growing.

If you looked at it pragmatically, Victor had succeeded in cloning himself; and even if something had gone wrong with the experiment, it was an extraordinary feat. He had shown that it was possible to clone humans, and from a scientific standpoint the resulting mutation of the telomeres was merely a side effect, one that did have dreadful consequences, to be sure, but in the end, just a side effect.

From what he had been able to gather from Victor, this experiment was only the beginning. It was Victor's way of proving that he could do it. The next time, he would strive to eliminate any genetic abnormalities or, as he had said, to correct any birth defects, as if all he had to do was take an eraser and rub them out. All things considered, his motives seemed noble, if it weren't for the fact that Victor had let something else slip. He wasn't doing it out of some noble or even scientific motivation: to him, it was war.

Father. That was the word one of the boys had used. *Fad-der-did-it.* Not Daddy or Dad, but Father. As in God the Father, of course. How could it be otherwise? Victor wasn't their natural father; he was their creator. That was why he had them call him Father. Just like that other creator, his adversary in this war. And already he had lost the first round. He, Victor Hoppe, had failed. The children had been born with telomeres that were too short. That mutation was far worse than the other one that had caused their facial disfigurement. The cleft palate had been in their genes from the start; it was a freak of nature. But not to Victor. In his eyes, his harelip was an error on God's part, an error that had to be set right, that *he* was going to set right.

That was the way it must have played out in his mind. Cremer understood it up to this point, or thought he understood it. But should he just let it happen? Should he allow Victor Hoppe to continue his work undisturbed, for the sake of science? Or should he halt a genius because that genius was also showing signs of madness?

Those were the questions that had been plaguing him, and he knew full well what his answer ought to be; but he'd been trying to ignore it, reluctant as ever to become involved.

But then came the woman's phone call. At first he had thought it was someone playing a trick on him, but soon he'd realised that this was in fact *the* mother. Not the biological mother; the surrogate mother. But he didn't say so. What he did do was tell her where she could find Victor Hoppe. And by telling her where to find him, he had solved his own predicament.

'They're boys. Three boys.' That was what Dr Hoppe had suddenly told her when she was eight months pregnant. Her stomach had been as round as a drum; a drum that was constantly being pounded from inside. The doctor had been doing a final ultrasound on her. He'd rarely told her anything while doing the procedure – until now. 'See that grey spot, there,' he'd usually say, but she had never seen anything but black specks, although she had never come out and said so because she didn't want to seem even more stupid than she already felt. When he told her that everything was fine, that was always enough for her. But that last time, he'd said, 'They're boys. Three boys.'

'*What?*'

'There are three boys in your stomach.'

'But it can't be! It's not possible. You're pulling my leg.'

'Do you want to see? I'll show you.'

He had pointed it all out to her in great detail. And she had looked, and counted, and grown more and more bewildered. Six eyes. Six hands. Three hearts. Three beating hearts. And three penises. That was the word the doctor had used.

'But you promised me a daughter,' she managed to blurt out. 'You always told me it was a girl!'

'I never said that. You convinced yourself.'

She felt as if she couldn't breathe.

'It can't be. It can't be.'

'There used to be four. At first. Four boys.'

She shook her head, confused.

'Here,' he said. He then traced something on the screen with his pen. A mouse. Or a hamster. That was what it looked like.

'That one died five months ago.'

She felt like vomiting. She wanted to spew out the entire contents of her stomach. But nothing came.

When the doctor went to wipe the gel from her stomach, she hit him.

'Out!' she yelled. 'Take it out! Take *them* out! Take them all out!'

'Tomorrow. I can't do it until tomorrow.'

'Now! Now! *Now!*' She began hammering both fists on her stomach. 'I don't want it! I don't want it!'

He grabbed her hands by the wrists and tied them to the bed frame.

'You must stay calm. This isn't good for the children.'

She began kicking with her feet, twisting her body from side to side. She screamed. She yelled.

Then he injected something into her intravenous tube.

'You don't have to see them tomorrow,' she heard him say. 'If you don't want to.'

It had been impossible for her to forget the children, no matter how hard she tried, because they had left an ineradicable souvenir, from one side of her stomach to the other.

It had turned into an ugly scar. Some parts of the incision had become infected, and she had left it untreated for quite some time. Out of shame, but also because she had wanted to punish herself. It wasn't until the pain was so bad that it felt as if she was being stabbed by a thousand daggers that she'd gone to the hospital. The stitches had been left in three weeks longer than they should have been.

She told them it was a miscarriage. An emergency Caesarean section, while on a trip abroad. The physician who removed the stitches asked if the surgeon had been a butcher. He'd never seen such a mess. She had to clamp her lips shut. It was the only time she ever showed her scar to anyone.

The scar was still her Achilles heel. Even at the slightest touch it hurt. She could no longer bear to wear tight clothes. Her stomach was often terribly bloated. That was why it didn't really feel like a scar. Instead of having something taken *out* of her, she felt as if she'd had something put *inside* her.

She had never tried to have another relationship either. How could another person take pleasure in her body when she was so revolted by it? And as long as she remained celibate, there was no need to explain anything. She had accepted the loneliness that came with it.

The financial compensation she had insisted on – which the doctor had promptly paid – had done little to ease her pain. She had hoped that it would still her conscience. She had put her body at his disposal, not her soul. But afterwards it had made her feel like a whore. Worse than a whore.

She'd needed the money to live on and to pay off her debts, and so she had kept it and spent it. But it meant that her conscience had never stopped festering either.

Several times she had made up her mind to look for the children. She wanted to know how they were, if they were well. That, at the very least. It was the only way she'd ever be able to clear her conscience. But she had changed her mind every time. As the children grew older, the urge to see them only increased. She counted the months. She counted the years.

The worst day of the year was always 29 September. The ache in her stomach would grow unbearable around that date. The day the children turned four, and for the umpteenth time, she made the decision to try to find them. They were now old enough, surely, to start wondering about their mother – who she was. At that age, they needed a mother. Yet still she had waited a few months; gathered up her courage. And finally she had taken the big step.

6

She arrived on Sunday, 14 May 1989. Whitsun. She had taken the train from Salzburg to Luxembourg the previous day, and had spent the night there. Early the next morning she took the train to Liège, where she boarded the local connection to La Chapelle, from which she found a bus departing hourly for Wolfheim.

She asked the bus driver to warn her when they got to the village.

'Where do you want to get out? At the church?'

She was gratified that he spoke excellent German.

'Napoleonstrasse. I'm on my way to see Dr Hoppe. Dr Victor Hoppe.'

She had set out on the off chance that he would be home. She had found his address and telephone number a few weeks ago through international directory enquiries, but had not rung him in advance. She was afraid of hearing his voice. She thought it would make her lose her nerve. Even now, having come so far, she wasn't sure if she would find the courage to ring the doorbell. She had brought enough money and clothes to stay a couple of days in the area if need be.

'Dr Hoppe,' the bus driver repeated. 'In that case you will need to get out at the church. He lives right there.'

She was speechless. She hadn't expected to meet anyone who knew him so soon. She immediately felt paralysed with fear.

'Have you ever met him?' she asked in a quavering voice.

The driver shook his head. 'No, I haven't. But I've heard people say that he is an excellent doctor.'

She wanted to ask if he knew anything about the doctor's children, but then she might have to explain herself, which she wanted to avoid at all costs. Besides, she was afraid his answer would be a disappointment, so she said nothing more. She tried not to think of the upcoming encounter, but without much success. Every time the bus rolled to a halt she expected the doctor to climb aboard. It was the same feeling she'd had some months before, when she had tried to find him in Bonn. She had hoped back then that she might accidentally bump into him, in the street or in a shop – but now that it might actually come to pass, she hoped it wouldn't.

The bus left the municipality of Kelmis behind. They had already traversed the villages of Montzen and Hergenrath.

'We'll be in Wolfheim any minute,' said the driver, glancing at her in the rear-view mirror.

She nodded at him. 'Your German is quite fluent,' she remarked in the hope that a chat would get her mind on something else. 'I thought that in Belgium people spoke only French and Dutch.'

'In this part of the country most of the people speak German,' said the driver. 'But many also know French, and some can speak Flemish as well. The languages and the borders here have been jumbled up together for centuries. Do you know about the three-border junction?'

She shook her head.

'It's just a few kilometres from here. At the top of the Vaalserberg. It's where the borders of Belgium, the Netherlands and Germany converge. You really must go and have a look. If you stayed on the bus, you'd see it. My route takes me up to the three borders; I make a U-turn up there. If you like, you could get off at Wolfheim on the way back.'

'Another time, maybe,' she said, smiling. 'I don't have the time today.'

She had no idea how much time she had, or might need. She didn't even know what she would say when she saw the doctor, even though she'd rehearsed many an opening sentence on the long train ride.

The bus swerved to the right, past a sign that said Wolfheim. The road was paved with cobblestones and the wheels of the bus rattled over them in a jouncing rhythm. A church steeple appeared through the windscreen.

'There's your stop,' said the bus driver, slowing down.

She began buttoning her coat.

'A few months ago a tragic accident happened here,' the driver began. 'A colleague of mine ran over a boy, with his bus.'

She felt the blood drain from her face. It was what she'd always been afraid of but had tried to think about as little as possible. She was sure it had been one of her children. She was too late, then. A cold chill went through her. She heard what the bus driver said next, but it barely registered.

'My colleague has been staying home ever since. He doesn't have the nerve to drive a bus any more. I'm replacing him for now.'

The bus swerved right, and screeched to a halt.

'Here we are,' said the driver, as the doors swung open. 'The doctor's house is over there.'

He pointed through the windscreen to a tall house a bit further on.

She nodded mechanically, stood up, picked up her suitcase and shuffled towards the exit.

It had just rained, and a breeze brushed her face. She turned her coat collar up and waited, looking at the ground, until the bus left. When the sound of the engine had almost quite died away, she heard the shouts of children playing. She turned round and saw across the street a group of small children splashing in a puddle. There were four boys, and she guessed they were about five years old, perhaps a little younger. For a long-drawn-out minute she stared at the children, motionless, listening to their voices. From their shouts she was able to make out the names: Michel, Reinhart. She felt her heart beating faster, and took a deep breath. Slowly she exhaled through her nose. Then, just as slowly, she set herself in motion. The wheels of her suitcase, rolling along behind her, made a rattling sound. She walked on until there was only the street between her and the children.

Then she recognised them, even though she had never seen them before. The boys were the spitting image of each other. The posture. The stance. The shape of the face. And they were wearing the same blue anorak and woolly hat, which enhanced the likeness. But there were only two of them. Not three. She began to feel dizzy. And in that moment, as everything started spinning around her, one of the boys glanced her way; and then suddenly everything settled down again, as if someone had pulled a lever.

The boys had *her* eyes. She had seen it in a split second: the dark iris set in an expanse of white that was so quintessentially *her*.

As if in a trance, she had let go of her suitcase and crossed the street.

'It's my fault! It's all my fault!' She must have cried something like that. Then she had grabbed hold of one of the boys' hands, clutched it in hers, and fell to her knees so that her face was level with his and she could look him straight in the eye.

'I should never have left you alone!' She had said something like that. Or perhaps, 'I should never have left you!'

She was more sure of what she had said next: 'I'm sorry! I'm so sorry!'

But she did not remember *when* she had said it. It might have been when the boy had tried to pull free and started screaming. It might have been when she'd apologised to the women.

'Let go of him!' the woman who was the first to come running had yelled. 'Let go of him!'

'I'm their mother!'

'You're crazy!'

Another woman had reached them by now, 'Let go of my son! In the name of God, let go of my son!'

The second woman had pushed her and, tumbling backwards into the puddle, she had let go of the child.

'Michel, Marcel, go inside. And take Olaf and Reinhart with you!'

She had stretched out her arms, but the children had run away. She'd burst into tears, sitting on the ground, in the puddle. It was then that she'd realised she must have made a mistake.

'I'm sorry! I'm so sorry!'

Then she had said all sorts of things. She had tried to explain. But finally she'd scrambled to her feet. 'I have to go to the doctor's,' were her last words.

She had rung the bell three times before the front door was opened and Dr Hoppe stepped outside. His physical appearance immediately evoked such revulsion in her that she shuddered to remember the times his fingers had poked and prodded her, both inside and out.

She was determined not to mention the children straight away. She had vowed to herself that she'd be more careful this time.

The doctor glanced at her. His face betrayed not the slightest reaction. Perhaps he did not recognise her.

'Doctor,' she began. The sound of her voice made her realise how nervous she was. She had wanted to come across as strong and determined, but she sounded like a child who had come begging.

'Doctor,' she said again, rather more forcefully, 'I want to speak with you . . . I *must* speak with you.' She had not introduced herself, she suddenly realised.

'I am no longer seeing patients, madam. For the time being.'

His voice was like fingernails scratching down a blackboard. She pulled a face and turned her head away. Then she shook her head and looked up at him again.

'This is urgent,' she said. 'It can't wait.' She was shivering, but didn't bother to hide it from the doctor.

'Then you had better step inside,' he said.

Following him up the garden path, she began to seethe. She had lain bedridden in his house for months and months and he didn't even recognise her! And that despite the fact that she had scarcely changed over the past few years. Her unlined face, her short hair, even her weight – they were all the same as the day she had given birth; she had never managed to lose the nineteen kilos she'd gained.

He's just pretending, she suddenly realised. He wanted her to think that they had never met. He would say that she was delusional, so that he could keep the children for himself. That was what he intended to do. But it wouldn't work. Not this time.

'Why are you pretending you don't know me?' she asked as soon as he shut the front door behind her.

He was startled, but said nothing.

'You know what I'm here for,' she went on. 'That's why you're acting this way.'

She saw that he felt cornered and decided to keep up the pressure. 'I am their mother and I have the right to see the children.'

'You are not their mother,' he said.

Her instincts hadn't let her down. He wanted to make her believe that she had dreamed the whole thing up. 'How *dare* you?' she said, raising her voice. 'How dare you lie to me, after all you've put me through!'

'I am not lying, madam,' he said calmly, which only infuriated her more. 'They don't have a mother.'

'You are lying! You do nothing but lie! You pretend that I don't even exist! You just want to keep the children for yourself!' She had deliberately raised her voice in the hope that the children would hear her and come out of the woodwork. 'You've been lying to me from day one! I don't believe a thing you say any more! I want to see my children. Now! Do you hear? I want to see my children, right this minute!'

She noticed that the doctor was avoiding looking at her. That proved he was lying.

Then suddenly he gave in. 'You want to see them? OK, you can see them. If you really want to see them, you may do so.'

She fell silent. All of a sudden she did not know what to say. She hadn't expected him to give in so soon. All the courage she had mustered vanished in an instant.

The doctor stepped forward and squeezed past her. 'Follow me,' he said, and began climbing the stairs.

'You can see them,' she heard him say once more, muttering, as if to himself. 'But you are not their mother.'

He took her to see the children, as she had demanded. He unlocked the door and told her she could go in.

She stuck out her hand. 'The key. I want the key. I don't want you locking me in.'

He wondered what made her think he'd ever want to do that. Nevertheless, he did give her the key, which she dropped almost as soon as she'd gone in, leaving him to pick it up again. He saw that she was hyperventilating, and waited until she had got her breathing under control. Then she asked what was wrong with the children – if they were ill.

'Something like that,' he replied.

She pointed at the unmade bed. Her hand was shaking.

'Where is . . .'

'Michael?'

That was who she meant. He told her the truth, but she said it wasn't true.

'It can't be. It can't be. You're lying.'

He was not lying. He was sure of that.

'When? Since when!' she asked.

He could not tell her exactly, but approximately. So it wasn't a lie.

'A few days ago. Or so.'

'You're lying! You're lying!' That was what she started yelling, louder and louder, and he didn't understand why. So he decided he should provide her with a more thorough explanation.

'I am not lying, madam. And they' – he pointed at the two other boys – 'they are going to die too.'

That she did believe, for she asked how long they still had.

'A few days. A week, maybe.'

'It isn't true,' she cried. 'Tell me it isn't true.'

But it was true.

Then she began to cry and, gazing at her shoulders, he wondered why she was crying so bitterly. She wasn't their mother, after all.

'Could you leave me alone with them for a while?'

The doctor shrugged, and nodded. Then he turned around and left the room. He pulled the door shut behind him but didn't lock it. She wouldn't have minded if he had. Maybe she deserved to be locked up, as punishment for having left the children to their fate. Although that was too mild a punishment.

Eyes closed, she breathed slowly, in and out. She'd been ranting and raving like a lunatic, she realised, and in the presence of the children too. She ought to apologise. For that, as well as for everything else. She didn't know where to begin.

She opened her eyes again. Not for a moment did she think she could possibly have been dreaming. The stench was too pungent, even with her eyes closed. She had smelled it as soon as Dr Hoppe had opened the door, while she was still out in the hallway. The smell was so strong that it took your breath away.

The two boys, in short-sleeved shirts, were sitting side by side in one of the beds. The middle bed. The left bed had been slept in, the sheets were turned down; the right bed had been stripped, and its mattress had a yellow stain in the middle that had spread outward.

She had to force herself to look at the boys, and once again the words came into her head that had first occurred to her a few moments ago: papier mâché. Their heads seemed to be made out of papier mâché. Only by their level gaze could you tell that there was any life in them. She did not recognise herself in that gaze. Nose, mouth, ears, chin, jaw – everything was different from what she was used to seeing in the mirror. Nor did the boys have her skin, her clear, smooth skin. Their illness had deformed them. There was no other explanation.

She had to say something, she realised. The boys seemed frozen. Maybe they were afraid of her. She took a step forward and said, 'I'm sorry about yelling just now.'

She'd taken a quick breath in through her nose, which made her aware of the dreadful stink once more. She whipped her head around to find out where the smell was coming from. As she did so, she noticed that the walls were almost completely bare. There were just a few shreds of wallpaper left, or mostly just the dull lining, so that it was clear that the paper had not been stripped off by soaking or steaming, but had been ripped down. Here and there black lines or smudges were visible on the remnants, as if they had been written or drawn on.

She walked up to the foot of the bed, where the boys were still sitting upright, side by side, not the slightest emotion on their faces, like commuters waiting for a bus. Even without sniffing, she could now smell the stench that was rising, from the bed, the sheets, the blankets, the children.

She felt sick and knew that she would faint if she didn't get away from that putrid smell. She also knew that if she walked out now, it would all be over. Any chance she had to *do* something for them, for herself, would be gone.

She looked at the children. At *her* children. Then she acted fast, holding her breath, and without thinking. In two steps she was by the bed. She yanked off the blankets and sheets, which were heavy and wet. The boys were naked from the waist down, stick-thin and covered in a thick layer of brown, caked-on shit.

She picked up one of the boys, and it felt as if she was holding nothing in her arms. That too was a shock, but it did not deter her. Nothing could stop her now. She picked up the other boy, threading one arm through his armpit, from the back. The bed sheet had stuck to his body and let go with a tearing sound.

She ran from the room, the two children in her arms. She didn't even look to see where the doctor was; even if he had been in her way, she would just have marched past him, without scolding or screaming, because – opening the doors along the corridor one by one – she had taken all the guilt upon herself. If she had not rejected them, then this would never have happened. She was convinced of it. It was her fault. Entirely her fault.

In the bathroom she made a beeline for the bath and deposited the children in it. She yanked off their shirts, grabbed the shower head and turned the tap all the way on so that the water gushed out in a hard stream. She held her hand under the tap and gradually began to breathe again. A great lethargy stealthily crept over her.

'I'm so sorry, I'm so sorry,' she started yammering.

Newly hatched fledglings – that was what the boys reminded her of as she dried them off. Not only because they seemed so vulnerable, so fragile, so helpless, but also because they were pink and bald and seemed to have far too much skin. And because the large, bulging eyes took up practically their entire faces. And because their mouths opened and closed like little beaks as they gasped for air. They did so greedily, as if they had kept their breathing to a minimum all this time because of the stench.

They had submitted to the bath without any reaction. They had not cried, they had not yelled, they had not struggled. But as soon as she started to dry them, they slowly began to revive. They were coming to life, almost literally. Carefully, as if picking up baby birds that had fallen out of the nest, she lifted them out of the bath one by one, and settled them down on a little bench, because they were unable to stand. Just as carefully, using only the tips of her fingers, she starting dabbing the boys' fragile bodies dry with a towel. Wherever she touched them, she felt their bones.

A few days. A week, maybe. The doctor's voice kept droning inside her head.

'It's going to be all right,' she told them, trying to get rid of that voice in her head. 'It's all going to be all right. I'm here now.'

Like drowning souls returning to life, they started to breathe.

And then one of the boys spoke up: 'Is-My-gal-in-ev-ven?' A voice that sounded like shattering glass.

'Is Michael in heaven?' she echoed, to give herself time to come up with an answer. Did the children know their brother was dead? Had they seen him die? Or had Dr Hoppe taken him away before it happened?

She decided to tell them the truth. Perhaps it would help the boys to feel less distressed about their own impending deaths. That was why she went on to say another thing. 'Yes, Michael is in heaven. He's waiting up there for you.'

She could detect neither grief nor fear in their eyes. The boys just nodded. For her it was harder to control her emotions. To give herself something else to think about, she asked them their names.

'Ga-bree-el.'

'Raf-fa-el.'

Their names sounded strange to her, just as the name Michael had. She would never have chosen such names for them. All these years she had been thinking of names, and in the end she had settled on Klaus, Thomas and Heinrich. Klaus, Thomas and Heinrich Fischer. Because they would have her surname, of course.

'My name is Rebekka,' she said. 'Rebekka Fischer.'

She had wanted to add that she was their mother, but didn't, because she did not want to upset them further. She would tell them later, when they were used to her. First she had to make them understand that she would not just abandon them to their fate. The way the doctor had.

How *could* he?

As she was hunting for clean pyjamas in the bedroom, the answer suddenly came to her. He did not love them. That was it. He did not love them because they weren't his. They were *her* children. That was why he had neglected them so. The thought made it even plainer to her than before that she should never have given them up. It was the worst mistake she had ever made, and she could not make it right any more. The only thing left for her to do now was to make sure that she was *there* for them, for the two that were still alive.

She dressed the children. Underpants. Undershirt. Pyjamas. With care and tenderness; the way she used to dress her dolls when she was little. She wished she could take them away from this place, but she hadn't the foggiest idea where she would go. Home? That was much too far. They were too weak. The hospital? If she did that, she would in all likelihood lose them immediately, and for ever. Anyway, why should anyone believe her, that she was their mother? If even the children themselves had never seen her or heard from her, *she'd* be the one they'd accuse of neglect, not the doctor.

'Is it OK with you if I stay?' she asked them, just to be sure.

They shrugged their shoulders. She did feel a pang of disappointment as she had expected the boys to be grateful.

She decided to stay anyway.

That was what she told the doctor a short time later. She had tucked the children into bed in another room; they'd almost fallen asleep on her shoulder. Then she had gone downstairs to find something for them to eat. The doctor was sitting in the kitchen eating a bowl of soup. Soup from a tin, one of the legions of empty tins that littered the worktop, spilled out of the dustbin and lay scattered all around it. Then she noticed the flies. There were flies crawling over every surface; they even landed on the doctor, who did not bother to swat them off.

'I'd like you to tell me what exactly is going on here,' she began, ignoring the rubbish and the flies.

'What exactly do you want to know?'

The fact that he was so calm made her blood boil. 'Their illness. What's the matter with them?'

'The telomeres were too short.'

'In layman's terms, Doctor, in layman's terms!'

Then he told her all sorts of things, but the only part she really understood was that the boys were growing old too fast; that every year of their lives was more like ten to fifteen years. She had no idea what made her think of it, but a picture came into her head of an apple that's been rotting in the fruit bowl for weeks. Maybe it was the smell that hung in the kitchen.

The doctor was adamant that the phenomenon could not be reversed.

'Who says? The specialists?' she asked.

'Do you doubt me?' He sounded as if he were insulted.

'How *dare* you ask me that?' she exclaimed indignantly. 'After all you have done to me?'

No response. She wasn't waiting for one, either.

'I am staying,' she said. 'Do you hear? I'm staying! I'm not leaving them alone ever again!' And as he still said nothing, she added, 'And I don't want you to come near them, do you hear? I won't have it! You've done enough harm as it is!'

That she had said it, had had the guts to say it, felt like having a great weight lifted off her shoulders, even if she wasn't sure how she would or should care for the boys. From his expression she could tell that the doctor was dumbfounded. So he had finally come to realise that she would not let herself be kicked around this time.

He asked himself why she was accusing him of doing harm. He had only tried to do good, hadn't he? He had thought about it long and hard, certainly, but in the end he had done what was expected of him. He had stopped feeding the children, thereby placing their fate in God's hands. For it was clear that God had been calling them from the very start, and he had not been able to delay it, no matter how hard he had tried over all these years. And since he had in the end surrendered the children to God, it was now up to God to decide when to take them. The fact that He was taking his time about it and had not taken all three at once – that was God's own decision. So the evil – it was God's doing. Surely there was nothing Victor could do about it? So why was the woman accusing *him*? Or could *she* be the one who was doing evil?

As soon as the doctor had left the kitchen, she began clearing away the tins. She stuffed them into rubbish bags and piled them up outside the front door. Then she hunted around for some fresh food, but all she could find was more tins, some stale bread and a couple of bottles of milk.

She heated some vegetable soup and took it up to the boys, who reacted with mild surprise when they saw her come in, as if they'd already forgotten that she had saved them from their horrible plight just an hour ago. They stared at her as she fed them, spoonful after spoonful, mouthful upon mouthful. The children had trouble swallowing, but they were apparently so hungry that they didn't refuse a single bite.

'Eat, eat, it'll make you grow big and strong,' she said.

When they had finished, she tucked the boys in for a nap, even though she still had so many questions. As soon as they were asleep she headed straight for the room she'd discovered in her quest for another bed for the children.

It was a classroom, with desks, a teacher's lectern, a blackboard and a map of Europe on the wall. She gazed round in wonder, and began poking about apprehensively. In the top drawer of the teacher's desk she found exercise books labelled with the boys' names. She leafed through some of them. The handwriting was difficult to read, but what she could decipher astounded her. The boys, it seemed, already knew how to write and do sums. She saw words of two, three, or even more syllables. There were even some sentences running the width of the page, and not only in German but also in another language that was foreign to her. They also knew how to add and subtract.

She thought it rather odd, but also extraordinary. She did for a moment ask herself how she, who had not completed secondary school, could have produced such bright children. But soon enough that very fact – that *she* had managed to produce such bright children – made her feel very proud.

Nevertheless, it raised more questions. Who had been teaching her children? She didn't for a moment imagine that it had been the doctor himself. And then, she thought, it didn't make much sense at all that the children had been schooled. Why would the doctor have gone to the trouble of paying someone to teach them, if he didn't care a fig about them?

She found the likely answer to her first question in a children's Bible she found lying in the bottom drawer of the teacher's desk. She hadn't glanced at a Bible in years, but did remember a few stories that had been read to her at school, like the one about Noah's Ark, or the story about Jesus and the publicans. She was quite religious, but only in fits and starts, when it suited her. When she'd been pregnant the first time, she had thanked God, but when she'd had her first miscarriage, she had cursed Him. In one and the same breath, as the aborted foetus had left her in a gush of stench and pain, she had called out to Him to help her.

It had been the same the second time. At first she had thanked Him for the divine miracle; then, when the children were born, the repudiation, because He had forsaken her. Later she had gone to church once or twice, to light candles, not for herself but for the children she had left behind. But it had been no use. What kind of God was He, if he allowed even little children to suffer so? That thought came to her as she leafed through the children's Bible, her eyes skimming over the colour plates. Then she discovered the name – at the back of the Bible, in an elegant, flowing hand. She read the name aloud to herself a few times. Was she the one who had taught the boys? If so, then she would like to meet her. The sooner the better.

When the boys woke up, she asked them about it. Not straight away, because first they needed to be changed again.

'Never you mind,' she said, because she could tell that this time they were ashamed of what they hadn't been able to control. Fresh sheets, clean clothes – all over again. But the smell wasn't as bad this time.

'Do you know who Charlotte Maenhout is?'

They both nodded.

'Was she your teacher?'

Again, a nod.

'Where is she? Where does she live?'

'In . . . hev . . . ven,' Gabriel said, laboriously.

The answer startled her.

'You mean she's dead?'

She had said it before realising how painful it might be for them to hear those words.

'She . . . is . . . an . . . ang . . . el,' Gabriel answered.

'My-gal too! My-gal too! Look!' Raphael suddenly piped up. The boy lifted his head and opened his eyes wide, as if he were seeing his dead brother. The next instant, something seemed to have got stuck in his throat. He started gasping for air, like a fish on dry land.

'Raphael!' she cried, panicked. She wanted to gather him in her arms, but didn't dare. 'Raphael! Raphael!'

Then she rushed from the room.

'Doctor! Doctor!' She ran down the stairs. 'Doctor!'

The office door opened just as she reached the bottom of the stairs.

'Raphael!' she cried. 'He can't breathe! He's dying!'

The doctor nodded.

'You have to *do* something!' she screamed. 'Help him! Why won't you help him!'

Again he nodded, and then stirred himself. But slowly. Very slowly. She stormed up the stairs again, hoping to get him moving. At the door to the room, she stopped. The doctor was coming up the stairs. One tread, then the next. Peering into the room, she saw that Raphael was flat on his back in the bed. As soon as the doctor had made it up the stairs, she stepped aside to let him pass.

He leaned down over Raphael and checked his pulse. Anxiously she clapped her hands to her mouth. Minutes seemed to pass before he let the arm drop. Then he turned to her: 'It is not yet time. God wants to torment him a while longer.'

That night and all the next day she barely left Raphael and Gabriel's side. She sat on a chair by the bed and kept watch. The boys slept almost the entire time, and they were very restless in their sleep. They kept moving their hands about, as if they were trying to climb onto something. They were also breathing heavily – so heavily that every time one of them stopped making any noise, she feared that he had stopped breathing altogether. Every so often she'd wipe the drool from their mouths and chins, or dab the sweat from their foreheads. Every so often she'd simply reach out and touch them.

During those hours of vigil she tried to read the Bible, but she couldn't concentrate. She kept having to stop and gaze at Raphael and Gabriel, even though it just tore her up with grief.

The boys woke up a few times. Then she would change them and give them something to eat. A sip of milk, a mouthful of soup or a bite of bread that she'd soaked in the soup. But they took in very little. A crumb of bread, a teaspoon of milk or soup.

'Come on, eat something, please eat,' she said, but insisting did not help. Swallowing seemed to hurt them, as did sitting up. She even had the impression that opening their eyes was arduous.

Their deterioration was faster than she'd ever have expected.

A few days. A week, maybe.

She grew more and more desperate. She felt it as an ache in her belly. She had the constant urge, as she used to have, to punch herself in the stomach, as if that would make everything all right again. At a certain point she even wished that she could just pick up the boys as they lay there and stuff them back inside her stomach, so that she might give birth to them again, and so give them a fresh chance at life.

She was waiting for the right moment to tell them she was their mother. She felt she *had* to tell them. But every time the opportunity presented itself, she faltered. Maybe the boys wouldn't want to know. Maybe they had a picture in their minds of what their mother was like and would be disappointed, just as she had walked around with a picture of what they were like, only to find out that they were quite different. Yet she wasn't disappointed. So maybe they wouldn't be either.

She told them late the next day, a Monday. She had not seen the doctor, as he'd stayed downstairs all day long, mostly in the office or in the room next to it. At five o'clock he'd had some visitors: a man and a woman. She had heard their voices, but hadn't been able to follow the conversation.

When the couple left the house, the boys woke up. She gave them some water to drink and wiped their faces clean with a facecloth. Both were burning hot.

'I have to tell you something.'

She had no idea if she had their attention. Their eyes were open, but they did not seem to be looking at anything.

'I'm your mother.' As she said it, she felt a wave of relief. As if she hadn't really been their mother until that moment. She instinctively started stroking her stomach as she gazed at her offspring.

She had not expected much of a reaction from them. But *something*. Just a nod, or a faint smile. That was all she needed.

'Your *mother*,' she said again.

If only she knew that they had understood. That would have been enough.

Perhaps they didn't believe her. Perhaps the doctor had told them they didn't have a mother. As he had told her. Or perhaps they were simply incapable of taking anything in any longer. That would be even worse.

She felt as depressed now as she had been relieved just a moment ago. She wasn't their mother. She had never been, because she had never been there for them. In that sense the doctor was right.

She looked at the children again. She wanted one more night alone with them. Surely that wasn't too much to ask? Just one more night. And then she would go for help. She would give them up for good, and accept her penance.

7

They'd expected that the doctor would kick the woman out in two seconds flat. That he had even let her in had been quite a surprise.

'We've got to warn him about her,' said Maria Moresnet. She had forbidden her sons to play in the street as long as that woman was still around.

'Oh, he'll realise soon enough that there's something not right with her,' Rosette Bayer reassured her. 'Let's just wait and see.'

Two hours went by before they saw her again. She suddenly appeared in the doorway.

'Over there. Look. There she is.'

She deposited some bags of rubbish outside the door and went back inside. Rosette and Maria were flabbergasted.

An hour later they decided to call the doctor. Maria dialled his number and he did pick up, which was fortunate, since several villagers had recently tried to reach him but with no luck.

She came straight to the point: 'Doctor, you'd better watch out for that woman who's in your house. She says things. She claims . . . all sorts of things. She bothered my boys.'

'Is that so?'

'She thought that *my* kids were *your* kids. She says she's their mother. But it's not true, is it?'

'No, it isn't true. She is not their mother.'

'Just as I thought. But in that case you shouldn't be letting her near them.'

'She is with them, and she's staying. That's what she says.'

'Watch out. She'll do more harm than good.'

There was silence on the other end of the line.

'I'll try to remember that,' the doctor finally said, and then he hung up.

For the next few hours the conversation in the Café Terminus revolved around the woman who had just appeared out of nowhere, as Maria put it. They soon decided that Dr Hoppe must know the woman, because he would not have let her see his children otherwise. But she wasn't the mother, no matter what she said.

'I bet she can't have children of her own, and she's talked herself into imagining all sorts of things,' said Léon Huysmans, who'd once read that the desire for a baby can drive a childless woman insane.

'Women really can't help it,' said Maria. 'It's because of their . . . what's it called . . .?'

'Hormones. Their hormones,' said Léon Huysmans.

'That's what I meant. In her case they've run amuck, probably. She even told us there was no man involved. Totally off her rocker. And yet – just think, wouldn't that be something? If women no longer needed a man, to have children? Then we'd be free to do as we pleased.'

'You wouldn't get through a single day without a man, Maria!' Jacques Meekers shouted at her.

'Oh yes I would, Jacques, easily!'

'I think it's going to be possible, in the future,' said Léon Huysmans. 'Women will be able to have children without a man. They're already close to that in America.'

'In America they can do anything,' said René Moresnet.

'Ah, so the women over there get preggers by immaculate conception!' cried Meekers, snorting with laughter.

'Meekers, behave yourself!' responded Maria, but she too couldn't help laughing.

The sound of the door opening and closing made everyone look up. Lothar Weber had risen to his feet and left without a word. Looking out of the window, René Moresnet saw him cross the street with his head down.

'We shouldn't have been talking that way,' said the café' owner. 'How would *you* like it if you suddenly had to go through life childless, and all anyone around you ever talked about was having kids and more kids?'

'I thought he was doing better,' said Jacques Meekers. 'He'd started smiling again, once in a while.'

'These things keep festering, Jacques. Take his wife, for instance.'

Meekers nodded, but said nothing. Vera Weber had been visiting the doctor almost every week over the past few months. Everyone knew she was suffering from depression, but no one dared say so. The closest they came to it was to say she had fallen into a funk.

Lothar Weber hadn't liked the whole idea from the very start.

'You can be present during the procedure,' Dr Hoppe had said, 'but we won't be needing your sperm.'

Not only didn't he like it, he didn't get it either. How could the doctor arrange for him to have a son, if his input wasn't necessary? At the next appointment he had asked about it again, just to make sure, but his mind had not been put at ease.

'It's simply a question of technique. Even your wife's eggs are not really necessary, in principle. It can just as easily be done with donor egg cells. But we'll try with your wife's eggs to start with.'

'But how, Doctor? How?'

'The hormones she is receiving now will cause the egg cells to ripen . . .'

'I mean, how are you going to make a baby? Out of what? Not out of clay?'

'Out of genetic material. DNA.'

'DNA?'

'Deoxyribonucleic acid.'

Lothar had nodded, even though he didn't get it at all. His wife had kicked him in the shins – twice. She was absolutely set on going ahead. It was the hormones that did it, Lothar thought, because in the beginning it was she who had been most hesitant. But once the doctor had given her the first injection, she'd quickly come round. It was true that she had turned quite moody, biting Lothar's head off over the slightest little thing, but that too was probably just the hormones.

The hormones were also responsible for her hefty weight gain: fourteen kilos in four months. She almost looked pregnant. She'd said it herself one day, and as she said it, he'd caught a glint in her eye.

He, on the other hand, still wasn't sure – until that afternoon in the

Terminus. What Léon Huysmans said had startled him. He had rushed out of the café to go home and tell his wife.

'In America they've been doing it for a while.'

'What?'

'What the doctor's doing. Without a man, or anything.'

'You haven't told anyone, have you?' she replied in dismay. She didn't want anyone to know that she was in treatment.

'No, no, they were the ones who started talking about it. Because there was a woman at the doctor's who—'

'Who said she was the mother of his children. I heard. Helga Barnard rang me. Is she still there? At the doctor's?'

'Yes, she's still there.'

'I hope she's gone by tomorrow.'

'She probably will be.'

The problem wasn't anything he had done. That Victor was sure of. He was being thwarted. God was just not going to give in without a fight. At least it did confirm that he, Victor Hoppe, was on the right track, because God would never have put up such a fight otherwise. It had all started with the questionable viability of Gunther Weber's cells. He had taken it as an omen. But then he had come to see it as an extra challenge, and since he did manage in the end to overcome that snag, he decided that that had been the worst of it. That was why he felt able to promise the parents they would have a baby in a year's time, identical in every way to Gunther, only without his hearing disability.

He'd been a bit overconfident, although he didn't see it that way. Or did not want to see it. Or could not see it. In any case, by Monday, 15 May 1989, one week before the four months were over, he still had not succeeded in deciphering the DNA code, and so had not been able to identify the gene with the deafness mutation.

He could have farmed out that step – to Rex Cremer, for instance, who had better equipment in Cologne, and more experience with the new technique – but Victor wanted to do everything himself. And he might have done it, too, if he had given himself more time. For once, he had raised the bar too high.

The thought that he too might have his limitations, that he too might possibly fail some time, or run out of luck once in a while – none of that ever occurred to him. No, in his eyes, it was obstruction, pure and simple. God would not relinquish the code of life to him without a struggle. It was something Victor understood all too well. After all, he would never have dreamed of giving everything he knew away either.

But since God was putting up such resistance, he was forced into a decision in the end. For there was only a week to go before he would have to implant an embryo of at least five days' gestation into the mother's womb, which left him only two days to decipher the code *and* find the error. That was too little time.

For that reason, he decided to stop trying to find it. He wasn't admitting defeat – no, he was merely regrouping. As if God had tried to smite him, but had just managed to nick him a little with his sword. Nothing life-threatening. A stab in the arm. Or a cut in his side. Not a defeat but an injury. That was how he saw it. And since it was merely an injury, he could still strike back. He wouldn't win this time, perhaps, but he could at least take a swing at God. If he resurrected Gunther Weber, giving back the life that God had taken from the boy, then God and he would be quits. And the boy would have to have a full life, naturally. He'd be deaf, but he would not grow old before his time. Not this one! He'd have the one mutation, but not the other. That was what it came down to: deafness, but normal telomeres. The first was unavoidable; the second wasn't. That was the challenge. But it wasn't hard. For he practically had it in the bag.

Lothar accompanied his wife to Dr Hoppe's on 15 May. It was Whit Monday, but he had learned that the menstrual cycle did not take Sundays or holidays into account. Lothar would rather have stayed at home – seeing that he didn't have a role in this anyway – but his wife had insisted, because she was scared, she told him. The doctor was going to poke all sorts of things up inside her, and she wanted her husband to be nearby in case something went wrong.

'As long as I don't have to watch,' he'd said, under his breath.

Their appointment at the doctor's was for five o'clock. The date and time had been decided on weeks ago. After the first month, during which Vera had had to keep track of her menstrual cycle on a calendar, the doctor had mapped out a strict timetable. If it all went according to plan, their next appointment would be five or six days from now. That was when the doctor would put one, perhaps two embryos back into her uterus. Male embryos. They would look like Gunther. In the beginning that had been their fervent hope, but now that the momentous day was almost at hand, it no longer seemed to matter as much. As long as the child was healthy – that, after all, was the most important thing.

One time, Vera had mentioned this to the doctor. She had only wanted to make things easier for him. 'It doesn't *have* to be a boy. He doesn't *have* to look like Gunther.'

'It has to be. It will be,' the doctor had answered flatly.

After that, she'd kept quiet. Not only was she afraid of appearing ungrateful or of lacking faith in him; in saying aloud the name of her dead son, she had also suddenly seen him before her. Suddenly she missed him terribly, and the longing to hold him was so overpowering that she instantly regretted having told the doctor that the baby needn't look like Gunther.

Still, what she wanted more than anything was a healthy baby. No defects; no disabilities; and so no hearing impediment either.

Lothar and Vera arrived at the doctor's house at five o'clock sharp. Lothar felt a bit awkward, as if he, not his wife, were about to undergo the procedure. Now that the moment was at hand, he asked himself if they shouldn't have tried the natural way first after all. Come to think of it, the subject had never even come up between them in the past four months. Nor had he made any overtures to her in bed. Perhaps that was another reason he was feeling slightly ill at ease: it troubled him to think the doctor would be fiddling with his wife – with him sitting right there – whereas he had not touched her in ages.

In the examination room Dr Hoppe had already set out everything needed for the procedure. Lothar sat down next to the desk, his back half-turned to the examination table on which his wife would be lying. He'd taken in the stirrups at a glance, and that was enough for him.

'Just relax, Frau Weber,' he heard Dr Hoppe say to her.

The doctor had just finished recapitulating what he was about to do, but Lothar was barely listening. As long as it's over soon, he thought.

In the village, people assumed that his wife was in therapy with the doctor, being treated for depression. He had never contradicted them, because he knew Vera wouldn't want that. She would rather they thought that than learn the real truth. He felt the same way. They were both still grief-stricken, but now that they had something to hold on to, something to look forward to, their grief had become more bearable. The emptiness was a little less empty. Something like that.

Behind his back he heard the sound of metal instruments being dropped into a metal dish, but there were other noises too. There was someone walking around in the house. Could it be the doctor's boys? Or was it that woman? No one had seen her leave.

'You ought to ask him about her,' Vera had said on the way there, 'in a roundabout way.'

Should he ask the doctor about the woman now? He glanced at his wife. The top half of her body was shielded from the lower half by a dark-green sheet. Her eyes were closed, and her breathing was calm. The doctor had given her a mild sedative. She would scarcely feel a thing, he had said. Her profile reminded Lothar of his son's. They both had the same snub nose and high forehead. He used to be glad that Gunther had not inherited his big broad nose. Thinking of his son made him shiver. He took a deep breath. Somewhere in the house he heard someone banging around. The doctor's sons? He wondered how they were doing. They had cancer – that was the rumour. But the doctor had never confirmed it. What was worse? To lose a child after a long-drawn-out illness, or to lose a child in an accident? He wished he could have had a chance to tell Gunther some things. Still, it was bound to be just as terrible for the doctor. Children weren't supposed to die, neither in an accident, nor because of illness.

'Why couldn't God have taken me instead? I've had my best years. He still had his whole life ahead of him,' his wife had sighed more than once in those first days after Gunther had died. In the doctor's case, of course, God *had* taken the mother's life first. But even that hadn't been enough of a sacrifice, apparently. So now God wanted the children as well.

You need not abide by God's will. Lothar could still hear Dr Hoppe saying those words. But now even he, the doctor, would have to abide. Or were the boys not as poorly as everyone seemed to think? It was true that no one had seen them since Charlotte Maenhout's accident, but was that enough reason to write them off for as good as dead?

'Seven, Frau Weber,' he heard the doctor announce. 'I have been able to harvest seven mature eggs. That is an excellent outcome.'

Lothar heard his wife sigh. She turned her face towards him. Her eyes were wet, but there was a smile on her lips. Like the sun coming out after the rain.

'You can get dressed,' said the doctor, starting to remove the green screen. 'It's all done.'

Lothar felt this might be the right moment to ask the doctor about his boys. All the tension had dissipated and they were all feeling palpably relieved. The doctor might even tell them about the woman who'd arrived on his doorstep yesterday. Lothar cleared his throat. Out of the corner of his eye he saw his wife sitting up. The doctor was taking off his gloves.

'How are the boys, Doctor? Gabriel and . . .' He couldn't immediately think of the other names, but the doctor spoke before they came back to him.

'Their fate is now in God's hands. God will decide what's to become of them.'

Zapped by a thunderbolt – that's how Lothar felt.

'I – I didn't know . . . It must be . . .' He looked at his wife helplessly. Her face had gone pale and there were tears welling up in her eyes.

Lothar averted his gaze. The doctor had his back to him. It was natural that he wouldn't want to show his feelings in their presence. Lothar wondered if he should tell him he was sorry, but he knew that if he did, he too would burst into tears.

'I'll give you a ring Friday or Saturday,' said the doctor, 'as soon as the embryos are ready to be implanted.' He had turned round, but wouldn't look either of them in the eye.

Lothar nodded. 'We'll be waiting by the phone, Doctor.'

God had another thing up his sleeve. Nothing, not even a lightning strike, could have been as devastating to Victor as this was. He had harvested seven ripe eggs, and not one of them had survived the procedure. So he discovered that evening. He collapsed into a chair, overcome with dizziness. He had been so certain the eggs were mature enough to be harvested. The ultrasound had shown him that they were. But, once removed from the woman's body, they had expired in no time in the Petri dish. He'd seen it happen. It wasn't really a matter of viable human life yet at this stage, of course; and yet it felt as if he were watching life being snuffed out before his eyes. One by one. Like balloons being popped with a pin.

Watching it happen, he knew: it was the hand of God. God was not going to let him do as he pleased; his all-seeing eye was fixed on Victor. God would brook no competition.

But he, Victor Hoppe, would never capitulate. God should have known he wouldn't.

So, the very next morning, he began making calls. He rang the universities and the hospitals. Judging from his tone, you'd have thought he was ordering a loaf of bread.

'Egg cells. Mature human eggs. That's what I said, yes.'

They'd hung up on him almost everywhere. A few asked him to call back later. One place told him that they couldn't find any reliable information on him.

No reliable information!

It was a plot. He was convinced of it now. God had mustered all His power and fomented a conspiracy! He had entered into a covenant! And all just to bring Victor to his knees!

Then the woman suddenly appeared before him. He still had the receiver clamped to his ear. The people on the other end of the line hadn't understood what he was asking. Didn't *want* to.

'Ripe egg cells. *Urgent*,' he was saying.

The woman started ranting and raving: 'Are you *still* at it? You don't know when to stop, do you! Haven't you caused enough suffering? What else do you want to happen? What, in the name of God, will it take for you to stop? Do you hear me? Stop this, right now! You're insane! Insane!'

In the name of God – that was what she'd said. That was how she had given herself away. But he'd already known it for some time. God had sent her here. It was that simple. Why else would she have come just at this time – when he was on the verge of taking God on at last?

She said she had come for the children, but she had nothing to do with the children. She wasn't their mother. She was nothing to them.

She'll do more harm than good. That was what was being said about her. So he wasn't the only one who knew. Everyone knew.

He went upstairs. He found her in the bathroom.

'I know why you have come,' he told her. 'You *didn't* come for the children. You came for *me*. You were sent. You were supposed to make me stop. But you won't succeed. *He* won't succeed. I'm going to go through with it, no matter what.'

Then he turned on his heel, and looked in on the children. They were still in the bed in that other room. He knew that room and that bed. That was the room where God had taken another life years ago. He'd prayed to God that time, the way the nuns had taught him to. But he hadn't known back then that God was evil. They had kept that from him.

He leaned over the two children and felt their pulse. It would not be long now.

8

'Rex Cremer speaking.'

'Herr Cremer, you have to help me! He's still doing it. Dr Hoppe – he just won't stop! And the children, my God, the children!'

'Madam, I can't hear you very well. Could you please say it again?'

'I'm at Dr Hoppe's house. I was just there. I've been there since the day before yesterday. I wanted to see the children, remember? You told me where he lived.'

'Good, so you did find him.'

'But the children . . .'

'What's the matter with the children?'

'One is already . . . Michael is already . . . And the other two . . . They could go at any time. I don't know what to do! You have to help me!'

'I don't know how . . .'

'And the doctor just won't stop! I heard him ordering egg cells – mature human eggs. That's what he told me. *I'm going to go through with it.* That's what he said! And he said *I* was trying to stop him! He's gone mad!'

'. . .'

'Herr Cremer?'

'I'm thinking, madam. I'm trying to think what I can do.'

'He's capable of anything! The children. When I found them . . . they . . . Terrible! It was terrible! He's insane! Dr Hoppe has gone insane! You have to . . .'

'Madam?'

'. . .'

'Madam, are you still there? Madam?'

The woman had been standing outside the Café Terminus, yelling and banging on the windows. Martha Bollen had heard her all the way from her shop and had hurried outside. The woman had turned to her in a panic: 'I have to make a phone call! It's urgent!'

Martha had taken her to the little office at the back of the shop and shown her the phone. She had left her alone, but listened at the door. She supposed that Dr Hoppe's sons had passed away; perhaps his phone was out of order. But the woman began to rant and rave. She was saying terrible things about Dr Hoppe, over and over. That he'd gone mad – that was what the woman yelled. At least three times! At that point Martha had heard enough. She marched into the office, snatched the receiver out of her hand and slammed it down.

'Out!' she shouted at her. 'Get out of here! You're the one who's insane! Go on, get out of here, or I'll call the police!'

The woman had run off.

Jacob Weinstein was deadheading flowers in the churchyard that morning when he spotted the woman. He didn't yet know who she was. She was wending her way along the graves, reading the names on the headstones, shaking her head each time. She was coming towards him but had not yet noticed him. When she came close, he hailed her: 'Excuse me, ma'am, are you looking for any grave in particular?'

She stared at him as if he had risen from the dead.

'I am the sexton,' he tried to reassure her. He saw that she was in a panic. 'If you'll just tell me which grave you're looking for, I may be able to help you.'

She looked around skittishly.

'Michael,' she said. 'Michael . . .'

'Who?'

'Michael.'

'Do you know the last name? The Christian name itself doesn't give me enough to go by.'

'Hoppe. Hoppe, maybe.'

'Hoppe? Like the doctor? Perhaps you are looking for his father. He is here, you are right. He was a doctor too. But his name wasn't Michael. I can—'

She shook her head vehemently. 'One of my . . . One of the children. The boys.'

'Oh, *that* Michael, you mean? As in Michael, Gabriel and Raphael? Like the archangels?'

She did not seem to understand the reference. She probably wasn't even religious.

'Michael Hoppe,' she said again, 'the doctor's . . .'

So he had understood her correctly. But she must be mistaken. 'He isn't dead yet, madam.'

Now she was nodding her head. 'He is,' she said. 'He is. It was over a week ago.'

'I think you must have misunderstood. They are very ill – that much I know. But dead? And a week ago? In that case he'd have been buried by now, and we haven't had a burial here in four months. I really do think you are mistaken.'

'No, the doctor said so. I'm sure of it.'

Suddenly the sexton realised who she was. She was the woman everyone was talking about, who had assaulted Maria Moresnet's children and claimed she was the mother of the doctor's sons. No one had seen her since the doctor had let her in. It must be her! And she was crazy – that's what they said.

'There's no Michael Hoppe here, madam,' he said firmly. 'You are imagining things. He is not dead.'

'You're lying! Everyone's lying!' she cried loudly, flinging her hands hysterically in the air.

'This is a churchyard, madam. I cannot allow . . .'

But she had already turned on her heels and was running towards the exit. Hurrying after her, he saw that she was making straight for the doctor's house. She even had a key. It took her a few moments to get the gate open, but then she scurried up the path to the front door. Not looking back, she disappeared into the house.

The door to the bedroom was open. She was sure she had closed it when she left.

'Gabriel? Raphael?' Her voice sounded reedy. She felt her temples throbbing and her stomach ached.

'Gabriel? Raphael?' She stuck her head round the door. The bed wasn't empty, as she'd expected.

She stepped into the room, halting at the foot of the bed, but saw only one child. The side Raphael had occupied was empty. And soiled. It was as if someone had plunged a knife into her belly.

In a daze she walked to the other side of the bed. Leaning down over Gabriel, she gathered him carefully in her arms.

'Where is Raphael? Gabriel, where is Raphael? Look at me!'

Gabriel gave no indication that he'd heard her. He was still breathing, thank God he was still breathing, but he did not open his eyes.

She lowered him onto the bed again. He was so light that his head barely made a dent in the pillow.

Her breath was coming out ragged and her throat felt as if it was being pinched shut. She looked round, but knew she would not find Raphael here in this room.

He isn't dead.

The doctor must have taken him to another room, it occurred to her. And Michael would be there too. A straw she could clutch at.

She left the room, turning back one last time.

'I'll be back in a minute,' she said. 'I'll be back with your brothers, Raphael and Michael. I'm going to fetch them.'

She was driven by hope and despair. And, increasingly, hatred. Hatred for the man who had caused all this. And who just merrily went on doing it.

She found him in the consultation room. He was standing with his back to her, washing his hands.

'Where are they?'

Her voice was hoarse. She had not had anything to drink in quite a while and no longer had any sense of time. She had no idea how long she'd been gone.

The doctor glanced over his shoulder but went on washing his hands. Then he turned off the tap.

'Where are they? Where are Michael and Raphael? They aren't dead. I know they aren't.'

He reached for a towel and began drying his hands with meticulous care. The palms. The backs of the hands. Each individual finger. In between each finger.

She glanced around the office, taking in the examination table with the stirrups. Again she felt a stab to her stomach. As if to feel her hate more intensely, she ran her fingertips across the swollen scar on her belly. Through the cloth of her blouse it felt like a branch with thorns. Forty-eight thorns. She had counted them often.

'Where are they?' she insisted.

The doctor hung up the towel. 'They are dead,' he said. 'They are both dead.' He would not look at her.

'You're lying. You're always lying.'

Snorting audibly, he shook his head. 'Do you wish to see them? *Then* will you believe it?'

She hadn't expected him to give in so easily. She nodded, however. 'I want to see them. At once.' Her throat had closed up almost completely.

'I'll show them to you. Come with me.'

He walked over to the door behind his desk, opened it and disappeared into the room behind.

For a moment she hesitated. She tried to picture what she would see. The boys lying there, together in one bed, perhaps oxygen masks over their noses, intravenous lines in their arms. Surrounded by all sorts of equipment, probably. That was quite possible. She steeled herself, then stepped into the room.

They were placed next to each other, in brotherly togetherness. He had set them up side by side, fraternally, on an empty table in the centre of the room, and he'd stepped back for her to see.

They were floating. Backs bowed, heads down, eyes closed, hands balled into fists; they were floating in water. Two great, liquid-filled glass jars, and in each jar, a body.

She couldn't get any air. She could only breathe out. In short puffs. She couldn't even tear her eyes away from what was on that table.

She clutched the cabinet beside her for support. Her hand hit one of the metal dishes and sent it toppling. The sound startled her. It seemed to be coming from somewhere else, as if she were in a dream. But she did not wake up. She *was* awake. And the voice she heard was flat and cold, but all too real: 'You see, they're dead. I'm not lying.'

If he had kept his mouth shut, if he hadn't said anything, then perhaps she'd just have walked away.

She caught sight of the scalpel lying on top of the cabinet. It was impossible to miss seeing it; it was impossible to miss picking it up. Receptacles everywhere, and in every receptacle scalpels, and scissors, and needles. She picked up the scalpel, raised her hand in the air and charged at the doctor. She did not slash at him. She didn't have the strength. She simply let the scalpel descend. Her arm came down in a wide sweep and the scalpel plunged into his side. It sliced easily through the cloth of his coat and drove deep into his flesh.

9

Father Kaisergruber had twice gone round to Dr Hoppe's with a flask of sacred oil. Both times the gate had remained shut to him. Since the priest knew that Dr Hoppe had not been opening his door to anyone, he did not take it personally. In fact, he didn't mind in the least, since he'd been reluctant to go in the first place and had only gone because several parishioners had urged him to. They wanted him to administer the last rites to the doctor's dying sons. He had objected at first, saying the children were too young, and besides, he wasn't sure they had been baptised, but Bernadette Liebknecht then reminded him of the story of the Canaanite woman, whose faith was so strong that Jesus had healed her sick child for that reason alone.

'The Gospel according to St Matthew, chapter 15,' Bernadette had said, reminding the priest that Dr Hoppe had declared that the children's fate was in God's hands. Did that not indicate that he hoped his sons would find peace in God? The extreme unction would surely help them find it, and it would also grant the doctor the strength to bear his loss.

The first time Father Kaisergruber had rung the bell at the doctor's gate was Wednesday afternoon, and the second time Thursday afternoon. He had tried calling beforehand, but the doctor had not answered the phone. Some villagers were becoming concerned, since Dr Hoppe had not been seen or heard from for several days. It seemed that he had taken in some madwoman to look after his children, and there had been no sign of her either since Tuesday morning, when she had raved at Jacob Weinstein in the churchyard, spewing all kinds of drivel.

Irma Nüssbaum had even been on the verge of asking the police to break down the door, but the others warned her not to because, they said, the doctor was probably keeping vigil by his children's deathbed. Irma wasn't reassured, however, and when she hadn't detected any sign of life at the doctor's house all day, she rang Vera Weber on the pretext of asking her how she was feeling. Casually, as if in passing, she asked Vera if she had any more appointments with Dr Hoppe.

'Yes, tomorrow or Saturday,' Vera told her, after some hesitation. 'He was going to phone me first.'

'I wonder if he will,' Irma said. 'I'm really starting to worry.'

She didn't probe any further as to the reason for the appointment, because she didn't want to cause Vera any embarrassment. Besides, she'd been told all she needed to know for now and decided to wait until Saturday night before taking any further action. If no one had heard from the doctor by then, she would call the police.

But she did not have to wait that long. Finally, on Friday evening came the sign of life she had been hoping for. That was when Father Kaisergruber made his third attempt. The next two days he would be too busy to call on the doctor because he was preparing for the following Sunday's annual pilgrimage up to Calvary Hill at La Chapelle, an event that was always held around 22 May, the birthday of St Rita, patroness of Wolfheim.

That evening the priest pressed the bell twice, and was already, with some measure of relief, turning to go when the doctor suddenly appeared. From the kitchen window of the house across the street Irma Nüssbaum was happy to see it. Two minutes later, as soon as the priest had followed the doctor inside, she began calling all her friends to tell them the good news.

Father Kaisergruber felt rather ill at ease. Dr Hoppe had greeted him in his customary businesslike manner. The priest had not announced his mission, but was immediately led into the doctor's office, as if he had come to be treated for some ailment or other. As the doctor took a seat at his desk, the priest dug his hand into his coat pocket to make sure the flask of oil was still there. It had been two years since he had traded in his old cassock for a dark suit. The Church had to go with the times, but he was still having trouble adjusting, especially with all these pockets.

Now that he and Dr Hoppe were seated across from each other, he couldn't help being reminded of years past. Of Victor's father. His son looked very much like the Karl Hoppe he remembered towards the end of the old doctor's life: the narrow, rather gaunt face, the unkempt red beard and the scar, the flattened nose and the blue eyes. It was almost exactly the same face. Except that Victor wore his hair differently, longer, much longer than the priest had ever seen him wear it, in fact. It was almost down to his shoulders.

The priest, coughing, decided to break the ice. He instinctively put his hand on the bottle in his pocket, as if to draw courage from it.

'The reason I came—' he began.

'Why did Jesus die on the cross?' Dr Hoppe interrupted him.

Father Kaisergruber was startled, but then he saw that the doctor was looking at the little silver cross he always wore pinned to the collar of his jacket. He did initially find it an odd question to ask, especially for Victor; but then he surmised that, as the death of his sons drew near, the doctor might yet be turning to the Faith for comfort.

He replied the way he always did: 'To redeem our sins. He sacrificed himself for mankind.'

'But then did He choose to die?'

The priest raised his eyebrows, immediately on his guard. The way Victor's father had died came back to him all of a sudden. The doctor was probably trying to get him to say that suicide was a good thing.

'No, Jesus was sentenced to death. A great injustice, to be sure. But He did not resist. He submitted to his punishment with resignation, to show that He bore no malice – that He had only good intentions.'

He wanted to find a way to put an end to this discussion, but the doctor went on pressing him, still staring at the little cross. 'But in that case why was he condemned?'

'He was not understood. The people did not believe Him.'

Now the doctor was nodding his head. He leaned back in his chair and put a hand to his side.

The priest took advantage of the silence to change the subject. 'But how are you—'

'But why the cross?' the doctor broke in again. 'Why did He have to die on the cross?'

The priest sat back and sighed. 'Why the cross?' he said, echoing the doctor's words. 'Because back in those days that was the way they executed criminals. That's why.'

'It wouldn't be done that way today.'

'No, thank God.'

The doctor looked up at him briefly.

'Today, He would have been incarcerated,' the priest went on, avoiding the doctor's eyes. 'Or else exonerated, in a court of law.'

'And then He wouldn't have died.'

'No, probably not.'

'In which case He would no longer be able to absolve us of our sins.'

'Possibly,' the priest said, nodding.

'And Jesus being resurrected, being risen from the dead – wasn't that for the sake of mankind, too?'

He is definitely searching, thought the priest. Perhaps I was wrong about him. Perhaps he has decided to repent, after all.

'It was Jesus' way of showing that He would always be there for all mankind,' he explained. 'He exists above life or death.'

He was getting the sense that he was being asked to initiate someone into the Christian faith – even though Victor had spent years at the monastery school in Eupen. All the religious instruction and all the prayers must have bounced off him like a spear bouncing off a shield. Or perhaps he had turned his back on religion at school because he had not been receptive to it back then – not mature enough.

'Oh, *now* I get it,' said Victor, for all the world like a student at the end of a lesson.

'I'm glad,' said Father Kaisergruber, and he meant it too. 'But now tell me, how are the children, Doctor?'

'Fine,' the doctor answered curtly.

'So everything's all . . .'

Dr Hoppe nodded.

The priest was relieved. 'Then there is no need administer the last rites? Because that's why I came, actually.' He tapped his finger lightly on the little flask in his pocket.

'No, certainly not,' said the doctor.

'Well! That *is* good news, Doctor,' said Father Kaisergruber, getting up, ready to leave. 'That is good news indeed. Now we'll know what to thank Jesus for next Sunday. On our pilgrimage to La Chapelle. There . . .'

The priest did not finish his sentence. It had occurred to him, too late, that the name of that village might well stir up unpleasant memories for Victor. But the doctor showed no reaction whatsoever. He probably remembered very little of his time at the convent of the Clare Sisters. How could it be otherwise? He had been less than five years old when his father had removed him from the asylum. And yet those years must have had some effect, the priest decided. The evil had finally been driven out, it seemed.

And they shall look on him, whom they have pierced.

Victor had been keeping the wound open for days. As soon as it started to heal over, he would scratch the scab away and then stick first one, then two and finally three fingers deep into the cut, as far as the middle joint.

When the wound was still fresh, even he had found it hard to believe. But he had looked, and he had felt. The wound in his side was real.

It had set something in motion.

It happened shortly after he'd vanquished the evil.

It wasn't until Saturday night that Lothar and Vera Weber finally received the phone call they had been anxiously awaiting: 'I'll be expecting you tomorrow morning at nine o'clock.'

'Did it work?' Lothar asked enthusiastically.

'It worked. I have three embryos.'

'Three? Isn't that too many?'

'We can't be sure that all three will continue to develop. We do have to take that eventuality into consideration.'

'Ah, I see.'

Then he asked how long it would take, and if his wife would have to rest afterwards, because they would like to take part in the pilgrimage to La Chapelle that afternoon. This year Lothar had been chosen to carry the church pennant. The doctor told him that it would only take a few minutes. It was a simple procedure. Vera wouldn't even feel it, and he didn't expect there to be any after-effects.

That night they lit a candle next to the portrait of their son Gunther.

The following morning they rang the bell on the doctor's gate at five minutes to nine. It was Sunday, 21 May 1989 – a special day. They were both nervous and tired. The heat had been oppressive that night in the bedroom, which had made it even more difficult for them to fall asleep. Over the past few days the temperature had been rising steadily and the heat had filtered into every corner of the house. That Sunday was promising to be a summery day too, but according to the forecast the spell of good weather would be over after that.

Vera Weber wasn't feeling at all sure as they rang the bell. Should she not have abided by God's will, after all? Wasn't she risking her own health? As well as that of her child-to-be? Such thoughts had been plaguing her over the past few days. Her nerves were largely to blame, naturally. She did realise that. But she also knew that there was still time to change her mind. Maybe they ought to wait. A month or so. To be absolutely sure.

'Lothar . . .' she began. But then the doctor appeared. 'Oh, nothing. Tell you later.'

Dr Hoppe looked pale. He always looked pale, but this time he was even paler. White. As white as chalk.

'Are you OK, Doctor?' asked Lothar, as soon as they were inside.

'Yes,' he replied, but to Lothar he didn't sound very convincing. The doctor was probably nervous himself. Naturally: the occasion must be just as momentous to him as it was to them.

'I heard the good news about the boys,' said Lothar to ease the tension, swatting at a fly that was buzzing round his head.

The doctor nodded. 'It was high time,' he said. 'God took his time over it. They were just skin and bone. If you like, I'll go fetch them for you. Then you can see for yourselves.'

Lothar shook his head. 'Another time perhaps. Let them rest.'

He did understand the doctor's relief that the worst was over, and that he was anxious to show everyone how well his boys were doing, but what Lothar wanted now was for the procedure to be over as quickly as possible. Besides, his wife was already half undressed.

'The evil has been vanquished, anyway,' said Dr Hoppe. 'That task is done.'

Lothar nodded. It was reassuring to think that the doctor had both sought and found solace in faith. He has God on his side right now, he thought; so perhaps God will also smile on us. 'I am happy for you,' he said, and he meant it.

He saw the doctor pressing his hand to his side. His white doctor's coat had brown stains there, and there was a fly crawling across it. Another fly was perched on the doctor's hand. Suddenly it struck Lothar that there were quite a few flies in the room. There was also a strange smell that he couldn't place.

His wife had climbed onto the table and placed her legs in the stirrups. He turned his gaze to Dr Hoppe, who went and sat down at a little table, where he bent over a large microscope and slid a Petri dish under the lens.

There's life in there, thought Lothar, and in a minute he'll put it inside my wife. *Immaculate conception*. He could still hear Jacques Meekers shouting it, that time, in the Terminus.

Shortly thereafter Dr Hoppe got up again and walked over to Vera, carrying an instrument that seemed to consist mainly of a long, thin metal rod.

'Doctor?' Lothar suddenly heard his wife say in a pinched voice. He looked at her, frowning. She was lying down, her head resting on a pillow, her eyes staring up at the ceiling. Again came her voice: 'Doctor, couldn't we postpone this for a while? Until next month, maybe?'

Lothar was startled. Had she lost her nerve, all of a sudden? He looked at the doctor wide-eyed; but the doctor lost no time in responding.

'No, we can't. It isn't possible. It has to be done now.'

'But is everything really ready to go?' she asked. 'I'm so worried that something could still go wrong.'

'Don't worry,' said the doctor. 'I will do good by you. And you are blessed.'

Lothar had no idea what the doctor meant, but his wife didn't bother to pursue it. She wanted to know something else.

'But the child, Doctor? Will the child be healthy?'

'He'll be healthy, Frau Weber. He will definitely be healthy.'

'So he won't be . . . deaf?'

'No, he won't be deaf.'

Lothar heard his wife give a sigh. She seemed reassured and her head sank back further into the pillow. He still had questions, but he decided to keep them to himself. His wife was calm, and the doctor was ready to perform the procedure. What he would really have liked to know, however, was what would happen if two, or even three, of the embryos developed into babies? Would they look alike? Would all three have normal hearing? And what if his wife didn't get pregnant after all? Would the doctor try again? But would they even want to? He and his wife had not discussed that eventuality. Perhaps, in that case, they would just have to abide by God's will.

'That's it,' he heard. Dr Hoppe leaned back and again placed his hand on his side.

'Is it done – already?' asked Lothar.

'It is done,' said the doctor, but with scarcely any excitement in his voice, as if he had done no more than his duty. He had done his part. Now it was up to Vera.

Lothar Weber watched his wife sit up slowly. There was life in her stomach now – new life. He could scarcely believe it. He felt himself becoming quite emotional at the thought. He hadn't expected that. He couldn't help thinking of Gunther, and had to steel himself not to burst into tears.

10

When Rex Cremer got to the top of the Vaalserberg, he was surprised to note that the Boudewijn Tower had vanished. He drove on a bit further, then stopped the car. The area where the tower had once stood had been transformed into an enormous building site enclosed inside a security fence. A huge hole had been dug there, so deep that Rex could not see the bottom, and massive cement blocks rose up from its depths with long metal rods sticking out of them. A rectangular sign on the fence showed a picture of the new tower, the legend written in four languages.

'The new Boudewijn Tower being built on this site,' he read, 'will be fifty metres high, with a lift and a roofed platform at the top that will offer a unique panoramic view.'

The drawing of the new tower showed a lofty structure with a series of stairs winding up around it. It made him think of a giant rendering of a DNA spiral, a double helix braided together in perfect harmony. The platform at the top of the tower was an octagonal structure with vertical glass walls and a metal-braced roof shaped like a pyramid, a flagpole at its peak.

Fifty metres high. You can't stop progress, thought Rex, thinking nostalgically of the old tower. A boyhood memory had been razed to the ground. The thought suddenly made him feel very old. It was a feeling he was having more frequently these days, as if time were slipping through his fingers. The years seemed to have turned into days. Case in point: he had last come this way six months ago, yet it felt like only an hour ago. The four years he'd been in Cologne, too, seemed scarcely to amount to anything. And, looking back, even those years at the university were condensed into just a few snapshot moments – snapshots in which Victor Hoppe, naturally, played a prominent role; but how could it be otherwise? Their first meeting had been nearly ten years ago. And the first occasion he had contacted Victor even earlier than that. He could still remember the exact date on which he had written the card that had started the whole thing rolling: 9 April 1979.

Sighing, he moved his foot from the brake to the accelerator. The car began to move forward again, driving at a slow crawl past the gaping hole that had been scooped out of the top of Mount Vaalserberg. He glanced at the clock on the dashboard. It was five to eleven. The day was Sunday, 21 May 1989.

Ever since the abruptly disconnected phone call from that woman, five days earlier, Cremer had been unable to relax. Part of it, of course, was not knowing what had happened, but the main reason for his anxiety was his own sense of guilt, which had suddenly returned with a vengeance. He just couldn't shake the thought that he was partly responsible for everything that had happened, even if he did not yet know the full scope of the consequences. He should have stepped in from the very beginning. He shouldn't have been such a chicken. That wasn't the kind of man he was. He had never been that way before, though perhaps – and he fervently hoped this was true – perhaps he was getting himself all worked up over nothing. But if something terrible had indeed happened, if Victor Hoppe really had gone too far this time, then he, Rex Cremer, would have to accept the responsibility.

It was with that mindset that he had left Cologne that Sunday morning at 10 a.m. Resolute. Determined. But, driving down the Route des Trois Bornes an hour later, all his resolve seemed to have evaporated and he was, more than anything, paralysed by anxiety.

He rolled into the village just as the church bells began to toll. He saw a few people hurriedly crossing the street and running towards the church, where Sunday Mass was presumably about to begin. He slowed the car to a snail's pace, driving on to Victor Hoppe's house once everyone was off the street.

Getting out of the car, he was struck by how oppressively hot it was. A thunderstorm was forecast, which was supposed to put an end to the heat of the past few days. He felt himself break out in a sweat.

He wiped his forehead and began walking towards the gate. But before he could reach it the front door opened and Victor came out. Rex stopped and took a deep breath. He wasn't sure if the doctor was coming to greet him, or if he just happened to be on his way out.

'I have been expecting you,' said Victor before Rex had a chance to say a word. The doctor unlocked the gate and flung it open. Rex saw that something had changed about his former colleague's appearance. His hair and his beard. His unkempt red hair, especially, struck him. It was almost down to his shoulders.

'I know why you have come,' said Victor. 'You have come to betray me.'

'Excuse me?' Rex stared at him in astonishment, but the doctor avoided his gaze.

'You have come to betray me,' he repeated. 'You will return with a great mob and then you will betray me.'

There was no menace in his voice, but Rex felt his anxiety rise. Victor had always had a peculiar way of behaving, but the way he stood there, swaying slightly, his head bowed, one hand pressed to his side, the other hand clawing the air – Rex had never seen him act this way before.

'They don't understand me,' Victor went on. 'They don't believe in me. Do *you* still believe in me?'

Rex decided the best thing was not to answer him. He didn't want to provoke him. But Victor wasn't waiting for an answer. He went on stonily, 'They mustn't lock me up. They must not. If they lock me up, I will not be able to fulfil my task. I have a mission.'

'Victor, perhaps—'

Victor whipped his arm up into the air and pointed his forefinger at Rex menacingly.

'*You* will betray me!' he said, raising his voice. '*You* will be the one! But woe unto him who betrays me, he shall wish that he had never been born. You will hang, don't you know? You will *hang* for this!'

Rex, flinching, took a step back. For just a second his eyes met Victor's. The gaze was empty, like that of a blind man. Rex took another step backwards. The outstretched arm came down; Victor began tugging at the bottom of his shirt tail.

'You don't believe me, do you! You *still* won't believe me,' he said, pulling his shirt out of his trousers, higher and higher, until his chalk-white, hollow stomach was exposed.

Rex shook his head.

'Do you want to see? Then will you believe it?' cried Victor. He pulled his shirt up another notch. There was a laceration in his side almost ten centimetres wide. 'Do you want to feel it? *Then* will you believe?'

Victor brought his hand dramatically to the wound and stuck two, three fingers inside the gash. He began to pull – no, he tore it open.

Averting his gaze, Rex tried to back off a little more, as inconspicuously as he could. He was starting to feel seriously nauseated and his head began to spin. Then he turned on his heels and darted to his car. He yanked open the door, got in and jammed the key into the ignition. He glanced over his shoulder to see if he was being followed, but Victor was still standing at the gate, his fingers plunged deep inside the wound.

He stopped the car at the three borders, because he felt as if he was going to be sick.

The voice. The words. The wound. The fingers inside that wound. And on top of it all, the stifling heat. The nausea. It was all too much for Rex. He stopped the car and threw up. Gradually the sick feeling began to pass. But Victor's voice wouldn't stop ringing in his ears.

You have come to betray me. You will return with a great mob and you will betray me. You are going to betray me.

The ravings of a lunatic. Rex had no idea where Victor had got that idea from, or who might have put the thought into his head.

You will hang for it!

That threat was even more worrying. The more he thought about it, the more those words began to feel like a real noose around his neck. He interpreted them to mean that Victor would drag him down with him. Victor would try to deny his own responsibility and fob it all off on Rex. He would say that Rex Cremer had known what he was doing and never tried to stop him; had encouraged him, even. And, besides, Rex had set the whole ball rolling, on 9 April 1979. And he would show them the proof. Black on white, dated, in his handwriting:

You have certainly beaten God at his own game.

Tormented by such thoughts, Rex Cremer paced round the summit of Mount Vaalserberg. He walked to the three borders. Then to the highest point in the Netherlands. Back to the three borders. He paced around the marker. Netherlands. Germany. Belgium. Nowhere could he find peace.

Finally he headed over to the fenced-off building site. Peering down, he could just glimpse the bottom, at least ten metres down. The four cement pylons with their metal stakes seemed to have been thrust up from the earth's core with diabolical force, as if trying to reach for something. He stood there for several minutes staring into the pit, his fingers threaded through the chain-link fence.

'Don't jump, mister!' he suddenly heard someone yell.

Startled, he looked round. A man walked by, laughing.

The man's voice had jolted him out of his reverie. Of course he wouldn't jump. The thought had never even occurred to him. He'd merely been thinking about what he should do next. Whether he should go home, and wait passively for what came next – as was his wont. To wait patiently – only this time it would be until they came for him. And even if he denied everything a thousand times, they still would not believe him. He too would not be believed. Misunderstood. Just like Victor.

Or should he go back to Wolfheim? Should he try once more to bring Victor to his senses? Perhaps it wasn't that terrible. Perhaps the thing he feared the most hadn't actually happened.

He left the building site and walked back to his car. He had to do something. Waiting was no longer an option. He had to try to persuade Victor to seek help, and he had to find out how the children were faring. He couldn't just leave them to their fate. He couldn't do that any longer.

So Rex tried to pull himself together and buck up his courage as he started the car and slowly began the drive back down the Route des Trois Bornes, down to the bottom, under the bridge, into the village, up to the house.

The gate was still open, and the front door too. Victor had vanished. Rex got out of the car and looked round. The village square was deserted. The pavements empty. He glanced at his watch. It was 12.15.

It was still stiflingly hot. Clouds had started forming, obscuring the sun, but that only made it feel even more oppressive.

You will come back with a great mob. You will betray me.

He had indeed come back; Victor was right about that. But he was alone. And he had not come to betray him. He had come to help him.

Cautiously he walked up the path to the front door and went in. It stank to high heaven. The stench took his breath away. Clapping his hand over his nose and mouth, he looked round. The front hall was deserted but one of the doors was open: the door to the office.

Besides the stench, there were also the flies – everywhere he looked. Bluebottles. There was something rotting in here. That was where flies laid their eggs: in rotting meat, so that when the eggs hatched, the larvae would have something to eat. The thought came to him in a flash as he stepped into the office. But it too was empty. Behind the desk another door stood open, as if showing the way. It might be a trap.

He sidled over to the door, one hand over his nose, the other swatting at the squadrons of flies zooming about his head. For a split second he thought he would find Victor in the room. Alive, or dead. The latter might be best.

But Victor wasn't in there. And yet he was. Three times over, in fact. V1. V2. V3. That was how the first, second and third glass jars were labelled.

They were barely children any longer. He saw that when he got closer up. They seemed to have reverted to the foetal stage. So skinny. So tiny. So bald. And the way they were curled up, just like a foetus in the womb. As if Victor had left them to stiffen in that position before preserving them in formaldehyde.

It was a terrible shock, which only grew when he saw the dates written on the labels. Three different dates: 13 May 1989. 17 May 1989. 16 May 1989.

He was too late.

His nausea returned. But at the same time he felt the urge to smash open the glass jars. Not to release the children, but to destroy them. To erase the harm and the shame. To obliterate all traces of it. Quickly. He took a step forward and stretched out his hands.

Then he spotted . . . her.

She was lying on the floor, half under the table. As he lunged forward, the movement caused the flies crawling on and inside her corpse to take flight in their thousands, like a lid suddenly being lifted off a pan. She was lying on her back, and although he could not recall her face clearly, since he'd seen her only once, he knew that it was her. She was naked from the waist up, and even though there was a second laceration that was quite a bit larger, the first wound he noticed was the smaller one. His eyes moved down from her face to her chest, where there was a cut, no bigger than the breadth of a thumb, but that cut was so exact, so surgically exact, that he knew that that one thrust, there in that spot, right by the breastbone, had dealt the death blow. She must have died within seconds. And so he realised that the other, much larger wound, had been made later. It followed the line of an older scar neatly, right along the incision. And he knew at once that Victor must have removed something from that stomach – the very thing, in fact, that was being redeposited in there by the flies, the hundreds and thousands of swarming bluebottles, laying their eggs in the putrefying womb in order to hatch new flies.

Rex took it all in in three seconds. In those same three seconds he felt the earth opening up under his feet and dragging him down into the abyss. He wanted to scream, but couldn't, because of the nausea. His stomach was on fire, as if it too was seething with thousands of flies trying to come out.

He threw up for the second time that day. He was bawling, too – for the first time in years. He felt like someone who has succumbed to a moment of insanity, and then realises what he's done. As if he had done it all himself. The children in the jars. The woman on the floor. *He* was the one who had done it. He didn't give Victor Hoppe a moment's thought. He looked, and he saw only what *he* had done. He let it all sink in, as if to punish himself. And as he stared, sobbing all the while like a little kid, it occurred to him that what he was looking at must never be seen by anyone else. That the only way to reverse all of this was to erase it completely. All of it.

Then he did what he had wanted to do from the start. He twisted the lid off the first jar and poured out the contents. Over the woman. All of it. The formaldehyde, and with the formaldehyde, the corpse, which landed whence it had come. The flies flew up in a black, seething mass, only to settle down immediately, driven by their instinctive urge to procreate.

His urge too was instinctive. He was doing this for his own survival. He was conscious of it; and yet not quite conscious. Everything he did was deliberately thought out, yet largely unconscious in its execution.

The contents of the second and third jars followed those of the first. The children were being returned to the womb, as foetuses. He saved some of the formaldehyde in the third jar and used it to dribble a liquid trail to the doorway. Then he went back for some more chemicals, which he sprinkled all around the room. He knew that that quantity of chemicals, in that combination, was more than enough to wipe all of it from the face of the earth.

And all this time, as he was busy with these preparations, he never once wondered where Victor was, nor if he was close by. It didn't matter.

Even as he performed his final deed, which was to erase everything and blow it sky-high, he wasn't thinking of Victor. He was only thinking of himself. As he had always done, in fact.

22

The days when the villagers of Wolfheim used to make the pilgrimage to La Chapelle on foot were long gone. These days even the heavy statue of St Rita, which six men used to carry in procession on their shoulders, was left behind in the church, and the marching band, once twenty musicians and twenty instruments strong, had shrunk to just a drum and a tuba. The one annual tradition that was still kept, however, was the parish committee's selection of a deserving burgher to carry the church standard in the procession of the Stations of the Cross. On Sunday, 21 May 1989, that honour had been reserved for Lothar Weber. He had been chosen because people felt he needed something to cheer him up after the loss of his son. At first he had turned it down, since he hadn't really done anything to deserve it, but his wife had said, 'Lothar, just do it. Gunther would be proud of you.'

And so he did it for Gunther; for, if truth be told, Lothar didn't really like being the centre of attention.

First, at eleven o'clock, they celebrated Holy Mass. Father Kaisergruber asked St Rita to watch over the village and its inhabitants over the coming year, and protect it from the sort of calamity that had struck some of its inhabitants these past few months. The priest did not mention any names, but Lothar knew that he meant his family, amongst others. He took Vera's hand in his, and kept it there for the entire service.

After Mass they drove to La Chapelle in a long motorcade. Almost every one of Wolfheim's two hundred-odd burghers was in attendance, and as they assembled at the Calvary gate, people kept coming over to Lothar and patting him on the back to wish him good luck. It made him feel quite moved, actually.

At twelve o'clock on the dot everyone was in position and the pilgrimage was ready to start. Father Kaisergruber, carrying a large silver cross on a pole, was in front, and right behind him came Lothar Weber with the church standard, embroidered with the name of their village and a likeness of St Rita. Jacob Weinstein and Florent Keuning, each carrying a votive candle, fell in behind. The rest of the villagers formed two long lines, the eldest in front. Josef Zimmermann and some of the other elderly were in wheelchairs. Bringing up the rear was the two-man band: Jacques Meekers on tuba and René Moresnet with the marching drum.

Lothar felt a shudder go up his spine as Father Kaisergruber lifted the pole with the cross high in the air, which was the sign for the procession to begin. At the rear Jacques Meekers and René Moresnet began playing 'You have called us, Lord', as the rest of the parishioners started reciting the Our Father. The muttering of so many voices sounded to the standard bearer like the buzzing of a swarm of bees.

It was sweltering hot that afternoon, but the sun was already hidden behind looming clouds. The weather forecast had predicted a thunderstorm by nightfall.

When the procession drew to a halt at the first station, '*Jesus condemned to death*', the beads of sweat were starting to drip down Lothar's face. The banner was heavier than he'd expected and his Sunday suit was much too warm for this hot weather. But he did not own any other suit. It was the same suit he had worn at Gunther's funeral.

'*We worship Thee, O Christ, and praise Thee*,' said Father Kaisergruber. The music had stopped.

'*Because by thy holy cross Thou hast redeemed the world*,' chorused the villagers.

'*My Jesus, I know that it was not only Pilate who condemned You to death*,' the priest began to read from a prayer book, '*but my sins too have caused thy death . . .*'

Lothar's thoughts began to wander. He thought about his son Gunther, but also about that other son, the one who was coming, and who was supposed to look like Gunther. He still had his doubts. Just as in these past few months he'd never been able to come to terms with the fact that he was no longer a father, he now found it impossible to believe he would soon be a father again. His wife seemed to be feeling something already. He had seen her run her hand over her stomach when she was getting dressed, the way she used to do when she was expecting Gunther. According to Dr Hoppe, the embryos that had been transferred that morning would still have to implant themselves in the uterus in order for the pregnancy to take, but Lothar was almost certain that it had already happened. Maybe it would even be twins, or triplets. But even that thought didn't yet invoke any paternal feeling in him. It would come, he supposed. He hoped.

The dull beat of the drum roused the standard bearer from his musings. The procession started up again. The villagers had already started mumbling the Our Father again. Lothar looked up at the sky, where grey clouds were accumulating. It didn't look as if the thunderstorm was going to wait for nightfall.

At the eighth station, '*Jesus comforts the weeping women*', he finally caught sight of his wife. He had tried to find her in the throng several times before, with no luck. She was staring dreamily into space and again he saw her putting her hand on her stomach. Oh yes, she was pregnant all right.

'*Give me the strength*,' he heard Father Kaisergruber read, '*to forget my own grief so that I may comfort others*.'

Well put, he thought, and when his wife happened to look his way at that very moment, he felt a shudder go up his spine for the second time that afternoon. He smiled at her and she smiled back. Then she gave him a curt nod, as if to say he was doing great, and that gave him the strength to march on with pride, his back straight and his nose in the air, as if suddenly the church standard didn't weigh a thing.

Forty-five minutes later the procession arrived at the eleventh station: '*Jesus is crucified*'. Lothar stared at the relief sculpture. Even though the figures were carved of white stone and were relatively small, they seemed very lifelike. It was almost as if they were just taking a break, before springing into action. The emotion in the faces, especially, was strikingly real. The haughty judges, the grieving women, the dutiful workmen wielding hammers, and, finally, Jesus himself, stoically allowing himself to be nailed to the cross.

'*Patiently didst Thou bear this suffering*,' read the priest.

Lothar tried to find his wife again, but did not spot her this time. He would see her later, presumably, when they arrived at the clearing in front of the twelfth station. That was always a wonderful moment – not only because the procession was nearly finished, but also because it was such an impressive sight, every time. After walking the eleven stations along a narrow, winding path, hemmed in by towering trees, you suddenly came into this enormous, wide open space. It was truly as if the heavens had parted and great shafts of light came pouring down on you. Lothar also found the twelfth station's statues awe-inspiring. Those seven life-size figures on the hill, with Jesus on the cross in the middle, and the two murderers on his left and right hand. Those statues too were lifelike; as real as flesh and blood. They seemed so real that he always found himself wondering how long they'd be able to stick it out up there on that cross.

'*We worship Thee, O Christ, and praise Thee*,' said Father Kaisergruber. The prayer of the eleventh station was coming to an end.

'*Because by thy holy cross Thou hast redeemed the world*,' said the villagers.

The procession started up again. The two-man band began playing 'Lord, grant us your peace'. Lothar took a deep breath and lifted the standard even higher in the air. He glanced over his shoulder, and catching sight of Florent Keuning, nodded at him. The handyman gave him the thumbs-up. For the first time in his life, Lothar felt truly supported by everyone, and it made him feel good.

Close on Father Kaisergruber's heels, he turned the last corner and suddenly found himself in the large empty clearing. The explosion of light he had been expecting, however, was muted by a menacing, inky cloud that obscured the sun. But the second, perhaps even greater disappointment came when, shuffling forward, he raised his eyes to look at the hill where the twelfth station was depicted. Two of the statues were gone! He noticed this immediately, for it was the two murderers that were missing. They were no longer there, nailed to the cross; only Jesus remained. Lothar glanced over his shoulder at Florent Keuning, whose blood was draining from his face until he was as pale as the statue of Jesus on the cross. Turning his head forward again and walking on, Lothar suddenly heard muttering behind him, soon followed by the first exclamations. Women's shouts, especially. Screams. And then he too saw it, like a bolt from the blue. And he heard it as well. Everyone heard it. And at that very moment, big fat raindrops began to fall.

Father Kaisergruber knew that Jesus and the two murderers would not be displayed on their crosses this year. The sandstone sculptures had grown porous and were threatening to come loose. That was why the Clare Sisters had had them taken down and had commissioned a sculptor from La Chapelle to make three new statues, of bronze this time. The four remaining sandstone figures, at the foot of the cross, were still in place: Mary, Mary Magdalene, John and the Roman soldier. But he didn't know that one of the statues had already been finished, and seemed to have been reinstalled. It was the first thing he saw when, at the head of the procession, he came out into the clearing before the twelfth-station grotto. It was a rather extraordinary sculpture – astonishingly lifelike. But it wasn't made of bronze. If it had been, it would have been a green or brown cast. This sculpture had to be sandstone again. Its pallor was sharply set off against the black clouds that had gathered above the hill. It was an imposing sight.

Slowly Father Kaisergruber took several steps forward. So realistic! The sculptor had done his best to make Jesus as true to life as possible. He could tell from the wound in his side, where Jesus had been stabbed by a Roman soldier's spear. It actually *looked* like a gaping wound. The sculptor had even daubed it with red paint, to enhance the effect. The same red had also been used on the flesh wounds, where the hands and feet were nailed to the cross. And the sculptor had made Jesus' hair and beard almost the same shade of red, if of a slightly lighter hue. That was rather surprising. Artistic licence, he thought – but a split second later, the truth began to dawn on him. He refused to believe it at first, even though he was seeing it with his own two eyes. But then he heard muttering behind him, and then a name being yelled out, over and over. In that instant, as he heard the screams behind him, he saw the head on the cross lift up and the eyes open for a second, and those eyes looking at him, looking right through him. And then he heard a voice, and the voice was unmistakable: '*It is finished!*'

Father Kaisergruber felt as if someone had stabbed him with a spear, not once, but a thousand times; but the worst was yet to come. The head on the cross sank down, down, and as the head sank, so did the body bend forward, farther and farther. So far that the hands began to tear free of the nails, ever so slowly, sinew by sinew, bone by bone, and once they were free, everything happened very quickly. The body pitched forward in one smooth arc. The feet were ripped from the nail that held them, and then there was nothing to keep the body up there. It tumbled all the way down the hill, landing with a thud between the railings and the altar grotto.

Father Kaisergruber felt everything go dark before his eyes. He felt dizzy. Looking behind him, he saw the procession's straight line falling apart: a couple of women had fainted. As he looked, several others collapsed. He recognised Vera Weber among them. Then the thunderstorm broke overhead. And to him that was, just possibly, the worst thing of all.

All the people of Wolfheim were convinced that the woman had done it – that she was the one responsible. She had drugged Dr Hoppe and nailed him to the cross. To do that required brute strength, of course, but the woman was well built. Anyone who'd set eyes on her could tell you that. But she must have murdered the children first – or maybe later. One or the other. Whatever the case, after nailing the doctor to the cross, she had returned to the house, set fire to it, and then she'd committed suicide. So: first she had drugged the doctor, then she had drugged the children or else killed them, then nailed the doctor to the cross, then gone back, set the house on fire and killed herself. In that order. That was how it must have happened. That was what the villagers told the police. The woman was responsible for the whole thing.

But little by little this theory began to crumble. The medical examiners kept discovering new things. That the woman had been dead for several days by the time the fire had broken out. Later they determined that the children, too, had already been dead. They must have weighed less than nothing by then. But the people of the village refused to believe it. The bodies had been reduced to ashes. How could the authorities know how long the woman and the children had been dead? Perhaps she had had someone to help her. Further investigation was called for.

Later still, the villagers were told that the hammer found next to the cross had the doctor's fingerprints on it, but that too was discounted by everyone; it must have been a trick. The real perpetrator had pressed the hammer into the doctor's hand to get his fingerprints.

The patrons of the Café Terminus considered just once the possibility that the doctor might have nailed himself to the cross. But the discussion petered out quickly, since no one could imagine how that might be done, from a practical standpoint.

'You'd have to have at least three arms,' René Moresnet declared.

So it was impossible. Everyone could agree on that. Except one man. But he had not joined in the discussion. Florent Keuning had kept quiet and would continue to hold his peace – partly out of respect for the doctor, but mainly because he felt that he himself was in some way guilty. He ought to have realised, but it hadn't raised any alarm bells in his mind at the time. He'd even chuckled to himself over it. And now the knowledge of it kept gnawing at him.

Sometimes what might seem impossible is merely very difficult.

Victor Hoppe had thought about it long and hard. That he would sacrifice himself was a given. That he would die on the cross was a given too. The evil had to be vanquished, but the harm the evil had done would first have to be set right. All sins had to be washed away. That was why he'd have to take his own life, and at the same time *offer up* his life. He would do it for mankind. And later, he would have to rise from the dead. He had seen to it that that would come to pass as well. He wouldn't be able to accomplish it in three days, of course, but it would definitely come to pass. He had made sure of that.

But to die on the cross? How would he do that? He had thought about it, and suddenly had an inspiration. He had walked over to Florent Keuning's house.

'A hammer and three nails,' he had said to the handyman. 'I need a sturdy hammer and three long nails.'

'Do you have something heavy to hang?' Florent had asked. 'If you like, I can come and help you, you know.'

'Thanks, but I can manage by myself.'

The handyman had given him what he needed, and Victor had thanked him and told him that his sins would soon be forgiven.

He knew that the entire village would be going to Calvary Hill that afternoon. He had taken it as a sign. The reason they were going there was to see *him*, so he must get there on time. But then Rex Cremer had arrived. Cremer was out to betray him. That too was a sign. What he, Victor Hoppe, was about to do, was the right thing to do. It was good.

As soon as Cremer had gone, Victor set out. It took him three-quarters of an hour to reach Calvary Hill on foot. The hammer weighed heavy in his hand. He stumbled and fell a few times, but always managed to get back on his feet.

The entrance to Calvary Hill was shut but not locked. He followed the path meandering past the eleven grottos of the Stations of the Cross until he reached the twelfth station.

Jesus was no longer up there! He saw that it was so, and again, *again*, he took it as a sign. The cross was waiting for him. For him alone.

He scaled the hill, taking the same route as the one he had taken as a boy, so many years ago. A young child, but already predestined, he now realised.

Again he stepped into the clearing from the right, but this time there were no spectators. Not yet. He took off his clothes, down to his underpants. He pried the wound in his side open again with his fingers. It began to bleed. That was good.

Then he stepped up to the cross. He saw that if he stood on tiptoe, his arms just reached the crossbeam. The cross was just the right size for him. He picked up the hammer and nails. For a moment he wondered if the nails would hold his weight. But in Jesus's case they had held, so then he stopped worrying.

He was left-handed. That was why he first hammered one of the nails into the left crossbeam, where his left hand would go. He heard snatches of music in the distance.

Then he crouched down, placing his left hand on the ground. He grasped the hammer in his right. Picking up a second nail, he pounded it through his left hand. It was easy. It hurt, but that was all part of the deal. He had to bear it stoically. He beat the nail all the way through and then picked up his hand. He yanked the nail out of his hand, which now had a hole right through it. He peered through the hole then wrapped a bandage round it.

Then he leaned back against the cross, his feet still on the ground. Standing on tiptoe, he crossed his feet, leaned forward and, using his left hand, hammered another nail through both his feet. The pain was excruciating, both in his hand and in his feet. But still he persevered. He had a mission.

Straightening up again, he stretched out his right arm until his right hand was at the far end of the crossbeam. Then he pounded a nail into it with his other hand. He hammered until the nail was anchored deep in the wood of the crossbeam. The pain was already growing less acute.

With a last effort he tossed the hammer into the pines on the hill. Next he tore the bandage off his left hand with his teeth, again peered through the hole in his hand, and then hooked it over the nail he had hammered into the cross earlier. The nail slipped easily through the hole.

Now he was hanging on the cross.

He waited patiently as the music came closer.

He knew that if he leaned forward and lifted his feet off the ground at the same time, his legs would snap and his lungs collapse. He had considered this. He had also considered what his last words should be. But he hadn't had to think about it very long. John, chapter 19, verse 30. There it was written.

And then he saw the procession come forth, with Father Kaisergruber in the vanguard. Even he would now have to believe in Victor's goodness. He was quite confident of it as he stared at the priest, and the priest stared back at him.

12

'Right here, at the three borders. That's where the last victim died. A certain Rex Cremer. A German.' Jacques Meekers tapped his index finger on the map of Wolfheim and its environs. 'Actually, the accident itself had already happened before the doctor's death, but the victim didn't die until later that night, in hospital, in Aachen. And of course we didn't hear about it until afterwards. Because what had happened here and at La Chapelle eclipsed everything else, naturally. Anyway, the chap must have been driving much too fast. There were several witnesses who saw it happen. He was gunning it, at top speed, from this side of the Vaalserberg up to the border, just as a coach came barrelling down from Vaals. The driver honked his horn, and it must have given this fellow, the German, such a turn that he spun the wheel in the opposite direction. He just managed to avoid the coach, but he couldn't steer clear of the hole. You know, the huge excavation, the foundations for the new tower. The poor man crashed right through the fence and plunged down into the pit. One of the cement pillars went—'

'That's enough, Jacques. You've told that story a hundred times. And that accident had nothing to do with the other events, surely? It was just a coincidence.'

'And look here,' Jacques Meekers went on, ignoring the interruption; 'if you draw a line, see, from here, the doctor's house, where the walnut tree used to stand, to the three borders, you can see how all the disasters seem to branch out from that spot, just like the roots of a tree.'

On Saturday, 19 May 1990, the new Boudewijn Tower at the three-border junction was officially inaugurated. Among the numerous attendees were Lothar and Vera Weber. They had a carrycot with them for their baby, who was four months old that day. It was a boy. They had named him Isaac.

They had been given the good news two days earlier. The hospital tests had shown that young Isaac's hearing was normal. It came as a great relief, especially after the nasty shock they'd had at his birth.

It was the first time they had shown their son in public. There was no reason not to any more, now that the surgery was over and done with. They'd done a beautiful job, really. Perfect. They'd used the very latest techniques. Later you'd barely be able to see a thing, just a discreet scar. Nothing like the way it had looked at first.

Many of the villagers came over to admire the baby that afternoon, and all discreetly took in the deformity. No one said anything about it, however. Just as no one had mentioned it in the past four months. Yet everyone knew exactly when and where it had happened. That day on Calvary Hill, when Vera had had such a terrible fright. That was when it had happened. For she must already have been expecting then.